Praise for
The Color of Ice

"In Barbara Linn Probst's exquisite new novel, *The Color of Ice*, we are treated to a passionate tale of love, loss, redemption, and healing as seen through the power of glass and ice. Color, form, and light ignite this woman's journey by an artist who manages to open Cathryn's closed heart. Probst gifts the reader with a seamless, rich portrayal of Iceland and how its natural beauty reflects and transforms everyone who touches its magnificent landscape."

—**Lisa Barr**, *New York Times* best-selling author of *Woman on Fire*

"A brilliant novel of art and passion set against a stunning Icelandic backdrop. Through vivid descriptions and a keen insightfulness, Probst creates a seamless journey of self-discovery culminating in acceptance, healing, and ultimately, unconditional love."

—**Rochelle Weinstein**, author of *When We Let Go*

"Seamlessly portrayed, tenderly sculpted, *The Color of Ice* is an alluring, stunning literary vision that will stay in your mind long after you finish it."

—**Weina Dai Randel**, author of *The Last Rose of Shanghai*

"An engaging narrative with an ending you won't expect. A sensitive and sensual story of renewal."

—*Kirkus Reviews*

"Writing with beauty and insight, Barbara Linn Probst explores the power of landscape to influence the unfolding of artistic creation and the mysterious journey from passion to unconditional love and redemption."

—**JoAnne Tompkins**, author of *What Comes After*

"Once again, Barbara Linn Probst's lyrical writing takes readers on a splendid journey into parts unknown. In *The Color of Ice*, she combines the dramatic backdrop of Iceland's rugged volcanic landscapes and majestic blue icebergs with the delicate art of glassblowing to create an intriguing exploration of the re-awakening of passion. Nothing is predictable as the story unfolds through the nuanced magic of Probst's words."

—**Patricia Sands**, author of the *Love in Provence* series

"In *The Color of Ice*, Barbara Linn Probst has gifted us with another luminous story of art and passion—a tale of discovery and forgiveness that moves like a glassblower's rod, always turning, always moving, all the way to its stunning ending."

—**Diane Zinna**, author of *The All-Night Sun*

"In *The Color of Ice*, Barbara Linn Probst gives us a vivid travelogue, an ode to art, and a compelling journey of self-discovery—all in one remarkable, utterly engrossing novel. The two main characters—one cerebral and restrained, the other corporeal and instinctual—find in each other the key to unlock their artistic voice."

—**Katherine Gray**, award-winning glass artist and resident evaluator on the Netflix series *Blown Away*

Praise for
The Sound Between the Notes

✳ Gold Medalist, Sarton Award for Contemporary Fiction

✳ Silver Medalist, Nautilus Book Award for Fiction

✳ Named one of the Best Indie Books of 2021
by the editors at *Kirkus Reviews*

"In her second novel, Barbara Linn Probst delivers yet another powerful story, balancing lyrical language with a skillfully paced plot to build a sensory-rich world that will delight those who loved *Queen of the Owls* and win countless new readers. Offering a deep exploration of the search for identity and connection, *The Sound Between the Notes* reminds us to embrace everything we are—and everything that's made us who we are."

—**Julie Cantrell**, *New York Times* and *USA TODAY*
best-selling author of *Perennials*

"Beautifully told, *The Sound Between the Notes* is a story of tragedy and triumph, of the push and pull of family, of the responsibility we feel to ourselves and those we love. Once I started the book, I couldn't put it down until I reached the last gorgeously written note."

—**Loretta Nyhan**, author of *The Other Family* and
Amazon charts bestseller *Digging In*

"Family ties can bind or blind us—even with relatives we've never met. In *The Sound Between the Notes*, trails of music connect generations separated by adoption—while the same notes threaten a family believed sewn with steel threads. In this spellbinding novel, Barbara Linn Probst examines how the truth of love transcends genetics even as strands of biology grip us. Once you begin this story, suffused with the majesty of music and the reveries of creation, the 'gotta know' will carry you all the way to the final note."

—**Randy Susan Meyers**, international best-selling author of
Waisted, The Comfort of Lies, and *Accidents of Marriage*

"Probst writes very well and convincingly. The characters are well drawn and the tight plot is just one agonizing twist after another. . . . The climax, on the night of her performance, is a tour de force steeped in suspense, and Susannah's subsequent revelations are satisfying and authentic. A sensitive, astute exploration of artistic passion, family, and perseverance."

—*Kirkus, starred review*

"As soaring as the music it so lovingly describes, poignantly human, and relatable to anyone who's ever wondered if it's too late for their dream, *The Sound Between the Notes* is an exploration of our vulnerability to life's timing and chance occurrences that influence our decisions, for better or worse. Probst creates her trademark intelligent suspense as Susannah, an adoptee trying for a midlife resurrection of an abandoned music career, confronts lifelong questions of who she is. A story that speaks to our universal need to have someone who believes in us unequivocally, and how that person had better be ourselves."

—**Ellen Notbohm**, award-winning author of
he River by Starlight

"A great story that had me turning the pages nonstop, a tale of passion, identity, and art. . . . *The Sound Between the Notes* is so beautiful, so lyrical, so musical that it was hard to put down. It is a story that will not only appeal to fans of music but to mothers and anyone looking for a good read. This is a wonderful story from a skillful writer, one that appeals strongly to the heart. It features awesome characters, a twisty plot, and gorgeous writing."

—*Readers' Favorite Reviews*

Praise for
Queen of the Owls

✳ **Medalist for the Sarton Women's Book Award**

✳ **Independent Book Publisher's Award**

✳ **Finalist for the Eric Hoffer Award Grand Prize**

"A nuanced, insightful, culturally relevant investigation of one woman's personal and artistic awakening, *Queen of the Owls* limns the distance between artist and muse, creator and critic, concealment and exposure, exploring no less than the meaning and the nature of art."

—**Christina Baker Kline**, #1 *New York Times* bestselling author of *A Piece of the World, Orphan Train,* and *The Exiles*

"This is a stunner about the true cost of creativity, and about what it means to be really seen. Gorgeously written and so, so smart (and how can you resist any novel that has Georgia O'Keeffe in it?), Probst's novel is a work of art in itself."

—**Caroline Leavitt**, best-selling author of *Pictures of You, Cruel Beautiful World,* and *With You or Without You*

"*Queen of the Owls* is a powerful novel about a woman's relation to her body, diving into contemporary controversies about privacy and consent. A 'must-read' for fans of Georgia O'Keeffe and any woman who struggles to find her true self hidden under the roles of sister, mother, wife, and colleague."

—**Barbara Claypole White**, author of *The Perfect Son* and *The Promise Between Us*

"Probst's well-written and engaging debut asks a question every woman can relate to: what would you risk to be truly seen and understood? The lush descriptions of O'Keeffe's work and life enhance the story and help frame the enduring feminist issues at its center."

—**Sonja Yoerg**, author of *True Places* and *Stories We Never Told*

The Color of Ice

A Novel

Barbara Linn Probst

SHE WRITES PRESS

Published 2022
Printed in the United States of America
Print ISBN: 978-1-64742-259-2
E-ISBN: 978-1-64742-260-8
Library of Congress Control Number: 2022904038

For information, address:
She Writes Press
1569 Solano Ave #546
Berkeley, CA 94707

Interior formatting by Tabitha Lahr

She Writes Press is a division of SparkPoint Studio, LLC.

The end precedes the beginning,
And the end and the beginning were always there
Before the beginning and after the end.
And all is always now.

T.S. Eliot, *Burnt Norton*

Part One: Blue Ice

One

The view from the window of the Icelandair 757 wasn't at all what Cathryn had expected. She had chosen Iceland for her first truly impulsive act in fifteen years—rather than, say, Maui or the Bahamas—precisely because of its starkness, yet the glittering azure of the water looked more tropical than Arctic.

Until a week ago, the notion of going to Iceland had never crossed her mind. She had a full calendar back in America, no Icelandic roots, not even a bucket list of remote destinations. When she told Rachel where she was going, her daughter's first reaction had been a skeptical: "Really?" And then: "The northern lights—and Björk!"

Cathryn didn't know who or what Björk was, and Rachel had rolled her eyes at her mother's un-coolness, the latest example in an endless string of ways that Cathryn had failed to be the person Rachel thought she should be. "She's just about the most incredible musician on the planet," Rachel had said, finally.

Cathryn had tried to look suitably impressed. "On the planet. My goodness."

"I'm serious."

"I know you are. And I'll look her up while I'm there, I promise."

Rachel had given a pained sigh. "You don't *look her up*, like someone's cousin. I'm just saying she's from Iceland."

It was yet another conversation that didn't work, and Cathryn had changed the subject. That was a week ago. The days that followed had been filled with too many last-minute tasks to spend time courting her daughter's elusive approval.

Turning to the window again, Cathryn tried to catch a glimpse of Reykjavik, Iceland's capital, but the plane banked to the right and the view shifted. A trail of thin white clouds, delicate as shredded lace, obscured the sapphire shore she had been admiring only moments earlier. The brilliant coastline, gone already.

The clouds thickened as the plane began its descent. The cabin lights dimmed, and the flight attendants made their announcements, in lilting English, about arrival time and temperature on the ground and the carousel where their bags would be waiting. Cathryn had checked her suitcase through at JFK—something she almost never did—but it was impossible to fit everything she needed for ten days of unpredictable weather into her navy blue carryon. Two of those days were for a freelance job, an interview and photo shoot with a glassblower who had some sort of project about icebergs. The other eight were for her. Eight days in an unfamiliar country, doing whatever she wanted.

Whatever she wanted. As if she knew what that was.

She had told each of her children a different story. She'd told Judah that she had a demanding business assignment, and he shouldn't try to reach her unless it was urgent. It was partly a lie, but he was twenty-two years old, for heaven's sake. Surely he could manage for ten days without running to his mama to haul him out of a jam.

She'd told Rachel that she was taking a vacation, leaving out the part about the job. Another freelance assignment wouldn't elicit the admiration of her hard-to-please firstborn, but a trip to a wild and unfamiliar country might. And it *would* be a vacation, as soon as she finished with the glassblower person.

The landing at Keflavik Airport was as smooth and efficient as the flight had been. Within thirty minutes, Cathryn's passport had been stamped, her suitcase retrieved, and her dollars exchanged for krónur. Even the people at the Avis desk were pleasant and quick. Since she didn't plan on venturing far from the Ring Road, the well-traveled highway that circled the country, she opted for a two-wheel drive Kia.

The Avis representative handed her the keys and a special iPad that came with her Icelandair tour package, a combination guidebook and GPS. "Here you go, then. Have a wonderful trip."

"Thank you," Cathryn said, although *wonderful* wasn't an adjective she would have chosen. Safe, maybe. Or pleasant. She hadn't expected *wonderful* in a long time.

She had taken the red-eye from Kennedy, landing in Iceland at sunrise. That gave her a day to recover from jet lag and get to the meeting place at the iceberg lagoon, a spot on the southeast coast with an unpronounceable Icelandic name. She'd looked it up and had seen at once, from its turquoise splendor, why the people at Shades of Blue wanted it for their logo.

Shades of Blue was a new client, an organization of artists' representatives headed by a woman named Renata Singer who was pencil-thin, sleek, and stylish, with neon-blue hair. According to Renata, blue represented truth, wisdom, intuition, tranquility, and renewal. "So it's perfect for us," she told Cathryn when they met to discuss the job.

Renata had crossed her legs and swung a stiletto-clad foot back and forth. "Here's what we were thinking. Something dynamic—you know, art in the process of creation, artist getting inspired, that sort of thing."

Cathryn skimmed their list of blue nouns. Truth, intuition, tranquility. She pictured a cool expanse of water, sky, the sea. "Something blue. A blue place, a real one, that inspires one of your artists."

Renata's leg stopped swinging. "That's good. I like it." She turned to the two men seated across from her.

"Do we have any blue projects?" one of them asked.

"Actually, we do." It was the third partner, an older man with a silver goatee. "That blue lagoon place. I think it's in Denmark or something. That glassblower fellow is going there."

"You mean Mack," Renata said. "But I don't think it's Denmark."

The man with the goatee took out his phone. "Hey Siri, where is the Blue Lagoon?"

Siri's too-friendly voice chirped, "I found one option. Blue Lagoon near Grindavík on the Reykjanes Peninsula."

The man tapped on the link. "It's in Iceland." He showed Renata the phone.

"Iceland. Right," she said. "But that's not the place. He was talking about a different lagoon, something with icebergs."

She returned her attention to Cathryn. "It's an interesting idea but, as you can imagine, quite beyond our budget. We aren't about to fly you off to the middle of whatever just so you can take some photos."

Cathryn nodded. "Of course." But something seized inside her. Less than two days ago, when she'd met Rachel for one their rare Manhattan lunches, Rachel had propped her chin on her hand and gazed at her mother mournfully. "Really, Mom," Rachel had sighed. "You should jump off the high dive once in a while. Go someplace crazy and exotic. Bangkok, Marrakesh."

Someplace crazy and exotic. Easy for Rachel to say. What seemed obvious when you were a blithe twenty-four-year-old was impossible for a middle-aged loner like her.

And yet.

Cathryn stared at Renata. Not the heat and crowds, the spices and swirling colors of Morocco. The opposite. A place made of rock and ice, forged by glaciers and volcanoes.

"You have an artist going there?"

"We do. He's got some project. I can't remember the details." Renata gave Cathryn a pointed look. "As I said, we're not sending a consultant halfway around the world for a publicity gig. No offense."

Cathryn felt her spine elongate, as if her body were an arrow, aiming her where she needed to go. "I'll pay my own way."

"Excuse me?"

She fixed her eyes on Renata's. "It won't cost you anything, except the fee you were going to pay me anyway. I'll go there on my own nickel." She was speaking rapidly now, surer and surer of the rightness of her idea. "I'll interview your glass person while he's working or getting inspired or whatever he's gone there to do. I'll shoot him with that blue ice thing in the background. It'll be stunning."

Renata frowned. "Why would you want to fork over your own money?"

"It's something I've been needing to do. A mini-vacation. And if I can do some work while I'm there—well, so much the better."

Not just *some* work. Some extraordinary work, a portfolio centerpiece that could lift her career to a whole new level. The possibility hadn't occurred to Cathryn when she began speaking, but she could almost see it now, a portrait of the mysterious blue icebergs that merged the commercial and artistic. Shades of Blue. Ice and sky.

She offered Renata her best smile. "Consider it a lucky convergence."

Renata looked at her colleagues. "It's okay with me. Unless either of you has an objection?"

"You're not going to try to hit us up with your expenses, are you?"

"Not at all. As I said, just the fee we agreed on." Cathryn's heart was galloping wildly now. "I can't remember the last time I've gone on a vacation."

"If it were me," Renata said, "going off alone, I'd do a Club Med cruise."

The goateed man threw Cathryn a quick glance. "She can take it off her taxes. Works for everyone."

"Fine." Renata uncrossed her legs and stood. "Let's give Cathryn a thumbs-up and let Mack know when she'll meet up with him."

Cathryn felt something lift in her chest, opening like a pair of wings. She knew almost nothing about Iceland—northern lights, horses, and now this blue ice—but she was going there.

She'd had an impulse and, for once, she'd acted on it. Just because.

Two

All Cathryn wanted, as she pulled out of the Avis lot, was to go straight to the guesthouse and sleep off the jetlag that was making her feel gritty and foul, but her sunrise landing meant that check-in time was hours away.

She could head to the little town of Hvolsvöllur and wait for the guesthouse to open, or she could do what all the tourists did when they landed at Keflavik and visit the Blue Lagoon—not the iceberg place on the southern coast where she was meeting the glassblower, but the famous site near the airport that Siri had found for Shades of Blue. The Blue Lagoon was a man-made lake whose geothermal seawater was supposed to cleanse, heal, and undo the effects of aging. There was even a shuttle bus from the airport so Icelandair passengers could stop for a rejuvenating plunge on their way to Europe or the US.

Well, Cathryn thought, she *was* a tourist—or would be, soon enough.

She arrived at the Blue Lagoon just as the Welcome Center was opening. Dutifully, she extended her arm for the electronic wristband, then showered and stowed her flip-flops and robe in a locker. Edging into the steaming water, she saw that the Blue Lagoon was really a series of lagoons connected by bridges and waterfalls.

Even at this hour, it was filling with visitors. People clustered at swim-up bars to get silica and algae to spread on their faces, then disappeared into the sulfur-laden mist that rose from the water, faces covered with white goo, hair piled on top of their heads in alien-looking swirls.

Cathryn made her way from one pool to another and tried not to feel self-conscious as she realized that she was the only person who was there by herself. There were couples, families, friends, posing for selfies or toasting each other with plastic cups of seltzer and wine. She fought the urge to explain—to someone—that she was just passing through on her way to a business meeting, then told herself it was ridiculous to care what a bunch of strangers thought. She didn't, in America.

That was the advantage of being attractive. When you were attractive, people assumed you were alone by choice. She knew it wasn't fair, but it made things easier. The less she had to explain, the better.

Still, there wasn't much to do. She had gotten the mud mask and free drink that came with her pass; the only other activity was the spa. She remembered the sign at the reception desk. *Surrender to a transformational spa journey.* Well, maybe it would ease the jetlag.

"Our in-water treatments get booked months in advance," the receptionist explained when Cathryn asked if there were any openings. "But as it happens, we just had a cancellation for a regular massage." She reached beneath the counter. "I have to tell you that cancellations are very, very rare." Then she gave Cathryn a beatific smile, as if Cathryn's luck were her luck too, and passed her a clipboard with a set of forms and a glossy brochure.

Cathryn scanned the brochure. "Renewal, restoration, and relaxation in an exquisite subterranean setting. Experience the interplay of pressure and release as your masseuse unlocks hidden reservoirs of tension, and restores peace and harmony to body and soul."

She suppressed a Rachel-like eyeroll and scrawled her signature. Then she followed the receptionist through a maze of passageways to a small room with a massage table, sink, and adjacent shower. "You can shower and dry off," the receptionist told her. "Then lie down on the table, under the sheet. On your stomach, please, with your face in the cradle. Your masseuse will be here shortly."

Cathryn gave what she hoped was an appreciative nod. She had just arranged herself on the table when there was a gentle rapping on the door. She lifted her head. "Yes. Come in."

A young woman stood in the doorway, clad in a white tunic and pants. She greeted Cathryn with the benevolent smile that seemed to be de rigueur for the Blue Lagoon staff. "I'm Sigrún. I'll be providing your treatment today."

"Hello. Thank you." Cathryn let her head drop into the terry-cloth cradle.

Sigrún arranged a towel under Cathryn's feet and adjusted her shoulders. "Is there anything I should know? Any medical or other conditions?"

"No, nothing. I'm a perfect specimen." She'd thought the masseuse would laugh, but maybe it was an American sort of joke.

She could hear Sigrún washing her hands in the sink. "This is the oil I'll be using." She let Cathryn smell her palm. "It's a blend of sandalwood, ginger, and mint."

"It smells lovely."

"Just breathe normally," Sigrún told her. "Your body will relax more easily that way." She pressed firmly on Cathryn's back through the sheet, then lifted each leg to rotate it in its socket. Cathryn tried to do as she'd been told. Just breathe. Normally.

"Let me do it," Sigrún said gently. "You don't have to do anything." She peeled back the sheet and spread her hands across Cathryn's skin. Her hands were warm, moving across the muscles in long overlapping strokes. Cathryn let out a sigh.

The masseuse dug her thumbs into the base of Cathryn's spine. The knots rolled under her fingers like hard little pebbles as the intermingled scents of ginger and mint filled the room.

Cathryn shuddered. She liked the sensations she could predict—the sting of hot water from the shower, hard against her back; the satisfying *there* when she laced her running shoes tight, the way she liked them; the pleasure she knew how to give herself when she couldn't sleep.

This was different. It was an onslaught of smell and texture and touch. The fragrance of the oils, the terrycloth cradle against her face.

And then a memory—no, not a memory, but a moment lived anew, as if time had folded into itself. A spring day. Rachel was pushing Judah in a little red wheelbarrow. There was a *thump* as she tripped, dropped the wheelbarrow, and fat baby Judah rolled out. He didn't cry, just sat there with his wet open mouth, surprised to find himself on the damp ground.

Cathryn had gotten up quickly. She'd scooped up her baby as he stretched his arms to her. The warm weight of his perfect little body melting into hers. His need for her and her response, in the very same instant.

Longing washed over her like a tide—for something that had no name, no shape, no place in the world she had made for herself.

A groan rose from deep in her flesh. It was a foreign sound, low and animal. She gripped the edge of the massage table as tears slid from her eyes.

This wasn't supposed to happen. She'd been caught off-guard, that's all—naked and jetlagged and blindsided by a despair that wasn't supposed to be part of this trip.

It wasn't about sex. She could have that if she wanted. It was something else, like a cry for water from a parched land.

Cathryn squeezed her eyes shut. "Is everything all right?" Sigrún asked.

Yes. No. There was no answer to a question like that. But she said, "Absolutely."

Sigrún's voice was soft. "Just relax, then, and let me work these knots for you."

Cathryn loosened her fingers from the edge of the table and willed herself to survive the rest of the massage. A few more minutes. Then she could get up, leave. Drive to the guesthouse, sleep off the time change, and awaken restored to her familiar self.

The guesthouse was a chain of box-like structures that stretched across a bright green field. Each had its own little deck with a view of the mountains and sky. Cathryn climbed out of the Kia and turned in a slow arc, her exhaustion forgotten as she gazed in wonder at the expanse of pewter and charcoal and jade. She hadn't been prepared for the stark beauty of the landscape.

A woman hurried out of the closest building. "Welcome. I'm Guðrún, your host. You have a reservation, yes?"

"I do. Cathryn McAllister."

Guðrún glanced at the Kia. "It's just you?"

Guðrún's expression was neutral, her question simply a clarification, but Cathryn felt a flare of anger. *And what if it is?*

Then she flinched, startled by her reaction. She'd been traveling alone for years, ever since Brian died, and hadn't felt a need to explain. It was that damn Blue Lagoon. The heat and fog, the smell of sulfur and sandalwood.

"Yes, just me."

"I'll show you to your cottage." Guðrún led Cathryn to the fifth little cabin. "We have a hot dinner at eight, though you can go to the restaurant in town if you're hungry now. And there's the Saga Center, of course. Our most important saga took place right here, a thousand years ago." She opened the door and gestured at the room. It was tasteful and modern, with gray-and-white throw pillows and a sliding glass door.

Cathryn could feel Guðrún's expectant gaze, but she was still reeling from her response to the woman's innocuous question. Jetlag, she reminded herself, and an addled brain from the mineral-rich heat of the lagoon.

It certainly wasn't because of Brian. She hadn't thought about Brian in forever. He was shoved in a drawer of the bureau called her life. Not exactly forgotten, but not hauled out to explain away an awkward moment.

"The room is satisfactory?" Guðrún asked.

Cathryn blinked. "Yes, yes. It's wonderful."

"I'll leave you, then. Dinner is at eight, as I said. In the main building."

Cathryn closed the door behind Guðrún, stepped out of her shoes, and collapsed on the bed. Twenty-four hours ago, she'd been texting with Renata Singer about the final details of the trip; she hadn't even finished packing her suitcase. Tomorrow she'd sleep late and drive to the blue iceberg place for the job she had been hired to do. And after that—the solo vacation that she didn't need to justify.

She bunched the pillow under her cheek, trying to get comfortable. The one thing she wanted was a nap, but the bureau drawer had been flung open and she was wide-awake with memories.

When you had a husband with secrets, like Brian, it was easy to tell yourself that he was a rotten bastard, and maybe he was. But he had been other things too. The person who went out on Sunday mornings to get fresh bagels, and then did the breakfast dishes so she could curl up on the couch and finish the crossword. The person who spent six straight hours constructing the loft bed Rachel wanted for her birthday, and went to four different stores to find the computer game Judah absolutely had to have. He had done a lot of good things. It was the other things, the not-good ones, that had changed her life and ended his.

She hadn't really hated Brian, but she'd been furious at him for humiliating her, ambushing her with what she should have known. And then, for dying and robbing her of the chance to know what she would have told him when he returned from that fateful drive. What she would have done, what kind of person she would have been.

Cathryn rolled onto her other side, angry at Brian for intruding after all this time and keeping her from the nap she needed. She had done perfectly well without him. Raised his children, neither of whom was easy to deal with. Made a successful career. Kept her figure and her looks.

Oh, screw you, Brian. Go back to being dead.

She grabbed the pillow and threw it at the sliding glass door. She had ten days of glaciers and waterfalls and geysers; there was even a visit to a puffin colony on the Saga Tour itinerary. She was damned if a dead husband was going to ruin that.

Clenching her teeth, she snatched another gray-and-white pillow from the stack and shoved it under her head. Then she curled into a tight comma and, at last, dropped into an exhausted sleep.

Three

After breakfast the next morning, Cathryn texted the glass-blower to let him know she'd be arriving at the iceberg lagoon—Jökulsárlón, she spelled it carefully, mouthing the four syllables—around noon.

To her surprise, he texted back to say that it was impossible to have an impression in the middle of the day when the place was packed with tourists. If Cathryn wasn't going to arrive until noon, it would be better to do the interview this evening and visit the lagoon early the next morning, before the tourists arrived, for the photos.

Cathryn frowned at the message. This new twist would delay her vacation by half a day, though she supposed he was right. Reluctantly, she typed, "I'll be staying at the Fosshotel, about fifteen minutes west of Jökulsárlón, if you know where it is? Maybe we can meet there for the interview." Then she added, "This evening."

"I know where the Fosshotel is," he replied. "Let's say seven p.m. in the lobby, and then seven a.m. tomorrow at the lagoon."

Seven a.m.? That was three in the morning for her still-on-American-time body.

Well, she was the hired help. He was the artist.

Once Cathryn had settled into her room at the Fosshotel, she logged onto the Wi-Fi and pulled up the glassblower's website.

Renata had called him Mack, but his real name was Henry Malcolm Charbonneau. The website showcased a sample of his work—an eye-catching kaleidoscopic montage, one object merging into the next. "Glass is present and not-present," the text read. "Both window and object, glass allows us to look through it and at it. The artisan's task to offer an experience of both in the same piece."

Cathryn had never thought about glass like that—she'd never thought about glass art, period—but it was an intriguing idea. She reread the sentences, wondering about the man who had written them and how he saw the world. Did he really look *at* and *through*, at the same time? Maybe he did. If you were an artist, you saw things differently—not only for what they were, but for what else they could mean and be.

She rested her chin on her fist, allowing herself a single wistful sigh. It had been years since she'd thought like that. She'd given up art-for-art's-sake when Brian died, trading it for a career documenting other people's work. She was good at what she did, with a roster of clients—theater companies, filmmakers, edgy little galleries— and a solid reputation.

The glassblower was a serious artist, though; that was obvious from his website. Cathryn scrolled through his bio, commissions, awards. Nothing about Iceland or blue icebergs. She'd have to ask him to explain what he was doing here, and at Jökulsárlón in particular. Then she typed *Iceland* into the search bar, thinking she might throw a few interesting facts into the conversation to get him to open up. She'd interviewed enough artists to know they could be laconic and had learned to prepare.

Iceland, she read, was one of the most volatile places on earth. Forged by volcanoes that spewed out molten rock over millions of years, split in half by a massive tectonic plate, with more extreme geothermal activity than anywhere else on the planet—it was a country always in formation, largely uninhabitable, survivor of a volcanic cataclysm that had wiped out one-fourth of its sparse population. With an impossible language and an equally impossible climate, Iceland had earned its reputation as a country like no other.

It seemed like a captivating landscape for an artist. No wonder it had attracted Mr. Henry Malcom Charbonneau. If she had been a real photographer, like Ansel Adams or Imogen Cunningham, she would have wanted to come here too.

They had agreed to meet in the lobby of the Fosshotel, so Cathryn found a small seating area in the corner and tried to look alert and intelligent, despite her lingering wooziness. She kept her eyes on the door and, right at seven, saw a man enter the hotel and look around. It was him, clearly. He looked messier than his photo, and bigger, but the profile was the same. A strong nose, thick eyebrows over hooded gray-green eyes, unruly hair. She raised her arm to let him know where she was.

He strode across the room and extended his hand. "Mack here."

"Cathryn McAllister. Thank you for coming out of your way to meet me here. I take it you're not staying at the Fosshotel?"

"You're the one who's gone out of your way. Iceland's pretty far to travel for a story."

"Not really. I thought it would be a sort of adventure, that's all. A vacation. Once we're done, that's the plan."

"Aha. So I'm keeping you from your vacation."

"No, not at all. I wouldn't have even had the idea for the trip if the blue iceberg thing hadn't come up." She met his eyes. "They did explain, right? It's to have an exotic example for their new promotion. Here's one of our wonderful Shades of Blue artists. That sort of thing."

He laughed. It was a big laugh, robust and irresistible. "In other words, it's a nice blue coincidence. The lady's not here because your art is so great."

"Please don't take it that way. It was a good fit, that's all. I have no idea if your art is great or not. I'm just here to do a job."

He settled into the opposite chair. "As am I."

"And that's what I want to hear about." Cathryn cleared her throat and shifted into her best professional stance. "What do you think? Shall we talk over a drink? Is there an Icelandic wine you'd recommend?"

"Icelanders don't bother with wine. They go straight to Brennivín, better known as The Black Death."

"Sounds forbidding."

"It's a bit like vodka. One of those distilled drinks, and an acquired taste. Personally, I prefer Kvöldsól. It means Midnight Sun."

"That sounds much nicer."

"Actually, Kvöldsól *is* a wine," he said, "so I've misled you. It's made from crowberries, wild blueberries, and rhubarb. It's supposed to keep you from aging."

"They said the same thing about the Blue Lagoon. It's probably just to entice the tourists."

Mack raised an eyebrow. "Did it entice you?"

"It must have, since I went there."

"See? It worked." He smiled. "A glass of Kvöldsól, then?"

"Oh, why not? I definitely prefer eternal youth to the Black Death."

He signaled to a waiter. "Kvöldsól. *Tvö glös.*"

"You talk like you've been here for a while."

"Not really. But some things are easy to figure out, like what to order in a bar."

Cathryn nodded. This was turning out to be easier than she'd expected. She had imagined a sullen hulk or a prima donna who would need constant affirmation, but Henry Malcolm Charbonneau, glass artist, was an interesting man.

"So," he said, leaning back and crossing his arms, "since my agent has decided that I'm suitably exotic—that was your word, right? — what do you need from me?"

Cathryn couldn't help wincing at the word *exotic*, even though she had been the one to use it first. It was Rachel's word, shorthand for the kind of experience she thought her mother needed, yet it sounded offensive when Mack lobbed it back at her.

Then she told herself, *Stop it*. No one was getting exploited. Mack Charbonneau would get a ton of free publicity, Shades of Blue would get a gorgeous promotion, and she would get a nice paycheck—plus, maybe, a portfolio showstopper.

"Insight into why you're here," she said. "What you want. Who you are."

"Three different questions."

"Start with whichever one you like. Or skip them all." She waved a hand. "It's up to you. They're not required questions, they're just—"

He finished the sentence for her. "Icebreakers?"

Cathryn burst out laughing. "Exactly."

He laughed too, and she thought, again, that he had the most extraordinary laugh. "I think," he said, "that was what's known as a perfect moment."

"It was."

"Shall we try for another one?" Before she could respond, he said, "I'm joking. Obviously. I don't think it's something you can try for. It has to just happen."

"Of course." The silence hung between them, dense with something Cathryn couldn't name. Then she flicked her hair behind her ears. "In any case, if you give me whatever you're okay with, I'll make it work. You have the lead in this, I promise."

"I don't mind talking. I just want to be sure I'm heard rather than interpreted."

"I thought artists liked people to interpret their work."

"Some just want it to be experienced."

The waiter arrived with a bottle of Kvöldsól and two cone-shaped wine glasses. "Will you be wanting to order an appetizer?" he asked. "Or dinner, perhaps? I can reserve a table for you in the dining room."

Mack shook his head, then turned to Cathryn, "Sorry. I don't have a lot of time, so I'd better focus on answering your questions. If you're starving, though, please feel free."

"A drink is fine." She took a pad and pencil from her purse. "If you're pressed for time, let's get to it. Why you're here, in Jökulsárlón."

He eyed her keenly. "I hope I haven't offended you."

"Why would you offend me?"

"Not on purpose. But it's been known to happen."

"I promise to let you know the instant I'm offended."

"Something to look forward to." He reached for the wine bottle and filled their glasses. "Your timing is perfect, you know. I'm leaving the area tomorrow, right after I show you Jökulsárlón."

Cathryn set down the pencil. "You're leaving? You're going back to the States?"

"No, not to the States. I'm heading up to Akureyri, in the north. I met someone who has a hot shop—that's a studio for blowing glass—and he's letting me use it for a few weeks while he's away. It's a huge stroke of luck because I want to do the design work here, while I'm still in Iceland."

"Wait. You're finished with Jökulsárlón?"

"I spent four days there. I got what I needed."

Now she was confused. "So you came to Jökulsárlón just to *look* at it?" Somehow she had thought he was doing his glassblowing right there, next to the ice. It made no sense, of course, yet she hadn't thought beyond Jökulsárlón itself.

"Looking, experiencing, getting to know the thing you want to portray. That's half the work." He lifted his wine glass. "The other half is transforming it into your own incarnation of what you've seen—in my case, into glass. And for that I need a hot shop."

Cathryn struggled to keep up. "An oven, a kiln."

"There's no glass studio around here. In fact, officially, the only glass studio is in Reykjavik. But I met this fellow—well, it's a long story. The point is that he has a place, only he's just starting out so it's all unofficial. But he has the equipment I need, and he was glad to rent the space while he goes off on a holiday."

"So you're going there."

"I am. After I show you Jökulsárlón." He took a long drink of the wine, then added, "You won't be disappointed, by the way. The lagoon is hugely photogenic. Your promotional spread will be great."

Cathryn knew he meant the remark to be encouraging, yet the words *promotional spread* made her feel oddly deflated. That's what it was, of course. A promotion for the client who had hired her, nothing more. She remembered the image she'd had in Renata's office—and again, only moments ago—of a new *something* that would change the trajectory of her career, the perfect union of natural splendor and commercial message. It had been vague, flimsy as smoke. She could almost see it uncoil from the censer and drift away.

Cathryn shifted in the chair, straightening her posture. "It's not really my spread. I'm just doing what Shades of Blue wants me to do. You know, have camera, will travel."

"You're the one behind the lens. It's your vision."

"I wouldn't call it a vision."

"Why not?"

"Please. This is just an assignment. It's for the people who hired me."

"If they'd hired someone else, it would end up looking different."

She was starting to feel exasperated. He'd told her that he didn't have much time. Why were they wasting it talking about her?

"Let's get back to you." She moved her wine glass aside, untouched, to make room on the table to write. "Why *here*? Blue icebergs, glaciers. What drew you to this particular place, as a subject for your work?"

"If you'd seen the place, it would be easier to explain. We're doing this backward."

Cathryn tried to keep her professional composure, but this was getting ridiculous. Avoiding the tourists wasn't a priority for her; that was his idea. He was the one who had made the schedule, and now he was complaining that the order was wrong.

"Well, here we are." She could hear the curtness in her voice, not a good way to get someone to open up. She tried again. "Explain as well as you can, and I'll listen as well as I can."

"Fair enough." Mack took another drink, then set the glass on the table. "I guess I should start by saying that I'm someone who works best when I'm—well, obsessed. My last series consumed me for two whole years."

He gave her a look that seemed, for a moment, both open and opaque. Like glass, Cathryn thought. A contradiction, piquing her interest.

"What was it about?"

"Leaves," he said. "Awakening."

She felt a jolt, as if he had looked right into her. Not through her clothes, the way men did, but through her skin and flesh. She remembered what he had written on his website. Window and object, at the same time.

She shivered, then pulled her attention back to what he was saying.

"—leaves and buds, on the brink of uncurling. Life, about to emerge and reveal itself."

Cathryn picked up her pencil. "Life, about to emerge. I like that." She tilted her head. "Did you go somewhere special, the way you've come to Iceland?"

"I went to Costa Rica." A shadow crossed his face, disappearing so swiftly that Cathryn wasn't sure if she had imagined it.

She made another note on her pad. "Did you find a studio in Costa Rica and do the work there, close to the source, the way you're doing here?"

"It didn't work out that way."

His reply was terse, almost rude, but she wasn't about to give up. If he wanted her to work for every insight, so be it. She'd interviewed reticent artists before.

"So you had to wait before you could—what was the word? Translate."

"I had to wait."

"Is that a problem? The gap, while you wait?"

"That's an astute question."

Cathryn shrugged. "I'm just asking."

"It can be," he said. "Sometimes you need to wait for things to settle, but if you wait too long, something can get lost. Then it's like you're trying to depict a memory instead of the real thing. Make a copy of a copy." He matched her shrug. "It's not always possible to work on-site, but it's great when it is. The hot shop in Akureyri isn't exactly next door to Jökulsárlón, but it's here in Iceland."

"I'm looking forward to seeing it." Quickly, she added, "Jökulsárlón, I mean."

"It's an amazing place. The light through the ice, the other-worldly blue—well, you'll see for yourself." His face softened. "You might think of ice as fixed and frozen, but it's not. It changes all the time, depending on the movement of the water and air, the temperature and wind. It's always responding—which means it's always becoming something new, something unknown."

"About to emerge and reveal itself."

"From something that people don't think of as being alive."

"But it is."

"Of course."

Cathryn jotted down a few words. Then she laid down her pencil and reached for the wine glass. "And now you're ready to re-embody what you've understood. Do you have it all planned out—how you're going to convey the spirit of the icebergs?"

"It's not really like that. I do plan, but mostly I think on the pipe."

"On the pipe?"

"While I'm working."

Cathryn nodded. It was the same with photography. She tried on the notion. *I think on the camera.*

She took a sip of the wine, finally, and turned to him in delight. "Blueberries and rhubarb. Just as you said."

"You like it?"

"I do. I feel younger already."

"Told you so."

Cathryn took another sip before placing the glass firmly on the table. She had to admit that she was enjoying herself. He was an intriguing man, and it would be a good story. Eye-catching, with the photos of the blue icebergs.

"Okay," she said, leaning forward, elbows on the table. "You were obsessed with the leaves. So where did the icebergs come from?"

"A photo," he answered. "I saw a photo at a friend's apartment, and I was hooked."

"A photo can do that. The photographer witnesses something and lets you witness it too." A memory flickered across her awareness. "You saw a photograph, and then off you went. Straight to Iceland."

"More or less."

"I can't imagine being that unencumbered."

"Few people can."

"You're speaking from personal experience."

"Is there another kind?"

She couldn't help herself. "No family, then?"

"Is that a required interview question?"

"No. Sorry." Somehow they had slipped into territory that had nothing to do with Shades of Blue. Yet she was curious and wished she'd had the nerve to say, "Yes, it is. Tell me."

Instead, she picked up the pencil. Back to the task she had come here for. "What challenges do you foresee, as an artist, in trying to capture Jökulsárlón in glass?"

Mack folded his arms. "First of all, I'm not an artist. I'm an artisan."

"Okay I'll play. What's the difference?"

"An artist thinks he has something meaningful to express. The material—whether it's clay, paint, stone—is simply the tool for expressing it."

"I'm not sure I agree, but fine. And an artisan?"

"An artisan listens to the material, to what *it* wants, and lets it teach him its language."

"I thought you said you were trying to show leaves unfurling, et cetera. You had an idea, and you set out to make pieces that would convey your idea. Isn't that what an artist does?"

"No, it's not. I'm trying to convey the essence of something that already exists, outside of me. I'm not trying to use glass to make a personal statement about the futility of human existence or the timelessness of maternal love or whatever irrelevant idea I happen to have in my head."

"Whoa. Did I hit a nerve?"

"You asked."

She pushed the pencil and pad away, yet again. "This is the most complicated conversation I've had in a long time."

"Maybe you need to get out more." He looked at his watch, then unfolded his arms and stood. "That sounded prickly. I just meant, I don't see myself as all that complicated. Anyway, we can talk more tomorrow, at Jökulsárlón. It's too abstract, sitting here in a hotel."

"Tomorrow, then." Cathryn rose too, extending her hand. "Thanks for making yourself so available."

He took her hand. She felt the pressure of his fingers, the warm roughness of his palm. "Tomorrow," he echoed.

"Seven o'clock in the damn morning."

He laughed. He had a wonderful laugh.

Four

When Cathryn arrived at Jökulsárlón the next morning, there was only one other car in the parking lot, a dark-green Jeep that she assumed was Mack's. She got out of the Kia, zipped up her jacket, and pulled on her hat and gloves. It was ten minutes before seven, and she was proud of herself for being early. The sun's rays lit the ice, but the air was cold. A sharp wind sliced through the water.

She crossed the parking lot and saw a lone figure walking along the gravel that bordered the lagoon. "Hey!" she called. "Good morning!" He stopped and waited for her.

Aware that he was watching, Cathryn picked her way across the rocks, gripping her camera strap with one hand and holding her hat in place with the other. "I'm here," she said when she caught up. "I mean, obviously I'm here. But it was a cliffhanger to see if I'd really get up that early."

She smiled up at him. He seemed taller, silhouetted against the sky. A black cap framed his face, making his features more distinct. Bones, eyebrows, mouth.

"Of course you got up," he said. "You weren't about to tell your client that you'd slept through your appointment and blown the whole job."

Cathryn flinched, her smile fading. She didn't know if he meant to be dry or just plain rude. She thought of saying, "Okay I'm officially offended. Letting you know, as requested."

He was right, though. She'd been put in her place for saying something stupid and glib and not even true. Still, he'd thrown her off balance. Maybe she ought to explain that she was just trying to be—what? Charming?

Oh, the hell with it. She'd never see him again, after today.

"I could have faked it," she quipped. "Slept in, had a nice warm breakfast, and photo-shopped you against the icebergs without ever leaving the room."

He laughed. It was a big laugh, bigger outdoors than it had been at the Fosshotel. "Since you did leave the room, and you really *are* here, let's go for it." He motioned toward a rocky path that led to the edge of the water.

"Wait." Cathryn put her hand on his arm, stopping him, and raised her eyes to the lagoon. A flock of birds skimmed the surface of the water, a silvery shimmer against slate-colored silk. Then, as if on cue, they lifted their wings and veered left, toward the ocean.

Stillness settled over the landscape. Only the silent blue icebergs, stately as kings and queens. Sculptures made of turquoise and crystal, the colors of milk and sky.

"You were right," Cathryn said, her voice quiet. "There was no sense talking too much until I'd seen it for myself." She released her breath. "I can't begin to imagine how you're going to capture this in glass."

"No one can capture something like this. Evoke, maybe."

"Evoke. Whatever." Quickly, she dropped her hand. A gust of wind snapped through the silence. She adjusted the camera strap, then followed Mack across the boulders and down the slope. The view changed with each step. A jagged piece of aquamarine, framed by a dark mountain. Bands of black and white and teal. Blue dancers, raising their glittering arms.

Mack paused, hands in his pockets, and gazed at the frozen landscape. As if reading her mind, he said, "It's different every time I come here. Every moment, really. It depends on the light and the tide and the wind. If we could get close, you'd see that it's not just our perception that keeps changing, it's the icebergs themselves. They shift. They even bubble and crack."

"You mean, they make noise?"

"They do."

"I never heard of such a thing. As in, actual bubbles?"

"Actual bubbles. Like champagne."

"From melting, when the temperature rises."

"Exactly. And when it drops. When a chunk breaks off, they moan. It's a shredding sound, like a sigh." He indicated the expanse of lagoon. "We're only seeing about ten percent of what's really there, you know. The other ninety percent is below the water line."

"The tip of the iceberg."

"Just so."

Cathryn wanted to say something clever and coy—*Another perfect moment?* But she didn't, only stood next to him as the stillness lingered. Light glinted on the ice.

Then, suddenly awkward, she slid the strap from her shoulder and took the camera out of its case. "Okay, " she declared. "Off to work we go."

She turned to peer at the ice. "I think I'll shoot the icebergs themselves, then get you in a few shots. You know—artist, about to be inspired."

"Whatever you need." He eyed her closely. "Do you know why the icebergs are blue?"

"I'm sure you're going to tell me." She knelt and focused the lens, zooming in. She took a dozen shots of the ice, one after another. Different angles, different close-ups. Each seemed both astonishing and insufficient.

"It takes over a hundred years," Mack said, "and it happens deep inside the glacier."

Cathryn looked up. "Really?"

"Of course, really."

"Why does it take a hundred years?"

He pointed at a slope of ice that bordered the lagoon. "It's because of compression. Snow falls on the glacier, and the air get squeezed out by its weight. The more the snowflakes press down on each other, the smaller the air pockets become. Over time, the whole thing gets incredibly compact, until eventually it's so dense that it absorbs every wavelength except blue. Then, when a chunk of glacier breaks off and that ultra-compressed center gets exposed to the light, the blue is refracted off the crystals, and that's what we see."

"How did you learn all that?"

"It's probably in *The Lonely Planet*."

"Seriously."

"Seriously, it's science. We think of icebergs as being white, but that's because they're usually covered in snow. Strip away the snow, and you see the true color."

"Which is blue?"

"Not always. It can be green, black, striped. It depends on how the ice interacts with the light. Pure ice absorbs the reds and reflects the blues back at us, the way it does here." He lifted a shoulder. "Like I said, science."

"Phooey. I'd rather it was magic."

"Science is pretty magical." When Cathryn didn't reply, he said, "Think of it this way. Each layer of ice contains a certain amount of time, the time it took to form. When those bubbles appear on the surface and drip away, it's like the iceberg's losing a bit of time, a bit of its own history."

"Goodness. You've got an answer for everything."

"Hardly." Cathryn saw the shadow cross his features again, the same one she had seen the evening before, at the hotel. Well, everyone had secrets.

She stood, brushing off her jeans. "I need some photos with you in them. I'm supposed to be here for Shades of Blue, not *National Geographic*."

He surveyed the lagoon. "What did you have in mind?"

"I'm not sure." She moved a few yards to the left, then stepped back, squinting at the ice. "I don't suppose you could sort of hover next to that pyramid-shaped iceberg?"

"You mean, in the middle of the lagoon? As in, walk on water?"

"Oh well. Figured I'd ask."

"Here," he said, touching her elbow. "I think this could work. You wouldn't even have to photoshop it."

Cathryn let him lead her to a cluster of rocks that jutted into the water. Behind them, she could hear the sound of cars pulling into the parking lot. "What do you think?" he asked.

"Yes, I see it." Then she turned to him again. "That's what you're trying to convey, right? The blue we can only see when everything else is absorbed. The blue that only happens when light penetrates the hidden crystals. How can you do that, if it takes a hundred years of whatever?"

He met her eyes. "I can try. It's the only thing worth trying."

A car door slammed, and children's voices rang out. The wind picked up, slapping against their bodies. Cathryn wet her lip. "I'd better take those photos."

He stepped back, a stark figure against the twisted turquoise shapes. His face seemed both hidden and exposed.

She was about to take the picture when something made her stop. "Take off your hat," she said. "I want to see your hair." She knew it was cold, knew the bitter wind would blow the hair across his face, but she didn't care.

"Take off yours," he said.

She yanked the cap off her head. The wind lifted the strands, whipped them into her mouth. Her skull was bare now, free. There was nothing between the top of her head and the beginning of the world.

She stuffed the hat in her pocket and snapped his picture.

A moment later, three children came racing across the gravel. Anxious voices called after them in a language Cathryn didn't recognize. More cars arrived.

"I'm glad you made me get here so early," she told him. "It would have been impossible when the place was full of people."

"I thought it would be better. In any case, I didn't really have an option. I have to be on the road by eight."

"By eight?"

"I need to get to Akureyri so I can pick up the keys from Einar—that's the person who's renting me his studio—before he has to leave. It's a seven-hour drive."

"Oh. Right." He'd told her that, over the bottle of Kvöldsól.

Cathryn shivered. She was cold, suddenly, her hair wet with spray from the lagoon. "I need to leave too. The sooner I send my stuff to Renata, the sooner my vacation can start."

Mack nodded. She put the camera away, and they walked in silence to the parking lot. He stood next to the Kia while she chirped it open.

"Does your route take you through Akureyri?" he asked. "I expect it would, as part of the Ring Road."

Her fingers were curled around the silver door handle. "I think so. I think it's Day Four." She feigned an airiness that she didn't feel. It was hollowness, not airiness.

"The Icelandair people are incredibly organized," she added. "Guesthouse reservations, an iPad with daily instructions. They've practically ordered my meals for me."

"You're welcome to stop by when you're in Akureyri," he told her. "You could see a glassblower in action, round out the story."

Cathryn tightened her grip on the door handle. "It would be interesting, but I think my schedule's pretty tight. You have to make advance appointments for those *go-inside-a-glacier* and *wander-the-lava-tube* things."

"Understood."

"It seemed sensible, with only a week." She swallowed. "Anyway, thank you again for making yourself available."

"No problem, as they say."

"I hate that expression."

He smiled. "So do I. I always qualify it. *As they say.*"

"Whoever *they* is."

"Someone. Not me."

She smiled too. "Well, safe journey to Akureyri, and good luck with your project."

"Thanks. You too."

Cathryn watched him walk to the dark-green Jeep and climb inside. He backed out of the parking spot, angled the car in a quick V, and pulled onto the main road.

Around her, the parking lot was filling with cars, but Jökulsárlón felt emptier than it had when she arrived.

Part Two:

Blue Fire

Five

By the time Cathryn came to the intersection of Route 87 and Route 1—Húsavík to the right, Akureyri to the left—she was tired of waterfalls, lava fields, and the coastal fog. She had enjoyed hiking in Vatnajökull National Park, but nothing had come close to the magic of Jökulsárlón.

According to the iPad, she was supposed to head north to Húsavík, a picturesque fishing village with colorful houses, a view of the snow-capped peaks, and a whale-watching trip she had booked for six thirty the next morning—another insanely early expedition but, as the tour company explained, the best time to see the whales. The guesthouse had confirmed her reservation and asked if she would require breakfast.

It was still early when she came to the intersection, not even three o'clock. If she took a slightly indirect route to Húsavík, Akureyri would only be a twenty-minute detour. Twenty minutes each way, thirty minutes or so to have a look at the glass studio. Two hours at most.

Mack's invitation had seemed genuine, and it would be interesting to see glassblowing up close. It might even add to the project, although she had already emailed her design, along with an invoice.

She had his phone number from the messages they'd exchanged. And if he was too busy—well, she'd head to the fishing village, as planned.

"Yes, please come," he said. "I'd hoped you might."

"I'm not interrupting anything?"

"Your timing's perfect. I have an idea I want to try, but I'll wait till you're here so you can watch."

Cathryn felt a surge of happiness that she told herself was ridiculous. "Sounds great."

"Be forewarned. It's pretty primitive. Shower and cot at one end. Glory hole, bench, and marver at the other."

"I'm guessing that a glory hole is some kind of furnace, but I have no idea what a marver is. You'll tell me, I'm sure."

"Whatever you want to know."

Everything.

She inhaled, restarted the engine, and turned left, toward Akureyri.

Akureyri wasn't on her itinerary except as a pass-through. Other than its view of the Eyjafjörður fjord, it didn't have any *can't-miss* sights, no volcanic craters or photogenic puffins. Still, Cathryn told herself, it was worth visiting for the chance to learn about glassblowing. A perfect way to round out her Shades of Blue experience.

She found a place to park in front of the building and rapped on the door. "It's open," he called. "Just be careful not to slam it. You never want to startle someone who's working with hot glass."

Cathryn pulled on the handle of the heavy wooden door, and it swung wide. She guided it shut and looked around.

It was another world, as mysterious as Jökulsárlón. "Oh," she said. And again: "Oh."

Mack was bent over a metal sink, holding an oversized ladle under the running water. "I'll take that as hello."

"Yes. Hello." She turned slowly. An open furnace along one wall, glowing orange. A pile of tools next to a bucket of water. Blue shapes on a high shelf.

"They're experiments," he said, catching her eye. "A way to explore, play with some ideas. I don't think any of them are going to be usable, but glass is forgiving that way. You throw it back in the furnace and start again."

"This is incredible. I've never been in a place like this."

"And here you are."

Here she was. Cathryn felt the flush spread across her cheeks.

Was she doing something wildly inappropriate? No, why would it be inappropriate? It was a natural follow-up to the project. And he had invited her. He'd even said, *I'd hoped you might come.*

It was only inappropriate if she added another motive, and there wasn't one. He was five years younger than she was, for heaven's sake. She'd figured that out from his website.

Mack placed the wooden ladle on the bench and wiped his hands. "Have you been cooped up in a car for hours? Do you need a coffee or something?"

"Coffee would be great." She added another thirty minutes to the detour, but there was still plenty of time. The guesthouse didn't expect her until six.

"There's a café across the street. I'll tell you a bit about glassblowing before I show you how I do it." He gestured at the barn-like space. "I'm not really set up—or, rather, Einar's not set up—to entertain a guest. It's barely a half-step above camping out, but it's fine for me. I don't do much except work."

"And I'm keeping you from that."

"You're not. I'm glad you came. Besides, I'm a caffeine addict."

Cathryn dared to smile. "As am I."

"Come, then. It's just down the block. An authentic Icelandic coffee bar. Consider it part of your Saga Tour."

The café was nearly empty, only a family with two small children who were fighting over a chair with a plaid cushion. Cathryn angled her own chair so her legs wouldn't accidentally brush against Mack's. He was a big man, long-limbed. His knees stuck up like hills on either side of the little table.

The waitress spoke English, like everyone else Cathryn had encountered. "Two coffees," Mack told her.

"And a sweet?"

Cathryn shook her head. "Nor for me," Mack said.

The waitress left, and Cathryn leaned forward, resting her chin on her palm. "So," she said. "Tell me. What do you love about glass?"

"What do I love?" He tilted his head, as if considering how to answer. "I love the way glass is alive."

The light from the window illuminated his features, sharpening the crags of his cheekbones. "And like everything that's alive, it's full of contradictions. Fragile and strong. Liquid and solid. When it's hot, you can pull it, twist it, cut it. When it's cold, it's immovable."

"Glass is present and not-present. We can look through it and at it."

"Quoting me back to myself?"

"It was an intriguing statement. It stuck with me."

The waitress returned with their coffee, a matched cup and saucer in each hand. "Now don't you go switching those cups," she told them.

Cathryn frowned. "Do people do that?"

"Some troublemakers might." The waitress put a hand on her hip and gave Cathryn an arch look. "You've heard about *prælapar*? No? Well, if you serve your guests in a cup and saucer that don't match, it means they'll have an affair. Someone in my position has to be careful."

"Goodness. You have an awful lot of power."

"Oh, there's more. If I refill your cup before you've finished, you'll get an unbearable mother-in-law." She gave a philosophic shrug. "Well, that's what they say. But do wait a bit to drink. If you drink your coffee while it's hot, you'll get ugly. More beauty to you if you wait till it cools."

"I'm definitely waiting," Cathryn said.

"Glad you've explained it," Mack added. "This will revolutionize the cosmetics industry."

Cathryn bit her lip, trying not to laugh. When the waitress had left, she asked him, "Do you think she actually believed all that?"

"Shall we switch saucers and find out?"

Her eyes widened. He was joking, of course. Quickly, she plucked a packet of sugar from a jar in the center of the table, flapping the tube back and forth to loosen the crystals. "Okay," she said. "Glass is full of contradictions. What about glassblowing? There are other ways of working in glass, right?"

"There are," he replied. "Flame-working, with a hand-held torch. Using a mold, crackling. Pulling out long threads of glass, and then chopping or twining them. But it all starts with that first orb."

"That you create by blowing."

"That you create by blowing," he repeated. "That's what makes it so intimate. After all, what other art form requires the breath of its creator?"

Cathryn set the sugar packet on the table, unopened, and met his gaze.

Mack reached for his coffee cup. "On the other hand, blowing's just a small part of it. It's mostly about heating and shaping, softening and twisting, with an occasional puff of air to give it some volume."

"Still."

"The thing is," he went on, "you're working with a substance that's been heated to over two thousand degrees—ten times as hot as boiling water—so you're always on the edge of that place where it's all beyond your control. It means you can't daydream or think about anything else. You can't lose your attention for a second."

"Can you really do that?"

"Come. I'll show you."

"I can't. Not yet." She gave him a solemn look. "I don't dare drink my coffee. I have to wait for it to cool down."

His eyes were solemn too, with none of the irony there had been in hers. "No worries. You'd have a long way to go to approach the outermost rim of ugly."

For the second time that afternoon, Cathryn flushed. He couldn't be flirting, though; there was nothing flirtatious in his voice. He was probably speaking aesthetically. Cheekbones, eyes. She'd had enough experience to know the value of that currency. Initially, at least. Nothing, not even good cheekbones, guaranteed happiness.

"That's kind of you," she managed. "Down the hatch, in that case."

Mack drained his cup and left a pile of krónur on the table, shaking his head when she reached into her purse. "It's just coffee."

Exactly. Just coffee. It meant her heart was thundering for no reason.

They returned to the studio, and he told her, "I'm glad to let you watch and explain what you're seeing. But once I start a piece, I can't stop until it's done. If you need to leave, it's okay, just leave, but I can't stop what I'm doing to say good-bye."

"Of course."

"You were there," he said, pulling his sweater over his head as he strode across the room. He tossed it onto a chair. "In Jökulsárlón. So you can understand what I'm after. Color and form and light—those three things, working together." She watched as he laid a row of tools on the bench. "Three elements to convey something that's endlessly changing, endlessly becoming. Layers of light and glass in exactly the right relationship, so the piece is different every time you look at it."

"Like the iceberg itself." She stepped closer and peered at the tools. Metal and wood, some with pointed tips, others with blades or rounded cups. She pointed to an elongated paddle with a square end. "What's that?"

"We call it a tag. You use it to shape the glass." He indicated a pair of oversized tweezers. "Every glassblower has his own tools; it's unthinkable to use someone else's, but I didn't have much choice. I couldn't very well hide my jacks and shears in my suitcase. Even if I'd checked my bag, what are the odds that the person scanning the luggage would know they were a glassworker's tools?"

"Wait." Cathryn furrowed her brow. "You knew, when you came here, that you'd be staying to work? I thought meeting Einar was a stroke of luck."

Mack flashed a quick grin. "I planned on waiting for the right bit of luck to strike."

"Because you didn't get lucky in Costa Rica?"

The grin disappeared. The transformation was swift and total—as if the light, the very source of the light, had been drained from his face. "Because I didn't get lucky in Costa Rica."

Cathryn was certain he wasn't talking about finding a studio. It was something personal, something that hurt. She longed to ask but knew she couldn't.

It was impossible to know where the hours had gone. Cathryn had watched, entranced, as Mack swung the pole, and the molten glob clung to its tip like a living creature, always changing, always on the verge of falling. Features emerged, receded. With a deft twist, he pulled what was inside to the surface, exposing a new depth.

Finally, when he was finished, he put the piece in a small oven. "The annealer," he explained, as he set the timer. "It has to cool slowly."

Cathryn glanced at her watch and was stunned to see that it was seven forty-five. You couldn't rely on the fading light to warn you about the passage of time, not this far north. If the annealer hadn't prompted her to look at her watch—if Mack hadn't wiped his hands on his jeans, signaling that he was done—she never would have guessed how late it had gotten.

She felt a spike of alarm. Her reservation in Húsavík. Surely they would hold it for her; it was part of her prepaid Saga Tour.

"Want to try it yourself?" he asked.

"Now?"

"True, it's probably too late. But if you want to come back in the morning, I'd be glad to let you have a try. You can't understand something by watching someone else do it."

She stared at him. "You really mean it?"

"Of course I really mean it."

Cathryn grew still. She could. Instead of looking for whales, who might not even show up, she could play with fire.

It was a minor swap, glass for whales, and she'd pick up her itinerary in the afternoon. "All right," she said. "What time?"

"Early would be good. Let's say eight o'clock."

Her mind was racing now. Why go to Húsavík anyway, only to come right back here in the morning? Why not just stay in Akureyri? There had to be a room in one of the hotels.

"And wear layers," he told her. "It's hot by the furnace."

"Yes. Eight o'clock."

"And layers," he insisted. "You'd be surprised how warm you can get."

"Layers," she repeated. "Right."

She was warm already, lit with the fire of what she was doing.

Six

Twelve hours later, Cathryn was knocking on the door of the studio again. The sun was bright overhead, and the street smelled of the harbor.

She had abandoned the reservation in Húsavík, despite a polite reminder from the owner of the guesthouse that she would still be charged for the room, and found a nondescript hotel in the center of Akureyri.

After Húsavík, she was supposed to head south to visit a volcanic crater and a field of mini-geysers, but that didn't make sense anymore. Akureyri was fifty miles northwest of the crater. It seemed foolish to backtrack so far—simpler to skip that part of the trip and head straight up the fjord after her morning in the hot shop. It was her vacation, after all. She could do whatever she wanted.

Mack opened the door, a coffee mug in his hand. His hair fell in a disheveled heap across his forehead, and he clearly hadn't shaved. Steam rose from the mug in a hazy spiral.

Cathryn tensed. Had he just woken up? Forgotten that she was coming?

"Morning," he drawled. "Ready to not lose your attention for a second?"

She let out her breath. He hadn't forgotten. "I think you described it as being on the edge of out-of-control."

"The best place to be." He lifted the mug, as if in salute. "Do you realize that you always quote me back to myself?"

"I do? I guess it's an interviewer's device. You know, to establish rapport."

"Don't," he said. "I'm not your interview subject. Not now."

"What are you, then?" The words slipped out. Mortified, she wanted to grab them back.

"Your glassblowing teacher, of course." He was still holding the door with his other hand. "Were you planning on coming in?"

"I thought you'd never ask."

The place looked different in the morning light. There was a yellow glow over everything, even the line of tools, as if each item had been dipped in butter. Mack gave her an appraising glance. "You have something else on, under that heavy shirt?"

Cathryn met his gaze. "I do. As instructed."

"I just wanted to be sure. It gets hot in front of the glory hole."

She kept her eyes on his as she ripped open the row of snaps on her flannel shirt and flung it on a chair. She still had two layers underneath. "There you go. Ready to blow glass, captain."

Mack laughed. "We need to do a few things first." He shut the door with his heel and set the mug next to her shirt. "Come. Let's set up."

Your glassblowing teacher. Fine. She followed him across the room. A bench, steel table, and a small furnace formed a triangle at the far end. "What do I need to do?"

"Mostly, you need to pay attention. There's a saying about glass-work: Be quick, but don't hurry. You have to stay alert, because the glass never stops moving—which means you never stop responding. It's like a dance."

"With a partner you can't predict."

"Exactly. That's why you can't daydream. Ever."

Cathryn felt herself tighten again. "What if I do?"

"I'll be right here. We'll do it together." His expression was kinder than she'd expected. "I'll show you how to make a paperweight, give you a taste of what it's like. That way, you'll understand better when you do your write-up for Renata."

For her write-up, only she'd already turned it in. Mack didn't know that. Or maybe he did.

"Let's start by picking the colors you want to use," he told her. "You don't have to stick to the Jökulsárlón colors."

"I'd rather stick to them, actually."

This was for the job, for Shades of Blue. To make sure that was clear, she added, "Like you said. I want to understand how you get that silvery-blue."

"You don't have to," he insisted. "You can do whatever wild thing you want. Red. Bronze. Aubergine."

Whatever wild thing she wanted.

Cathryn tossed her head. "Fine. Red and bronze."

"Pick a third. Three colors work well for a paperweight."

"Lord, you're bossy. Dark blue."

"That's good. The cobalt will balance the other two." He pulled out a cart that had been pushed underneath the metal table and removed a tray of pans. "These are called *frits*. They're tiny grains of colored glass that we'll roll your piece in, one layer at a time. Personally, I prefer color bars, but Einar has frits so we'll use frits." He glanced at her, as if checking to be sure she was really listening. "Everything's in layers, step by step. You can't be impatient."

Cathryn raised an eyebrow. "Do I come across as impatient?"

She was aware, suddenly, of how close he was standing, how his body seemed to fill the room. "I don't know," he said. "I don't really know you."

He motioned her to a rack where a half dozen metal rods were arrayed and selected one, handing it to her. "Hold it this way." He placed her fingers on the top and bottom of the rod. "You'll be collecting the glass at one end—that molten blob is called a *gather*—and carrying it back and forth between the glory hole and the table with the frits, so it has to feel comfortable. You have to feel confident when you're holding it."

Cathryn balanced the pipe between her hands, feeling its heft. "Comfortable, check. Confident, not so much."

"You'll be fine." He took the pipe from her. "Actually, speaking of comfort, you should probably get rid of that long-sleeved shirt. You'll get much hotter at the glory hole than you might think."

She remembered telling him to take off his hat when they were at Jökulsárlón, and the way he'd said, "Take off yours." It had felt shocking and wonderful.

"All right." She pulled the long-sleeved tee shirt over her head. Mack took off a thick denim shirt and put their garments on the metal chair. The dark blue tank top was the only layer she had left. She had thought it would make her feel vulnerable to be so bare, but it didn't. It made her feel powerful.

"Ready?"

She nodded.

"We'll take it step by step," he said. "And once you start to work in the colors, you'll see that the glass is very pliable and responsive. Some people say it's like warm honey." His expression grew stern. "No matter what, though, the pipe can't stop spinning. You might worry that the gather's going to fall off, but it won't as long as you keep it moving."

"Promise?"

The sternness seemed to deepen, darkening his features. "I don't make promises, not anymore."

Then he took a pair of iron tongs and placed them in a bucket next to the bench. "Your jacks. They're an extension of your arm, like a conductor's baton. Some people even travel to Murano to buy their jacks from one of the master glassmakers."

"Did you do that?"

"I did. It's like a rite of passage, when you're ready to make the commitment." He motioned at the row of tools. "Einar's stuff is pretty basic, but I'm grateful to have it."

She eyed the pole again. "What if it *does* fall off, though? The gather."

"We pick up the pieces, throw them in the furnace, and start over."

"Ha. Wouldn't it be nice if life was like that?"

She'd meant it as a clever remark, but suddenly she longed to know how he would answer. Even when she had been a kind of artist herself, all those years ago, her photographs hadn't been alive the way glass was alive. If a photo didn't work, you got rid of it. You didn't melt it down and turn it into something new—no more than you could take an experience that didn't work out the way you had hoped and toss it into the glory hole of your life. The layers of your life accrued, adhered. What was it like to have an art form that let you start over?

She gathered her courage, ready to speak, needing to speak— when, without warning, Mack sagged and slumped forward. Cathryn jerked, her hand flying to her mouth.

Before she could move, Mack had righted himself. He shivered and wiped his face. "What is it?" she asked, confused. It had been so quick, the sagging and then the recovery. "What happened? Are you all right?"

He waved a hand. "It's nothing. I get these dizzy little blips once in a while. Probably from my intemperate habits. Or, more likely, my bad karma."

"Don't be glib."

"I'm not. It's no big deal."

"Bad karma doesn't give you dizzy little blips. Bad karma gives you pangs of conscience that tell you to act more benevolently toward your fellow human beings."

"Good to know. I'll start soon."

"Hey, you can start with me."

"I thought I *was* treating you benevolently."

She felt the telltale flush creep up her neck. "You are."

"Whew." Then he bent and placed two more tools in the bucket, along with a wad of wet newspaper. "One of our most finely crafted pieces of equipment. It's perfect for holding the glass while you shape it."

"You sure you're okay?"

"I'm fine. Come, let's gather your glass."

He placed her hands on the pipe again and guided her to the mouth of the furnace. "Let the glass come to you. Keep the pipe turning, and it will."

Cathryn could feel him behind her, surrounding her, as his hands hovered near hers. The heat poured over them. She moved her fingers, rotated the pipe.

"See?" he told her. "It won't fall off, even if it looks like it's going to, as long as you keep it moving."

"It's magical." She'd said that about the icebergs too. Glass and ice, both alive.

"That's because it's molten. Not liquid, which would spill. And not solid, which wouldn't let you shape it." He stepped away from the furnace. "You've got enough now. Remember what I said about being quick but don't hurry?"

"Permission to quote you, sir?"

He laughed. "Carry it over to the marver and roll it along the red frit. It's okay to press down hard. It won't break."

She pressed the gather into the frit and moved it back and forth, collecting grains of red glass. "This is amazing. When do I get to blow through the pipe?"

"No one does that, their first time. You have to learn to understand the glass. How it moves, what it needs."

"Darn."

"Air's only one of the factors. Not even the main one."

Cathryn raised her head. "Air, fire, water, and earth—because glass is made of sand, right? And water to cool it down." She gave him a smug look. "All the primordial elements."

"You're not spinning the pipe." He laced his arms through hers to give the rod a twist. "Nothing, not even the most interesting thought, can be more important than keeping the glass in motion."

Chastised, she looked down. "You're right. I'm sorry." But she wasn't sorry that her lapse had made him twine his arms through hers. The muscles moved below his skin as he rotated the pipe and then, carefully, took it from her.

"Let me show you how to use the tweezers and jacks to work in the colors. Sit at the end of the bench. I'll bring the pipe to you."

She sat, and Mack placed the pipe with its molten bulb across her open palms. She could see the sheen of sweat on his arms, the dark moist hair that made a trail from elbow to wrist.

"Here's the interesting thing," he said. "You're going to be pulling the colors in and out of each other, but you won't know how your paperweight will actually look until you open the annealing oven the next day. It looks red-orange right now because it's molten, but when it cools you'll see the colors of the frits you chose. They cool separately because they're made from different elements. You can't blend them, the way you'd blend paint. You can only make them interpenetrate. That's what the jacks and tweezers are for."

"Wait," she interrupted. "You can't see what it looks like until the next day?"

"It has to cool slowly or it won't be stable. I like to reduce the heat in stages, over twelve hours or so."

"But I won't be here in twelve hours."

He shrugged. "Then you won't know what you've made."

Cathryn grew quiet, her lungs caught between the in-breath and the out-breath.

"Does it matter?"

She knew she was supposed to say *no*, it was for the experience, not to take home some silly paperweight. But she said, "Yes." Because it did matter.

She wanted him to tell her, *Then stay.* It was a crazy thought, and of course he didn't.

Instead, he took the pipe again. "I'll make sure it cools properly and send you a photo. But first you have to finish it. Let me heat it up for you. It's gotten cool while we've been talking."

She watched him walk back to the glory hole, struggling with a wave of disappointment she hadn't foreseen. She didn't know what she'd foreseen, but not this feeling of utter desolation. As if the best part of the trip, the whole point of the trip, was already over.

When he returned to the bench, she held the rod while he used a long-handled wooden cup to shape one end of the sphere. Her neck and shoulders were covered in sweat. She wanted to lift the hair off her neck but couldn't take her hands off the rod, not right now. Why hadn't he mentioned the hair part? She could have tied it back. No, he'd been too busy telling her to take her clothes off.

She knew she sounded irritable, but couldn't help it. "I don't understand how you get from a round little paperweight to a replica of Jökulsárlón."

"It's not a replica. I told you that already."

"Fine. How you get from a round little whatever to the mystical essence of an iceberg lagoon?"

Instead of getting annoyed, he gave a Mack-sized laugh. "There are a hundred ways to work with glass, like I told you. That's what makes it fun." He handed her the jacks. "I'll keep the pipe turning for you. Take this and see what you can do."

Cathryn took the jacks and pinched a section of the molten glass. Despite herself, she felt a surge of delight. "It's like taffy." She remembered what he had said. "Or warm honey."

"Play with it," he told her. "I'll adapt to your movements."

"What should I do?"

"Whatever you feel like." He tilted the rod to catch the glass as it shifted. "Follow your instincts, but don't do too much. Overdoing doesn't make it better."

She wanted to ask what too much was, but knew he couldn't, or wouldn't, tell her. Anyway, too much wasn't her style. Her style was more like not enough.

It didn't seem fair, not to know how her piece would come out. Well, that was her life. One more item in the bin called I'll never know.

She drew out a thick strand of glass and pushed it into the hot sphere. "You really have no idea how you're moving the colors around? What it will look like?"

"You learn to tell, with experience. I just meant that you won't be able to tell, your first time."

Would there be a second time? Of course not. It was an explanation, that's all.

She twisted the glass, catching the moving shape as he rotated the pipe. She could feel him next to her, responding to her gestures. His mass, the movement of his arms and chest.

After a while he said, "I think the piece is ready to come off. It's called controlled breaking. Come, I'll show you."

Cathryn followed him across the room, forcing her feet to move. Once her piece had been freed from its perch and settled in the annealing oven, there would be no reason for her to linger.

Mack placed the pole in a V-shaped holder. "The last step is to remove what you've made from the blowpipe. If you don't break it off intentionally, it'll shatter when it cools."

"That sounds very profound. To survive, you have to break free."

"It is profound." He gave the paperweight a sharp rap, and it broke away from the pipe. "Look," he said, lifting it with the tongs to show her the underside. "You see this little mark on the bottom? It's the imprint that's left. We call it a punti scar, the mark of its origin. It proves that the piece was made by hand and not from a mold."

Then he opened the small metal door to a box-like structure next to the table and placed the paperweight inside. "The annealing oven." He flipped a dial, then turned to Cathryn again. "Each glassblower has his own special punti mark. It's like *Kilroy was here*."

She smiled, though something was squeezing her ribs so hard that it hurt. Her paperweight was in its twelve-hour cooldown oven. It meant they were done.

She looked at her watch and saw that the day was half gone. No doubt he had things to do and was waiting for her to leave.

As if he had read her mind, he asked, "Where do you go next?"

Cathryn tried to remember what was next on the route up the peninsula. A little island for bird-watching, and then a town on a fjord known for its herring festival. Not that she gave a shit about a herring festival.

She gave what she hoped was a casual shrug. "Oh, off to search for the northern lights." It sounded better than herring, and it wasn't a lie. The guidebook said it was the wrong time of year, but everyone who came to Iceland hoped to catch a glimpse of that iconic splendor.

"Aha. You've ferreted out my heart's desire."

"Really? It's mine too."

"Who knows, then? Maybe we'll fulfill our desire together."

Cathryn's pulse jumped, a ping-pong of excitement and fear. Then she told herself, Idiot. It was like his remark about the outermost rim of ugly. A flirtatious bit of repartee, flip and meaningless. Men did that, and women loved it.

She kept her voice light. "As you say, who knows? Meanwhile, thank you again for giving me so much of your time."

Mack studied her with an expression she couldn't fathom, then touched her arm before striding to the metal chair and handing her the shirts she had discarded. "You'll want these."

"Right."

Somehow they were walking to the door, and he was holding it open. "Safe travels," he said. "I'll text you the photo tomorrow."

"That'd be great. Thanks."

She didn't want some damn photo, but that was all she was going to get. Well, what had she expected? Her face impassive, Cathryn stepped through the doorway, into the street.

The gaudiness of midday assaulted her. A cacophony of people in their brightly colored coats. The glaring yellow sun, the smells of diesel and fish.

It took all she had to stride to the Kia, grab the handle, and stumble inside.

Seven

Cathryn left Akureyri and headed north, along the eastern edge of the Tröllaskagi Peninsula. The road wound past glacial valleys, horse farms, and cliffs with jaw-dropping views of the fjord. Sheep dotted the hillsides. Bales of hay, wrapped in Easter-egg pink and blue, were scattered across the fields like giant marshmallows.

Her plan was to drive the thirty-five kilometers from Akureyri to Árskógssandur and take the ferry to the little island of Hrísey. Known as the Pearl of the Fjord, Hrísey was home to forty species of bird, with a scattering of hamlets and a family-run restaurant that served seafood they caught themselves. Cathryn parked the Kia near the harbor and bought a ticket for the ferry. Then she found a seat in the café until it was time to depart.

Someone had left a flyer on her table—an advertisement for a local beer spa, Árskógssandur's other attraction. The spa featured wooden bathtubs filled with a special blend of beer and yeast that was supposed to cleanse, soften, and neutralize the effects of aging.

Cathryn pushed the flyer to the end of the table. Another Icelandic claim of effortless renewal. Rhubarb wine. Silica facials. Broken glass you could throw in the furnace for an instant do-over.

She drained the cup of coffee she'd bought to justify her seat in the café and tried not to let bitterness seep into the afternoon she had planned. She would have two hours on Hrísey, plenty of time to watch the birds and enjoy a plate of the island's signature blue mussels, then back to her car and onward to the next pre-booked guesthouse.

When she began the trip, a drive around the land of fire and ice had seemed like a daring adventure. But now she wondered: How daring was it, really, when everything was booked for you by a Saga Tour agent and programmed into your personal iPad?

Rachel had missed the point. *Crazy and exotic* didn't have to do with rain forests and spice markets. It had to do with you.

Whatever wild thing you want.

A bell sounded. Cathryn rose quickly and joined the line of people waiting to board the ferry. She found a spot by the railing as the boat pulled away from the dock.

They were halfway to Hrísey when she heard the jingle of her cell phone. Her heartbeat quickened, then righted itself. It was a call, not a text. Anyway, it couldn't be the photo; the paperweight would be in the annealer for another ten hours. She felt in her purse for the phone and squinted at the caller ID. Judah.

The squint deepened to a frown. Why would her son be calling? He knew she was in Iceland—on a business trip, she had told him. Unless it was an emergency, although a Judah "emergency" could be anything from a minor impediment to a serious screw-up.

"Hey Jude." It was her standard greeting and always made her think of the Beatles song, released long before her own Jude was born. *You're waiting for someone to perform with. Don't you know it's just you?*

She stepped away from the railing, into the privacy of a sheltered corner. "What's up?"

"Mom. I need your help."

Cathryn's mind flipped through the possible scenarios. An accident. Arrested. Trapped in a burning building. "What happened?"

"They towed my damn car and I can't get to work." His voice rose, cracking. "How was I supposed to know they would really do that? The sign was practically hidden by the branches. You couldn't even see it."

Cathryn closed her eyes in relief. A towed car, not a mangled one. "You remember I'm in Iceland, right?" Then she added, "On a job."

"Yeah, I remember." Judah let out a sigh. "But I thought maybe I could borrow your car, just for today. I have to be at work in half an hour. I thought maybe you had a spare key."

Now that she knew he was all right, not dead or held hostage, Cathryn had to stifle the urge to scream. Her Peter Pan son had followed her to Iceland with his endless passivity, or lack of confidence, or whatever it was that made him assume she would rush to pave every road before he even stepped on it. She knew she had encouraged that dependency after Brian died, feeling badly for her poor fatherless son, but she had never meant it to go on so long.

And, of course, the words *car key*. Judah had no way to know what those words meant.

"Mom? You there?"

She opened her eyes. "I'm here."

There was a long silence, and she knew he was waiting for her to tell him where the key was. Finally, Judah cleared his throat. "You took car service to the airport, right? So your car's still at the house?"

The urge to scream got stronger. Judah was her son and she loved him, but she wanted to throw the phone over the side of the boat. Why was it her job to solve this? What would he have done if she hadn't answered?

"Actually, I don't have a spare key," she said. "I left it with the dealer the last time I brought the car in."

"Shit. What am I supposed to do?"

Cathryn closed her eyes for another excruciating moment. "Call into work and tell them you'll be late. Find out where they took your car. You can figure it out."

"You sure you don't have a key somewhere?"

"I don't have a key somewhere. I'm in the middle of a fjord."

Her heart was pounding—not with anger but with fear, as if she were doing something frightening. "You can figure it out," she repeated. "You're a smart guy." She could feel him struggling, even from twenty-seven hundred miles away. "Just tell your boss the truth. People respond to the truth, you'd be amazed."

"I guess. I mean, yeah, okay." Then he added, "How's your trip?"

"Oh, working hard, but thanks for asking. I'll try to squeeze in a geyser or two."

Then, suddenly, Cathryn realized that she did have a spare key. The dealer had given it back to her, and she'd dropped it into the Navajo pot on her desk where she kept her flash drive and extra batteries.

Wait, she wanted to tell Judah, but stopped with the word still forming on her lips. He'd already accepted that he had to handle it himself. To give him the key would undo that.

"Geysers sound pretty cool," he was saying. "I mean, cool as in *cool*, not as in *cold*."

Thoughts careened across her mind. Wouldn't a good mother, a kind mother, tell her son about the key? It would save him a lot of trouble, and he would be grateful.

On the other hand, maybe a good mother would help her child grow up, even if he didn't thank her for it.

"Anyway," Judah said, "have some fun, if you can. Sorry I bothered you."

Cathryn blinked. "It's fine."

"I think this happened to Garrett once, you know, my roommate? He can probably tell me where they towed it."

"Good idea." Cathryn heard the slapping of water against the boat, the screech of a bird. Judah was going to do it. He was actually going to handle it himself. "You'll deal with it," she said. "I have faith in you."

She had never told him that before and wasn't sure, now, if it was entirely true. But he was twenty-two years old, and both of them had to start sometime. If Brian had been there all these years—well, Brian hadn't been there. He'd been dead, smashed on the highway before he could humiliate her in front of their family and friends.

Everyone had been so kind and supportive. The shocked widow, at such a young age. The lovely couple. It was all such bullshit. Rachel knew that, even at nine years old, and had distanced herself from the tense mother and nerdy little brother who cramped her style. But Judah, only seven, had needed her, and Cathryn had let him.

If he assumed, even now, that she would provide the fallback, the Plan B, the spare key to unlock whatever jam he was in—that was her doing, not his. Fifteen years had passed. It was time to stop being a parent who was needed and become one who wasn't.

She realized that Judah had been telling her a story about Garrett's car; she'd missed most of it, though the punchline seemed to be that Garrett eventually retrieved it. Then she saw that the other passengers were gathering at the front of the boat. "I have to go," she said. "I'm supposed to see an island with a lot of birds. But text me when you've got the car back, okay?"

"Will do. Say hi to the penguins for me."

"Puffins. No penguins in Iceland."

"Puffins. Ptarmigans. All avian species that start with a P."

Cathryn smiled. "I'll tell them Jude the Dude sends his regards."

She dropped the phone into her purse and joined the other passengers as the island, Hrísey, came into view. She was already losing interest in the birds and blue mussels, but it seemed silly to go right back to the mainland. Resolving to make the best of it, she joined a tour led by a man with a handlebar mustache who pointed out the hidden nests and explained why there were so many birds. "We've banned all hunting and all gathering of eggs," he told them, "and there aren't any natural predators. No mice, no skunks. Not even man. Less than two hundred people on the whole island."

Cathryn listened to his recitation of bird species and found the monologue oddly calming. By the time she boarded the ferry for the return trip to Árskógssandur, something had settled inside her. Deal with it, she had told Judah. Figure it out. That went for her too.

From Árssko´gssandur, Cathryn continued up the winding coastal road until she reached the entrance to a shockingly narrow tunnel. It barely looked wide enough for one car but was, apparently, meant for two-way traffic. There was no way to turn around or take an alternate road. Grimacing, she flicked on the headlights and inched forward.

The tunnel was carved out of rock, dimly lit, and endless. Every so often, she noticed a little pullout on one or the other side. There were signs with circles and arrows in different colors, but she had no idea what they meant and there was no one to ask.

At first, it seemed to work out. She drove slowly, despite her impatience to emerge on the other side. Each time she approached a pullout, she saw a car waiting for her to pass—thank goodness, although she didn't know if or when she was supposed to be the one to pull over. Maybe she could just keep going and let everyone make way for her.

That seemed like a reasonable plan until she saw the approaching beams of an enormous truck. How had that thing even fit into the tunnel? But there it was, accelerating toward her with no pullout in sight.

Was she supposed to stop, back up? What good would that do, in this skinny little tunnel? Cathryn gripped the steering wheel, her heart pushing against her ribs. What the fuck was she supposed to do?

The driver seemed to have no intention of slowing down. The headlights grew brighter, larger, closer. She thought *this is it*, and *fucking Icelanders*. What were they thinking, building a tunnel like this? Another sign bloomed on her right, a white arrow and then a big letter M. What the hell did M mean?

Just as the truck seemed about to crash into her, Cathryn saw the pullout, a little bay hacked out of the rock. She jerked the Kia into a space that couldn't possibly be big enough. It skittered along the rock wall, throwing her against the steering wheel as she jammed her foot on the brake. The truck whizzed past.

Her heart was thundering now, so huge and loud it would surely burst through her flesh. Did Icelanders really live with this kind of insanity, or was it just that she hadn't taken the time to understand the rules? She put the car in neutral and sagged against the seat. She didn't think she could drive another inch.

Three more cars sped past, two going in the same direction, a third in the opposite. Cathryn waited, but there was no crashing sound, so the drivers were probably Icelanders who knew what to do and understood when they had to give way. Clearly, the pullouts weren't meant for the huge trucks.

It was all she could do to keep breathing—to stay there, still alive, as the air moved in and out of her lungs. Finally, she forced herself to shift the car into gear. She couldn't stay in the little pullout forever. As she moved forward, back into the lane, a crazy joy swept over her.

I did it, she thought. I saved my own fucking life.

Another car shot into view, but this time she saw the M sign and moved out of the way. After another kilometer, there was a burst of light at the mouth of the tunnel, and Cathryn could see the road widening into two lanes. She craned her neck, eager to know what would appear when she emerged.

The view of Ólafsfjörður, where she'd booked a guesthouse for the night, made the terror recede. Snow-topped mountains, brilliant in the sunlight. An expanse of bright green fields, blue water so abundant that it almost hurt.

The owner of the guesthouse greeted her warmly. "This used to be the post office, you know, but I think we've made it rather appealing. We're pleased to offer a full breakfast from seven to nine, as well as soup whenever you like."

"That sounds wonderful," Cathryn said.

"Let me show you to your room." As he led her to a room on the top floor, he told her, "Actually, you're in luck. There's a chance we may be able to see the northern lights tonight. It's early in the year, but we're quite far north, and they say we've got good odds." He opened the door, then handed her a brass key. "I'm asking each of our guests: would you like me to knock and wake you if it happens? It could be late. Two, three in the morning."

Cathryn stopped on the threshold of a room with a slanted roof and whitewashed floorboards. The key rested in her palm. "Yes. Please."

My heart's desire.

Maybe we'll fulfill our desire together.

"Very well," the owner said. "If the lights start to appear, someone will knock on your door. If they don't, we'll let you sleep in peace."

For a wild, impossible instant, she thought she might text him: *Come. We can see them together.*

"Thank you," she said. "That's sensible."

She didn't want to be sensible. She wanted the northern lights. She wanted her heart's desire.

When Cathryn awoke the next morning, sunlight was spilling into the room. At first she was confused, until she understood: no one had woken her because the aurora hadn't appeared.

She shouldn't have expected it. It was the wrong season, and even in the winter the northern lights were unpredictable. She flung the blanket aside and sat up. Instinctively, she reached for her phone.

There were two messages. Her pulse spiked, then tumbled again, as it had on the ferry. Judah, followed by Rachel.

Judah's message was long and sincere. "I wanted to let you know that I worked it all out. They were awesome about covering for me until I got the car out of the impound place, and I got docked a few hours' pay, but I can do some overtime so it's all good. Sorry for calling you in the Land of Ice."

Rachel's message was shorter. "Just saying hi and hope you're having fun. Can you bring me back one of those wool scarves? Any color, but maybe red."

Her pleasure dimmed. She hadn't even bought a souvenir for herself. Maybe she should bring home a paperweight. One she had made.

He was supposed to text her a picture so she could see how it turned out. Twelve hours had come and gone; the photo should have arrived by now. He'd forgotten.

Then she realized: No, twelve hours would have been the middle of the night. Unlikely that he had been up then, or was up now. It was barely six in the morning.

She swung her feet onto the floor and pushed off the bed. The terror she had felt in the tunnel—and the power, the gratitude—came back to her, as if someone had seized her by the shoulders and shouted, *Don't you understand?*

She'd been certain that she was going to die, but she hadn't.

She was still here, right now. She wasn't finished.

Her phone buzzed. She wheeled around and saw the photo. A sphere that looked like a planet, with swirls of red and cobalt and gold.

Below it, three words. "To remember. Mack."

There was a dot between the second and third words, the tiniest of marks. If she took the dot away, it changed everything. It meant that it was *him* she needed to remember, the man, not the glass-blowing lesson.

She looked at the photo again. She wanted the real thing, not a picture of it.

That meant she was going to turn around—head south, instead of north—and go back to Akureyri to get it.

Eight

The single-lane tunnel wasn't nearly as terrifying as it had been the day before. Maybe it was because she knew the rules, more or less. Or maybe it was the fierceness that coursed through her body, shoving the fear into a little M pullout so she could rush past and get to Akureyri.

When Cathryn emerged at the southern end of the tunnel, she pulled onto the shoulder to consider—belatedly—what in the world she was doing.

He had said good-bye, with no suggestion that they would see each other again. *Safe travels.* That was it. Even the photo of the paperweight was a remembrance of something that was over, in the past. Not an invitation. Not, even obliquely, a call to return.

Well, what was the worst thing that could happen? He'd be embarrassed and annoyed? Maybe even angry?

No. The worst thing that could happen would be for her to turn around and head north again, afraid to take the risk.

She thought of texting: "I'm coming back. Is that okay?" Or nothing at all, and simply appearing. Finally, she wrote, "On my way back."

If he told her not to come or asked her to leave once she got there, she'd reverse direction yet again and pick up the itinerary the

Saga Tour had planned for her. She could drive through the damn tunnel a third time if she had to.

The sky was a flawless blue, matched by the blue of the fjord. Snow-covered mountains rimmed the horizon as Cathryn wound down the coastline into Akureyri. The parking spot she had vacated less than twenty-four hours earlier was still there. She slid the Kia into the space, shut off the engine, and reached across the seat for her phone.

He had answered her text. One word. "Yes."

Yes what? She hadn't asked a question.

Then she shivered, part thrill and part the terror she had kept at bay while she drove through the tunnel. *Yes* wasn't a reply to a question. It was an affirmation of what her own message had implied.

She shoved the phone in her purse, locked the Kia, and rapped on the studio's heavy wooden door. Like the first time, he called, "Come in. It's open." She pulled on the handle and stepped inside.

Mack was bent over the bench, deep in concentration, his face streaked with sweat as he brought two bubbles of glass together until the edges touched, fit, fused. Each was a different shade of turquoise, one lucent, the other opaque.

"Give me a minute," he said.

Suddenly Cathryn felt like a fool. What was she doing here? What did he think she was doing here? She remembered what he had told her about not being able to stop, once he started a piece. "Shall I come back later?" Or not at all.

Mack raised his head. "No. Stay."

She sat down on a metal chair, watching as he moved a small torch around the perimeter of the fused object. Then he picked up a pair of tweezers and drew the end of the piece into an elegant tapering curve. After what seemed like hours, he put the finished sculpture into the cooling oven and turned to her.

"You came back. I wasn't sure if you really meant it."

"I guess I did."

"Why?"

She brushed back her hair. "I wanted my paperweight."

"In that case, I'd better give it to you." He wiped his face with a towel, then walked to a shelf and plucked an object from the back. "Here you go. I think it came out pretty well."

Cathryn rose to take it from him. "It did. I can't believe it."

"The cobalt was perfect."

"The cobalt was perfect," she echoed.

"Why are you really here?

Her heart was like a jackhammer. "I don't know. I wanted to come back."

He was facing her, only inches away. The glow from the glory hole illuminated the crags of his wonderfully unbeautiful face. "I'm glad you did."

She gave the barest nod. If she moved more than that, the moment would shatter. Like glass.

"I don't know much about you," he said.

"What do you want to know?"

He lifted a shoulder. "How long you're going to be in Iceland. Your favorite ice cream flavor. Whether you have a husband waiting for you back home."

"I fly back on the twenty-third. Cherry Garcia. No husband."

"Was there ever a husband?"

"There was. He died."

"Are you grieving?"

It was an odd question. Intimate and demanding, old-fashioned in its syntax. "No," she answered. "It was a long time ago."

"That doesn't mean you're not grieving."

"Trust me, I'm not."

He indicated the paperweight she was still holding. "Do you have a bag to put this in? There's a decent pub down the street. I'll buy you a Viking Gold."

"Really? At this hour?"

"There's a special dispensation in Iceland. You can have a Viking Gold whenever you want."

"That's not the Black Death drink, is it?"

A smile lit up his features. "Not at all. It's like a cross between coffee and caramel and a Coors Lite. It's for those of us who've decided that we want to live."

Cathryn met his gaze. His words were a declaration and an invitation. Yes, she thought. She wanted to live.

The pub was like a pub anywhere: beer on tap, pendant lights, a mirror on the wall. They settled onto stools at the end of a cherry-wood bar, and Mack held up two fingers. "Viking Gylltur."

Cathryn tilted her head. "Essential vocabulary for a stay in Iceland?"

"Actually, there are three essential phrases. There's *Þetta reddast*, which either means everything will be just fine, or I really don't want to think about the shit that's about to hit the fan. And *Gluggaveður*, which means weather that looks great when you're inside looking out the window, but actually isn't. And *Vesen*, for something you're making more complicated that it needs to be."

"The Icelandic are pretty cynical."

"Or realistic."

The bartender placed their beer on the cherrywood counter, gold bottles with the logo of a Viking ship. Mack extended his bottle in a brief salute. Cathryn raised hers in response but didn't drink. She was already light-headed, even without alcohol.

"I guess you need a few choice phrases if you're going to be here for a month," she offered. "That's what you said, right?"

"Or as long as I need. I have the studio for a month, and then we'll see." He gave one of the hooded glances she had come to recognize. "It's hard for me to think too far ahead, but for now I've got this place while Einar treks around Scotland. After that, who knows?"

Cathryn made a noncommittal murmur. It was hard for her *not* to think too far ahead. Maybe it was from raising two children—the way the orthodontist made you book the next check-up while you were paying for the last one, the way time was organized into semesters and sports seasons and cycles of summer and winter clothes. She couldn't imagine giving an answer that consisted of *we'll see* and *who knows?*

On the other hand, she was sitting in a pub in Akureyri having a Viking Gold when the iPad wanted her to be in Siglufjörður touring a herring museum. There was nothing about this moment she could have foreseen.

She raised her bottle again. "Þetta reddast." Mack gave an appreciative grin, and Cathryn sat back, pleased with herself.

She hadn't really thought about what would happen after she appeared at his door. Appearing had seemed like the important part, doing something that might be insane, yet felt so urgent and right. He had seemed glad to see her, and he had used her arrival to take a break from his work. But then? He wasn't about to drop his project to go off on a sightseeing tour, so what did she have in mind?

To stay here, she thought.

And then: Lord, how pathetic. If she had no other reason to be in Akureyri, then she was chasing a man. Period. And worse, hoping to distract him from the very work she had come here to chronicle.

It seemed so obvious, but she hadn't stopped to consider her actions—or how they might look to him—when she threw her suitcase in the Kia and headed back to Akureyri, past the horse farms and the sheep and the Easter-wrapped bales of hay. She had simply come, driven by an instinct that was so unlike her usual way of being that it had seemed, for that very reason, beyond question.

Now that she was here, she needed an explanation that would make sense to him. It came to her at once, because it was the truth.

She had come for the man, and for the glass too. To be part of that. To understand what its mysterious quality of being molten, always in transition, could teach her.

And what are you, then? she had asked him.

Your glassblowing teacher, of course.

Something wondrous shot up her spine, spreading into her tendons and bones. Joy and panic and power, braided together.

She could do this. Would do this.

Mack set down his beer. "So," he said. "You reversed your route."

"I thought I might spend a couple of days learning about glass." He gave her a quizzical look, and she lifted her chin. "I'm here on a ten-day adventure. I can do whatever I want with my time."

"And you want to spend some of that time in a hot shop in Akureyri?"

Cathryn faced him, steady as steel now. "I do. When would I ever get another chance like this?"

"I can't stop what I'm doing to give you glassblowing lessons."

"I'll watch. I can learn that way too." Then she shrugged, turning it into a joke. "I could even be useful. I'm sure there are things that even a tenderfoot like me could do. Clean the tweezers. Mash up wads of wet newspaper—I could definitely manage that."

Mack traced the edge of the beer bottle and didn't answer. The longer the silence went on, the more her confidence began to fade. Fine, she thought. Forget it. As wonderful as the idea had seemed, she wasn't going to beg. If he didn't want her here, she would take her paperweight and leave.

She opened her mouth to say *just kidding*, but Mack pushed the Viking Gold aside and regarded her with a look that made her stop, wait. Her heart banged against her ribcage. *Just kidding* changed to *Please*.

"You're good company," he said, at last. "If it's what you want to do, I won't turn you away."

Cathryn was flooded with a relief that seemed out of proportion to his reply, but she managed to keep her voice neutral. "Name me a girl who could refuse an invitation like that."

"Not you, I assume?"

"Not me."

"I'm counting on you to mash up huge quantities of newspaper."

"Enormous quantities."

"I might even let you hand me a tool now and then."

"Sounds heavenly." Then she frowned. "It's really a yes? I don't want you to feel as if I've forced myself on you."

He reached across the polished wood of the bar and picked up her hand, moving his thumb slowly across her palm. "It's a yes."

The sensation washed over her again, the same sensation she'd had in the Kia when she read the single word he had written. *Yes.*

Nine

Cathryn made her way back to the hotel where she had stayed before. A couple of days in Akureyri, with an early morning departure on the third day—straightforward enough, yet the reasons *not* to do it grew more convincing with each step.

The extravagant *go-inside-a-glacier* tour she'd paid for in advance, for one thing. Not to mention three nights of prepaid accommodations between Akureyri and Reykjavik that she wouldn't be using, and the folly of announcing that she could learn about glassblowing by watching someone else do it. Besides, she had her own art, if she wanted it—which she didn't. She'd made her choice fifteen years ago. The camera was a way to earn a living. Period.

The worse folly of chasing after a man, which had to be how he saw it. She hadn't done that since she was an adolescent. Even Brian had pursued her, when they first met. And when she sought men out, after Brian died, it was always for a purpose—for sex, adult conversation, a dinner companion.

Mostly, the fact that this impulsiveness was just *not her*. If she booked a Saga Tour, she carried it out, down to the last viewing spot. Her children knew that about her, and that was how the three of them had survived.

Fifteen years. You couldn't throw away fifteen years just because a man drew his thumb across your palm.

Especially when all he had said was, *If it's what you want to do,
I won't turn you away.*

Her unease mounting, Cathryn stepped into the hotel's revolving glass door and let it guide her from the street to the lobby. She
could hear the ding of an elevator, a woman's voice.

A strange sensation welled up inside her as she placed her foot
on the thick floral carpet, and her doubt lifted as quickly as it had
descended.

Whatever had brought her back to Akureyri, it couldn't be
entirely *not her*—because she was here. If you did something, that
meant it was you, or part of you.

Cathryn booked a room for three nights, splurging on a suite overlooking the town square. She threw her suitcase on the bed but didn't
unpack; she could do that later. Instead, she changed into her boots
and jeans, and hurried back to the hot shop.

This time she didn't knock. She grabbed the handle of the big
wooden door, yanked it open, and went inside. Shafts of light from
a row of windows near the roofline cut the barn-like space into rib-
bons of silver and gray; an angular blue sculpture, lit by one of the
beams, rested on the table. The smell of beeswax and wet newspaper
mingled with the smell of the furnace. She looked around, but Mack
wasn't there.

She hadn't said she was coming back as soon as she checked into
the hotel, but she'd assumed that he would be there, working, when
she did—that he would be *there*, like the marver or the glory hole.
A foolish assumption, clearly. He wasn't impatiently awaiting her
return. He'd acquiesced to her request but hadn't altered his plans,
whatever they were, to accommodate it.

Embarrassed now, Cathryn bit her lip and pushed the door open
again, ready to disappear into the street. Instead, she collided into
Mack. The coffee cup he was holding shot out of his hand, spewing
hot liquid. He stepped aside as the coffee arced past him.

"Oh no." She reached out in dismay, fingers wide, as if she could grab the coffee and bring it back. "I'm so sorry. I can't believe I did that."

"Wait a minute," he said. "Shouldn't I be inside the hot shop, and you're the one who wants to come in?"

Cathryn tried not to feel more chagrined than she already did. "You should. I went in without knocking. I'm sorry for that, too."

"Don't be sorry. But you do need to buy me a replacement coffee. And a new *kleina*." He held out a coffee-soaked bag. "That's a fried donut, for you tourists."

Cathryn winced. "I was barreling ahead without looking. I want to say *sorry* a third time, but *sorry* won't bring back your coffee. At least it didn't burn you. And yes, of course I'll get you another donut."

"I'll redeem it later. For now, let's just go inside. I'll make us some fresh coffee on the hot plate." He gave her an appraising glance. "Or you can, if it makes you feel better."

"I'm happy to make fresh coffee. It's the least I can do."

He held the door, and she ducked under his arm, reentering the hot shop. Her eyes darted from the glory hole at one end of the long room to the cot at the other. There was a clothes rack and a cupboard next to the cot, a little door that probably led to a bathroom. She assumed that the hot plate was nearby but wasn't sure she wanted to go back there, behind the cot. Where he slept.

"Actually," Mack said, "my caffeine addiction has decided to behave. It was obviously the donut I wanted."

"Rain check, then. Whenever you like."

"Rain check." He dropped the ruined bag of kleinur into a wastebasket, then strode to the table with the sculpture that Cathryn had noticed earlier. He studied it for a long minute, hands in his pockets. "Nope," he said, finally. "No good."

"I like it," she countered. "It's bold, fresh."

"I don't care about bold and fresh. It has to have feeling. And it doesn't."

She frowned. "You told me it was all about the material, the glass, what *it* wanted, not some feeling you're trying to *make* it have."

Mack turned to her with a look of delight. "You're going to make me work for every pronouncement, aren't you?"

"Only if it doesn't make sense."

"That probably fits a lot of what I say."

"I'm serious."

"And I'm glad you are." He gestured at a metal folding chair. "Here. Sit, and I'll try to answer your question."

He leaned against the table, and Cathryn lowered herself into the chair. She brushed back her hair, lifting it off her neck, and raised her eyes to his. He seemed huge and male, filling the space around her.

She swallowed, then squared her shoulders. "No mansplaining," she told him. "Real 'splaining."

"It's an interesting question, you know. I'm not sure I've ever had anyone ask me so explicitly." He crossed his arms, serious now. "It would be one thing to set out to create a piece that would evoke the notion of—say, agony or envy. The idea would come first, and you'd use the material to convey your idea."

"Okay. And what would the other thing be?"

"Ah. The other thing." His face softened. "That's when you let yourself be in the moment, feeling whatever you're capable of feeling, right then, and let that truth pour itself into the piece you're making."

Cathryn could only stare at him. What he had said was so extraordinary, so different from what she had imagined when she flung her challenge at him.

Phrases slid through her mind like sheets of silk, none of them right. Yet she needed to speak, to respond. "Mack," she began.

Before she could form the next word, she saw his eyes lose their focus as he slumped forward, nearly slipping off the edge of the table. She jumped to her feet. "Mack!"

He shivered, righting himself in an instant. Then he scowled. "It's fine." He wiped his neck, as if wiping away whatever had just happened. "Like I told you, it lasts for a second. It's nothing."

Cathryn faced him, ready to argue. "How can it be nothing? Everything is something."

"It *is* nothing. It only seems dramatic because you're not used to it."

"I think you're blowing me off. Tell me the truth."

"Cathryn." It was the first time he had said her name. "Cathryn," he repeated. "We all have our quirks. This is one of mine. That's all."

Her eyes narrowed. The bullshit-detection meter she'd developed as the mother of teenagers was on high alert. Whatever he was telling her, or himself, wasn't the whole truth.

Then a second alarm sounded. This wasn't like teenage Rachel trying to avoid punishment. It was more like the intuition she used to have when something was wrong. She would know, even before she got the call from the school nurse or heard the sobs behind a closed door.

Her hand quivered, as if the need to touch him came from her fingers themselves. *Something is going on. You need to find out what it is.* She started to move—until she saw the look on his face. Its message was clear: This wasn't her business.

Slowly, Cathryn released her breath. Mack had let her into his studio, but not into his secrets. And why should he? She was only staying for two days.

"I hope it doesn't happen while you're spinning a blob of molten glass."

"I'm sure it has. But that second when gravity takes over can give the piece an extra little creative twist."

"You're joking."

He smiled. "I am. And it's called a gather, not a blob."

"Fine, a gather." Cathryn realized that her fists had clenched. She let her hands open, her body relax. She could feel Mack relax too. Whatever line she had almost crossed was still intact.

Mack regarded her with amusement. "Glass deserves our respect, you know. There's hardly a more ancient substance. People have been making objects out of glass for over four thousand years."

"But never an iceberg lagoon."

"Not that I know of."

"And I'm keeping you from doing that. I promised I wouldn't."

"It's all right. I haven't taken any time off since I got here. Maybe I need to do that. Let my ideas percolate."

"That sounds like a teenager's excuse for skipping school. I need to let all that algebra percolate."

His laughter filled her with an absurd joy. "You're a handful, Cathryn McAllister."

"Is that a complaint?"

"Not at all." Then he folded his arms again, watching her. "Actually, I think it's true. Your arrival is probably well-timed. A sign from the gods that I need a break. Not just a coffee break, but a real one. Away from the hot shop."

"Why do I think you're going to blame me for that later?"

"I won't. I don't blame other people for my decisions."

As he spoke, she saw the change in his face that she had come to recognize but didn't understand— a withdrawal and a darkening, taking him as far away as the lapse of consciousness he had called a dizzy little blip. This disappearance was just as swift, but it wasn't little. It was the tip of an enormous iceberg, like the very forms that had captivated him.

Cathryn tossed her head, trying to restore the lightness that had been there between them. "Maybe I don't want you to take a break. I came here to learn about glassblowing."

"And you will."

She could see Mack struggling to remain in the present, to be there with her. The effort, so evident in the tightening of his shoulders and the twitch of his jawline, pierced her with an unexpected tenderness.

"But for now," he said, "you need to indulge me. A small detour. A tourist stop."

"A detour? Why would that be indulging you? I'm the one who's a tourist."

"Because I'm the one who feels guilty for depriving you of your itinerary. If I hadn't invited you to visit Akureyri, you'd be off on your Ring Road adventure. Hiking around the Snaefellsnes Peninsula, shopping in Reykjavik. Strolling through the Phallus Museum."

"Is that actually a museum?"

"It actually is."

"I can't believe the Icelandair people didn't tell me about this."

"I think it's formal name is the Phallological Museum. From what I understand, there are more than two hundred specimens belonging to around fifty different mammals. Whales, walruses. Homo sapiens."

"No. Not Homo sapiens."

"Indeed. There are four legally certified human specimens." Mack gave her a merry grin. "The museum also claims that its collection includes the penises of elves and trolls, although, since elves and trolls are invisible, the specimens have yet to be verified."

Cathryn burst out laughing. "Don't tell me that's where you want to go on your tourist jaunt."

"*Our* tourist jaunt. And no, the museum's in Reykjavik. I'm thinking of something closer to Akureyi."

"I really wanted to see the elves."

"I'm serious. I don't want you to miss every single sight in northern Iceland."

"It was my choice. I'm like you, I take responsibility for my decisions."

"What if I just want an excuse to goof off?"

Cathryn shook her head. "You don't seem like the goofing-off type. You told me you like to be obsessed."

"It might not be a virtue. That's the point."

"Aha. So you want me to help you be a better person by giving you a noble reason to play hooky?"

"I couldn't have said it better."

"Mack," she began. The whole conversation was making her dizzy. It had taken too many turns—and now this one, about how she could help to cut through his obsession.

Then she grew quiet. Maybe it was true. And if it were, it meant she could help him, be more than a supplicant. "Did you have something in mind?"

Mack thought for a moment. "I've been wanting to go to the mud pots of Hverir ever since I got here. It's only an hour or so from Akureyri."

"I think that was on my Saga Tour. I was supposed to go there after the whales."

"But you didn't."

"No. I wanted to make a paperweight."

"You made your paperweight. Now you can see the boiling mud."

"Are you inviting me to go to the hot pots of Hverir with you?"

His eyes held hers. "I'm inviting you to go to the hot pots of Hverir with me. It won't take long. Just be prepared for the smell. Apparently they stink of rotten eggs."

"You do know how to show a girl a good time."

"You're sure you can handle it?"

She raised her chin. "I can handle it."

As she said the words aloud, she knew they were true. She could handle anything.

The wondrous feeling spread through her body again. It was like falling in love. Not even with Mack, but with the Cathryn McAllister she might become. Was starting to be.

Ten

They took Mack's car, a dark-green Jeep with four-wheel drive. Cathryn curled against the passenger door and watched the passing scenery. The terrain was brown and flat, rimmed by a jagged line of mountains. Not like the spectacular coastlines she had seen earlier. No enormous black rocks jutting into the sea, no waterfalls or glacial valleys.

After a while, a sign appeared on the right. *Lake Mývatn Nature Baths.* "What's that?" she asked.

"It's a thermal lake," Mack said. "A less commercial version of the Blue Lagoon. I haven't been there, but we can stop on the way back if you like."

"Good idea. Rid ourselves of the rotten egg smell."

"Maybe not. I think the thermal baths have the same smell. It's the sulfur." He glanced at her. "Did you visit the Blue Lagoon, when you landed?"

"I did. I remember the sulfur, now that you mention it. And the swim-up bars."

"Mývatn has the same water but no swim-up bars. And no bus-loads of tourists."

"Even better." Cathryn peered more closely out the window "Looks like it might rain, though."

"The lake's still open, since it's—well, a lake. It'll be fine if it drizzles. It'll keep the tourists away."

She arched an eyebrow. "Oh? And what am I?"

"Whatever you want to be."

Hardly, she thought. No one's life was like that—unless Mack thought his was. She had no idea what he believed. About art, maybe, but not about people. Her. He'd said he felt guilty that his invitation to stop in Akureyri had interrupted her perfectly planned itinerary. She wondered, now, if he had really thought she would come or if it had just been something polite to say.

Maybe it had been a kind of test. If she heard the secret message and came, as beckoned, he would open the door. She would enter, become a new person.

Whatever you want to be.

Well, she had come. And come back.

Cathryn felt her heartbeat quicken. What was she? That was the question.

When they pulled into the parking lot at Hverir, the first thing she noticed was the sky. It stretched across the horizon, an iridescent expanse streaked with black and silver and topaz. Below it, steam spouted from mounds and craters scattered across a gray-and-ochre landscape that seemed more lunar than earthly.

Mack got out of the car and Cathryn followed, glad she had worn jeans and what she called her ugly-cowgirl shoes. It was clear, even from the parking lot, that the ground was sticky and wet. "I can smell the sulfur," she told him.

"You're still game?"

"Of course I'm still game."

They made their way slowly to the thermal field. Cracked mud and thick gray ooze surrounded the steaming fissures. Farther away, pyramid-shaped mounds, like miniature volcanoes, spat twisting columns of smoke. The ground gleamed purplish-red, hellish and magical and unreal.

"It feels like we're on Mars," Cathryn whispered, "or the Moon."

"Not on Earth, anyway. Not in a place that was meant for humans."

As they got closer, the smell grew stronger. Cathryn could hear the bubbling and roiling of the mud pots, the hissing of the vents. Clouds of steam rose into the sky, billowing over the rocks. A family of tourists crowded around one of the gurgling yellow spouts, taking photos. A woman in a North Face jacket grabbed the arm of a small child. "Don't get so close. I told you that in the car."

As if by tacit agreement, they veered in the other direction, toward a barren expanse at the edge of the field. Beyond it, a red ridge streaked with sepia zigzagged upward. A wooden sign said *Námafjall Trail*.

"Shall we?" he asked. "It might be interesting to get an aerial view."

"Yes. Good idea."

There was no one else on the trail, and Cathryn could see why. It was an unforgiving path, with nowhere to rest and nothing to soften the starkness. No trees or vegetation, no birds. Loose gravel clattered down the side of the hill as they wound their way to the crest. The sky loomed above them, charcoal and amber.

When they reached the top, she brushed back her hair and surveyed the landscape below. From their perch at the top of the ridge, the mud pots and fissures seemed like a single boiling presence, pulsing in a rhythm, a language of their own, as the subterranean heat forced its way to the surface. In the distance she could see the Viti crater, cradling a teal green lake as it spewed columns of thermal gas. "It really is like a science fiction movie," she said, her voice dropping again.

She could feel Mack standing next to her, hands in his pockets, tall and silent. A gust of wind wrapped itself around them.

After a while, he turned to her. "I'm glad I didn't come here earlier. It's good to share it."

"It is." Then she gave him an impish look. "And I'm glad I opted for the paperweight. This way, I get both."

"You do indeed." He kept his eyes on hers. "A clever ploy."

Cathryn's heart began to knock against her ribs. It was like a hand knocking on a door, the way she had knocked on the door to the studio. She pushed her hair back again. "I try to be. Clever, that is."

Seconds passed. She felt the weight of her feet, braced on the rocky crest. The breeze, the expanse of sky. The rise and fall of Mack's breathing.

Then he said, "Ready to head back down?"

"Yes, I think so."

He nodded at the trail. "You go first. That way I won't kick up dust in your face."

"You're very gallant."

"I try to be."

"Quoting me back to myself, are you?" She tossed him an arch look and strode ahead of him down the path, sashaying from rock to rock—really, that was the only word for the extra little flounce of her hips that he would surely have to notice as he walked behind her.

For a moment, it was exciting to play like that. And then, a moment later, shame washed over her, sweeping away the playfulness.

What in the world did she think she was doing—this lapse into sophomoric flirtatiousness, this inane bit of contrived sauciness? She had claimed to be in Akureyri for the glass, and she was. But she had come for him too.

Admit it, she told herself. And admit that Mack had done nothing to encourage her fantasy. A meaningless quip about fulfilling their heart's desire that had to do with viewing a celestial light show. A single ambiguous word in a text, and a single touch on the hand. This wasn't junior high school. A grown man had more direct ways to signal his interest, if that interest was there.

Disgusted with herself, she resumed her regular gait, swift and scissor-like.

The descent to the base of the ridge was quicker than the ascent had been. The sky was changing rapidly now. By the time they reached the thermal field, it had begun to drizzle, a sharp cold spray that made the steam hiss as it spewed from its underground source. Most of the visitors were already hurrying to their cars.

Cathryn glanced over her shoulder. Behind her, Mack was covering the final yards of the trail with long brisk strides. "Want to make a mad dash?" she called. "Maybe we can beat the rain." She took off at a run—desperate, now, to get back to the car, to Akureyri, to the vacation she had planned before this insane impetuousness derailed her.

She had forgotten what the terrain was like. Her shoes slapped against the ground but the slick gray ooze didn't offer enough traction, especially in the rain. Within seconds her feet slipped, and she crashed to the ground, smack on her rump. Her hands flew out to break the fall. Mud splattered on her arms, clothes, face. "Shit," she cried.

Mack was there at once. "Should I laugh or commiserate?"

She glared at him. It wasn't funny, and she didn't want sympathy. "Oh, just be *gallant*."

"That I can do."

Before she had a chance to realize what was happening, he had lifted her up in his arms, out of the ooze. His hands on her body—into her armpits, under her knees—were shockingly intimate. Desire rose up in her, stunning her with its force. It obliterated the rain, the steam, the stench.

When he set her down, his eyes were hooded, unreadable. "You're all right?"

"I'm all right."

He wiped his hands along the sides of his jeans. "Let's get you back to the car. It can't feel pleasant to be standing here like this."

Why can't it? she thought—although pleasant wasn't a word she would have chosen. On fire, maybe. Helpless. It was hard to believe he hadn't felt what she did, but there was no indication that he had.

She tried to swipe the mud from her arms. "I'm sorry about this. It's going to mess up your upholstery."

"Don't be sorry. It's a rental and the seats are vinyl." He tilted his head, eyeing her as she swatted at her elbows and legs. "Another reason to stop at Mývatn. You can shower, get clean, take a dip in the thermal lake."

"Fine." Cathryn kept her gaze averted—unable to look at him now, certain that he'd sensed her absurdly unwarranted arousal and that she'd made a fool of herself in a far more humiliating way than landing on her backside. She picked her way across the field to the car. There was nothing to do but see the day through. Actually, it wasn't day anymore; it was early evening. The fading Icelandic light made it hard to know what time of day or night it was.

Mack started the engine, and Cathryn retreated against the passenger door. A thermal pool would be good; she could wash away the whole mortifying experience, along with the mud—only she hadn't brought dry clothes, much less a bathing suit. Everything was in the Kia. She stole a glance at Mack, wondering if he had thought of that, but it was too dim to see his expression and she didn't dare ask. Well, they probably rented suits at Mývatn, like they did at the Blue Lagoon.

It was only a six-minute drive to Mývatn, and Cathryn could see that it was a much simpler facility than the Blue Lagoon, with only a dozen scattered cars in the parking lot. The lake—two lakes, really—glowed an eerie blue in the receding light. Beyond the perimeter, the landscape was rocky and barren.

They got out of the car. It was raining steadily now, a slanted patter of ice-tipped needles. For the second time that day, Cathryn wondered what she was doing. And for the second time, she had no answer.

They hurried inside, where the lone receptionist was engrossed in a book. She lifted an eyebrow at Cathryn's mud-covered appearance, but her voice was polite. "Be sure to shower thoroughly before entering the lagoon. And keep your bracelet on." Efficiently, like a nurse, she fastened the paper bracelets around their wrists. "And be aware," she added, "that we require all guests to leave the lagoon if it starts to thunder. If it's merely rain, we stay open until twenty-one hundred." She looked from Cathryn to Mack. "You're American, yes? That's nine o'clock."

"Thank you," Cathryn said. "Also—well, this is a bit of an unscheduled stop. Do you happen to have bathing suits for rent?"

"We do." The receptionist reached behind the desk and took a plastic bag from one of the shelves. "Here you go." Her eyes flicked to Mack. "And you, sir?"

"Please."

"Women's changing area to the right, men's to the left."

Mack nodded, then turned to Cathryn. "I'll meet you outside."

"Yes. Fine."

She headed for the changing area—eager, now, to immerse herself in Mývatn's restorative heat. The day had exhausted her; it was hard to believe that it had only been twelve hours since Mack sent her the photo of the paperweight.

She pushed aside the curtain to the women's dressing room, stripped off her muddy clothes, and spread them on a bench to dry. Then she took the required shower, glopped the special conditioner on her hair, and ripped open the plastic bag containing the rented swimsuit. It was skimpier than the suits she usually wore, but she knew her body looked okay Well, more than okay. Anyway, what the hell. She had shown him things about herself that were far more revealing than a few extra inches of midriff.

Cathryn stowed her towel and flip-flops in an outdoor locker, then followed the walkway that led to the first pool, scanning the area with a growing anxiety. He wouldn't have gone in without her, would he? Then she thought: You have no idea what he would do.

A moment later, she spotted him, waiting for her. Of course he had waited.

He looked taller and broader without his clothes. She remembered her first impression when he walked into the Fosshotel lobby near Jökulsárlón. Bigger and messier and more raw-looking than the photo on his website, that was what she had thought. He saw her and raised a hand in greeting. *Hello, you.*

She crossed the walkway to where he stood. "Well, here we are. More sulfur."

"You can never have enough sulfur." He smiled. "Interesting hairdo, by the way."

Cathryn lifted a hand to her head. She'd slopped the cream on the way she was supposed to and then heaped the strands on top of her head, pulling them into vertical tufts so they wouldn't fall. "Hey, people pay top dollar for this look in New York." She couldn't help smiling back. Maybe everything would be all right.

"Let's give it a go," he said.

Holding onto the parallel railings, they lowered themselves into the hot pool. Cathryn gave a small gasp. "Oh my."

"Is that a good *oh my* or a bad *oh my*?"

"A good one. It's fabulous. I know I was at the Blue Lagoon and this shouldn't feel quite so surprising, but I wasn't so cold and wet and muddy." She stepped farther into the water until her shoulders were covered. "This is pure bliss."

Mack gestured at the second pool. "Let's get away from the crowd."

"Crowd? I don't think there are ten people in here."

"I'm practically feral, if you haven't figured that out yet. More than three is a crowd for me."

"I don't know what I've figured out about you."

"Join the club. I don't know what I've figured out about myself either."

A bolt of annoyance shot through her. "And that gets you off the hook? No need to be anything except conveniently enigmatic?"

The outburst startled her. Why was she so angry?

Yet Mack seemed to understand, even if she didn't. "Come," he said. "Let's go to a quieter part of lagoon. It's easier to talk that way."

Cathryn followed him around a jetty that divided the lake into separate lagoons, half-striding, half-bobbing through the thick mineral-laden water. His instinct had been right; there were only a handful of people in this part of the lake. The water seemed cooler, as well. She'd read about that, the way the temperature could vary even in a single lagoon, though maybe it was from the icy rain that continued to fall.

She surveyed the little cove where he had led them. Steam rose from the surface of the water, wrapping the bathers in swaths of gauze. From above, fog began to penetrate the rain. There was a languor to the rain now—viscous, like the Karo syrup from her childhood. It hit the water with a hiss. The two vapors met, fog and steam, moving toward each other until she couldn't tell which was which.

"What do you want to talk about?" she asked.

Mack leaned against the rocky edge, and Cathryn moved next to him. She didn't want to face him like an interrogator. She wasn't here to interview him for Renata Singer and Shades of Blue, not anymore.

"Remember I asked if you were grieving?" he said.

"I do. It seemed odd."

"And you said you weren't."

"I'm not. It was too long ago."

"Too long ago," he repeated. "How do you get to the place where the grief is so far behind that it belongs to the past?"

"I don't know. Maybe you come to terms with it. Maybe you get caught up in other things. I suppose it's different for different people."

Cathryn shifted so she could see his face. The truth was written there so clearly that she was amazed she hadn't seen it before. "I think you're the one who's grieving."

"I guess I am."

"You lost someone you loved?"

He looked right at her, and something seized in her heart. She was almost afraid to ask who it was. Who he lost would tell her who he loved, and might still love. Yet she had opened the door—the door to him, Mack—instead of being the one to glide through a door he had opened for her, the way she had imagined. Now she had to enter. She had asked if she could, and his face told her *yes*.

Her voice was soft. "Who was it?"

"It doesn't matter. What matters is that I let it happen."

"Guilt doesn't help. Believe me, I tried that."

"It's not just guilt. It's realizing that you're not the person you thought you were. And seeing the consequences of that mistaken belief."

"The person didn't die?"

"A part of me died." His face twisted. "The part that kept the rest together. The illusion that I'm a good man."

She wanted to assure him that of course he was a good man, but how did she know? She knew so little about him. And even if she knew everything there was to know, it wasn't her place to tell him if he was good or not-good.

"I don't think a person can be good in general," she said. "You can only be good specifically. In a specific moment."

"That sounds remarkably wise."

"It does, doesn't it?"

"How did you figure that out?"

Cathryn pulled in her breath. She had accused him of being enigmatic instead of open, but she had done the same thing herself. "Life," she said. "Mistakes. A failure to be good, when I might have been."

"Everyone has experiences like that."

"The longer you live, the more of those experiences."

Be brave, she told herself.

"I've lived longer than you might think. I'm forty-eight years old."

"You're a beautiful woman, Cathryn. No one cares how old you are. Certainly not me."

Had he really said that? The receptionist had warned *no thunder in the pool,* but that hadn't meant the thunder in her chest, the lightning that was coursing through her body.

The rain was pelting her now. Fog descended over the steaming water. Dimly, she could see the other people moving away, back toward the entrance to the lagoon.

Then he spoke again, his voice quiet. "Someone did die." She almost asked *who,* thinking he might tell her now, but his eyes stopped her. "I can't talk about it. I've never talked about it."

"It's all right. There are things I've never talked about either."

"Do we really need to talk?"

"No." The word was an exhalation of everything she had been keeping at bay. They moved toward each other in the same moment. His mouth felt for hers as hers opened to him. He pulled down the top of her bathing suit, moving his hand across her collarbone, her nipples, her skin.

She didn't know who she was or where she was, and she didn't care. The desire she had felt at Hverir split open, exploded. He moved her against the side of the pool where he'd been leaning, and she wrapped her legs around him. She could feel him through the nylon. Nothing else mattered.

He raised his head to look around. "I don't care," she said. "If anyone's here, they can't see." She couldn't believe herself. Never, ever had she acted like this. She thrust her fingers into his hair. His mouth found hers again as he moved his hands over the bikini bottom. She didn't want to unwrap her legs, it was impossible to unwrap herself from him. She felt the fabric tear as he ripped the suit aside.

For an instant she thought, *The rented suit.* Then: fuck the suit.

Yes. Fuck me. Fuck me forever.

Tears streamed down her face.

She was annihilated. Burned through.

Baptized in the silicon waters, and born anew.

Part Three:
Glass Rain

Eleven

When Cathryn talked about Brian's death, she called it tragic, devastating, a freak accident. Privately, she thought of it as the final disappearance of someone who had already removed himself from her life in just about every other way, long before he crashed into the back of an eighteen-wheeler.

A person would have to be completely obtuse, which she wasn't, not to have felt Brian's withdrawal. At first, she hadn't been sure. There were small things that might not have meant anything, like the way he slept on the edge of the bed so they wouldn't have to touch, a vagueness in his *have-a-good-day* kiss. And other things that she wanted to ask him about but couldn't. An evening when she'd been unable to reach him, an errand that took a ridiculously long time. To question him would make her seem needy and insecure, traits that Brian despised.

Then it got harder to pretend that he wasn't removing himself, bit by bit, and accumulating secrets. There was the new cell phone she found behind his socks, with a different password. She knew the password was different because she tried the regular one, the one he used for everything else, and it didn't work. And the late nights and last-minute meetings—trite predictable bread crumbs that he seemed to be leaving on purpose, as if he wanted her to know.

Yet she hadn't confronted him, because life was too complicated. It was like one of those Jenga towers that Judah liked to build;

if you disturbed one block, the whole thing tumbled. She had two children with elaborate schedules and needs, a big house, and her own work as an abstract photographer trying to gain traction in a competitive art world. Peaceful coexistence—even if it meant closing her eyes and pretending that everything was fine—was a necessity.

And everything would have been fine, or fine enough, if Rachel hadn't found the photo. The irony didn't strike Cathryn until later, after the funeral. A double irony, because it was Rachel, Brian's favorite, who was the agent of his undoing. And a photograph, symbol of the domain that was supposed to be hers, that led to the end of her marriage, and the end of Brian's life.

It started because Rachel needed money for her classroom book club. It had to be the exact amount, and Cathryn didn't have any fives. "Go ask Daddy," she told her.

Rachel ran off, returning a few minutes later with Brian's wallet. "Daddy was on the phone." She handed the wallet to Cathryn with a smug look that meant, "See? I didn't take any money without permission."

Cathryn flipped open the wallet and felt inside the billfold. Her fingers touched something slick and unfamiliar. Curious, she pulled it out.

It was a photo of Brian and a woman she had never seen before. They were standing in front of a big horizontal mirror; a cream-and-white shower was reflected behind them, like a frame within a frame. The woman had long dark hair and almond-shaped eyes. She was wearing a black lace mini-bra and leaning into Brian's chest. Brian had one arm around her; the other arm held an iPhone up to the mirror. He was laughing.

Rachel crowded next to her. "What is it?"

Part of Cathryn thought: This is my fucking *husband*. But another part—bizarrely, as if the person in the photo had nothing to do with her—was assessing the way the shot had been cropped and lit. It was clever and effective. Artistic, really.

"What is it?" Rachel repeated.

Cathryn began to shiver as the meaning of the photograph penetrated her awareness. She didn't resist when her daughter took the photo from her quivering fingertips.

Rachel looked at the picture and frowned. "Who's that lady?" Before Cathryn could reply, she said, "I'm asking Daddy." She whirled around and yelled, "Dad! Dad!"

Cathryn's arms dropped to her sides and the wallet slid to the floor.

When Brian strode into the kitchen and saw the photograph in his daughter's hand, his first words were to Rachel, not Cathryn. The words were as hard as stones. "You don't know what you've done."

Turning scarlet, Rachel flung the photo onto the kitchen floor and fled. Cathryn's eyes went from the photo, face-up on the Mexican tile, to Brian. "How could you?" she whispered. She heard a door slam and could almost feel the bounce of the mattress as Rachel threw herself across the bed.

She took a step, needing to go to Rachel. Unforgiveable, to make Rachel feel that it was her fault for finding the photo, rather than Brian's for taking it in the first place, for having a reason to take it. Then she stopped, frozen in mid-gesture. Because this was it. Right now, right here. The moment she had known was coming, yet never believed would really come.

She turned to Brian again. "Blaming your daughter? Your nine-year old daughter?"

"I wasn't blaming her. I was telling her the truth. That she had no idea what she'd done."

"*She* didn't do anything. She was just looking for her fucking book club money."

"In *my* wallet."

Cathryn wanted to smack him. "Oh for fuck's sake. I was the one who was getting a five-dollar bill for her." Why were they making this about trespassing? "What does it matter? You put the photo there. She wanted to know why. Who the *lady* was with her father."

Her heart was pounding so fiercely she could hardly breathe. Wrongness piled on wrongness. You didn't lie. You didn't put a picture of a whore in your wallet and think that no one would dare to invade your sacred space, as if it were the invader's fault for finding what was there to be found.

Brian bent to retrieve the photo and wallet. "I did think that Rachel, of all people, would give me a minute before she got hysterical."

"You mean, you thought her loyalty to her beloved Daddy had no limits." Cathryn watched in disbelief as Brian tucked the photo back into the billfold. The casual way he did it, right in front of her, felt worse than finding it.

He looked up and met her eyes. "We need to talk."

The most dreaded phrase in a relationship. Well, she didn't need to talk. She needed to go to her daughter.

She remembered when Rachel was small and they were on a camping trip with Brian's brother and his family. It was late at night. The children were asleep in the tent, and the adults were gathered around a campfire with a bottle of Cabernet. Rachel had woken up crying, and Cathryn had jumped up to go to her. It must have been frightening for Rachel, waking up in a strange place in the dark, with the unfamiliar sounds and smells.

She had hurried into the tent and knelt beside her three-year old daughter. "It's okay, sweetie. Mommy's here."

Rachel had shoved her away. "I don't want *you*. I want Daddy."

Cathryn had turned it into a funny story when she returned to the campfire, but it stung. Even now, Rachel would have probably liked Brian to be the one climbing the stairs and opening the door to her bedroom to explain away what had happened. But no one, not even Brian, could be the source of a child's pain and also its healer. It was up to her, the second-choice parent.

"Rachel," she said softly, as she twisted the knob and opened the door. "It's me."

Rachel was curled on the bed clutching her stuffed monkey, a comfort object she had abandoned years ago but stowed on the top shelf of her closet "for an emergency." Well, Cathryn thought, this definitely qualified as an emergency. The room was growing dark as evening approached, but she resisted the urge to turn on the light. "Sweetheart," she began. Rachel grabbed a pillow and covered her head.

Brian's words echoed in her mind. *We need to talk.* If you really cared, you didn't say that. You just talked.

Cathryn lowered herself onto the edge of the bed. She didn't try to remove the pillow but simply stroked Rachel's arm, the one holding the monkey. Rachel twitched, as if she wanted to pull away, but she didn't.

"You know, honey, things aren't always what they look like."

Rachel's voice was muffled by the pillow. "A lady in her *under-wear*? I know exactly what that means. I'm not *stupid*."

Did a nine-year old really know about things like that? Being Rachel, she probably did.

Cathryn chose her words carefully. "The picture was taken somewhere else, probably on one of Daddy's business trips. And when people are away from home, silly things can happen—you know, like you might act a little crazy at camp and have food fights and things you would never do at home? It's like that for grown-ups too. But it doesn't mean anything. Daddy is still Daddy, and he still loves his family."

Rachel jerked her arm away and threw the pillow across the room. "I could see her *boobies*. And so could he." Her face was bright red. "You don't look at a person's boobies who isn't your wife."

Cathryn couldn't say, "Lots of men do." *Lots of men* weren't Rachel's father, the man she idolized.

She touched Rachel's hair. "I know it's not so great, but it was just a mistake. Even grown-ups make mistakes. It's not like he's in love with this woman or something."

Rachel pulled the monkey closer. "Duh. She's ugly."

"I'm sure Daddy is very sorry."

Was he? Maybe he was just sorry he'd been caught.

"I hate him," Rachel said.

"You're angry at him, I understand." *I am too.*

"I'm never going to talk to him again." Rachel thrust out her lower lip. "I wish he was dead."

Cathryn was pretty sure she was supposed to say *you know you don't mean that* and *don't say such things.* Wasn't it bad parenting to let your child make a pronouncement like that, no matter how angry she was? She had no idea. There was nothing in the parenting books about what to do when your child finds a photo of her father with a hooker.

The photograph flashed across her mind again, mocking her and filling her with rage, as if photography itself had betrayed her. "Yeah," she muttered. "Me too."

Appalled by what she had just said, she began talking—louder now, as if the volume of her new words would obliterate the prior ones. "Daddy might want to talk to *you*, though. Maybe in a little while, before bedtime."

"No!" Rachel shouted. She pushed herself to a sitting position and crossed her arms. "It's my room and he doesn't get to come in."

What the hell, Cathryn thought. She wasn't handling this very well, but at least she could honor her daughter's need to defend her own space. "It's okay. If you don't want to talk to him tonight, you don't have to. You can stay here and read in bed. Just wash your hands and brush your teeth. I'll check on you later."

Rachel's eyes widened. "Really?"

"Yes, really."

Let her daughter have her anger, at least for tonight. Cathryn wished she could do that too, stroke her anger in a silent little cave, but knew she had to face Brian and the painful unfinished conversation that awaited them.

Then she thought about how she had framed it for Rachel, as a mistake. If she took it like that herself, they would have a way to go on. Brian would be contrite. She would be cold for a while—to make her point—and then they would spend some quality time together and reconnect. In the end, it would be a good thing, the way disruptions often were. Later, they would remember it as the best thing that could have happened.

And yet, when both children were in bed, and she and Brian were settled onto opposite couches, face-to-face across the coffee table, her image of a blessing-in-disguise seemed as far away as the Moon. She could feel Brian's scrutiny, neither remorseful nor defiant but oddly calm, as if he were considering her for a job interview. His gaze unnerved her. She shouldn't feel so exposed; she wasn't the one who had done something wrong.

Brian looked at her for a long time, then gave a tired sigh. "You know as well as I do that we haven't been happy."

Cathryn eyed him warily. This was about *him*, not *we*. How he'd betrayed and hurt her.

"We've drifted our separate ways," he went on. "You've buried yourself in your photography—I don't blame you for that, don't get me wrong. We should pursue what we want, what we need. We all deserve a chance at happiness." He lifted a shoulder. "I took mine. This is someone I've known for quite a while. I haven't been sure what to do."

Wait, she thought. What was he saying?

"I've tried to be discreet. But now that you know, it's probably for the best."

Cathryn gave a violent twitch—as if he had flung her upside down, thrown her into an Alice-in-Wonderland world where words meant the opposite of what they were supposed to mean. For the best? *His* best, so he wouldn't have to keep covering his tracks. Not *her* best.

Her legs were vibrating, two jiggling appendages that had nothing to do with her.

"I kept putting it off," he said. "I didn't want to hurt you."

Dark angry waves lashed at the pylons that held her life in place. Who cared if he didn't *want* to hurt her? You didn't get any credit for *not wanting* to be a bastard. All that mattered was if you actually were.

The shaking grew stronger, seismic tremors that rippled from her heels to her teeth. This couldn't be happening. It didn't belong in a world made of sidewalks and trees and stores, because houses didn't just fly apart and apples didn't fall up. She had a life, and a future. A future he had promised her.

For quite a while. How far back did *quite a while* stretch? How long had her husband been acting the role of someone content to let things be as they were, someone without a parallel life? How much of their shared history was a sham?

"Cath—"

She needed him to stop talking. She needed everything to stop. She needed the world to stretch itself out and give her more time, more possibility, a way to make this un-happen.

It was too big. It was bursting the seams of the present. The world was going to explode.

"Cathryn."

Shut the fuck up.

"I'm sorry."

Brian apologizing, at last. What difference did it make?

"We've been together a long time. This isn't easy."

She didn't want to hear about how hard it was. She wanted to know what she was supposed to do.

All the things she had chosen to not-see. She had drawn a sharp impenetrable line around the signals that had been there for months and years, banned from her awareness, deflected before they could pierce her with their knowledge. And Brian had encouraged it. Whenever she'd been brave enough to venture a question, he had made her feel small and stupid and paranoid, as if it were something in her, some defect, that made her invent reasons to doubt him.

Well, maybe he hadn't *made* her feel that way, but she had. Not trusting herself. Slipping from day to day in a fog of denial.

"What are you saying? You want a divorce?"

He looked surprised. "I hadn't thought of it like that. Does it have to be so black-and-white?"

Oh, for god's sake. Was he a child? Did he actually think he could have it both ways?

"She has something I need," he said. "But I need my family too. You. I need you."

Cathryn wanted to smack him—shove him off the couch and kick his infantile arrogance across the room. "News flash. You don't get to have both."

She almost said *you have to pick.* But a different thought seized her. *No, I get to pick. Me, not you.* She could grab the moment and choose what came next.

Fight for her marriage, even if it meant a showdown with Little Miss Lingerie. Win, and then make it better.

Forgive him with an open heart, no strings attached, and release the sorrow and pain like smoke into the sky.

Tell him to go to hell and walk away.

The very thing she had wanted—time, stretching in every direction—was suddenly there for her. As if someone were holding a camera to this precise instant, centering her in the viewfinder, waiting for her to signal that she was ready for the action to resume.

But she wasn't. She had no idea what to do.

She had a vision of herself, her body, at the edge of a curb. Cars sped past, red-and-white streaks of light, but she herself was outside of time, she could walk between them, through them, do whatever she wanted. And what was it she wanted?

The vision passed. She blinked, her attention caught by the key to the Honda that she'd dropped on the coffee table earlier that evening. A black oversized key with little icons for lock, unlock, and trunk. It lay in a heap of smaller keys to places she could no long remember, on a chrome ring with an ornament that Judah had made at summer camp.

"I need to get out for a while," she told him. "I need to be alone. To think."

Brian looked startled. Maybe he had expected her to tell him to get out. Cathryn didn't know what he expected. "I'll go, if you want," he said. "Give you some space."

She narrowed her eyes, distrusting his offer. Maybe he wanted to run over to Miss Lingerie's house and tell her that their secret was out. Or maybe he just didn't want to have to deal with one of the kids waking up and needing something.

Oh, who cared? Let him go.

"Fine," she said. Impulsively, she tossed him her keys. "Get me some gas while you're out."

He caught the keys. "All right. I'll take your car."

"Give me a couple of hours," she said. She stood. "*Now*, if you don't mind."

Then she walked out of the room. She didn't need to watch him leave, as long as he did.

They hadn't talked about how long Brian would be gone. Cathryn had thought that being alone would help her decide what she wanted to do, yet three hours had passed and she still didn't know. Fight, forgive, or leave. All the choices were terrifying.

And yet, strangely, *I love Brian and don't want to lose him* didn't seem to figure into the bizarre equation she was trying to solve. She understood the other elements. Who will repair things around the house if he's gone? What will I tell people? What if I forgive him but he cheats on me again? What if I fight for him and lose?

If you loved someone, surely the pain of being without him would be your guide. *I love Brian and don't want to lose him.* What was wrong with her? Why wasn't she tortured by the thought of that impending loss?

Her head started to throb. She looked at her watch. Maybe she should call him on his cell, find out when he was coming back?

As if on cue, the phone rang. She ran to get it. "Mrs. McAllister?"

"Yes. Who is this?"

"This is Officer Bellamy of the State Police. Am I speaking with Mrs. McAllister?"

Had that idiot Brian gotten himself *arrested*? "Yes, this is she."

Then she thought: No, if he'd been arrested, he would be the one calling. Didn't people get to make one phone call?

"I'm sorry to be calling you like this, ma'am, but I'm afraid there's been an accident involving your husband."

"An accident?"

The officer cleared his throat. "It was on the Thruway. We believe he was trying to move into the exit lane when the truck in front of him slowed down. Apparently his brakes failed and he was unable to stop."

She leaned against the wall, her heart racing. "How badly was he hurt?"

"I'm sorry, Mrs. McAllister. A patrol car got there right away and called an ambulance, but he was already gone. At that speed, it was probably instantaneous."

This made no sense. "That can't be true. I just had an inspection."

"Ma'am, I'm so sorry."

"I'm sure they checked the brakes." She needed to argue, explain that this was a mistake. She had sent him off to repent. Not to die.

"I understand," the officer said. "Something went wrong, I don't know. You'd have to get a mechanic to look at the car."

Those fucking Honda people, screwing it up. Unless Brian had done something stupid, hit the gas instead of the brake?

"I'm very sorry, ma'am. We found your number by tracing the registration. Someone will be calling you about making a formal ID."

He meant the body. Bile rose in her throat. Her legs gave way and she slid down the wall to the floor. "Are you absolutely sure?" she whispered.

"I'm afraid I am."

She was afraid too. Crazy thoughts collided in her brain. She had been the one to send him off. It was supposed to be her, but she'd been glad to let him take her place. That way, she could stay home and decide what to do. Only she hadn't decided.

"Mommy?"

It was Rachel, on the stairs, clutching her monkey. "Is Daddy back? Is that him on the phone?"

Cathryn stared at her in horror.

"I'm ready to talk to him now. Can I talk to him, please?"

She looked at her daughter and opened her mouth to speak—to cry, or scream—but there was no sound. Nothing. Just the terrible unending silence.

Cathryn wanted to assure Rachel that her words couldn't possibly have caused Brian's death—no more than Brian's words, earlier that evening, made Rachel the reason their Jenga-world had toppled. Yet she couldn't find a way to talk about it. Telling Rachel that her outburst had no power to bring about real events meant reminding her about the conversation, which meant risking that Rachel would hurl the accusation back at her, "You said it too. I heard you."

She *had* said it. In that moment, she had even meant it. Unforgivably careless, no better than Brian's remark to Rachel.

She couldn't talk about it, just as she couldn't talk about the way she had flung her car keys at him. The memory was buried in the coffin along with his mangled body.

After the funeral, Cathryn gathered her children and told them that they were a team and would pull together because that's what Daddy would have wanted. When Judah asked if they were going to get a new dad, Rachel shoved him against the refrigerator and screamed that he was a stupid ignorant turd. Cathryn didn't have the energy to reprimand her.

She thought one of them would ask why Daddy had been driving her Honda instead of his own Subaru, but they never did. There was too much going on. Aunts and uncles hovering over them, people arriving with flowers and casseroles. No one mentioned it, and why would they? No one cared which car was hers and which was Brian's.

She thought, briefly, that she ought to find the woman, the one in the picture, and let her know what happened, but she had no idea how to do that. She couldn't check Brian's phone for a call history because it was destroyed in the crash, along with the photo in his wallet. When his credit card bill came, she ripped it open and, as she had expected, there were charges for hotels and restaurants and florists, but nothing that told her who had been with him at the hotels or who the flowers were for. Maybe there was a way to get Verizon or FTD Flowers to go through its records, but that was more than she was willing to do. She was the widow. No one would expect her to go that far out of her way for the mistress. It was all she could do to take care of her children.

Even her artistic aspirations—the series she had been working on, about light on stone, a huge installation that would take her work to a whole new level—seemed too meaningless to pursue. Instead, she lingered over all the *ifs*.

If she hadn't buried herself in her artwork.

If she had opened to Brian, looked for a path for them, together, instead of wanting him to leave so she could do something called *think and decide*.

If she had been the one to go for a drive.

If she hadn't wanted him dead for betraying and rejecting her.

She had a closet full of sophisticated photography equipment that was too expensive to throw out, so she found a new way to use it. Small jobs, carrying out other people's visions. Commercial, not artistic. She was finished with that.

She had a good eye, and it didn't take long for her to get busy and known. Cathryn McAllister, freelance photographer and graphic designer. Cutting-edge concepts for print, internet, and social media, with an occasional high-profile assignment for a theater company or museum. She liked the brevity and variety, the range of clients. Her business flourished.

Rachel grew into an aloof, self-contained adolescent, while Judah, two years younger, became increasingly petulant and demanding. Cathryn was never certain what they needed from her, except to keep life from falling apart again, so she made sure that didn't happen. People told her to sell the house, move to a condo in one of those gated communities, but she thought it was better not to change their environment. She worked hard to preserve the family rituals. Fresh bagels on Sunday. Pizza and s'mores on Friday.

After a while they didn't want to get up early on Sunday, even for freshly baked bagels, and Rachel announced that s'mores had too much refined sugar. A distant and critical teenager now, she refused to be seen with her mother or "weirdo loser brother," and Judah was more interested in his video-game characters than the people he lived with. Understanding that adolescents needed to break away, Cathryn tried not to mind, yet it pained her to see how much her children disliked each other.

Without their sports and playdates to structure her calendar, she joined a book club and a hiking club. She watched documentaries on Netflix, went for a two-mile run every morning. Had a string of low-key, manageable affairs with appropriate, well-groomed, and reasonably interesting men, but there was always a reason not to take that extra step. She could never say *yes, I want you*, and after a while she'd end the relationship with an amicable expression of regret and a promise to stay friends that she never kept.

Rachel went away to a good college. When Judah graduated from high school two years later, he announced that he wanted to be a carpenter. Cathryn found a trade school and helped him settle into an apartment with three other apprentice carpenters. With both children gone, it really did make sense to sell the house, but she didn't. It was a wonderful house, and she liked walking from room to room, feeling the wide-plank floors and the warmth of the sun through the skylights.

If she was lonely, she didn't let herself think about it. She was good at being alone. Anyway, there were business acquaintances, alumni luncheons in Manhattan that she sometimes went to and sometimes didn't, seasonal cocktails with the neighbors. Her siblings, a brother and a sister, were a decade younger and on the other coast. Each year, they promised to get together for Thanksgiving, and every few years they actually did.

Gradually, the affairs stopped; it hardly seemed worth the effort. In her mid-forties now, Cathryn gave thanks for her good cheekbones, efficient metabolism, and orderly life.

Two weeks after her forty-eighth birthday, Shades of Blue hired her to go to Iceland to do a promotional feature with an award-winning glassblower. Cathryn bought a round-trip ticket, packed a suitcase, and told her almost-grown children that she would be back in ten days.

Twelve

The plan was that Cathryn would spend a couple of days helping Mack in the hot shop. Small tasks, like handing him shears or a paddle, sweeping up the broken glass. An extra pair of hands for him, an interesting interlude for her.

Becoming lovers hadn't been part of that arrangement, yet it had happened. Sitting next to him in the Jeep, on the way back from Mývatn, Cathryn didn't know if it had changed Mack's feeling about her presence in the hot shop. Maybe it was just the kind of thing he did. She'd made it easy enough—bursting into the studio, offering herself, asking if she could stay. Two or three days, she had assured him, and then she'd be gone. He wasn't a monk. If her glassblowing adventure included some no-commitment sex, why would he refuse?

People had sex for all sorts of reasons. Lust, loneliness, obligation, power. To prove they were desirable. To make a baby. She'd had sex for each of those reasons, at one time or another. She had even indulged in the very maneuver she was ascribing to Mack, back when she was young and greedy and vain—signing up for a weekend trip with the local Sierra Club, going to bed with the person leading the hike, and parting company when the hike was over. It was the privilege of being pretty: the best-looking female got to share the tent of the alpha male.

It wasn't the kind of thing she did anymore— yet it might be exactly what this seemed like to Mack, a quick trophy fling with the star of Shades of Blue before she left for Keflavik and her flight home. That might be the way he saw it. Saw her.

Tears stung her lashes. That wasn't what this was.

And what was it?

Not that. Her mouth opening to his, their bodies finding each other in the rain and steam—it wasn't a notch on her bedpost, a vacation perk.

She couldn't pretend that she'd been seduced or surprised. She was the one who had turned the Kia around. She had known exactly what she wanted to happen. But not why, or if it would.

Cathryn wiped her eyes—quickly, so he wouldn't notice—and made herself focus on the road ahead. The headlights of the Jeep cast parallel beams into the darkness but there was nothing to see except the road itself, no cars or billboards or towns. In an hour, maybe less, they would be in Akureyri.

She looked at Mack, remembering what he had told her at Mývatn and the glimpse of his pain he had let her witness. She longed to know the rest of his story, but she couldn't ask. He'd made that clear.

Well, they could talk about art. That was a safe subject.

She pushed back her hair, still damp from the lake. "I've been wondering," she said, her voice as casual as she could make it, "how it all started, your interest in glass?"

"Are you interviewing me again?"

Cathryn crossed her arms, feigning indignation. "Can't I be interested?"

"You can."

"And?"

"And," he said, "I discovered it one summer, when I was at camp."

"You mean, when you were a kid?"

"I was—I don't know, maybe twelve? My parents sent my brother and me to this hippie sleepaway camp, one of those places that lets twelve-year-old kids play with hot glass and use real axes to chop wood. We loved it, of course, but the place shut down a few years later when someone discovered that they didn't have any insurance."

"Wait a minute," Cathryn said. "You actually blew glass when you were twelve years old?"

"I did."

"You just figured it out?"

"It's a bit harder than that." Mack laughed. "There was a counselor who knew a little, and I asked him—well, begged him—until he let me try."

"And you adored it."

"Who wouldn't? Glass is amazing." He gave her a quick glance. "Think about it. Glass is the only substance that lets you see front and back, surface and interior, at the same time. It shows you everything, all at once."

Unlike a person, Cathryn wanted to reply. But she said, "I hadn't thought of it that way, but yes, you're right."

"There's nothing like it. It's the best art form there is."

"You're not an artist, though. That's what you told me. An artist imposes his ideas on the material, et cetera, et cetera. You don't do that."

"I try not to do that. I try to watch, wait, let it come to me."

"Let it come to you," Cathryn repeated. "Is that your philosophy about everything?"

She knew, as soon as she heard her question, that she was asking about more than glass. It seemed painfully obvious: she had come to him; he hadn't pursued her.

She braced herself to hear him say, *Yes, about everything.*

Instead, he told her, "It depends. With hot glass, there's a moment when you have to act and seize what you need. If you hesitate, gravity will take over, and you'll lose it."

Cathryn remembered how he had swung the pipe to let the gather slide back into place. Another time, he'd let it hang, elongate, before catching the molten strand with a twist of the tweezers.

"Unless you *want* gravity to take it. An extra little creative tweak, that's what you called it. The silver lining when you lose the attention that you're never supposed to lose, not even for a second."

Mack's voice was full of delight. "You're a force to be reckoned with, Cathryn McAllister. You don't forget a single word."

"I guess I don't." Then she set her jaw. "I'm serious. How do you know which it is, wait or seize?"

"You just know. Except when you don't, of course, and then you throw your mistake back in the furnace."

"What an easy out. You glassblowers are spoiled."

"Glass isn't unique that way. Anyone can rip up a photo or poem."

"There's no ripping anymore. You just hit *delete*."

"Actually, isn't photography all about wait-and-seize? You wait, and then you capture the moment before it's gone, like capturing time."

"You make it sound all mystical and existential."

"Isn't it?"

She shook her head. "What I do is much more ordinary."

"I'm sure that's not true."

"And you know this because?"

"Nothing you do is ordinary. I think we just proved that."

Cathryn turned crimson. Then a memory darted across her mind. A day at the ocean, when she had crouched for half an hour by a tuft of grass that was growing right out of the sand, waiting until the wind lifted its three perfect strands so their shadow made exactly the composition she wanted. She had leapt to her feet and spread her arms, feeling huge as the ocean.

It was a long time ago. She had been pregnant with Rachel, though she hadn't known it yet. Nearly a quarter-century ago.

She shifted in the seat to face him again. "What happened after summer camp? Did you study with a teacher?"

"You want my story as a glassblower?"

"I want the story of your life."

"It's the same thing."

"I don't believe you. You're more complex than that."

"Believe it. I'm a simple man."

"I doubt that," she said. "You strike me as anything but simple."

"Why is that so hard to accept?"

"Are we arguing?"

"If I say *no,* you'll say *yes, we are.*"

Cathryn had to laugh. "Fine. Tell me your story as a glassblower."

"That's pretty simple, too." Mack dropped his hand from the steering wheel and stretched it across the seat. "When I started out," he said, "there was a right way to do everything. Each step had a name and a particular tool. Everything was meticulous, exact."

"So you rebelled."

"It wasn't a rebellion, more like an expansion. I started to assist someone who opened me to all the ways you can work with glass. Fusing, flocking, sandblasting. Improvisational and eclectic, like jazz. I stayed with him for ten years, and he showed me that I didn't have to follow the rules. That there weren't any rules, except the rules of the material itself. Gravity, like I said. The chemical and optical properties of glass. You can't blend colors the way you can with paint; the molecular structure won't let you. But no rules about what's beautiful or ugly. You can be minimalistic or baroque, utilitarian or abstract, whatever you want."

"And that's where you are now?"

"No, not that either. I'm glad I tried all those things, but I had to let them go."

"No jazz, then." Cathryn raised an eyebrow. "What's left?"

"Just two things, really. Form, and the space inside."

She thought of the blue icebergs. Always in movement, Mack had told her. Water and molten glass, alike that way.

An orb, in transition between liquid and solid. A single drop of water. A perfect globe containing nothing at all.

"That's harder than you might think," he added. "It means taking everything away except what's actually needed."

Then she thought of Michelangelo. *I saw the angel in the marble and carved until I set him free.*

Cathryn moved her gaze to the window. The sky was alive with stars.

Mack dropped his arm, returning it to the steering wheel. "What about you? Tell me your story."

"Me?" He meant her story as a photographer, but there was nothing to tell. She had three or four templates that constituted the McAllister brand. She adapted them to suit the client's needs, set a reasonable price, and everyone was happy.

"I'm just a camera-for-hire. I don't have an interesting story like yours."

"Why don't you let me decide if it's interesting?"

Because. For the merest instant, Cathryn let herself remember the panels she'd been working on when Brian died. Sunlight on stone, each square with its own subtle beauty. Even more beautiful as a group, as the interplay of texture and light.

She'd deleted the entire file. Not recycled into something new, like glass, but erased.

"How about if I tell you a story about Iceland?" she countered. "I bought a book of Saga tales at the place I stayed my first night."

"I think you're dodging my question."

"Hey, some of the stories are pretty wild."

Mack gave her a wry look. "What red-blooded male could resist a wild Saga tale? I assume there are axes and spears and plenty of Viking bloodshed?"

"It's a woman's story. But yes, there's a battle." Cathryn settled against the passenger door. "I'm sure I'll butcher the names, but here goes." She watched Mack to see if he would resist her diversion, but he seemed to be waiting for her to continue.

"So," she began, "there was this woman named Hallgerður who was incredibly beautiful, so beautiful that people would stop whatever they were doing, just to stare at her. But some of them could tell from her eyes that she had the soul of a thief, which was a big deal because stealing was one of the worst things you could do in Viking society. Anyway, she met this Saga hero named Gunnar, and of course they fell madly in love. Gunnar's friend warned him about Hallgerður, but he was too gaga to care."

"Is this a story about how stupid men are around beautiful women?"

"Quiet. Let me tell it." Cathryn lifted her hair from her neck, feeling the beads of water from Mývatn that still clung to her skin. "So they got married, and everything was fine until there was this huge famine. Everyone in their village was starving, so Hallgerður sent one of her servants to steal food from a neighboring farm. When Gunnar came home and saw the table heaped with food, he asked her where it had come from. And then he got furious at how she'd dishonored him and made him a thief's accomplice, and he slapped her across the face, right in front of everyone."

"Aha. It's a story about what brutes men are."

"Just wait." Cathryn tucked her legs beneath her and continued. "So Hallgerður gave him this cold-as-ice look and told him she would never, ever forget that slap. Fast forward a few years, when Gunnar's preparing for a big battle. He needs a lock of her hair to make this special bowstring that's going to protect him from getting wounded, but Hallgerður refuses. 'Remember that slap?' she tells him. 'No way am I giving you a piece of my hair.' He begs and begs, because his life is really at stake, but she won't budge. So he goes into battle with a regular old bowstring, where he's struck by an enemy arrow and killed."

"That's one hard-hearted Viking woman."

"It's a really famous story," Cathryn said.

"Is there supposed to be a moral? As in: Never slap a beautiful woman, even if you're a great big Saga hero."

"Something like that. Or else, make your own damn bowstring."

Mack laughed. "I can hardly wait to hear your other stories."

Cathryn drew in her breath, as if inhaling his words—because they meant he wasn't simply permitting her to stay but wanted her to. He'd said she was good company. A force to be reckoned with.

Someone who could temper an obsession with glassblowing that might not be a virtue.

Then, in the next moment, fear replaced the relief—because of what she had just revealed about herself, through Hallgerður. A woman whose soul didn't match her outer beauty, who never forgave her husband for hurting her and sent him to his death.

She tried to calm her racing pulse. Mack had no idea what the story meant to her. There was no reason for him to think she'd been speaking about herself.

If she'd been speaking about herself. She wasn't sure now. Too much had happened today; she couldn't think straight.

I can hardly wait to hear your other stories.

Whatever else the story meant, he had liked hearing her tell it. That's what she would do, then. Like Scheherazade, she would offer a story each night, swapping stories for time.

Up ahead, the lights of Akureyri came into view. "You can drop me at my car," she said. "I'm parked in front of the studio. My hotel is only a few blocks away."

She wanted him to hear the message behind her words: I can fend for myself. I'll report for duty in the morning.

He pulled up behind the Kia and shut off the engine. Then he reached across the seat, touching her hair. "When you're settled in your room, text me if you want a visitor."

Her carefully crafted neutrality fell away—crumpled, burnt through, as if a match had been lit, and that match was her.

"It's not too late?" She meant, in the evening. Surely it was after ten o'clock by now.

"Not for me."

"Nor for me."

They were speaking literally, of course.

Yet she added a silent word, the word that contained everything she needed to say.

Yes.

Thirteen

When Cathryn opened the door to let Mack in, she felt a wave of inexplicable terror, as if certain, suddenly, that he would look at her and realize that he didn't want to be there after all. But there was nothing of that on his face. It was a complicated look, raw and shrouded and sharp with a desire so palpable that Cathryn felt herself give way before he had even closed the door.

Fleetingly, she thought: I barely know him. But the thought was like the flutter of a curtain, and it seemed to her that she did know him, as if she remembered his body from a dream. The flesh of his shoulders, the hollow at the base of his spine.

A man she recognized, in some mysterious way. And yet, equally, an unknown country that she could step into, right now, at once—or merely pretend to enter, without really yielding.

The Cathryn McAllister she used to be would do that—grasp the rudder of her own desire and steer the ship of her body along the channels she knew how to navigate. Take what she needed, choose pleasure instead of surrender.

She could do that now. Or she could let go entirely. Here, with this man.

What was said to the rose that made it open, was said to me. Rumi had written those words eight hundred years ago.

Mack took her face in his hands. Cathryn thought she might speak, ought to speak—syllables were forming in her throat—but his mouth was already on hers.

Mack lay beside her, afterward, and traced the line of her collarbone. His voice was quiet as he told her, "I can't spend the night. I have to go back to the studio. It's the only way I can sleep. Alone."

Cathryn could almost feel her skin contract, pulling away from his fingertips. All she could think was: If he was leaving so easily, it meant she had misunderstood what had happened between them in the tritest, most humiliating way.

"I don't understand." The three words were all she could manage.

"It's just how I am." He turned her shoulder, made her look at him. "I told you, I keep to myself."

"Meaning?"

"Meaning I'm a hermit."

It was another label, like feral, that told her nothing. "Why?"

His eyes darkened. "A lot of reasons."

She wanted to swat away his non-answers, force him to give her a real answer. Then a second question pushed its way into her awareness. *If that's true, then why did you break your isolation to be with me?*

There were too many ways he might answer, and she wasn't ready to hear them. Not now, when she was naked and vulnerable and drained from a day that felt as long as a week.

Exhaustion overwhelmed her, and all she wanted to do was sleep. Let Mack go back to the damn studio if he wanted; she had no idea what was going on in his mind. He seemed unknown again, maybe even unknowable.

"I need to be alone when I sleep," he repeated. "Please don't take it personally. It's one of my quirks, that's all."

Quirk. Another convenient excuse, the same word he'd used to dismiss the moment when he lost consciousness. She couldn't push for a better explanation, not now and maybe not ever. She was only a visitor, with no claim on his private world.

"Oh fine. You won't get to hear how magnificently I snore."

"I'm sure your snoring is beyond compare." He withdrew his arm gently, then slipped out of bed and bent to gather his clothes. Cathryn watched him through half-closed eyes, too tired to say anything more.

She felt his palm on her hair. "I'll see you at the hot shop," he told her.

After all that had happened, it was impossible to picture herself arriving at the studio like a pupil—cleaning the jacks, wetting the newspaper, watching him work—even though that was why she was here.

Two days in a glass studio meant two more nights with Mack. Cathryn wondered if the nights would make the days awkward or the other way around, but they didn't. Mack was focused and professional in the hot shop, making it easy for her to be that way too. Only the glass mattered, with its demand to watch and respond, always attentive, never assuming. There was no time to think about anything else.

She wondered, too, if it would be hard to be someone's assistant instead of the one in charge, but it was surprisingly enjoyable. There was a freedom in playing a minor role, a sense of purpose in being ready with the right tool at the instant it was needed.

At the end of the day, they parted. Cathryn went back to the hotel, showered, had a bowl of soup, and occupied herself with reading or catching up on email until she heard the buzz of her phone. A text from Mack, asking if she was free. His courtesy touched her—as if there was anything she wanted more than to open the door of her room and let him in.

She longed to wake up next to him but knew he wouldn't waver. Anyway, it was only for three nights, the length of a freelance job. There had never been an implication that it would be anything else.

And yet, when she awoke on the last morning—raising her eyes to the dove-gray wall, with the fluted sconces and old-fashioned armoire—the knowledge that this was her final day in Akureyri slammed into her with a force that made it hard to breathe.

She didn't want to move, get out of bed, start the day. If it didn't start, it wouldn't end. She remembered how she had felt when she realized that she wouldn't be there to see her paperweight come out of the annealer. This was ten times worse. Stupidly, she hadn't seen it coming. The hot shop had felt like the universe, the hours she spent there like time out of time. Her immersion had been so complete that its brevity hadn't seemed real.

It was Iceland's fault. She never would have let herself fall into this kind of spell in America.

Blue icebergs that moaned when a layer of their history melted away. Steam that spewed from underground cracks. Lakes and wine that kept you from aging, made you think you could freeze time and be its master.

She willed herself to inhale. Her distress was absurd. She'd known from the beginning that she would leave after a three-day interlude that would, soon enough, become a vacation anecdote and a paragraph in her resume. *I often go the extra mile, learning firsthand about the subjects I document for my clients.* The pain in her chest was melodrama, unworthy of her.

She hadn't mentioned the specifics of her departure to Mack, and he hadn't asked. Maybe he thought it was up to her to speak, since she was the one with the return ticket. Or maybe he was too absorbed in making glass to care if her flight was today or tomorrow or the day after. He'd still be making glass after she left, still focused on his project. Obsessed.

Cathryn pressed her fingertips against her temples, trying to quiet her throbbing brain. Stop it, she told herself. Just. Stop. It.

She swung her legs over the side of the bed, squaring her feet on the braided rug. Then she let her hands drop, bracing them on the mattress as she readied herself to stand and begin the day. But her own body made her halt. It was the stickiness between her thighs, the swollen languor of her flesh.

She wanted to scream. Stop. Please.

It was time to go home. She had a plane ticket, a life. Another freelance job, awaiting her return. A hair appointment, brunch with an old friend.

Most of all, there was the obvious fact that he hadn't asked her to stay.

Cathryn finished her bowl of oatmeal and *skyr*, the Icelandic breakfast she had come to enjoy, and set out for her final day in Akureyri. It was a bright, sunlit morning. Two girls ran across the street, their braids flapping against their knapsacks. The smell of freshly baked bread mingled with the smell of the harbor.

She was halfway to the studio when she heard the buzz of her cell phone. Icelandair, canceling her flight? Mack, telling her not to go? Hardly. Grimacing, she reached into her purse and felt for the phone. It was Rachel.

"Hey, sweetie," she said, surprised. "How nice to hear from you. And an actual call, instead of a text." She spotted a bench outside one of the shops and sat down, holding the phone to her cheek.

Rachel's voice was uncharacteristically tense. "Where *are* you?"

"I'm in Iceland. Like I told you."

"Not *like* you told me. You always send us these little updates when you go somewhere, and you haven't sent *anything*. Plus, you never even answered me about the scarf. I mean, just to say *all they had was green*. So of course I got worried. I thought you'd fallen into a volcano or something."

"Silly girl. And I'm sorry. I figured I'd text when I found one."

"It's not like you," Rachel insisted. "You always answer."

Like me, Cathryn thought. It was the koan she'd been carrying in her pocket for three days.

She wanted to remind Rachel how she herself had complained,

more than once, about having to provide what she called *constant updates on her coordinates.* Even as a teenager, Rachel had hated to divulge her plans or make any commitments, but would become furious if Cathryn didn't answer *her* texts immediately. Where *are* you? she'd type, followed by an irate emoji, as if she had dropped her mother somewhere and expected her to stay right where she'd left her until she was needed.

"I got busy, that's all."

"Doing what?" Rachel demanded.

Cathryn took a deep breath. "Learning about glassblowing."

"Glassblowing? WTF?"

"Hey, why not?"

"You're not making any sense. And you really don't sound like yourself."

"I don't? How do I sound?"

She waited, and then Rachel said, "Happy."

"That's the nicest thing you've said to me in years."

"*Mother.* You are being seriously weird. Are you sure you're okay?"

"I'm sure I'm okay."

Rachel let out a sigh. "I guess I'm acting like an old lady."

"I'm touched, actually."

"Whatever." They were silent again. Then Rachel cleared her throat. "So you're flying home tomorrow, right?"

Cathryn hesitated. "I don't know. I might stay a bit longer."

"Why would you do that?"

Cathryn wanted to tell her all-too-imperious daughter that it went both ways and she didn't have to disclose every movement and motive either, but she kept her voice even. "I can stay if I want, honey. It's not like I'm expected back at a desk on Monday morning. That's the nice part of being a freelancer."

She hadn't imagined that Rachel would care, one way or another, but Rachel startled her by saying, "I really need you to come home."

"What's the matter?" Her mind sped through the possibilities, the same way it had when Judah called, when she was on the ferry to the island with the birds. An accident. Arrested. Trapped in a burning building. Because Rachel was a woman, she added, pregnant.

Rachel didn't answer, so she asked her again. "What's the matter, honey? Are you in trouble?"

"I'm not *in trouble*. I could just use a little parental assistance."

Cathryn still didn't understand. "What kind of assistance? Financial?"

"Just assistance. For a change."

The muttered *for a change* made Cathryn bristle. Rachel had been remote for years. She didn't get to accuse her mother of refusing help that she'd never asked for.

Yet she was asking now, and she got to do that. There was no expiration date on activating your right to be a needy child.

"Tell me what's going on, sweetheart."

"It's not important." Rachel gave a dismissive sniff. "I just thought you might want to tag along while I move out of this crap apartment and back on my own."

"You're breaking up with Ryder?" Ryder was Rachel's live-in boyfriend, although she had never let Cathryn meet him.

"That's the plan."

"Am I supposed to say *what a relief* or *I'm sorry to hear that*?"

"You're not supposed to say anything." Cathryn could almost see Rachel tossing her head. "It doesn't matter."

"Of course it matters. It matters how you're feeling."

"But not enough to stop *glassblowing* and come home. Like you *said* you would, which is why I figured you'd be around this weekend."

Cathryn tried not to react. "Is there something specific you need me for?"

She regretted the remark at once. What a lousy, manipulative way to put it. Rachel didn't need her to carry furniture. She needed her for something far less tangible and they both knew it.

"Nothing. Whatever. Enjoy your vacation."

Cathryn sagged against the bench. There was no way to pretend that this call was anything less than awful. It was the very gesture she had longed for, when Rachel was a haughty adolescent—and before that, when Rachel turned her back, pointedly, to snuggle with her beloved daddy. For so many years, she had wanted her daughter to say *I really need you.* And now, when she finally did, the timing was wrong—or else Cathryn herself had made it wrong, because she didn't want to say, *Yes, of course, I'll be there as soon as I can.*

She searched for the words that would fix this, but there wasn't time. The silence was already too long.

Her gaze darted from a teenager on a bicycle, his jacket flapping behind him like a sail, to an old woman sweeping the steps with a red-handled broom—as if one of them had the answer, as if the answer were out there, on the streets of Akureyri.

Rachel was feeling needy and alone. But she wasn't in danger. She wanted company while she ended a relationship, that was all.

Well, relationships ended. For any number of reasons. Sooner, later.

Cathryn swallowed and tried again. "When are you moving out?"

"I don't know," Rachel said. "The weekend."

"Call me if you need anything, okay?"

"I thought I just did."

"I meant, if a problem comes up, something you didn't foresee."

"I don't go around *foreseeing* problems. That's your thing. I just do what I have to do."

Try, Cathryn told herself. It was just how Rachel talked. "You have a place to go to, right?"

"I have a place. It's not available until Saturday, so that's why."

"Got it." Then she made her voice as sunny as she could. "I have faith in you, sweetheart. I know you're doing the right thing."

"Really? And how would you know that? Based on what?"

"Rachel. Are you trying to make me feel bad for not running home?"

"*Do* you feel bad for not running home?"

"I guess I do, if I had to ask."

Rachel's voice softened. "Don't. It's okay. I wanted to be a baby for a minute. You know, regress. But I'm fine, really. I'll just toss my stuff in a U-Haul."

"Are you just saying that?"

"I'm saying it because I'm meaning it. Ryder didn't kick me out; I'm leaving because I want to."

"You sound pretty sure."

"I am sure. Go have your glassblowing adventure. It's about time you did something random. You know, not a job or, like, self-improvement. Just because."

"Just because," Cathryn echoed. Then she said, "Will you call me later, honey, so I know how you're doing?"

"I will. And have fun, really."

It wasn't until they said good-bye that Cathryn realized what had just happened. She'd told her daughter that she was staying in Iceland. It was what she wanted, but she hadn't known that she'd actually do it until she spoke the words aloud.

She was certain that Mack hadn't expected her to do that. He hadn't said, *I wish you didn't have to go. Can't you change your flight?*

Maybe it wasn't what he wished. Maybe he'd be relieved when she left.

Shit. What if she was making a horrible assumption?

She needed to find out—now, before she did something pathetic, like canceling her fight to be with a man who was waiting for her to leave.

Her mind was racing. If she told Rachel that she was coming home after all, Rachel would make a flippant remark about her swift *one-eighty*, but she'd be grateful, and Cathryn would feel like a good mother. If Mack didn't want her to stay, that was what she would do. It would be a positive outcome—for her daughter, and for their relationship.

And if he did?

She already knew the answer. Her imaginary devotion and Rachel's imaginary gratitude would dissolve in an instant.

As they should. It was absurd to fantasize about sacrificing yourself for a child who wasn't in danger and had told you not to. It was self-deception, or worse—using your child as a ploy to make your wounded pride seem noble and brave.

Cathryn rose from the bench. Slowly, she began to walk to the studio.

She wanted a new relationship with her daughter, not the defensive sparring they'd gotten accustomed to. But it couldn't be a do-over of a relationship they'd never had when Rachel was small. It had to be with the real Rachel, as she was now.

If she wanted to open, like Rumi's rose, she had to open to everything—to Rachel, the woman with the red-handled broom, the man standing in a doorway shaking out a rubber mat. And to her own self. Someone who dared to offer herself and could handle whatever she got in return, even if it was nothing. Someone she had glimpsed, with Mack.

She liked who she was in Iceland. She didn't want to stop being that person.

When she got to the studio, she didn't wait for Mack to finish what he was doing and greet her. She had to talk to him right now, before something false crept into her words. Already, half-truths were fighting for space in her mind.

Since I don't have any job commitments until—

It turns out that my flexible fare will let me—

I thought it might be interesting to—

No. They were safe little excuses. She had to tell him the truth. And then, if she saw him flinch, she'd leave as planned.

Mack looked up from the marver, his forehead creasing. "Are you all right?"

"I need to talk to you."

"Yes. Of course." He motioned to the metal folding chairs. Cathryn sat down and waited for him to wipe his hands and join her.

She hadn't thought about how to put this enormous new feeling into words; it was too immense for any of the ways she knew how to speak. *I feel, I realized, I decided.* It needed the crack of an iceberg, the roar of a seismic shift.

And then it came to her. A piece of Icelandic history that she'd read about, while she was having a bowl of soup. A tale worthy of Scheherazade.

"I have a story to tell you," she said. "It's about Laki, the volcano that erupted in Iceland almost two hundred and forty years ago."

She fought to keep her voice steady. "There were dozens and dozens of boiling craters, spewing lava and poisonous gas all over the country for eight solid months. Eight million tons of sulfur dumped into the atmosphere. Half the cattle and horses died, eighty percent of the sheep. The whole country was covered in darkness, and everyone was starving."

Mack watched her carefully, and Cathryn felt a tremor pass through her body. Then she straightened, steeled herself, and continued. "It wasn't the eruption itself that led to such terrible devastation. It was the aftermath, the darkness and ash, long after the lava had cooled. They called it the Móðuharðindin, the hardship of the fog. It took twenty years for the darkness to lift and the country to recover. To feel the warmth and light, and be whole again."

He reached across the table and took her hand. "What are you trying to tell me?"

Her military posture crumpled. He was going to make her say it. "I've been in the darkness for a long time."

"That's not the woman I see."

"I know. That's why I want to stay. Here, in Akureyri."

He turned her hand palm-up and traced her fingers, one by one. She watched the slow movement of his thumb, hardly daring to breathe. "It's all right with me if you stay," he said. His voice was quiet. "That's the best I can do right now."

Cathryn released her breath. His best was fine. It was all she needed.

Fourteen

This time, Cathryn didn't list all the reasons her plan was crazy. Maybe it was crazy, but she didn't care. She told Mack she had to make some arrangements and needed her laptop, back in the hotel room, and would return to the hot shop later.

Walking quickly, she retraced her steps through the city. It was mid-morning now and the sidewalks were filled with tourists peering at the window displays or posing with the oversized sculptures of Grýla and Leppalúði, the grotesque Icelandic trolls who ate badly behaved children at Christmastime. Cathryn made a mental note to return to Hafnarstraeti, the street with the souvenir shops, to find a red scarf for Rachel and maybe a CD of Björk.

The cleaning staff hadn't gotten to her room yet, so she put the *ekka trufla*—do not disturb—sign on the doorknob and threw open the curtains. Let the day come in. She didn't fear it now.

She called Icelandair first and said *yes*, she understood there would be a hundred-dollar penalty for changing her flight but *no*, she wasn't sure when she wanted to rebook. Then she went on the Avis site and extended the rental of the Kia. A prompt appeared, alerting her that she would be charged the regular rate, not the rate that came with the Saga Tour, for both the car and the special iPad.

Whatever, Cathryn thought. She was done with the iPad and its programmed pleasures. She stuffed it in her suitcase.

She had a job lined up for the week she got back, a dance company that wanted new photos for their upcoming season. They were one of her oldest and most faithful clients; the director, Nora Lang, had become a kind of friend. She emailed Nora to say, regrettably, that she couldn't do the shoot right now; did Nora want her to refer them to someone else, or could it wait a bit? Confident that Nora would rather wait than trust the job to someone new, she signed out of her email and called each of her children to let them know she was staying in Iceland longer than she had planned.

Judah seemed confused. "Why are you staying in Iceland? I thought you had a business thing and then you were coming back."

"I did have a business thing, but there's a lot to see and do, so I figured I'd hang around for a bit. You know, be a tourist." Cathryn could already hear the question he hadn't asked. *What if I need something?*

Maybe she should have gone away sooner, somewhere truly inaccessible, so her lovable-but-helpless son would have to fend for himself.

Then she had an idea. Ask *him* to help *her.* Judah lived a few miles away, in an apartment with three man-boys from his technical school. "Actually," she said, "I have a favor to ask. Can you keep an eye on the house while I'm gone? Come by every couple of days to make sure everything's okay? You can even stay there if you want. Just you, though."

"As in, no Dungeons and Dragons orgies in your living room?"

"As in that."

"Joke, Mom. And yeah, sure."

"And my car," she added. She remembered her excuse about leaving her spare key with the dealer. "I do have another key, I'd forgotten. It's in the little Navajo pot on my desk. Maybe you can start the car when you come over, drive it around the block or something?"

"You really did have a key?"

"I know, I'm sorry. But you worked things out, so that's good. Anyway, can you do that for me?"

"Sure. I'm on it."

She had already told Rachel that she was staying in Iceland, but she needed to tell her again, now that it was true. And she wanted to make sure Rachel was all right. She tried calling, but Rachel didn't answer. Finally, she sent a text: "Not exactly sure when I'll be back, but call/text any time and let me know how you're doing."

That didn't feel like enough, but Cathryn knew so little about Rachel's relationship with Ryder that she didn't know what to add. Rachel had always kept the parts of her life from overlapping—the same way, when she was small, that she had insisted that the items on her dinner plate couldn't touch. All Cathryn knew about Ryder was that he did something with electronic music. Rachel had been quick to move in with him, but that was her pattern. There had been a series of live-in boyfriends, none that lasted, and none whose disappearance seemed to affect her for long. Cathryn had tried to talk about it, but Rachel had cut her off. Cathryn didn't blame her. She couldn't expect her daughter to take relationship advice from a mother who wasn't in one.

She switched back to email and saw that Nora Lang had already replied, asking if Cathryn knew someone who could fill in, since she hadn't specified when she'd be back. Cathryn read the message twice, unhappily. She'd been looking forward to the job—it was an interesting chance to shoot the dancers in motion, and Nora always included a prominent credit line—but she couldn't blame her. Nora had a season to prepare for and needed someone who would show up.

Cathryn reminded herself that it was just a bump in their long history. She emailed a colleague, someone she met for drinks now and then. Elliott Fischer had passed extra work on to her a few times when he was overbooked, so it seemed like a chance to repay the favor—or bail her out, whichever way he wanted to take it.

She reread her message to Elliott, deleting the second *I really appreciate,* and hit *send.* She couldn't think of anything else she had to do. When you lived the way she did, there weren't many people who would notice if she were gone for a while.

It's all right with me if you stay.

Uttered in a different moment, by a different man, the words might have sounded arrogant and cold. It was the way Mack said them, so quietly, as he traced her fingers with his thumb. As if he were already giving her more than he had planned to, or thought he could—not reluctantly, but with a sense of wonder.

It became obvious, now that she was staying for a while, that she couldn't hover in the hot shop eight hours a day. Mack needed time alone. Part of the process, he explained, was thinking through what he wanted to do—sketching, visualizing, choreographing the sequence of movements. Cathryn filled in the rest of the sentence: without the distraction of an unskilled apprentice who was waiting to be useful.

"Makes sense," she said. "Let me know when there's something for me to do, and I'll show up then."

"Why don't you come in the afternoon?" he suggested. "Around one, one thirty? That'll give me a chance to work out my ideas."

"Yes. Good." Cathryn nodded. The division of the day just might make this work. It would give him the creative solitude he needed—and give her a chance to explore and assure herself that she wasn't missing the whole of Iceland after all.

"I'll show you how to let yourself in," he added. "I usually keep the door unlocked, but you should have a way to get in if you need to."

Cathryn followed him outside. He shut the door and pointed to the bolt. "You see that little gap, right below the top latch? Push it up and to the left, and you'll pop the lock."

She tried it. "Hey. It works."

"Of course it works." He motioned them inside again and showed her how to ease the door shut. "Remember not to slam it. First rule in a hot shop: no sudden noises."

"Got it." She tilted her head. "What's the second rule?"

She thought Mack would make a joke, but his expression was stern. "Pay attention."

She decided to spend the first morning at the Lystigardurinn, Akureyri's famous botanical garden, a park-like anomaly only fifty kilometers from the Arctic circle. Founded in 1910 by the women of Akureyri as a way to beautify the city, it had expanded to become a center of scientific research. Cathryn skimmed the brochure she'd plucked from the rack, astonished to learn that the Lystigardurinn was home to over seven thousand species. People had thought that many of the plants would never be able to survive on the edge of the Arctic, but they had. They did more than survive; they flourished.

Intrigued, she wandered along the paths. Beds of purple and red flowers. A meadow of bright blue poppies. Color, abundance—so different from the starkness of the glaciers and lava fields.

She followed a side path that led to a graceful bridge and, from there, to a little pond. A boy was pushing a toy sailboat into the water. He looked about three, clad in a striped shirt and those overalls with straps that Cathryn remembered Judah wearing at that age. OshKosh, they were called. Judah had liked boats too, anything that moved. A woman sat on a nearby bench, watching the boy. She had short brown hair and a round face. Spotting Cathryn, she smiled. "Lovely morning," she said, in English.

"It is," Cathryn answered. She gestured at the little boy. "My son liked to do that, when he was small."

"The simple toys are nice, aren't they? No batteries, just wind and water."

The boy leaned toward the pond to grab the boat before it drifted away. Cathryn wanted to say, *Careful, he might fall in.* It wasn't her child, though, and the woman said nothing. The boy snatched the boat and sat back on his haunches, examining the sail. After a minute, Cathryn said, "Well, enjoy your morning."

"You also," the woman told her.

Cathryn made her way along another side path. On her right, there was a cluster of purple flowers unlike anything she had ever seen. Each had a tall, dotted center, like a pineapple, surrounded by narrow violet blades that fanned out in dragonfly wings. She bent closer.

The light was different here, so far north. With the sun resting lower in the sky, there were no hard shadows; each object was distinct, fully lit. Slowly, Cathryn reached into her purse and found her phone. She hadn't brought her camera, but there was a camera on the iPhone. She hardly ever took photos that didn't have to do with a job she was paid to do. An occasional *Hi from Mom!* snapshot, but nothing just because she wanted to. Not anymore. That was the price she had elected to pay. And yet.

She stepped carefully into the flower bed and crouched next to one of the purple blooms. It had been a long time, but the feeling returned at once. A clarity in her mind and body. The perfection of exactly what she was seeing—here, now, offering itself in the intimacy of the present.

She thought of something the American painter Georgia O'Keeffe had written, *When you take a flower in your hand and really look at it, it's your world for the moment.*

Cathryn peered at the image on her phone. It wasn't a viewfinder on a camera, but the call was the same—to be quiet and receive what was there to be received.

She knew what to do without having to think—zooming in for a close-up of the feathery petals, adjusting the filter, waiting for the perfect instant when the petals lifted. Yes. Right there, as if the flower was praying. She took seven shots in a row, certain that one of them would capture the quality of movement and light she had witnessed.

Then she stood and backed out of the flower bed. Eagerly, she opened the photo app to see how they looked. Oblivious to the other visitors who were strolling along the path, she flicked through the images on the screen.

Her eagerness faded. They were crap. Something you'd find on a Hallmark card.

Angry at herself for being so naïve, she deleted them, one after the other. Then, on impulse, she saved the last one.

A souvenir of her time in Akureyri. Something to look at when she wasn't here anymore.

Fifteen

Cathryn went back to the botanical garden the next morning, drawn to the trees and color and quiet paths. The early morning fog had lifted, and a bright blue sky, speckled with white, arched over the greenery. She found the same pond where she had seen the mother and little boy, and had just sat down on a wrought-iron bench when she heard a child's bell-like laughter. She looked up and saw that the pair was back. The boy ran to the edge of the pond, waving his boat.

The woman dipped her head in greeting. "I see we both like this spot."

"All three of us." Cathryn nodded at the boy.

"I'm Eva," the woman said, "and this little scamp is Pétur."

"Cathryn," she said, pronouncing it like the Icelandic Katrin.

The woman, Eva, settled next to her on the bench. "So," she said. "You can't be a regular tourist. No tourist would return to the Lystigardurinn two days in a row. What brings you here?"

"I'm here with—" She hesitated, not sure what word to use for Mack. Finally, she said, "—my companion, who's rented a studio in Akureyri for an art project."

Eva looked at her with interest. "And you? Are you an artist too?"

Cathryn waved a hand. "No. I was, once. I mean, sort of."

"And why not now?"

"Oh, you know. Children. Time. Life."

"All good subjects for art."

"Perhaps." There was an awkward silence, and then she asked, "What about you? Is Pétur your only child?"

"No, my daughter is in school. She's practically grown, but I wanted another baby, so I thought—well, as you Americans say—it's now or never."

"Goodness, you're courageous. Once my two got to be self-sufficient, there was no way I would have started all that again."

Eva shrugged. "I wanted one more. Might as well have what you want."

Cathryn suppressed the urge to roll her eyes. As if it were that simple.

On the other hand, she did have what she wanted. An image of Mack's naked body flashed across her mind, and she felt a swell of desire, right there on the garden bench, so sudden and sharp that she could hardly bear not to thrust her fingers between her legs.

She turned quickly, fearful that the lust in her expression was all too evident, and focused her attention on the little boy. He was squatting by the pond again, moving his boat back and forth by the shallow edge. "You did well," she said. "He's adorable."

Eva gave another shrug. "He's very self-sufficient, as you put it. He can play quietly like that for a long while."

Cathryn kept her eyes on the boy. "Mine never could. They were always quarreling. That's what siblings do, of course, but they were so different in temperament that they could never get along."

"A shame," Eva said. "And still?"

"Still. Like oil and water."

"What is oil and water?"

"Two things that can't mix. Even if you try, they stay separate."

"That seems all right. To be one's own person, not mixed."

Cathryn started to tell her that it was just a figure of speech, but Eva cut her off, calling out sharply. "Pétur! *Taktu eftir!*"

Cathryn saw the boy step back from the water. He turned to his mother and pointed at the boat that was drifting away, his features twisted into a look that meant he was about to cry. "Yes, yes," Eva said, slipping back into English. "I'll get it." She rose and strode to the pond. She waited by the edge until the boat came to her, then plucked it from the water. "Here you go, little one." She gave Cathryn a mother-to-mother look. "He likes to let it go, and then he's surprised when it floats away."

"What does *taktu eftir* mean?"

"It means pay attention. He was about to step right into the pond, as if water was air."

"I remember that age," Cathryn said. "They're little scientists, testing to see how the world works."

"It's true. But my Pétur is a sly one. You think he's sitting there quiet as a lamb, and then he leaps like a fool."

"I remember those days. They see something, and off they go."

Eva settled on the bench again. Then she gave Cathryn a curious look. "Your children are older now?"

"They're huge. In their twenties."

"Ah. Then you have time for your art."

Cathryn gave a start, and Eva said, "Time, life. You have that again." Cathryn stared at her. "You have that again," Eva repeated. She smoothed her hair and offered an encouraging smile.

As if from far away, Cathryn saw herself sitting on a filigreed bench, her hands in her lap. From above, she could hear the call of the terns as they flew in and out of the canopy.

Then she inhaled sharply. The woman had no idea what she was talking about. You couldn't have a child, a relationship, a resurrected career—poof, merely because *you might as well have what you want*.

"Perhaps," she said. Then she looked at her watch, feigning surprise. "Actually, I *don't* have time. Now, that is. I have to be getting back."

It wasn't true, but all she could think was: I have to get out of here.

"Yes, of course." Eva nodded politely. "Until we meet again."

Cathryn gave a return nod as she stood and brushed off her jeans. "Bye, Pétur," she called. The boy looked up with a cheerful wave. She waved back, then hurried down the path, as if she really were expected somewhere else.

When she was certain that she was out of Eva's vision, she stopped to look around. Surely there was another place she could retreat to, in all this bucolic greenery—a meadow or side path, a diversion that would seem like a purpose. There were seven thousand species, after all.

She became aware of voices, low and unhurried, as an elderly couple approached on the gravel path, heading toward the pond she had just left. The woman had a kerchief over her hair, and the man was wearing a herringbone cap. *Góðan dag*, they murmured. Twin smiles, peaceful and benevolent.

Cathryn inhaled, then shouldered her purse and began to walk again, still unsure of where she was going. Then she remembered that the botanic garden had a little café. All right, she could go there. She felt in her purse for the map, and her fingers grazed the edge of her phone. Rachel, she thought. The conversation with Eva had made her think of her own children. It was early in America, but maybe Rachel would be up.

Rachel had never replied to her message, and she needed to hear her daughter's voice, know she was all right. She pictured Rachel in a robe, her hair wet from the shower, pouring a cup of coffee—where? Her new apartment wouldn't be available until tomorrow. Was she still at Ryder's place? And where was Ryder while Rachel was having the imagined cup of coffee? Had she told him, or was she simply going to disappear?

Her children might be huge—the word she'd used, in reply to Eva—but that didn't mean they were grown. Safe.

According to the map, the café was on the right, just around a bend. Cathryn quickened her steps until she spotted the outdoor tables. She sank into the nearest chair, pulled out her phone, and tapped on Rachel's number.

To her relief, Rachel answered right away. "Mom? Hey. Are you still in Iceland?"

"I am."

"How's the glassblowing? Or are you done with that?"

"No, not done. I just wanted to know how everything was going. Are you all set for the move into your new place?"

The silence lasted a beat too long, and then Rachel sighed. "I'm not moving. I asked for my deposit back."

"You're not? Is that a good thing or a bad thing?"

"It's just a thing. It's what I did. Or didn't do."

"You seemed so sure."

"I guess I wasn't." Rachel's voice sharpened. She sounded belligerent now, as if Cathryn had accused her of lying. "I mean, why not *try*, for once? I didn't really try with Ryder. I just got pissed off and told him it was over. And then I thought: I'm going to end up like my mother if I keep this up, oh-so-beautiful and all alone. No offense, but that's who you *are*, Mom. You're the beautiful Snow Queen. *I don't need anyone, thank you very much.* We're all in awe of you, okay, but I don't see how that's made you happy."

Cathryn sat up straight—stunned and hurt, yet proud of her daughter for the fierceness of her declaration. She wanted to argue that it wasn't fair, she wasn't a Snow Queen. Maybe she had been, but not now. If she told Rachel about Mack, Rachel would see that—but she wasn't ready to share Mack, and definitely not with her daughter.

She moved the phone to her other hand. "I understand that you want to try, sweetheart. But does that make Ryder the right one to try *with*?"

"He's not the wrong one, if that's what you're asking. I mean, he's not perfect, but he has a lot going for him, and he can be cool to be with."

"Are you happy with him?"

"How would I know what happy-with-a-man even *looks* like? I mean, given the quote-unquote role-modeling I had in my formative years."

Cathryn closed her eyes. Not that again. "It wasn't all terrible between Dad and me."

"*Not terrible* isn't my definition of a great relationship."

Cathryn took a deep breath. When she opened her eyes, she saw that the patio was starting to fill with people. Families, couples. Lunch hour, on a beautiful day.

"Fine, Rachel. Point taken."

"I used to make up stories about her, you know." Rachel's tone shifted again, a mixture of candor and slyness. "I called her Miranda. I pretended we were best friends."

There was no use claiming she didn't know who Rachel was talking about. Cathryn could still see the photograph, the woman's almond eyes and black lace bra, and she had no doubt that Rachel could too. Another child might have forgotten, but not Rachel.

"I'm so sorry, honey."

"Don't be. I was a moron. It was my way of—I don't know, feeling in control."

"We've never talked about that night."

"I didn't think you wanted to."

"I probably didn't." Cathryn wet her lip. "Do you want to talk about it now?"

"What does it matter? It's so long ago."

"It does matter."

"Whatever."

"Rachel. Dad died because the brakes failed. He didn't die because he screwed another woman, no matter what it looked like in that photo."

"Let's hope not. Otherwise, every single guy is doomed."

The cynicism in Rachel's words sent a spike of pain into Cathryn's heart. Was her daughter really this hard? "Men aren't all like that." She hesitated. "Is Ryder?"

Rachel's laugh was dry, with none of the sweet happiness that Cathryn wanted for her. "He has his shortcomings, but that's not in the top five."

Something wasn't right about her daughter's decision; Cathryn could hear it in every syllable. "Are you sure this is what you want, honey? To stay with Ryder?" Before Rachel could answer, she said, "If it's about the hassle of moving, I'll help you. I can cosign a lease on a new place, get you some furniture, whatever you need. I'm sorry if I sounded like I was hedging on that before. But don't stay because leaving is too much trouble."

"I never said it was. That's your idea, not mine." Rachel's voice was firm. "I'm staying because I want to stay. Because for once I actually want to make something work, instead of running away when it gets tough."

"All right. Fine." A family descended on the table next to hers. A mother and father. Children, squabbling and giggling. Like the couple on the bridge, taking their connection to one another for granted.

"I even decided to do the Miranda thing," Rachel added. "You know, go all-out."

"What's the Miranda thing?" Sleep with a married man? God, she hoped not.

"The underwear," Rachel said. "I bought a little black lace number. To show him I cared."

"Oh." Cathryn didn't know if Rachel was criticizing her, even obliquely, for not taking better care of her man. No, that was absurd. Rachel had been nine years old. She couldn't possibly have blamed the destruction of their family on her mother's bedroom attire. Anyway, ardor didn't come from black lace. Mack saw her in dirty jeans, a tank top streaked with grime.

She kept her voice mild. "If you think it will help."

Rachel gave another mirthless laugh. "I'll keep you posted."

"Please." Then she said, "Not just about that, of course. About you. Everything."

She had to say it, one more time. "It was the brakes, that's all. Not divine judgment. Not because of anything you or I might have said or thought."

"Mom. Stop. I get it."

Cathryn watched the father at the next table hold the chair so a tiny girl could climb up and settle in her seat. The mother bent over the girl and fastened a yellow bib around her neck. She raised her eyes to her husband's and smiled.

Cathryn's heart caught. Had she once had, and then squandered, that kind of easy connection? It was impossible to be certain, after all this time.

It seemed to her, now, sitting in the little café, that it hadn't been all bad, even at the end. She still didn't know, not really, if Brian had been an unfaithful jerk who didn't appreciate her, or a lonely, confused husband who didn't feel that she appreciated him. Maybe he didn't want to pressure her into being something she wasn't, or couldn't be, so he did what seemed simplest and found the missing fire somewhere else. He had told her as much. She could hear his voice down the tunnel of memory. "She has something I need. But I need my family too. You. I need you."

What was it her husband needed, that the woman in the photo had?

She had assumed it was heat. But maybe it was warmth. Love.

Had she actually loved him?

Even in the horror of finding the photo, she hadn't been terrified of losing Brian. She had been furious at him for humiliating her—and then, for robbing her of the chance to embrace forgiveness and generosity, to know if she could have done that.

She probably wouldn't have, though; she'd been too cautious. Not a Snow Queen, but Snow White, asleep.

Cold, either way. Disconnected.

Rachel's voice cut into her reverie. "Anyway," she said, "don't worry about me. I'm a big girl. I shouldn't have whined about you staying in Iceland."

"I'll get you a scarf."

"That'd be great. Red, if they have it."

"Red it is. I love you, sweetie."

"Love you too, Mom."

"Talk to you soon."

Cathryn heard the click as Rachel ended the call. She was about to return the phone to her purse when she heard the echo of Eva's words, tossed at her with such blithe assurance. *Then you have time for your art.*

She could try again, right now. There were no beautiful flowers in the courtyard—yet Minor White had photographed peeling paint, a frosted window, feet. Edward Weston had taken pictures of cabbages and knees. If you were an artist, everything was art, or could be. If you saw it that way, opened yourself to be its vessel.

Cathryn stood and surveyed the patio. The treetops were a green calligraphy against the crayon-blue sky. If she twisted her body, she could shoot the tips, angled and asymmetrical, jutting into the wide blue dome. It wasn't a beautiful composition, but beauty wasn't everything.

She lifted the iPhone, squinted, and tapped on the little white circle.

Sixteen

The shelves of the hot shop were lined with blue and white shapes. Azure and teal, milky and clear. Some of the pieces had jagged edges, cold-sliced with a knife, while others were built in tiers, the interior giving way to delicate bands of light. Cathryn thought they were extraordinary, each in a different way, but she knew Mack wasn't satisfied. That was clear from the way he scowled at each new piece as it came out of the annealer and shoved it on a shelf.

She didn't dare to offer a suggestion; she was a greenhorn, a guest in his world. All she could do was wait until he was ready to try the next idea and had a task for her. It wasn't a role she had ever chosen before— doing one small thing at a time, instead of being the person in charge. Sometimes she grew tired of standing by, of attention without action. And then, out of nowhere, she would feel a huge swell of joy and want nothing more than to be exactly here, dipping a tool in water or sliding the warm beeswax along the length of the jacks.

Or *here*, in bed with this one particular man—a man with secrets, who moved her in a mysterious and inexplicable way.

Cathryn stepped out of the shower, glad to be free of the grime and sweat of the hot shop. She tried to remember if there were things she needed to attend to, back in America. It all seemed light-years away, but there *was* one thing—her neighbor, an overly zealous gardener who liked to leave tomatoes and zucchini on her doorstep. Well, since Judah was supposed to be keeping an eye on the house, she'd ask him to be on the lookout for a basket of vegetables.

She wrapped herself in a towel and reached for the phone as she lowered herself into the edge of the bed. Quickly, she typed out a long text. Then she added a PS: "They'll just spoil, so go ahead and use them."

She hadn't expected Judah to answer right away, but he did. "For what?" he texted back.

Cathryn rolled her eyes. Did he really need to be told what to do with vegetables? "For salad," she wrote. "Gazpacho. Ratatouille."

She had just hit the little blue arrow for *send* when her phone rang. Annoyed, she answered without looking at the caller ID. "Ratatouille," she said. "It's like a stew."

"Ratatouille. Sounds like a Disney character. A rodent with a French accent."

Her frown deepened. "Who is this?"

"It's Elliott Fischer. I thought I'd report back about the dance group."

"Oh, goodness. Sorry, I was texting my kid."

She had asked Elliott Fischer if he could do the shoot in her place—the dancers in motion, for the troupe's seasonal promotion—and had thanked him profusely when he said he'd be glad to. She hadn't thought about him since then, but she did want to know how it was working out.

"And yes, please. Nora Lang is one of my oldest clients, and I hated to let her down."

"No worries," Elliott said. "She couldn't have been nicer. In fact, I'm going to do the job tomorrow. She was grateful I could get it done so promptly."

"All's well that ends well, then." Cathryn tried to make it into a joke, though she was half-serious. "Don't go stealing my client, now."

"Would I do that?"

"Yes."

Elliott laughed. "Where are you, anyway?"

"Iceland." Cathryn looked around the hotel room. In a few short days, the room had become her home. The dove-gray walls and the pleated curtains, the glossy old-fashioned armoire with its belled doors and ornate handles—they were the landmarks of her world, anchoring her in place. "Iceland," she repeated.

"How about that? The place where my cousin ended the Cold War on a chess board."

It took Cathryn a moment to figure out what Elliott was talking about. "Is Bobby Fischer really your cousin? Or was?"

"Distant. Something-something-removed."

"He beat Boris Spassky in Reykjavik, right? Gosh, I can't believe I'm remembering that. I mean, remembering that it happened. I was hardly even born."

"World Chess Championship, 1972. It was touted as a Cold War confrontation between the US and the USSR, and Bobby nailed it."

"Bobby Fischer. Who would've guessed?"

Cathryn waited for him to say something more. She could hear a church bell in the distance, the dripping of the bathroom faucet. Then she tightened the towel and cleared her throat. "Anyway, thanks for taking care of my client while I'm away." She emphasized the words *my client*.

"My pleasure. I'll let you know how it goes."

Uneasily, she ended the call. There was nothing to be done about it. No one could be in America and Iceland at the same time, not even an expert multitasker like her.

She'd never really had to admit that before—because she *had* done it all, whirling from role to role, showing up everywhere. For over a decade, she had juggled soccer schedules and play dates and client meetings while she got the oil changed, the tires rotated, the leaves raked, the driveway plowed, her hair cut, and her nails manicured. If there had been a World Championship in every-where-at-once efficiency, Cathryn was certain she would have won.

We're all in awe of you, but I don't see how that's made you happy.

Rachel's words echoed in the hotel room—harsher, now, than the moment she had uttered them. They halted Cathryn anew, because her daughter was right.

She had taken pride in the number of plates she kept in the air without thinking about what they were or which plates mattered. *Find someone to clean the gutters* and *listen to Judah practice his oral report* had seemed of equal weight. Before that, *Swap out the snow tires* and *have sex with Brian.*

It was sad and terrible. Yet that was who she had been. Cathryn McAllister, someone who got things done. Cool and deliberate, weighing the cost-benefit of each step before lifting her foot.

She wanted to argue—with Rachel, or an invisible accuser—that she'd had to be that way as the breadwinner and single parent of two children whose complicated demands never seemed to overlap. And yet, another truth tugged at her awareness—because she'd been like that when Brian was alive too, measuring, organizing, figuring out the shortest path to what she wanted, whether it was a Lebanese restaurant or an orgasm for two. Keeping the world in order.

I don't see how that's made you happy.

It hadn't. Happiness hadn't been on her list.

And why not? It seemed like an obvious thing to want.

Heat crept up her shoulders, her neck. Because she wanted it now. That was why she had reversed her route.

And that was why her heart was flapping so wildly—like a bird against a window, seeing what it wanted through the glass.

She jumped up from the edge of the bed. So she was efficient. Well, she'd use that efficiency to make herself useful—because, really, she could help Mack in a much better way than handing him a paddle or wadding up newspaper. She knew how to navigate the online art world. She could find out what others had done, provide a context to help him situate his vision. It was the kind of thing she was good at.

Excited now, Cathryn adjusted the towel and moved to the desk. She opened her laptop and typed *glass art icebergs* into the search bar. There were some wonderful images, but they were all from Antarctica. She kept scrolling. No Iceland. No Jökulsárlón.

Even better, she thought; maybe Mack really was tilling new ground. She tried other combinations of *glass* and *Iceland* and *art*, to be sure, but there was nothing relevant. She was about to close the browser when she noticed an article that made her interest spike. She put her palms on the desk and leaned forward to read.

It had nothing to do with blue icebergs or blown glass, but it was important. She needed to tell Mack about it. He would be excited too, and thank her.

She waited until the next day, when they were in the studio. "I discovered this Icelandic artist named Rúrí," she told him, propping her elbows on the table where he'd spread the day's sketches. "It's pretty interesting. She did an installation for the National Gallery in Reykjavik back in 1984 that she called *Glass Rain*. It's still there, in fact."

Mack eyed her with interest. "She's a glassblower?"

"Not really. She uses different media, not just glass. It's all about creating an experience. When she built *Glass Rain*, she took five hundred pieces of glass, dagger-shaped pieces with razor-sharp edges, and hung them from the ceiling in a particular way."

"Don't tell me it spelled out her boyfriend's name."

"Hush. Hear me out." Cathryn laced her fingers under her chin. "There's a narrow little path through the daggers, but you can't see it when you enter the installation. You have to enter and move forward with these daggers all around you—without seeing the way out, or even knowing where to look."

Mack's expression remained skeptical. "But people know there's a way out. It's a gallery, not real life."

"They might know that intellectually, but if they can't actually *see* it, the terror is real."

"It's not. It's contrived."

"It's what they feel."

"And that's supposed to make it art?"

"Immersive art. Something you experience." She let her hands drop. "It's about the moment when faith turns into knowledge. You start with faith—because you're right, people do trust that there's going to be a way out—and then there's a moment when you see it, and you know."

"And that's the part you like? When you feel in control again?"

"That's a snarky way to put it."

Mack reached across the table and touched her hand. "I'm sorry. I didn't mean it like that. It's my lousy social skills. I warned you."

Cathryn was about to say, *a warning isn't a pass,* but something stopped her—because he wasn't wrong. She did like that part. It was the very thing she had been struggling to face, just before she came across Rúrí's work.

I don't see how that's made you happy.

Carefully, he picked up her hand—a touch so exquisite and gentle that Cathryn could hardly breathe—and threaded his fingers through hers.

She struggled to hold back the tears. That was the impossible thing about him. A brusqueness that made her wonder if her presence meant anything to him at all. And then, when she least expected it, a tenderness that pierced her to the bone.

Then she squared her shoulders, because she needed to finish what she had to tell him. "It's the moment of recognition," she said. "Apparently there's a bend in the middle of the installation that you can't see until you're fully immersed—and then, all at once, the path is right there."

"No hanging razors on the path to the exit?"

"No. It's free and clear."

"So everyone's safe and happy. Is that the point?"

Her defensiveness returned, even though his fingers were still twined through hers. "It's to get past the fear of not-knowing."

"Maybe the fear of not-knowing *is* the point."

"That's an extraordinary way to look at it."

"It's only extraordinary if you're hell-bent on needing to know all the time."

Cathryn's heart was pounding now. She had wanted to tell him how you could give people an experience that was much more powerful than simply looking at a beautiful object. It was an idea for his project, a gift. But it felt as if they were talking about her.

"Anyway," he said, "I'd better get back to work." He withdrew his hand, braced his palms on the table, and stood. Cathryn followed him, not knowing what else to do.

He strode to the annealer and opened the door. "Let's see how yesterday's experiment came out." He removed the object from the shelf and gave it a long deadpan appraisal. Then he flattened his lips and dropped it into the scrap bucket. It made a splintering sound as it hit the glass that was already there.

Cathryn drew back. "Are you sure?" Then she winced. A stupid remark. He'd already smashed it. She glanced at the sketches that were spread across the table. She knew, already, that none of them would turn out to be what he was looking for. He seemed to grow more frustrated each day, as if he'd gotten further and further from the flame that had ignited him at Jökulsárlón.

Solve it, Cathryn told herself. Finding solutions was what she did.

The answer seemed obvious, yet she was reluctant to put it into words. Still, there seemed no other way. Finally, she swallowed, met his eyes, and said, "Maybe you need to go back to Jökulsárlón. Renew the spark."

She said it for him, though it wasn't what she wanted. If Mack went back to Jökulsárlón, it would be time for her to go back to America. He had agreed to let her stay and help in the hot shop, not to follow him around Iceland while he got re-inspired.

"What I *need*," he said, turning away and striding to the sink to wash his hands, "is to stop being in such a hurry to produce something. If I've learned anything over the years, it's that you need to let an experience transform inside you before you can translate it into an object." He dropped the soap into a wire basket. "Hell, I didn't find my way to the Costa Rica series till I was back in the US for a whole six months. It needed time."

"To incubate. Like the leaves. Until it was ready to be born."

Mack jerked, as if she had slapped him. He twisted the faucet and grabbed a towel, swiping at his neck and face with quick angry strokes. All Cathryn could see was his back, the tightness of his muscles beneath the denim shirt.

She didn't know what she had done wrong. She'd been echoing his thoughts. Agreeing with him.

Then she frowned, confused, because he had made the opposite point, during their first conversation—about the way time could dilute and distort, turn a living impression into a static memory. *Something gets lost in the waiting*, he had told her.

Maybe Mack was confused too. Maybe he was searching for a reason to stay and keep trying.

She took a new breath, found new words. "You told me it was a shame you didn't have a glass studio in Costa Rica so you could work right then, before everything got lost. You didn't need time. Time got in the way. That was why you felt lucky to have Einar's place, here in Iceland. No gap between taking in the impression, and expressing it yourself. Impression, expression. A single experience."

She paused, pleased with herself for the last phrase. It was what a photographer did, captured an image in the instant of its existence. Not six months later.

Mack laid the towel next to the sink and faced her again. "I was wrong. I wanted things to be different, that's all. Working on-site had nothing to do with it."

Her pleasure dissipated. He was serious about leaving. If he stopped experimenting and went back to America, it was over.

It wasn't the moment to be an obedient assistant. She had to find a new idea, the one he'd missed that would make him stay. She might be a woman desperate to hold onto her lover—and her adventure— but she was also a consultant with a shrewd eye. If anyone could come up with the perfect idea, it was her.

It came to her by itself. A shift, like changing the focal length on a camera. The truth she had felt about Rúrí's *Glass Rain,* but hadn't expressed in a way he could understand.

"The problem," she said, "is that you're working on the wrong scale. You want to depict the essence of the icebergs? It's not about a shape. It's about the immensity."

Cathryn could see, in his utter stillness, that her arrow had hit its mark. Emboldened, she kept talking. "You want people to experience what you felt at the lagoon. Not just observe it, like an object on a plate. So it has to be huge. An installation. Not a room full of hanging razors, but something they can enter and be part of, like an ocean or a city, different for each person."

Mack stared at her. Then he threw back his head and laughed. It was a glorious sound. "Cathryn, my darling, you're a genius."

She flushed. All she could hear was *my darling.*

His gaze swept the hot shop, his face lit with excitement. "I can't build it here—I don't have the material, and you can't ship something like that—but I can make a model. Now, while I'm close to the source."

Cathryn dared to relax. She had done it. He would stay; they would stay.

He grabbed her arms. "Thank you."

It was the first time he had touched her in the glass studio, other than to adjust the punti.

Seventeen

Mack wanted to spend the morning working out the idea she had given him. "Making a miniature version of immensity," he joked. Then he added, more seriously, "It's not as odd as it sounds. We have a saying in glasswork: If you can't make it small, you can't make it big. A model helps you see what's there and what you still need. But first I have to design it."

By now, Cathryn understood what that meant. Sketches, calculations, and the precise choreography he would have to execute, later, in the triangle between marver, glory hole, and bench. If he'd had a real assistant, an apprentice who could do most of the things that a master glassblower could do, it would have been easier. But all he had was her, trusted only to reheat the gather or hand him a clump of wet newspaper.

"I'm not sure when I'll be ready for you," he said. "It might be later than usual."

"No worries. Just text when you need me."

It felt awkward—ridiculous, really—to linger in Akureyri, hoping to be summoned. Yet she'd been the one to offer the vision that was occupying his thoughts—and keeping him here, instead of in Jökulsárlón looking for renewed inspiration, or in America where everything could digest.

She could hardly complain. And it wasn't as if he were taking back something he had promised. *It's all right with me if you stay.* That was all he had ever said.

With so many hours at her disposal, Cathryn decided that it was a good opportunity to venture beyond Akureyri. She pulled the iPad out of the suitcase to look for a *must-see* Icelandic sight that she had missed to be with him. Not a picturesque little fishing village. Something different, and big.

She spotted it right away. Goðafoss, the hundred-foot wide waterfall known as the Waterfall of the Gods. It was only fifty kilometers from Akureyri, a forty-minute drive at most, and one of the sights the Saga Tour had intended her to see.

Before she left, she logged onto her email, just to check. Nothing from Elliott Fischer or Nora Lang. There were three messages from Renata Singer, though, who wanted her to see the final promotion with the photos she had taken at Jökulsárlón. Mack was there in profile, silhouetted against the sky. "It's perfect," Renata had written. "Can't you just feel him getting inspired by those amazing blue icebergs?"

Really, Cathryn thought; Renata was too much. Mack had already spent four days at Jökulsárlón when she took the photo. He'd been flirting with her, not getting inspired.

Well, she'd been flirting with him, even if she hadn't wanted to admit it.

"They look fantastic," she typed back. And they did. The spread really was the jewel in her portfolio she'd been hoping for.

Then, because she knew she was supposed to, she added, "It's been a pleasure working with you. Let me know if there's anything else I can do for you."

She deleted Renata's emails and scrolled through the others. Nothing that mattered. Then she checked her text messages and saw one from Judah. He had sent a few selfies, one of him waving from the driver's window of her car, another of him vacuuming the living room with a goofy grin on his face.

Cathryn couldn't help softening. He was trying, and wanted her to know. She texted back, "Great job, buddy, and thanks!" Then she collected her jacket, headband, and daypack. On a whim, she threw her camera, her real one, into the daypack and headed for the Kia, and Goðafoss.

The drive was easy, a flat plane of greenish earth on either side of the road, snow-flecked mountains in the distance, a Delft blue sky. Goðafoss was a popular tourist stop. In a country full of dramatic waterfalls, it was one of the most spectacular. Not the tallest, like Glymur with its six hundred and fifty-foot drop, or the most powerful, like the mighty Dettifoss, but a massive horseshoe-shaped curve that rose in the center, separating the waterfall in two. With its easy access from the main road, Cathryn knew the site would be packed with tour groups but hoped she could leave most of them behind if she ventured from the parking lot onto the trails.

She pulled into the nearest parking space, shut off the engine, and climbed out of the car. The roar of the water was the first thing that struck her, obliterating all other sound. The second thing was the force of the spray. It rose everywhere, caught in a rainbow that shimmered, faded, and reappeared across the river.

Goðafoss was broad rather than high. It descended from the mouth of the river in a mere forty-foot drop, yet its curved lip was nearly a hundred feet wide. Cathryn had parked her car on the west bank, but saw that there was a long footbridge across the water that connected the two sides.

The first viewing spot offered a panoramic frontal view from high above the falls. Families crowded by the railing, snapping photos. Cathryn edged to the front and craned her neck. The spilling water was streaked with turquoise, the color of the icebergs; foam rose up like glitter from the current below. After a few minutes she stepped back, letting others take her place, and descended along a rocky path to a second viewing spot.

She was startled to discover that the path ended at the edge of a cliff. No railing, nothing to assure a person's safety except his own common sense. "Attention," the sign read. "Attempting to climb down is forbidden." Good grief, Cathryn thought. Who would be stupid enough to climb down those slippery rocks toward a churning river?

She braced her feet on the rocky shelf and watched the water pour over the side of the falls. The sound was even louder here, filling the span of the river and the sky above. It was impossible not to be awed—and a bit frightened—as she clung to her tiny perch. Nothing but air between Goðafoss, Waterfall of the Gods, and her one small body. She felt the spray on her face, the air in her lungs. Then she stepped away from the cliff, her toes scrabbling for a wedge of firmer ground. Turning away from the river, she moved quickly from rock to rock, back to the main path.

Another trail led to the edge of the basin, where she could see Goðafoss from below. From this third spot, she could look across the river and see the whole of the falls. It was a different kind of view, tamer, less astounding, yet the light was wonderful. She hadn't taken any photos at the other two places—the first had felt too obvious, the second too unsafe—but this one seemed to beckon. She took out her camera. A wide-angle would be good here. A slow shutter speed, to capture the water in motion. Excited now, Cathryn knelt and adjusted the aperture, framed the shot. Then she held her breath and waited for the instant when the spray caught the sunlight like a handful of tossed coins.

She took a dozen shots, then a dozen more, before retracing her steps back to the parking lot. She looked at her watch. Plenty of time—although *plenty* was a meaningless notion, since she had no idea when Mack would need her—to walk across the bridge and view the falls from the eastern bank. It would be another perspective, which meant the angle of the light would be different.

Grasping the strap of her camera, she hurried across the footbridge. From the landing, she saw a trail that led down the slope, to the basin. It was narrow and steep, but no worse than the one she had taken on the western side. She picked her way carefully, one hand grazing the rocky wall. The wind was stronger here, lifting her hair and whipping it against the wool headband.

She paused to gaze at the water, its vastness and power. It was what she had told Mack he needed in his work. Scale. Enormity. Forces that had to be experienced, not just observed.

As if the word *experienced* was a finger of light, pointing her toward something farther up the cliff, Cathryn felt her attention jerked upward. Three figures were cavorting on a ledge above her. One wore a red jacket; the others were clad in khaki and green. It was the figure in red that grabbed her attention, not only because of the color, but because of the outstretched arms and the foot lifted in the air, like a dancing Hindu god, in a crazy extravagant gesture of defiance and glee.

They were boys, teenagers, with the stupid belief in their own invincibility that she recalled all too well from Judah's teenage years. She wanted to scream *No!* and *Don't!* but she knew they wouldn't hear, or else her scream might throw the one in red off balance.

Jesus and shit. She implored them with her eyes, begging them to come to their senses and *stop it, right now*. Didn't they understand? A person could slip, fall, drown. There was no reason that couldn't happen. Not just now, to them. But always, to anyone. The utter fragility—and how she never remembered that—filled her with terror.

It seemed like a miracle that her own children were still alive, surviving, against all odds, the incomprehensible vulnerability of being human. She took their survival for granted, as if they were immune simply because they were *her* children, the ones who mattered to her.

A tenderness rose in her chest, infusing her terror with pity. For them, and for herself too, so stunningly unaware. And yet it could be no other way—because how could you live, moment after moment, day after day, if you felt the narrowness of the perch that kept you aloft? You had to assume you were safe.

A rock flew across the air, right over her head. Her heart jammed into her mouth, and she was certain that more rocks would follow, and then a body in red, tumbling onto the boulders and the water below.

It didn't. Just the one rock, and then a peal of laughter. She dared to look up and saw that the boys were scrambling back up the trail, finished with their high jinks. No doubt she had been the only one who was so frightened.

Cathryn rested against a rocky shelf as her breathing slowed. The danger had been real, not just the overwrought reaction of a mother picturing one of her own children on that slender ledge. The danger was always real.

That was the other side of the immensity she'd been urging Mack toward. Immensity only had meaning next to your own smallness. The shock of your smallness, your almost-nothingness, was the price you paid for sensing that scale.

And yet, she thought, art didn't have to be small. A person might be small, but art—the impact of art—didn't need to be.

It was a wonderful thought, making her happy. And then it came to her in a burst of irony—right there on a skinny little trail in Iceland, with light and stones all around, after the terror of an incident that hadn't even happened—that *scale* was the very quality she had given up in her own work, fifteen years ago. When Brian died. The phrase that kept echoing, after all this time, as if it were trying to tell her something.

She had been working on a set of enormous panels, collages of light on stone, the same two elements that surrounded her now. She had wanted to show the same place at different times of day— not in temporal order, but arranged to disrupt the eye, calling the viewer to notice how different aspects of the stone were revealed and concealed as the sun moved. Six panels, twenty-four photos on each. It was going to be a huge installation that would take her work to a whole new level. It was over two-thirds finished, but she had walked away. Shut down her studio. Taken commercial jobs for other people. Gone small.

Cathryn shuddered. Then she looked at her watch again. It was almost noon. She needed to get back to the parking lot where she had cell service, check to see if there was a message. Inhaling sharply, she turned around and started up the trail.

As she ascended, sunlight spread across the sky, igniting the edge of the clouds and the beams of the foot bridge. From below, the bridge seemed tentative and insubstantial, a child's toothpick creation strung across the wildness of the river. Cathryn could see the stream of people moving in both directions, certain that it would hold them.

Too warm now, she pulled off the woolen headband. Her hair was matted with sweat.

Everything seemed connected, somehow, but she couldn't find the thread. Coldness, contraction, growing small. Expansion and heat. The vastness of the sky. Blowing into the molten glass and making it larger, just from your own breath.

Mack. She was at the top of the cliff now, by the eastern parking lot, and would have a decent signal. Eagerly, she opened her purse and took out her phone. No message. Maybe he wouldn't want to see her today.

Well, he'd warned her that he needed to think and plan. Yet she wanted to tell him about the boy in the red jacket and what she had felt about the sense of scale that she'd talked about with such blithe intellectual ease, as if she knew what it meant, and how the sensation of scale had brought such a fierce and tender love for her own children.

It struck her that Mack knew nothing about Rachel and Judah. He had never even asked if she had children. One question, the day she reappeared in Akureyri, about whether there was a husband back in America. But nothing about her children, and she hadn't volunteered.

There was so much he didn't know about her, and so much she didn't know about him. Why was that?

The wind whipped across her face. She remembered commanding him, *Take off your hat*. Show me who you are.

He hadn't, not really. She hadn't either.

Whatever was keeping them from revealing themselves had to end. Right now, this very second. She gripped her camera bag and ran to the bridge, back to the western parking lot, where the Kia was waiting.

Eighteen

Cathryn left Goðafoss and sped back to Akureyri. Urgency coursed through her body—made her press her foot to the gas pedal, lean into the steering wheel—as if that extra inch of closeness to the road would make her arrive sooner. She needed to talk to him, make him talk to her. Why didn't they know more about each other?

She pulled up in front of the studio, into the same spot that always seemed to be empty when she arrived, and shut off the engine. Her mind filled with memories of the other times she had pulled up to this very building, with its wide dark siding and the row of small square windows below the barnlike roof.

The first time, it was to accept Mack's invitation to stop by on her way through the region. A chance to see a hot shop, round out her project. She had returned the next morning to try it herself, a second invitation she hadn't expected. It was the third time, when she reversed her route and went through the tunnel again, that changed everything. Even then, she had let him know she was coming. *Yes*, he had replied. *Yes*, to everything that followed. This fourth time, though they were lovers now, felt the most audacious and fraught with danger.

She slammed the car door without bothering to lock it and strode up to the building, popping the latch the way Mack had showed her, and flung the heavy wooden door aside.

She was moving too fast, not thinking, and let go of the door instead of closing it carefully. It banged shut with a sound that seemed as loud as Goðafoss.

Cathryn recoiled. A noise like that, when someone was working with molten glass, was unforgivable; Mack had told her that. Anything could happen if you startled a person holding an object that had been heated to a thousand degrees. A spark flung into an eye, liquid fire dropped onto a foot.

But Mack wasn't at the furnace. He was sitting on a metal chair at the far end of the room, eating a sandwich. A sheet of greasy-looking paper dangled from his hand. Cathryn could smell the roasted meat and something spicy, like cumin. She let out her breath. "I'm sorry for banging the door. That was stupid of me."

"It was, but you got lucky." He motioned toward a second chair. "You hungry?"

It was like the moment at the waterfall, when the commanding finger of awareness ordered her to look at the boy on the ledge. The world narrowed to a laser-sharp spear of light, pointed at Mack's seated form. Yes, she was hungry. She was starving.

She ripped open her jacket and flung it on a bench near the door. Her daypack and headband followed, landing on top of the jacket in tangle of yellow and blue. Swiftly—and yet languidly, long strides slicing the space—she crossed the rectangular room to where he sat. Mack watched her with the hooded quality she had seen in his eyes before, heavy-lidded, private, and alert. He didn't move.

She had been to the Waterfall of the Gods, and she hadn't plunged to her death. What else was there to fear?

She took the sandwich out of his hand and placed it on the floor. Kicking off her shoes, she climbed onto his lap. In a single movement, fluid as the cat that was part of her name, she spread her legs around his waist the way she had at Mývatn, annihilating the unspoken boundary between the bedroom and the hot shop.

She picked up his hand and took his broad slick fingers into her mouth, one at a time. Five fingers, tasting of sweat and grease and the roasted meat he'd been eating. They filled the wet empty hollow of her mouth.

An unbearable lust exploded in the center of her body. She arched her back, and his fingers slid from her mouth, falling across her jaw and throat and the agony of her breasts, onto her stomach, between her legs. She thrust forward with a terrible cry as she pressed her body to his, opening everything—neurons, pores, flesh. The smell of cumin filled her lungs.

She didn't care if he responded, but he did. She could feel him through her clothes, the way she used to feel the teenage boys bursting through their jeans when she was in high school, making out in cars. But Mack wasn't a boy; he was a man. And she was— what? Nothing. She wasn't Cathryn anymore. Cathryn didn't exist, except as a wild endless need pressed against him. She was on fire, screaming in her head that this was more than a person could endure. She whimpered, then began to sob.

When her weeping had abated, Mack moved his hands, gently, and lifted her face to his. "Cathryn. What is it?"

"Everything. Nothing." He started to speak, but she shook her head.

She wanted to tell him: A boy could have died. My life is slipping away like the water.

Yet there were no words for the things she wanted to say, and she didn't know if he would want to hear them. For all she knew, he thought she was out of her mind. He'd been about to say something. Maybe he was going to remind her about the rules of the hot shop. Safety and attention. *Please don't do that again.* Or maybe he was going to turn it into a joke: *I guess you really were hungry.*

Or maybe: *God, you are an amazing woman.*

She looked into his eyes and saw the sorrow she had glimpsed before, something deep and private, but no judgment. "Where did you go this morning?" he asked.

Cathryn grew still. It was the first time he had asked what she did when she wasn't with him. "To a waterfall," she said. "Goðafoss."

She could sense him waiting for her to say more, but she couldn't. She felt dizzy, as if her skull was filled with air. What had felt so intense and irrefutable only minutes earlier—a force she had to obey, if she wanted to keep living—fell away like water sliding off a rock.

She unwrapped her legs and slid off his lap. Then she bent and picked up his sandwich, handing it to him. The gesture was like pushing open a door to another room, an ordinary room. The room she'd been in, where she had arched her back and whimpered with desire, shut behind her with a soft click, the way an image snapped into focus when she adjusted the lens. *There.* They were in a dingy hot shop in Akureyri, striped with beams of afternoon light that slanted down from a row of windows near the ceiling. At the other end of the rectangular space: the furnace, the marver, the bench.

Mack took the sandwich from her outstretched hand. "I'll eat it later." Then he stood. Cathryn watched him, wondering what he was thinking, what he would do.

The trance-like certainty that had drawn her across the room and the fervor that had flung her onto his body were both gone. She was depleted. Free.

He motioned across the room. "Want to see the design I came up with this morning?"

It seemed like a strange thing to say, after what had just happened. Then she thought: Maybe not. Maybe he wanted to reveal something too, share what he had discovered in her absence.

"All right." She stepped into her shoes and followed him to the marver.

A dozen sketches were arranged on the glossy surface, labeled with numbers that she realized were geometrical degrees. "To show where you'd be viewing it from," he explained. "It's hard to look at a two-dimensional diagram and visualize it in three dimensions. It'll be clearer when I make the model."

Cathryn studied the drawings. Her designer's eye went straight to the problem: The distance between the pieces wasn't right. There was something too predictable about the arrangement; it needed disharmony, a contradiction the viewer didn't expect. But she couldn't say that. Mack was the artist, not her.

Finally, she asked, "Will the pieces be blown?"

"For now," he said. "But when I do the full-size rendering, I'll have to use molds. You can't blow something that size with a pipe."

Cathryn's eyes moved to the rack of pipes on the wall. Emboldened, she asked, "Could I try blowing into the pipe? Just a little, to know what it's like?

Mack's expression grew stern. "To know what it's like isn't a sufficient reason in a hot shop. It's not like blowing soap bubbles."

Cathryn tensed, ready to push back. Then she remembered the carelessly slammed door, proof that her own impulses were stronger than her commitment to the rules of the hot shop. The hot shop was Mack's world; she'd have to convince him to trust her in it.

She peered at the drawings again. If she could offer an insight that would give them the power they lacked, it would be a way to prove herself. The artist in her wanted to do that—not only to show her worth, but to make it a better design.

And the woman in her? The woman had taken what she needed, on a chair at the other end of the room. She hadn't given him anything. Not really. Just a few stories, and an idea about immersive art that she'd stolen from another artist.

Mack stepped back, frowning at the sketches. "It's not quite right, after all. I hope you won't feel hurt, but I need to go back and think about this a bit more."

Cathryn almost said, "Why would that make me feel hurt?" Then she realized what he meant. He had told her that he would text when he was ready, but there had been no text. She had appeared, unsummoned, and now he wanted her to leave.

Mack turned to her, and the look in his eyes pierced her with a mixture of gratitude and alarm—gratitude for his concern, alarm because he seemed to need her less and less. Not that he ever had. He let her do minor tasks, but she didn't know enough about glass to be a true assistant. She was here with him because she had asked to be. Every extension of their time had come at her request, not his.

"Understood." She brushed back her hair. "You need to be alone."

"I don't know how to say it in a way that doesn't sound shitty." He didn't add, *after what happened in the chair*. He didn't have to.

"It's absolutely okay. Really."

"Why don't I believe you?"

"Believe what you want. Or doubt what you want." Suddenly she was pissed off. Not at Mack or anything he had done, but at herself, her recklessness and vulnerability. "It's fine if you want to be alone. I get it."

"You're angry."

"I'm not."

"Cathryn."

Just her name. Cathryn. A woman who was waking up. That meant: hungry, curious, alert. Not in charge, but not helpless either.

"It's all right," she said. "I can keep myself occupied. You don't have to apologize."

As soon as she spoke, she realized that he hadn't mentioned an apology. He had simply told her.

"I appreciate that," he said.

"The fact that I can occupy myself?"

"The fact that you don't need me to apologize."

"Oh?" She raised an eyebrow. "Is that unusual? Do most people need you to apologize?"

The question slipped out, and Cathryn knew from the expression on Mack's face that she had crossed another line, a more dangerous line than bringing her lust into the hot shop. She steeled herself for his withdrawal, or maybe his wrath.

Whatever she had seen on his face disappeared in an instant. He shrugged. "Do you know anyone who doesn't have something to apologize for?"

"True. We've all done something."

He'd finessed the question, the same way he had side-stepped her question about the moments when he seemed to lose consciousness.

She knew no more about him now than she did then—only that he had allowed her to use him in a way that she couldn't imagine any man being able to do, not without wanting to analyze it or turn it into a cartoon. A vamp in a black lace bra. A needy middle-aged woman humping a sexy glassblower in a chair.

She wondered, for a horrific instant, if she had done something insane. Then she pushed the thought away. There was no one to judge her except Mack, and he hadn't. "I think we've managed in this rather unusual situation because neither of us has resorted to apology."

"Well put." He nodded at her jacket and daypack, a blue-and-yellow heap where she had thrown them on the bench by the door. The message was clear.

Cathryn glanced at his design again. The problem she had spotted seemed even more evident. It wasn't her medium, but that didn't mean she couldn't see.

Mack made the most exquisite objects out of color and light and form, one beautiful thing at a time. But she understood space—how to situate the objects, the relationships among them. Maybe it came from raising a family and having to juggle all those separate personalities. Whatever the source, she knew.

Claim it, Cathryn told herself. Claim what you see.

She picked up her jacket and shook out the arms. "You might try moving the figures closer," she said. "I know you want to convey a sense of majesty, which can imply that the icebergs are far away, but people need to feel surrounded too, as if they're part of something a little bit dangerous. Like *Glass Rain*. As if they aren't sure there's a way out."

Mack narrowed his eyes. "You mean, move them closer in the center?"

"On the left, especially. It doesn't have to be so centralized."

He glared at the drawing, then burst out laughing. It was a huge sound, full of delight. "That's brilliant. You're good at this."

Cathryn reached for the wool headband and jammed it in her pocket. She had only needed it at Goðafoss because of the wind and the spray. "That's why Shades of Blue hired me."

She thought of Renata Singer swinging a stiletto-clad foot back and forth, the ridiculous streak of electric blue in her hair. It was hard to believe she was the same person who had sat across from Renata and her colleagues that day.

Because she wasn't.

Nineteen

Cathryn decided to visit Akureyri's other landmark—the Akureyrarkirkja, a towering Lutheran church that commanded a view of the city and harbor. More art deco than gothic, the Akureyrarkirkja boasted a thirty-two-hundred-pipe organ and a model ship suspended from the ceiling, homage to the tradition of offering gifts for the welfare of loved ones at sea.

Climbing—and counting—the hundred-and-twelve steps up to the church was, Cathryn learned, a required part of the tourist ritual. She was on step thirty-seven when she heard the marimba of her phone. Dropping a mental pin on the number thirty-seven, she stepped to the side, onto the grass, to answer.

It was Rachel. "Hey, sweetheart," she said, surprised by the call. It had only been two days since their last conversation, on the patio of the Lystigardurinn café. Rachel's pattern, for years, had been to text, not call—and even then, weeks could go by without more than a few crisp words, followed by an emoji that meant *just kidding* or *who the hell knows?*

"How are you, honey?"

"Oh, fine. Whatever. And what about you? Still cavorting around Iceland?"

"Well, maybe not cavorting, but still in Iceland."

"Are you going to see the northern lights? I mean, what's the point of being in Iceland if you don't see the northern lights?"

"They're on my list," Cathryn said, amused by Rachel's assumption that it was up to her. "It's not quite the season, but I'm told there's a good chance of seeing them in mid-September, around the equinox, so I've got my fingers crossed."

Her amusement faded. Mid-September was two weeks away. In two weeks, Einar would be returning from his holiday, ready to claim his studio.

"So you're just hanging out? Until the equinox?"

Cathryn hesitated. "More or less."

"Doing what?"

She had told Rachel that she was learning about glassblowing, but maybe she'd forgotten, or maybe Rachel thought that couldn't be enough to keep her *get-six-things-done-at-once* parent sufficiently engaged. "Actually," Cathryn said, "I started taking a few pictures. Real pictures. Not just for the job." She shifted the phone to her other hand. "It was fun, actually."

"Hey, that's cool. Can I see them?"

"They're nothing special. I'm pretty rusty."

"I don't care. I want to see."

Cathryn thought of the photo that she had taken from the base of Goðafoss, with the spray of water reaching into the air like a glittering hand. "There's one you might like."

"Email it to me."

"What a bully."

"Just do it."

"All right. But if it's trite, I don't want to hear about it."

"Mom." She could almost see Rachel shaking her head. Then Rachel said, "What about my scarf? Did you find it?"

The red scarf Rachel had asked for. Damn. She'd completely forgotten. "Not yet. I'm still looking."

"Don't let me down."

"I won't."

"Promise me."

"I promise. Really." She sent Rachel a silent pledge that she would go shopping the instant they ended the call. It was a minor thing, salvageable, but appalling nonetheless that she had forgotten her own child. "If they don't have red, what's your second choice?"

"I don't know. I really want red."

"I'll find red for you, then."

She heard the echo of Rachel's plea. *Don't let me down.* Then she understood, in a head-smacking burst of insight, that there was a reason her daughter had called again, so soon. Rachel had asked if she was still in Iceland and if she intended to stay through the equinox. *When are you coming home?* It meant, *I wish you would.*

Tread carefully, Cathryn warned herself. This was new territory for her aloof, independent child. "So how are things going?" She wanted to ask if the black lace underwear had helped, but didn't dare. Instead, she asked, "Are you finding your way with Ryder?"

"I guess."

The answer was right there, in those two weary syllables. Cathryn waited, but Rachel didn't offer more. Finally, she said, "Do you want to talk about it?"

"I don't know." Then: "Maybe."

This was more and more unlike the daughter Cathryn was accustomed to. For Rachel to even hint at uncertainty was so delicate that Cathryn was hesitant to probe further, but she gathered her courage and asked, "Is he taking you for granted, now that you've decided to stay?"

"Hardly," Rachel snorted. "I almost wish he would. Maybe then I'd be able to breathe."

"He's overbearing?"

"He doesn't leave me *alone.*" Her words seemed to explode though the phone. "He's *on me,* every second. Where am I going, what am I thinking. I actually have to tell him what I'm *thinking,* or else he thinks I'm withholding, or dreaming about some other guy, or who the fuck knows? It's like we're supposed to be some kind of fucking Siamese twins, sharing every single feeling and thought and experience, or else I'm not *committed* enough."

"It sounds pretty intense."

Rachel gave another snort. "That's putting it mildly. At first it was kind of a turn-on, I have to admit. Like, oh I adore you so much, I want to devour every part of you."

"And now?"

"And now I can't fucking *breathe*."

Cathryn flinched. This wasn't good. She glanced around the hillside, at the people making their way up the steps to the Akureyrarkirkja or back down again. Everyone headed somewhere.

Was she supposed to run home to rescue her daughter? No, that was probably the last thing Rachel wanted. Even as a tiny girl, Rachel had refused to let anyone help. She'd sit on the floor with a shoelace in each hand, shaking her head at Cathryn's suggestions. "I do it," she'd insist.

"You know what," Cathryn said, struck with a fresh idea. "If you need some space—for a day, a few days—go over to the house. You still have a key, right?"

Rachel's voice was cautious. "I do."

"Well, then. It's—what? An hour's drive."

"If that. Maybe less."

"Go on over, then. Any time you want."

"Huh. It's an idea. A secret bunker, for an emergency."

Cathryn's radar went to high alert. "You don't mean a real emergency, do you?"

"Like, if he threatens me or something?" Rachel gave a bitter laugh. "Don't worry, that's not his style. Ryder's weapon of choice is obsessive adoration."

"That doesn't sound so great either."

"Maybe not. But the house is a good idea, Mom. Especially since he has no clue where you live. So yeah, I just might do it."

"It's your home too. Always."

They were silent for a moment, and then Rachel let out a sigh. "I was kind of bratty when I said I wanted to make it work with Ryder because I didn't want to be like you. That wasn't fair."

"It was what you felt."

"Still. I didn't have to be so bratty."

Cathryn was about to say it was all right, she understood better than Rachel might think, when a sound rose from the top of the hill—the rolling, majestic tones of the Akureyrarkirkja's famous pipe organ. "Wait," she said. "Listen." She held up the phone, pointing it at the church. A Bach toccata, sonorous and lush, reverberated down the hillside and the hundred-and-twelve steps. She wanted Rachel to hear it with her.

As the toccata built to its climax, Cathryn kept the phone in the air, hoping Rachel was listening, hoping she had lightened her daughter's heart with this glorious gift. She yearned for Rachel to be happy, Judah too, but didn't know if either of them really was. Rachel had a degree from an impressive university and a plum job at a museum in Manhattan, but seemed to be drifting in some essential way. Judah, at twenty-two, expected less, but seemed so unformed.

Judah. She had told him that he could stay at the house if he wanted. Good grief. Had she double-booked her children for solo getaways at their childhood home?

She winced but couldn't very well rescind her offer. Anyway, she didn't know if either of them would actually go there. It seemed unlikely that Rachel, in particular, would do that, not if she wanted the relationship with Ryder to work. Ryder didn't sound like the sort of person who would accept her need for a day off in a secret location, yet Cathryn was glad she had offered. It was something she could do.

Then, abruptly, the music ended. Cathryn had thought she was paying attention, but her thoughts had drifted far from Akureyri when she realized that the final note was dying away. She hadn't known it would be the last one, and now the piece was over.

"That was awesome," Rachel said. "It must have been even more awesome in person. Where *are* you, exactly?"

"Climbing up to this big church. A hundred and twelve steps."

"A hundred and twelve? Whoa. You go, girl." Then Rachel's voice dropped, serious now. "And thanks about the house, really. I'll let you know if I take you up on it. I might or might not, but it's good to know it's there."

"It's always there, whenever you need it."

"I know. And don't worry about me. Go have fun in Iceland."

"I will. I am." She paused, then added, "Stay in touch, okay? And be happy."

She wasn't quite ready to break the connection, but Rachel had already ended the call. Reluctantly, Cathryn shouldered her purse and resumed her ascent. She couldn't remember what step she'd been on and didn't feel like beginning the count again from the bottom. Start from where you are, she told herself, though it sounded like the corniest of platitudes.

As she neared the top, she saw a young woman descending on the opposite side, holding a small girl by the hand. The girl had flaxen hair and a round, solemn face. One hand gripped her mother's; the other clutched a bright red apple. She was taking the steps in pairs, right foot first, joined by the left.

The little girl stopped and regarded Cathryn with a deadpan candor that made Cathryn stop too. The girl extended her hand, holding the apple. "*þetta er epli.*"

The mother gave the sweet, slightly embarrassed smile that Cathryn remembered from her own days as a young parent. "It means *this is an apple,*" she explained. "It's a new word for her. Epli. She's quite proud of it."

"As she should be." Cathryn squatted so she was the girl's height. "Epli," she said. "A beautiful red epli."

It was a Cezanne apple, luminous and alive—the brilliant skin both promising and protecting the life below, a life of flesh and seed and potential. The girl offered the apple to Cathryn. *Here.*

Cathryn understood, because her children had done the same thing when they were small. It didn't mean, *Take it, and then I will have none.* It meant, *Share my treasure. We can both have it.*

She took the apple, felt its perfect heft, then returned it to the child's outstretched hand. "How do you say *it's for you*?" she asked the woman.

"*Fyrir þig.* For you."

Cathryn kept her eyes on the little girl. "Fyrir þig."

The woman said something to her daughter in Icelandic. Then she told Cathryn, "I explained that the lady is admiring her splendid *rautt epli.*"

Cathryn assumed that rautt meant red. Red was the color of the scarf that her own daughter had asked her to find. The color of the boy's jacket, at the waterfall. The color of passion.

"Rautt epli." The girl echoed her mother's words.

A Snow White apple, Cathryn thought. Her insistence that she was more like Snow White than the Snow Queen. Asleep because of an apple she had misunderstood.

She had told Mack that she'd been in a fog for fifteen years, but it had started earlier. By the time Brian died, she had already withdrawn into her glass cage.

"She wants to walk all the way to the bottom by herself," the woman confided. "It's impossible, of course. Too many steps. But she needs to say when it's too much. If I say, she'll insist on continuing."

Cathryn's gaze went to the fold-up stroller slung across the woman's back. "Oh yes. I remember those days."

"They're stubborn, these little ones."

Cathryn thought of her own child and her choice of the man on whom she would, for better or worse, stake her claim to devotion. She was certain, already, that Ryder wouldn't merit Rachel's loyalty, yet she couldn't tell Rachel what to do or when it was enough. Who was she, anyway, to give advice about whom and how to love?

She touched the girl's silken hair. "I like your epli very much."

Then she stood, adjusted her purse, and continued up the steps to the Akureyrarkirkja. Its twin spires cut into the sky, like parallel staircases.

Cathryn placed her foot on the next step, and the next, though she didn't need to count them. Only feel them, one by one. Her foot, in the shoe. Herself, inside her foot.

Twenty

Cathryn returned to the hotel room, ready for her midday transition from tourist to—what? Apprentice? Groupie? No, she was more than that. She might not know how to etch or fuse, or even how to blow into the pipe, but she had seen what Mack needed.

She was slipping out of her jacket when her phone rang, yet again. This time it was Judah. Good lord, she thought. Her children never called when she was home, in America.

"Hey Jude," she said. "How are you doing?" She tossed the jacket onto the bed and stepped out of her shoes.

"Hey, Mom. And okay, sort of."

"What does *sort of* mean?"

"You're staying in Iceland for a while, right?"

"Maybe. Why?"

"I was thinking about the house." Judah cleared his throat. "I know you said I could stay there if I wanted, but I might need to stay there for, like, the next two weeks. I mean, if it's okay."

"Why?" she repeated. Two weeks wasn't like the evening's respite she had offered Rachel.

"It's just a fuck-up." He sighed, and Cathryn prepared herself for whatever was coming. "I kind of overspent, so I don't have the rent money for Garrett. It's his place, he's the one on the lease. We pay him, and then he pays the landlord." He paused, as if waiting for Cathryn to acknowledge what she already knew.

"Right," she said, finally. "You told me that when you moved in."

Judah gave another sigh. "He's usually cool, but he was already pissed at me because I was late the month before and I never did give him my share for the cable. So he said I had to get out until I paid up." Judah's voice rose, a plaintive mixture of self-recrimination and self-pity that made Cathryn cringe. "I don't get my next paycheck for two weeks, so I'm kind of stuck till then. But I figured you'd already said I could stay at the house while you were gone."

Cathryn clenched her teeth. She was damned if she was going to lend him the money to pay Garrett. Let him sleep on the street. How else would he ever learn?

Then she exhaled, frustration giving way to resignation. She couldn't forbid her child from staying at the home where he was always welcome. He might be pushing the envelope of her invitation, but she was the one who had extended it.

"Fine," she said, hesitating just long enough—she hoped—to make him understand that he couldn't take her bailout for granted. "I don't know exactly when I'm coming back, but it doesn't matter. There's plenty of room."

"Thanks, Mom. I really appreciate it."

Cathryn could almost hear the lyrics of the song that described her son. *Don't you know it's just you? The movement you need is on your shoulder.*

She could give him a few chores, at least, to let him know that it wasn't a completely free ride. "You can pull the weeds out of the garden while you're there. And take all the recycling stuff out to the road. They pick up on Fridays."

"Sure. Glad to do it."

She started ticking items off on her list. "Be sure to clean the lint filter if you use the dryer. And the icemaker on the refrigerator is kind of temperamental. If it's not working, it's probably just clogged. Take out the bin and empty it."

"Lint filter. Icemaker. Check."

It felt strange to be thinking about a house, and a life, that seemed so far away. Yet Cathryn had always loved her home, a sprawling maze that fanned out from a central living room with a two-sided fireplace and beautiful wide-plank floors. Bay windows let in a lemony afternoon light, and an arched doorway led to the extension they had built after Judah was born, a big family room with a sloping roof.

She and Brian had bought the house when she was pregnant with Rachel. It was beyond their budget but they'd done it anyway. Roots. A promise. If the marriage had soured later, it didn't mar the bright hope of the day they signed the contract. She didn't need all those bedrooms and bathrooms anymore, but it was her children's home—her home—and she saw no reason to let it go.

"One more thing," she said. "There's a chance your sister might come by for an evening, a little getaway, so don't be surprised if she shows up."

"When is she coming?"

"I have no idea. Probably not at all. I told her she could if she needed to."

"Okay. We'll try not to destroy each other."

"That would be nice." Cathryn had told Eva that her children were like oil and water, and it was true. But it was a big house, and they were adult enough to share it for a day.

"I really appreciate it," Judah repeated. "It's only for two weeks, I promise. Garrett's just sick of people—well, me—acting like he can just carry them if they have a bad month. He wants me to get the message. So yeah, I got it."

Not quite, Cathryn wanted to point out. Not if you have a nice clean room at Mommy's house as backup. But she didn't say it. Hopefully, he understood.

"So what about you?" Judah asked. "How's your trip? Did you see any volcanoes?"

"None that are erupting. But I saw a lot of cold lava. There's fields and fields of it."

"Did you go inside one of those lava tubes?"

"No, I haven't had a chance."

"I think you can go inside a glacier too. I saw it on Instagram."

She had booked a tour of the Langjökull ice caves, but canceled it to stay in Akureyri. "Not yet."

"Oh." Then, like Rachel, he asked about the northern lights.

"It's on the list," Cathryn told him. "At the very top."

"I hope you get to see it, then."

"Me too."

They said their good-byes, and Cathryn stared at the phone. Judah's perfectly reasonable questions had awakened the larger question that she thought she had already answered: What about all the things she had meant to see and do in Iceland?

She'd told herself that glassblowing—and time with the man who embodied it—was a fine substitute, and she hadn't been wrong. She had seen things she never would have seen otherwise—the transformation of a molten glob into an object of beauty, simply from the dance of movement and breath. It was no less miraculous than peering into the heart of a sleeping volcano.

Was it really enough, though, to assist with someone else's art?

When she met Mack, she had insisted that she wasn't an artist, but it was a lie. Only an artist could have known how the splashing water would look against a disappearing rainbow, or how shifting his design to the left would enhance its power. Maybe she hadn't acted like an artist for fifteen years, but it didn't mean she had forgotten how to see.

She needed to do more than help Mack with his art. She needed her own.

Her photography, freed from the fence she had tethered it to— reclaimed, welcomed back, opening her to the landscape she had traveled here to witness. A floating iceberg, a horse grazing on a green slope, steam hissing from the ochre mud.

And, of course, the northern lights. Rachel's first words, when she heard about the trip. The celestial phenomenon that Cathryn had called her heart's desire.

It wasn't her kind of subject. She liked to find odd compositions and unusual juxtapositions. Cropped segments of an absent whole, patterns of sun and slate. A huge sky rippling with sheets of gaudy electric green wasn't her style. And yet, the rightness of the idea was as undeniable as her own heartbeat.

She dropped into the desk chair and turned on her laptop. She had never photographed anything like the northern lights, so she needed to find out what others had done, what worked and what didn't. It was the kind of search she had undertaken for Mack when she looked for artists who had tried to capture the blue ice. But this time it was for her.

She leaned closer to the screen. Whenever you were dealing with the movement of light, you had to juggle aperture, shutter speed, and ISO—how wide the lens was opened, how long it stayed open, and how sensitive it was. But the aurora posed extra challenges. You needed to let in as much light as possible to capture a color that might not be visible to the human eye: the longer the exposure, the more the actual aurora could be revealed. Yet if the exposure was too long, you ended up with a greenish blur. It depended on how much the aurora was moving, which couldn't be predicted and could change in an instant.

Cathryn skimmed the websites of photographers who had traveled to Norway, Finland, Alaska. They told similar stories—of hours spent waiting for something that might appear without warning, or might not happen at all. It wasn't like photographing a maple tree or an iceberg, objects that were already there.

You couldn't plan; you couldn't even know. What seemed like a grayish haze, nothing at all, could rise up suddenly in a flashing column of liquid green—filling the sky with a writhing mass of magenta, emerald, violet. And then, just as suddenly, the dancing columns would collapse, and it would be over. A photographer had to be patient, and then he had to pounce. Like a cat, like her name.

It meant that your camera settings had to be in place ahead of time. You couldn't ponder and choose, not in the dark, and not when you might only have a few seconds to act. Each site had a different suggestion. Matrix metering, white balance, shooting in RAW. Every-one agreed, though, that you had to set your lens to infinity.

What made it so challenging was the nature of the aurora itself, a living thing constantly in motion. It had its own life cycle, shaped by solar forces more than ninety-three million miles away. Its own breath, an eleven-year period of inhalation and exhalation, expansion and contraction. People waited years for the right moment to capture its elusive splendor.

She didn't have years. There was no point tracking the activity on any of the special websites. She would have to meet the northern lights wherever they were.

On a whim, Cathryn typed *northern lights stories* into the search bar. She knew there was a scientific explanation for the aurora, the way there was a scientific explanation for the color of the icebergs. Mack had told her about compression and wavelengths and the refraction of crystals. She knew, vaguely, that the northern lights had to do with electrically charged particles and Earth's magnetic field. But that wasn't what she wanted right now; she wanted the legend, the magic, a story Scheherazade might tell to a king.

Norðurljós in Icelandic, the northern lights were known as the Dawn of the North, after Aurora, goddess of the dawn. Cathryn thought of Goðafoss, Waterfall of the Gods. The power of water belonged to the male gods, the power of light to the female.

Scandinavians thought the northern lights were the spirits of unmarried women. To the Old Norse, they were the glinting armor of the Valkyries, legendary females who chose who would live and who would die in battle. In Russia, the northern lights represented the descent of a fire dragon, coming out of the sky to seduce women whose husbands were away. Native Greenlanders believed they were the spirits of stillborn children.

The real lights came from solar forces colliding with the earth's atmosphere. From fire, like glass.

Cathryn closed the laptop. Every inch of her was vibrating, alive with purpose.

Later, Mack would text, and she would open her mouth to his, feel his hands slide down her hips and along her thighs. Their joined bodies, the molten glass, the radiance of a red apple. As if everything was leading her to this—to her own light, filling the night sky.

Goddess of the dawn, wind from the north.

Cathryn paid her third visit to the botanical garden the next day. The paths were familiar, yet the flowers seemed utterly new. Bright blue poppies with orange centers. A ring of spiky golden petals that shifted abruptly to magenta. Lavender fairy wings, opening into a bell of palest yellow. It was hard to believe that all this beauty existed, and thrived, so far north. She looked for the purple flower she had photographed on her first visit, but couldn't find it.

She wandered onto a side path, following it to a clearing. A shallow fountain in the center was surrounded by a ring of bricks, a wider ring of grass, and a border of shrubs. Tall trees, narrow and leafy, enclosed the circular space.

To her surprise, there was the woman again, Eva, with the little boy. He had a different boat this time, a wooden disk with a white sail like a folded handkerchief. He was kneeling by the edge of the fountain, pushing the boat forward and pulling it back again, intent on his game.

"Hello," Cathryn called.

"Ah, good morning." Eva stepped away from the fountain and gestured at the trees and sky. "This is the most beautiful spot in Akureyri, is it not?"

"It's lovely." Cathryn looked around for a bench. There weren't any, so she crossed the grass to join Eva where she stood. "I'm finding myself especially enthralled today."

"With anything in particular?"

"The flowers. I have to admit that I breezed past a lot of them, the last time I was here. There seem to be so many new ones, though it's probably because I hadn't noticed."

"It takes many visits to see them all."

"I suppose that's true." Cathryn thought of the photo she had taken with her iPhone on her first visit, the spiky purple flower with the dragonfly wings. It wasn't a particularly good photograph, but it was a flower she had never seen before and would probably never see again. A memory of Iceland. Maybe Eva knew what it was.

She felt in her purse for the phone. "This one caught my attention. Do you know what it's called?" She tapped on the photo icon and squinted at the screen, but the sun was too bright. All she could see was the glare of her own face. Turning to the ring of trees, she angled the phone until the image was clear. "Here it is."

Eva leaned over her shoulder. "I've seen it, but I don't know what it's called."

"Is there a way to find out?" Cathryn didn't know why it mattered so much, suddenly, but it did. It seemed important to know the name of each thing she had seen in Iceland.

"There must be a catalogue," Eva said. "You know, on the internet."

Cathryn tapped on Google and typed a few words. "Oh dear," she said. "It's all in Icelandic."

Eva stepped closer to view the screen. "Let me see. I can probably help." She took Cathryn's phone and began to swipe. "They seem to organize them by country of origin."

Cathryn peered at the gallery of flowers, each more exotic than the next. Eva laughed. "Now you have me—how do you say it? Hooked."

"Hooked," Cathryn agreed. "There's nothing like a good challenge."

"It's true." Eva laughed again. She wet her lip as she flicked through the pages.

Cathryn was about to speak when something pierced her awareness, as swift and sure as the spear of alertness that had pointed her to the teenager at Goðafoss. A knowledge out of time, like seeing past and present and future, together.

She wheeled around. Too quick for thought, too quick for her vision to process what her instinct already knew, she bolted toward the fountain where the little boy, Pétur, was face-down in the water.

She had grabbed him by the shirt before the sound of Eva's scream reached her ears. The shirt stretched, heavy with pondwater. Cathryn yanked the boy upward, out of the fountain, and shook the little body as she pulled him toward her. Water flew off him like shooting stars. She hit his back. Nothing. She hit him again. He gave a cry, angry and afraid.

Instantly, there was Eva, seizing her child. She threw Cathryn a furious look, as if it were Cathryn's fault, instead of Cathryn being the one who had saved him.

Maybe it was her fault. She was the one who had distracted his mother.

Time had felt so leisurely and expansive while they were looking at her phone, but time was a mirage, reflecting yourself back at you. The boy couldn't have been in the water for more than a few seconds, but it could have been forever. He could have been dead forever.

It wasn't her son. Her son was back in America, saved by her in a far lesser way. But he was someone's son.

A child needed you. You acted. That was all.

Cathryn was shaking now, her hands wet and empty. Next to her, Eva cradled her son. Eva's back was turned, pushing Cathryn outside the circle of their miraculous reunion.

She wanted to say *I'm sorry* and *aren't you going to thank me* and *he'll be fine.*

None of the sentences were right. There ought to be words—a few simple, perfect words—that would redeem this moment. But there weren't.

Twenty-One

Cathryn fled the Lystigardurinn. She couldn't imagine ever returning.

She walked rapidly, with no idea where she was headed or what she would do until one o'clock. Her situation felt absurd—a woman inventing ways to occupy herself until a man was ready to tell her, "Come. Hand me this. Fetch me that." It hadn't felt like that before. Each thing she had seen on her morning excursions seemed to have a purpose, a message.

But not now. Not compared to Pétur's limp little form.

Around her, people were hurrying to jobs, classes, appointments. She ducked into a space between two buildings and pulled out her phone, pretending she had something important to attend to. There were no messages. Not that she was expecting to hear from anyone, although she had thought Elliott Fischer might have written. Quickly, she swiped through her contacts. It was only seven in the morning for Elliott, but she could leave a message.

Despite the hour, he answered at once. "Fischer."

"Elliott," she said. "It's Cathryn McAllister."

"From the land of the midnight sun. Or is that Norway?"

"Iceland."

"Right. I can never tell them apart."

Cathryn hesitated. Maybe she ought to apologize for calling so early? Well, he'd answered, so she might as well get to the point. "How did it go with Nora Lang?" she asked. "I figured you would let me know."

"With Nora? She's a delight."

Cathryn tried to mask her annoyance. "I know Nora's a *delight*. That's not what I'm asking. I'm asking how the shoot went."

"Flawlessly," Elliott replied. "She couldn't have been more satisfied."

Shit, Cathryn thought. That was Elliott-speak for *I went to bed with her*.

She should have seen it coming. Nora's sex life was none of her business, but her status as a client was. And if Elliott Fischer was as slick as he was beginning to seem, Cathryn was in danger of losing her oldest and best client.

"Well, can you email the shots to me?" she asked. "So I can incorporate them into whatever we do later in the season? It's nice to ping back to images that are already out there. Credit line to you, of course."

"Hmmm." The murmur was meant to signify that he was considering her request, but Cathryn already knew what was coming. "Let's see how it goes, when you get back," he said. "It might be simpler to keep the momentum going. A more consistent look. You know, for the season."

It was bullshit. He'd already oozed his way into Nora's favor.

Frustrated, she couldn't resist a reciprocal jab. "You know," she told him, "that your something-something cousin Bobby Fischer was an anti-Semitic Holocaust-denier who applauded the attack on the Twin Towers?"

"So I've heard," Elliott said. "On the other hand, he was granted Icelandic citizenship by a special act of the Icelandic Parliament, and they let him live in Reykjavik until he died. In recognition of the 1972 match, which put Iceland on the map. As it were."

"Damn it, Elliott," Cathryn blurted. "Is Nora still my client?"

"You'll have to ask her, not me. All I can tell you is that she loved what I did for her."

Cathryn gritted her teeth. "Fine. I'll do that."

She jabbed the red circle for *end*. Even if she wanted to reserve a portion of herself for art instead of commerce, she still needed to make a living.

She had Nora's cell number but called the business line, knowing that no one would answer at this hour and she could leave a message. Messages were risky—you didn't know how they would be received without the give-and-take of conversation—but she needed to affirm her position without delay. Hers needed to be the first message Nora heard when she came in. It was only the one shoot, she explained. An unavoidable extension of her time in Iceland, and then she would be back, as available and devoted as ever.

Cathryn didn't know if it was true, but she had to tell Nora that it was. Then she drew in her breath. Should she warn her about Elliott?

A pause in the recording would be worst of all, signifying uncertainty. Instead, she kept talking. Appreciated his willingness to pinch-hit. Never meant to imply that she wasn't completely committed. Any indication Mr. Fischer might have given to the contrary was an inappropriate—

The robotic voice cut in. *If you are satisfied with your message, press one or simply hang up.* Cathryn hung up. She jammed the phone in her purse and resumed walking. She'd done what she could, and she didn't really believe that Nora would choose Elliott over her, not after their long history together.

The crowded streets—mostly tourists now, juggling cameras and guidebooks—made her realize that the one thing she hadn't done with her mornings was to wander through Akureyri like an ordinary visitor, browsing and shopping for souvenirs. She took out her phone again, consulted the map, and headed for Hafnarstræti, Akureyri's major shopping street.

At long last, she found a red scarf for Rachel. It wasn't pure red—amber and orange threads were woven into the fringe—but she thought Rachel would like it. Then she bought a scarf in forest-green for Judah. She doubted he would wear it, though he'd like hearing about the sheep that were everywhere, even along the slopes of the craters.

She glanced around the shop. Maybe she ought to buy something for herself?

No. She had the paperweight; that was her souvenir. On the bottom, where the sphere rested on a flattened disk, Mack had etched the words: *To remember*, and his name. When he wrote those words, he had already placed his time with her in the folder of experiences that were over. He hadn't expected to see her again. If she hadn't turned around and sped down the peninsula, he wouldn't have.

Had she been fierce and full of power, or pathetic? All the answers were clichés. *Time will tell. Only you can know.*

Cathryn paid for the scarves and took the bag from the cashier. Then she tucked the package under her arm and left the store. Slowly, she made her way through the shopping district. There were tiny boutiques that sold silica skin products, chocolates, birds carved out of wood, plastic trolls. There was even a music store with a framed poster of Björk. Brightly colored planter boxes lined the sidewalk: red rectangles, blue and green spheres. An enormous face was painted on a wall.

She spotted a bright blue building with circular towers ending in tall red roofs, like elves' hats. Outdoor tables were arranged on the cobblestones. Bláa Kannan. The Blue Can, with a bakery and bistro. Cathryn caught a glimpse of a wood-paneled interior with incongruously elegant chandeliers, but wanted the sun. She found an outdoor table and ordered a cappuccino.

"You must have one of our pastries," the waitress told her. "We bake every morning, right here."

Cathryn smiled. "I guess I must. Something simple, please."

"I'll bring you a kleina," the waitress said. "It's like a fried bun."

She returned a few minutes later with three knotted pastries on a blue plate—the donut-like sweets that Cathryn remembered from the day she came back to Akureyri. She had crashed into Mack and made him spill his coffee, ruining the treat he had bought for himself.

The waitress set a cup of cappuccino, topped with a star of whipped cream, next to the blue plate. "It looks wonderful," Cathryn said. She brought the steaming cup to her lips.

Then something made her stop. A feeling, like a voice calling her name. The way she felt when she knew someone was looking at her—as if a shutter had clicked and snapped her photo, superimposing it onto countless other photos taken over the years, in other cafés and other cities.

Herself, cool and controlled, a self-contained woman who knew how to dine alone. That woman could be anywhere, lifting a coffee cup, her perfect posture signaling *I don't need anyone, thank you very much*. Exactly as Rachel had said.

Cathryn set down the cup. She didn't want to be that woman anymore.

She wanted to be like the molten glass—swinging through space, on the brink of falling, her final shape unknown. That was why the glass had called to her. Not so she could master it. So she could be it.

And she wanted the rest of Iceland, the place she had come here to see. She wanted it with Mack. Not Mack or Iceland, but both.

Iceland's raw majesty, the rocky coastline and the sprawling ice—she wanted it with him. She longed to show him Breiðamerkursandur, the Diamond Beach where icebergs came to rest before drifting out to sea. She had gone there after they parted, that first morning, and surveyed the glittering shards of ice, some small enough to hold in your hand, others as large as a car, strewn across the black sand. Some of the frozen shapes were destined to melt and disappear into the sand; others would be swept out to sea. The Diamond Beach was a temporary home, a rest stop for the shimmering debris of Jökulsárlón.

There was so much she wanted to see, with him. The ice caves at Langjökull, a man-made tunnel into the glacier, five chambers carved from aquamarine ice. You could read the story of the glacier on the walls. Each layer represented a volcanic eruption or a shift as the lava cooled, a portion of the glacier's history. Like the tiered core of an iceberg, it was time made visible.

Snæfellsjökull in the west, with its twisted black rocks.

The Icelandic horses. The northern lights.

The day she made the paperweight, Mack had called the northern lights his heart's desire, adding, "Maybe we'll fulfill our desire together." She hadn't known if he was being flirtatious or serious, or both.

She grabbed a knot of fried dough and ate it in two ravenous bites. Her fingers were streaked with sugar and oil. She licked them greedily, then ate the other two pastries. They were warm and greasy, filling her with their voluptuous sweetness.

From what she had read, photographing the northern lights wouldn't be easy. It was too early in the season to count on their appearance, and this wasn't an optimal point in the eleven-year cycle of solar activity. And yet it happened, even in September. The guesthouse owner at Ólafsfjörður had told her there was a good chance the lights would appear the night she was there. They hadn't, but that didn't mean they wouldn't appear the next day, or the next week.

Cathryn wiped her mouth with a napkin. She'd do what she could to prepare. Select a location. Determine what settings she needed on her camera and teach her fingers how to move in the dark. The northern lights were unpredictable, requiring an instantaneous response—which meant that your fingers had to know how to find the buttons by themselves, to do what they couldn't see.

She'd have to manage with the equipment she had brought. If she had planned the trip around the aurora, she might have brought different lenses, but she had come to Iceland for a commercial shoot. Shades of Blue. And then an eight-day *Lonely Planet* sweep through the country's highlights.

She didn't want a *Lonely Planet* vacation. She wanted to see the northern lights, and she wanted to see them with Mack.

She could make it happen. She'd find a good viewing place outside Akureyri, free from the light pollution of the city. A little cottage, where they could watch the sky all night. He still wouldn't spend the night in her hotel room, but this would be different. It wasn't about sleeping; it was about being awake.

Ice and glass and light, three portals into an incandescent world. Colorless, yet reflecting every color. Invisible, yet illuminating what was there to be seen.

She could do this. A person who had careened down the Tröllaskagi Peninsula, taking the curves as breakneck speed, could make this happen.

Cathryn drained the cappuccino and used the cup to anchor a handful of bills. She reached for the shopping bag, ready to stand and move, when her phone buzzed.

It was a text from Nora Lang. "I got your voicemail," Nora had written, "and I have to say that I don't appreciate your telling me how to run my business, especially since you weren't even here for the job you contracted to do. And I really don't appreciate your badmouthing the person that you yourself referred me to. I know we've had a long association, but I'm not comfortable with these developments and I need to rethink what will serve me best, going forward."

Shit, Cathryn thought. She had mishandled this royally.

She wondered if the rift was beyond repair—then thought that it probably was, since Elliott Fischer had already claimed his place as Nora's savior. It was a bad blow, not only because of future work for the dance company, now lost, but because Nora was well connected, and people talked. Her whole brand was built on referrals and reputation.

Damn, damn, damn. She liked Nora, and it pained her to have Nora think badly of her. Her finger hovered on the screen, ready to type a reply into the message box asking if they could talk. She even started to write *I'm so sorry that this misunderstanding*

Only it wasn't a misunderstanding. Nora was right. Cathryn had let her down, and Elliott hadn't. End of story.

Cathryn bit her lip and typed *I'm so sorry but I wish you the best, always.* Feeling terrible, she hit *send.* Then she stood and pushed through the tables, away from the planter boxes and boutiques. Walking swiftly now, she turned off Hafnarstræti and wound through the smaller side streets until she came to one that led up a steep hill. She adjusted the bag of scarves and began to climb, past rows of brightly colored houses, yellow, red, blue. From the top of the hill, she could see the harbor and the fjord, an expanse of shimmering sapphire dotted with tiny white sails. It made her think of Pétur and his boat, the white triangle like a jaunty little flag as it bobbed on the surface of the water. No one, looking at the placid scene, could have foreseen what was going to happen only minutes later.

Sometimes you were caught by surprise, and sometimes you knew. With Nora Lang, she should have known.

Nora's message underscored a truth that Cathryn hadn't wanted to face. Her choice to stay in Iceland had consequences. She had abandoned her carefully constructed itinerary to heed a different call. In doing that, she had bound herself to a man who hadn't asked for her pledge and had promised nothing in return.

It's all right with me if you stay. That was all he had ever said. Trying to change that fact was as futile as trying to change what had happened with Nora.

The wind whipped her hair against her face. The only sounds were the moan of a distant foghorn and the screech of a tern.

Cathryn lifted her chin. It seemed to her as if she had been walking toward this very moment ever since she stepped off the plane at Keflavik Airport.

She had come to Iceland for him. She had told Renata Singer that she would pay her own way, and then she had crossed the ocean, into his arms.

And she had come for the person she was now, or might be.

A single phrase rose in her mind, rising like steam from the thermal lake. *Be brave.*

Twenty-Two

Cathryn knew the tasks Mack would ask her to carry out when she arrived at the hot shop—prepare a bucket of water for cooling the paddles, lay out the frits. Later, when he had started working, he might ask her to pull the cane into a thin strand while he twisted and snipped, or flash a chunk of glass in the glory hole so it would be soft enough to fuse. This time, though, he greeted her with a Cheshire Cat grin. "Today's the day," he said. "You get your wish."

"I do?" Diamond Beach, the aurora borealis. How did he know what she had been wishing for?

"You get to blow into the pipe. That's what you've wanted, right?"

Cathryn could only stare at him. He was offering a gift he had told her not to count on, and his kindness touched her. Yet it was a gift she no longer wanted, not in the same way. Mack didn't know that, of course. How could he?

"My goodness. I hadn't expected that."

"Even better. Come on, I'll talk you through it when you're ready."

His grin deepened. It was a Mack grin, big and confident and impossible to resist. Cathryn pulled off her sweater. She faced him in her tank top and twisted her hair into a knot. "I'm ready."

He selected a pipe from the rack. "It's a hollow steel tube, so the first thing you need to do is to blow through it to make sure there's no blockage."

She took the pipe from him, right hand on top, left hand underneath, the way he had showed her. Then she filled her lungs with air and exhaled into the end of the tube.

"Good," he said. "Did you feel it go all the way through? If there's any residue at the end, it'll interfere with a clean blow." She nodded. "Okay," he continued. "The most important thing, which you know, is to never stop rotating the pipe. Otherwise you'll inflate one side of the bulb more than the other, and the glass will be unstable."

Cathryn nodded again. She could feel her excitement mount. It did matter, after all.

Mack gestured at the glory hole. "Heat the tip in the glory hole first, so the gather can adhere. Then, once you have your gather, keep the pipe level, waist-high."

"Right." She did as he had told her, then stepped back from the furnace with the molten orb swirling at the end.

"You can balance it on the notch for stability," he said, "as long as you don't stop turning. You have to do two things, and both have to be absolutely even—your hands rotating the pipe, your breath moving forward in a steady stream."

"How do I know how much air to blow?"

"Keep your eyes on the glass. It'll show you."

Cathryn threw him a quick smile.

"Whenever you're ready," he repeated. "Just pay attention and blow evenly."

She drew the air into her lungs, and blew. The sphere began to expand. Joy filled her body, expanding with the glass. There, at last, was the magic she had sought. Her very breath, the source of transformation.

"That's good," Mack said. "You don't have to do a lot. Sometimes all you need is a single puff. It's called controlled blowing. Only what's needed."

"Should I blow some more? I mean, can I?"

"If you like. Just keep rotating the pipe. And keep it level."

Cathryn felt her fingers moving on the pipe, as if they understood their role and didn't need her to remind them. She inhaled, breathed out into the hollow tube, and watched the orb quiver and grow. When she took her mouth from the pipe, she laughed. "Oh, this is wonderful."

"It is."

"Thank you for this, Mack. Truly."

"You're very welcome. But that's enough for now." He took the pipe from her and carried it to the furnace, knocking the glass off the end. It dropped onto the molten heap.

"Hey!"

He gave her an amused glance. "You didn't really think we'd save this, did you? It was just for the experience."

"Phooey. I guess I did."

"You can't save everything, especially in a hot shop."

"Next you'll tell me the Easter Bunny isn't real."

He touched her arm. "Come. I'll buy you a coffee."

"A coffee?"

"All right, a Viking Gold."

"That's more like it. But let me treat you. It's my way of saying thanks."

Cathryn could see his shoulders tighten. It was his damn pride about money. He insisted on paying, no matter what she said or did.

She thought of the little girl holding out her apple. "One day you give to me, another day I give to you."

"It's not my way."

"Don't be so stubborn and retro. Why can't I pay, for once?"

A shadow crossed his face. "I'm paying off old debts."

She knew that look, but not what it meant. She wasn't giving in, though. Not this time.

"It's just a beer. You can buy me a great big glass of that Black Death stuff later, if it makes you happy."

"You're as bullheaded as I am."

"Shucks. You say the sweetest things."

Mack look startled, then burst out laughing. Cathryn could almost see the shadow lift.

It was a different pub, not the one they had gone to before, with mirrors and faded velvet couches and a wall made of white bricks. Shelves of craft beer and spirits made a gaudy backdrop for the polished wooden bar. Mack guided her to a table in the corner.

The bartender looked up as they passed. "*Drekka?*"

"Viking Gylltur," Mack said, holding up two fingers.

Cathryn settled into a ladderback chair with a woven seat. "Seems early for alcohol, but as my mother used to say, 'It's five o'clock somewhere.'"

"It only needs to be one o'clock for beer."

"That's a relief." She propped her elbows on the table, regarding him curiously. "You sure you can spare the time? I mean, in the middle of the day?"

He shrugged. "We're here."

Another evasion, she thought, annoyed and then troubled. Mack was obsessed with his project—his word—yet he had made time for her, right from the start. Why? It didn't fit with his description of himself as feral, a hermit.

The bartender set two bottles on their table. "You need glasses?" he asked. Mack looked at Cathryn, and she shook her head. "Okay," the bartender said. "You enjoy."

Cathryn reached for one of the bottles. Her unease grew. Now that she had let herself wonder, she had to know. "Mack." She hesitated, then gathered her nerve. "There's something I don't understand."

She thought he might say something clever like *join the club*, but he didn't. He wrapped his hand around the bottle and waited for her to continue.

"You have this burning vision," she said, choosing her words carefully. "That vision brought you to Jökulsárlón, and then to

Akureyri. You have a few weeks, no time for anything that's not going to support your vision. No whale-watching, no diversions. No family, as far as I know."

"No family."

"A single purpose." She wet her lip. "Why make time for me, then?" There. She'd said it. "Why let me into your world?"

He met her eyes. "Because you asked."

Cathryn flinched. She didn't know what answer she had thought he would give, but not that one. Because she showed up, like a star-struck groupie, begging for a chance to clean his tools? It could have been any woman who threw herself at him; that was what he was telling her.

Mack pinned her with his gaze. "You were so fierce and beautiful and true, when you came to get your paperweight. I couldn't turn you away."

"A woman asks, and if she's beautiful, you just can't say no?"

"I'm explaining how I saw you. How you were. Are. I had no intention of letting a woman into my work space."

"Or into your daytime hours."

"Or into my daytime hours," he echoed.

"It's not something you do, when you feel lonely?"

"I don't feel lonely. I told you that."

She nodded, remembering their conversation.

He gave her a look she couldn't fathom. "Don't underestimate yourself, Cathryn McAllister. You're quite a woman."

"Well." She exhaled, then picked up her bottle of Viking Gold. "I'll drink to that. At one o'clock, noon, whenever you like."

Mack raised his beer in agreement. "*Skál.*"

"Back at you."

Cathryn drained half the bottle before setting it back on the table. He had answered her question, in his oblique and strangely touching way—yet there was still so much she didn't know. Why he was so reclusive, and if he had always been like that. What he meant by debts. What those moments were, when he blacked out.

Mack knew as little about her as she knew about him. He hadn't inquired, and she hadn't volunteered, even after her determination at Goðafoss that she would. It seemed astonishing that he still didn't know about Rachel and Judah, yet there had never been a reason to bring them up. Her life in America, like her past, seemed irrelevant, but she knew that wasn't true. Like an iceberg, a person was built from the layers that accrued, each resting on the ones below.

"So," he said, signaling the waiter for another beer. "What did you do today, before you came to the hot shop?"

Cathryn grew still. The last time he had asked her that was after she had climbed on his lap. After Goðafoss. "Actually," she said, "something strange happened."

"Oh?" He moved aside to let the waiter take the empty bottle and replace it with a new one. The waiter looked at Cathryn, but she put up a hand.

"What happened?" Mack asked.

Suddenly she needed to talk about it. Not only to share something with him, but to say it aloud. "I went to the botanic garden," she told him, "and there was a little boy with a toy boat. He was playing with it in the fountain."

The scene unfurled before her, as if it were happening again. "I distracted his mother—not that I meant to, but I did. We were trying to find the name of a flower on my phone, and she forgot about him."

Cathryn could see it. The ring of trees. The circular fountain and the little white sail.

"And then—I *knew*. One minute I was looking at pictures on my iPhone, and the next minute I was pulling the boy out of the fountain." She looked into Mack's eyes. "I saved a child's life. But I was the one who had put him in danger."

Mack's reaction stunned her. He pushed away from table and stood, towering over her. "I need to get back to the hot shop." His voice was clipped, the voice of a stranger.

Cathryn froze. "What did I say?"

"Nothing. I need to get back, that's all. Take your time, finish your beer." Before she could reply, he was gone.

The space he had occupied was stripped of life, a Mack-shaped hole on the other side of a wooden table. The air was sharp in her chest.

Slowly, she finished her Viking Gold. When she went to pay for the beer, she discovered that Mack had already paid. She left the pub, not sure where she ought to go. Did he expect her to go back to the hot shop? Why shouldn't she? She had done nothing wrong.

As if in a trance, she placed one foot in front of the other and walked back to the studio. She popped the lock, the way he had showed her, and pushed open the heavy door.

Mack was there, illuminated by the light from the glory hole. He tapped the pipe, and the glass at the end fell into the anonymous molten mass. Then he turned around and laid the pipe on the rack. He walked toward her, his palms open.

It was the sorrow in his eyes. He hadn't let her see that before, not without the veil that always dropped, just when she thought he might let her see.

Her heart seized. It complicated everything.

Twenty-Three

When Rachel was five, she became infatuated with the Disney princesses—Ariel, Pocahontas, Belle, Mulan. It was one of the few things she allowed Cathryn to share with her, mostly because Brian wouldn't. Rachel liked Mulan, who became a warrior, and Esmerelda, who was sexy and dramatic, but had no use for Snow White, the original princess created over sixty years before her beloved Mulan. The babyish, high-pitched soprano cleaning the dwarves' house and singing "Some Day My Prince Will Come" wasn't Rachel's style, even at five.

The infatuation lasted for a few years, and then the Ariel and Pocahontas dolls were boxed up in the attic, along with their wardrobes and storybooks. It wasn't until the night before Rachel left for college that the subject came up again. Cathryn had forgotten about the conversation, just as she'd forgotten about the dolls and their tiny accessories. The only reason she remembered it now, in Akureyri, was because of Rachel's Snow Queen remark—and her own insistence that she was more like Snow White than an icy sovereign. Asleep, not aloof.

Rachel had been perched on the edge of her bed, tossing her childhood treasures into a carton destined for trash pickup the next morning. Cathryn, curled in the butterfly chair, had watched wistfully. It pained her to watch her daughter discard the relics of an entire childhood, although Rachel herself seemed indifferent.

"Oh, don't throw this out!" Cathryn jumped up to retrieve a glossy oversized volume that Rachel had flung aside. The cover had a picture of a sickle-shaped moon and a gem-studded coronet. "Grimm's Fairy Tales. This is a classic."

Rachel gave the book a cursory glance as she pitched a stuffed elephant into the carton. "Aren't they really violent? I mean, compared to the Disney ones?"

"Maybe a bit," Cathryn conceded, "but it's interesting to see the difference."

Rachel looked skeptical. "Like what?"

"Well, like Snow White." Cathryn laid the book on her lap. "You know the story, right? The evil queen creates this poisoned apple that will put whoever eats it into a kind of sleeping death. Snow White falls for the trick, takes a bite, and poof, off to dreamland." Rachel nodded, so Cathryn continued. "In the Disney version, she's awakened by the prince's kiss—which comes from sadness, by the way, not passion. He looks at the beautiful dead princess and feels sorry for her."

Rachel's eyebrow shot up. "True love's kiss is sad, but not passionate? What a message. No wonder most relationships don't work out."

"Actually," Cathryn said, "in the original story, Snow White's awakening was totally different."

"It was a hot kiss. I knew it."

Cathryn had to laugh. "Hardly. In the Grimm version, the prince decides to bring Snow White to her proper resting place, back at her father's castle. Then one of the servants who's carrying the glass coffin—you know, with the sleeping girl inside, although everyone thinks she's a corpse—trips on a rock. He loses his balance, the coffin jerks, and the piece of poisoned apple pops out of Snow White's throat, magically reviving her." She gave Rachel a pointed look. "It's an accident, not love's first kiss, that undoes the spell. The random stumble of a clumsy pallbearer."

"And the moral is—?"

"Maybe there are just accidents, like a stone on the road, and your whole life is changed."

Or a truck on the road. A set of car keys—tossed on impulse, caught by instinct.

She hadn't meant to invoke that memory—she hadn't even meant to think it, but Rachel didn't seem to make the connection. And why would she? No one had known about the car keys except Cathryn. And Brian.

Rachel shrugged. "Well, it worked out for old Snow White. The spell was broken, and she got her man."

"I suppose." Cathryn tried to match her daughter's shrug. "Anyway, it wasn't like she'd been suffering. She was asleep, not chained to a dungeon. Maybe she was having a happy dream that true love would awaken her."

"That is so retro. Maybe she needed to awaken herself."

"A feminist retelling? She didn't do that either. It was an accident. According to Grimm, anyway."

Rachel's interest was clearly waning. "Shit happens, but sometimes people get lucky. Is there something else?"

"I keep feeling like a more attentive pallbearer would have seen the stone and known enough to avoid it."

Rachel stood, took the book from Cathryn's lap, and tossed it in the carton. "Then Snow White would still be asleep."

Her daughter had dispensed with the quandary and returned to her sorting, discarding, and packing. But the question had lodged in Cathryn's mind, returning now.

This is an apple. A child, offering her rautt epli.

Eve, extending her hand with the fruit of knowledge. *Wake up.*

When Cathryn arrived at the hot shop the next day, she felt it at once. Mack was crackling with an excitement she had never seen before.

"I have an idea," he said, striding toward her as she entered the building, barely waiting for her to close the door. He took her purse and set it on the chair, then helped her take off her jacket. For a moment she thought he was going to take off all her clothes, make love to her right there, but of course that was insane. He wanted her to hurry so she could assist him.

"There's a piece I need to make," he told her.

"All right." Cathryn raised her arms to coil her hair into a knot.

Mack's eyes were fixed on hers. "I can't do it without you. I'm going to do something very specific with the pipe, and I need you to snip the excess with the shears exactly when I tell you. You can't be tentative. You have to cut the glass with a single movement, right that instant." His gaze was fierce, his eagerness electric. "Can you do that?"

Cathryn tried to picture what he was describing. It was more than he had ever trusted her to do. "Yes. I can."

"Here," he said, handing her a pair of shears. "Keep them nearby."

Cathryn took a seat at the end of the bench, feet parallel on the floor, and set the shears next to her. She waited while he gathered the glass from the furnace, rolled it in one of the frits, and laid the pipe across her palms. "Keep turning it while I draw the glass up, vertically." He flashed her a quick, wry grin. "I kept thinking about the horizontal relationship between the icebergs, but that's only one of the dimensions. I can't believe I didn't see it before."

Cathryn didn't know what he was talking about, but she didn't need to know. She just needed to be present, alert.

Her hands had learned how to rotate the pipe. She didn't have to watch them anymore, only keep part of her attention on the sensation of her palms. The rest of her attention was on Mack, as he coaxed the glass upward.

She had seen the quality of his work, but this was different. The form that began to appear was otherworldly, fluid as a dancer. The end tapered into a delicate unfinished arc, like a wing.

"I'm going to take the pipe," he said, "and I need you to be ready. You have to cut the glass exactly when I tell you. It has to be clean. One cut, on as sharp a diagonal as you can."

Cathryn transferred the pipe to his waiting palms, took the shears, and stood.

He gave the pipe a sharp, rapid twist. "Now." She wrapped the heavy blades around the molten shape, twisted, and made the cut.

"Knock it off the punti," he told her. "One tap." She struck the pole with the handle of the shears and the figure broke free.

"Open the annealer." In two long strides, she was at the annealing oven, opening the door for him. He thrust the object into the oven, and she closed the door.

He turned to her, beaming. "Thank you."

"It's good, what you did."

"Yes. It is."

"I think you found it." She shook her hair free, let it fall across her shoulders. "Not a shape, but a movement. Something in transition."

"Exactly. That's what I was missing."

"It's different from your other pieces."

"You see that, don't you?"

"Yes. I see it." Her heart was beating wildly. It was a new feeling, not lust, but joy—for him, because of his joy. With the same swift movement she had used to cut the glass, she wrapped her arms around his waist and lay her head on his chest. She closed her eyes. His back was warm from the furnace. A man's back, broad and firm, yet tender as a child's.

When the new sculpture came out of the annealer, Mack threw most of the other pieces into the furnace, recycling the glass so he could start the series anew. Cathryn couldn't help wincing at the destruction of so much time and effort, but he merely shrugged. "I see what I want now. Think of a musician. He doesn't make recordings of all the practice hours while he's learning a new piece and then save them, simply because they exist. They served their purpose."

She still didn't like it, but she was happy that he had found what he was looking for. She stepped around the table to view the figure from another angle.

Mack had set the sculpture in the center of the table where it could catch the light. It seemed to unfold as she moved, its facets opening to reveal new layers, secret depths. What she hadn't seen, when it was molten, was the way the colors were interwoven. They led the eye deep inside and upward at the same time—echoing, through variations in hue, the same yearning that was expressed in the delicate contours of the ascending, asymmetrical form.

Cathryn's voice was quiet. "I've never seen anything like it."

"I think I was approaching it too literally before. I was seeing the icebergs as objects in a static landscape. But they're not. They're like dancers."

She traced the figure with her fingertip. "I think each piece in the series will tell you what the next one needs to be."

He moved next to her, hands in his pockets. "You still think they need to be huge, an installation that people can walk through?"

"I'm not sure. I can see it either way."

"I like the idea that people can participate. I don't think you were wrong about that."

Her heart warmed, expanded, opened to this amazing man—a man who had recognized her, even before she recognized herself. "If the pieces are huge, then people can dance with them." She laughed. "Can't you just see it?"

He laughed too. "I suppose we'll need music."

"Wouldn't that be glorious?" Happy that he had found his way—that she had helped him, and that he was letting her be part of it—Cathryn stretched her arms over her head like a dancer opening to the sky. "Chopin, I think. Something gorgeous and lyrical." She arched her back and spread her arms, joyous and free. "We'll dance with the icebergs."

She lifted her face, raised herself on tiptoe to embody the way the piece made her feel. And then, quicker than a spark, she lost her balance and stumbled.

She knew, even before she stumbled, what was going to happen. Like the moment at the botanic garden, future and past changed places, didn't matter. She fell forward against the wooden table, crashing into it with the weight of her tumbling body. The sound of shattering glass went on forever.

Cathryn stared in horror. She was the clumsy servant, failing at the one simple task that had been entrusted to her: to pay attention. A destroyer of his dream, not a princess awakened by true love's kiss.

She wheeled around. Mack's face was ashen.

Glass Rain. Five hundred shards, each a dagger unless you saw the way to move through them. There was no difference, in the end, between accident and intention. She might as well have picked up the sculpture and thrown it against the steel marver.

Part Four:
The Punti Scar

Twenty-Four

"**P**lease leave," he told her. His face said *get the fuck away from me*. Cathryn backed away from the glittering mess on the floor, grabbed her things, and fled.

There was nowhere to go that didn't hold memories, hopes, reminders of his misplaced trust and her unearned joy. Not knowing what else to do, she walked. Down to the harbor, through the industrial part of the city, and up a steep hill with a view of the Akureyrarkirkja and its hundred-and-twelve steps. Pushing herself until her muscles hurt, needing to punish her careless, destructive body.

No, it wasn't her body's fault. Her body only did what her mind told it to do. If it had decided to cavort and rejoice, it was because something in her, Cathryn, had told it, *Sure, go ahead, no need to worry about the glass sculpture on the table*.

She clenched her teeth and kept climbing. The pavement gave way to a jagged line of cement squares, then to rocks and dirt. After a while she stopped to catch her breath. There were no trees, no houses, only tufts of dry grass pushing through the cracks in the cement and the shriek of the gulls. The fjord looked miles away.

After a while, shivering, Cathryn turned and retraced her steps to the center of town where she would have a better signal on her phone. What if he were trying to call? *I know you didn't mean it. Come back.*

There were no messages, no missed calls. She hadn't really thought there would be. What was broken between them wouldn't magically repair itself, no more than the pieces of the broken sculpture could find their way back into a restored whole. Sick with remorse, she wove through the streets again until she found the one that led to her hotel. She had to go somewhere. It was the hotel—or straight to the airport, and America.

The desk clerk regarded her with surprise; it wasn't her habit to return so early. "The room has been cleaned?" Cathryn asked. "I can go up?"

"Yes, everything is ready for you."

Thank goodness for that much. It was a place to wait. A place where Mack could find her. Slowly, she ascended the two flights of stairs to the room that had become her home. It was filled with Mack's presence. Despite the smooth new sheets, his imprint was on the bed, where he had come to her each night.

She closed the door and looked around, at the dove-gray walls and the tasseled spread and the heavy belled armoire, struggling not to give way to the desperate need to *fix this, right now,* the way she had fixed her children's skinned knees and missing buttons. She knew better than to text him, pleading for another chance. He would come to her when he was ready. When he had forgiven her.

She looked at her watch. It was only four thirty. Couldn't she go to sleep right now, and when she awoke everything would be healed, his trust in her renewed? How many hours until *later*?

Her phone buzzed inside her purse. Cathryn's heart soared with relief; she had never imagined that his mercy would be so swift. She grabbed the phone like a life vest, flinging the purse aside. But it wasn't Mack. It was a message from Rachel.

"So Ryder called me a fucking *cunt*, can you believe it? And then he ripped up the goddamn teddy I bought to make him happy and slapped the pieces in my face. He said I must be wearing it for someone else because it was in a different drawer—seriously?— and I was so quote unquote *distant.* As in, not telling him every single thought. That's it for me. I should have seen it coming, so color me stupid. And yeah, thanks for the offer of the house. I'm on my way."

A second text followed. "PS: I'm shutting off my phone. I blocked Ryder, but I need some space. Just wanted you to know I'm fine, and where I'll be. XOXO."

Cathryn stared at the screen for a horrified instant, then hit the R above Rachel's name and punched the telephone icon. *Call.* It went to voicemail right away. Shit. Couldn't Rachel have given her a minute to respond? Her hand shaking, she typed, "Please pick up, sweetheart. It's me." She waited, but there was no *delivered* message. Shit again. She hit *call* a second time; again, it went right to voicemail. She bit her lip and left a message. "Whatever you need, honey. I'm here. I love you." Then she dropped the phone on the bed and sank down next to it, her face in her hands.

Her darling girl. She wanted to claw the man who would do such an ugly thing to her daughter. How could a person who claimed to care about Rachel do something like that?

Cathryn felt her skin turn to ice. No doubt that was how Mack felt about her. She had ripped up his art, thrown it on the studio's concrete floor. To him, it was worse than slashing his flesh.

She was glad Rachel had left—or escaped, depending on how crazy Ryder actually was—and had a safe place to go. By a fluke of timing, Judah might be there too. Rachel wouldn't want to deal with her brother, especially right now, but it was a big house, and they didn't have to interact if they didn't want to. Still, she wished she could have given Rachel a heads-up that she wouldn't have the place to herself.

Aching for her child, Cathryn yearned to reach across the ocean and make everything all right. When Rachel and Judah were small, she had repaired each thing the moment it broke. After Brian died, that had felt more important than ever—to run behind them, sweeping, fixing, keeping the world intact. The heel on Rachel's special dyed-to-match shoes that snapped hours before the prom. Judah's crushing disappointment when he wasn't picked for the band that "everyone else" was in. Cathryn had paid a shoemaker triple his regular price to drop everything and fix the heel, found someone to cut a demo disk for Judah that made "everyone else" beg to be included. Now, all she could offer was a safe harbor, a place they could go to make their own repairs.

And where would Mack go, to repair what she had broken? Nowhere. She was the one who had to leave.

No. She wasn't ready to say that.

Yet the word screamed in her brain, loud as the gull that had circled overhead as she looked down at the city where she no longer belonged. *America*. Her daughter in America needed her. Mack didn't.

She pushed off the bed and yanked open the bathroom door. Her reflection in the oversized mirror was lit from bulbs on both sides, framing her against the tiled shower. There was something familiar and disturbing about the image. Angrily, she pulled her sweater over her head and kicked off her pants until she was standing nude in front of the mirror. Her body was different, since Mack. Her breasts were fuller, the nipples dark and thick. A body that had been touched, aroused, used well.

She ran her hands over her breasts, stomach, thighs. Her labia. Tears filled her eyes.

Then she realized why the image looked so familiar. A bathroom mirror, with side-lights and tiled walls. It was the photograph she had found in Brian's wallet, all those years ago, the evening that had changed her life. The woman her daughter had named Miranda, and thought she needed to be.

And where was she, Cathryn, in the composition? A woman leaning against her lover with such languid ease—or someone else, waiting outside the frame to find out what was going to happen now?

She wheeled around and yanked open the shower curtain, then twisted the knob as far as it would go. Steam filled the bathroom as she stepped into the compartment and thrust her head under the pounding water. A scorching Goðafoss, obliterating thought. She let the water pour down on her neck and back, then raised her face to the brutal stream. It was sharp as a rain of knives.

When she couldn't stand it anymore, she twisted the handle in the other direction and staggered out of the shower, collapsing onto the bed. She grabbed the edge of the tasseled bedspread and wrapped it around her body. Hot and shivering, too despondent to cry, she couldn't imagine moving ever again.

When Cathryn awoke, the sky outside the window was navy blue, flecked with stars. She had no idea what time it was. In June, Iceland had twenty hours of sunlight each day; in December, only four. Now, in mid-September, the day was divided almost equally into light and dark. It could be six in the morning or six at night.

She propped herself onto an elbow and felt for her phone. It was 4:43, well before sunrise, and long after Mack would have come, if he was going to. He hadn't come—had she really been stupid enough to think that he would?

Cathryn couldn't believe she had fallen into such a long, exhausted sleep; it seemed wrong, as if she ought to have been awake all night, keeping vigil. She reached up and felt her hair. It was still damp, a tousled mess. She remembered the shower, the mirror.

She pushed herself into a sitting position and tried Rachel's number, but the phone was still turned off. Judah? No, Rachel might not have told him anything or even spoken to him.

The person she really wanted to talk to was silent because he had nothing to say to her. Fresh tears stung her lashes. Had she actually thought he would come to her in the night?

America. The word rang in her ears. She needed to leave him alone. Go home. It seemed the only decent thing to do.

She stood, stumbled into the bathroom, and found her clothes. Her mouth felt thick and foul. She filled a glass with tap water and sucked it down like air. She needed to pack, call Icelandair, settle her bill with the hotel. There were too many things to do, and she had to do all of them right now—before a morning dawned when he didn't call, and she would know for certain that he wasn't going to.

Coward, she thought.

Face him. Tell him you're leaving. Don't just run away.

Cathryn trembled, because she knew that was right. It was the bravest gesture she could make, for both of them—so that later, if he thought of her, it might be with pity instead of bitterness. She would tell him good-bye to his face.

She threw on her clothes without bothering to comb her hair. It was a five-minute drive to the hot shop, but she couldn't bear the thought of getting in a car, making noise, having to stop at corners. Instead, she ran through the empty streets as the stars shimmered overhead.

Her usual parking spot in front of Einar's studio was vacant. The wide planks of the rectangular building and the row of windows just below the roofline were as familiar to her now as her own name. She popped the latch the way Mack had showed her and went inside.

The hot shop was dark, quiet—empty, without Mack moving between the furnace and bench. He had swept the floor; there was nothing to indicate that the sculpture had ever existed. Cathryn peered into the darkness and saw that he was asleep on the cot at the far end of the studio. Carefully, she crossed the room.

He must have heard her step because he bolted awake, alert as an animal. Cathryn's gaze locked onto his. She couldn't help thinking: Oh, he sleeps in boxers.

"What is it?" he said.

She felt too weak to stand. Could she really do this? She braced herself against the wall. "I came to say good-bye. And that I'm so sorry."

He didn't acknowledge her apology or argue with the word *good-bye*. After a long terrible moment, he said, "Where will you go?"

She looked at him. Sorrow and yearning, pain and desire—a formless mass of feeling welled up inside her. How could she possibly tell him everything she longed to say? All she could think of was what she had said the first time she left, after she made the paperweight—a stupid glib reply, because she'd been so unhappy.

"Oh, off to find the northern lights."

"Why?"

Why? She hadn't thought he would care what she did, much less why. Answers flashed across her mind, like the lights themselves. Because their source is ninety-three million miles away. Because they make you wait until they're ready to appear. Because it hurts to know that I won't be seeing them with you.

She had wanted the northern lights to be magic, just as she had wanted the blue color of the icebergs to be magic. There were so many stories about the mysterious green lights—stories she had saved to tell him, when they saw them together. She thought of the legend from Greenland that seemed so haunting and sad.

"Because they say that the northern lights are the souls of still-born children."

Mack's face turned ashen. "Why are you doing this?"

Cathryn stared at him. "Doing what?"

"Trying to break everything about me."

"I'm not." Her heart began to hammer. "I don't understand."

He shook his head. *No, you don't.* He was sitting on the edge of the cot, shoulders bent, arms loose between his knees. She crossed the room, tentatively, as if parting the air and claiming the space was more than she had the right to do. She knelt in front of him. "Tell me."

Her heart was pushing against her flesh. Seconds passed, each more endless than the one before. Finally, he spoke. His voice was low, inward. "I guess it's time to tell someone."

Cathryn watched his face but he looked away, toward the marver and the glory hole at the other end of the long room.

"I was married," he said. "Her name was Deborah. Well, it still is Deborah, as far as I know. I was thirty-nine years old, I hadn't planned on ever getting married, but the day I met her, I knew she was the woman I was meant to be with."

Cathryn was glad he was looking across the studio and not at her. It would have been too much to bear if he had seen her face, slapped with the truth she ought to have grasped by now. He appreciated her, enjoyed her, thought she was beautiful; maybe he even cared about her. But she wasn't the woman he was meant to be with. That place was taken.

She forced herself to keep listening. It was time to tell someone, he had said. She didn't know if it was her, specifically, or whoever had crossed his path.

"Deborah was a cellist—is a cellist, I have to stop using the past tense—and like me, she'd focused on her career. If I hadn't been in love with her already, I would have fallen in love when I heard her play. Bach's unaccompanied cello suites. You wouldn't believe that such a small woman could create such an incredible sound."

Breathe, Cathryn told herself. In. Out. Stay here for him. Don't leave, even in your thoughts.

"She was thirty-four, and neither of us felt in a hurry to change anything about the way we lived. But then she turned thirty-six, and something shifted. That biological clock. She wanted a child, and she worried that it would be too late if she put it off. I didn't especially want a child—I liked to stay up all night working, I went away for weeks at a time, I wasn't ready to limit my freedom—but I wanted her to be happy. I wanted that more than I wanted anything else. So I said yes."

Cathryn didn't move. It took every ounce of will she had not to picture Mack trying to get a woman pregnant. His wife. "Did she get pregnant?"

"She did." Mack's voice was quiet. He was still gazing across the room. Or somewhere, not at her. "It only took a couple of months. She was ecstatic. The baby was due in April, and I had a big trip to Costa Rica planned in March. It had been planned for ages, and the truth was that I didn't think she'd get pregnant so quickly. Deborah really didn't want me to go, but I told her I needed to. It was a project I was intent on carrying out, and she'd have me afterward, we'd have each other, and our child. Wasn't that enough? She argued with me, but my mind was made up. I felt like I'd agreed to the big thing, the child, so I deserved to have this." Pain rippled across his features. "The project was for her, too. I wanted to show leaves and buds on the brink of opening. As they were being born."

Cathryn remembered him telling her about the leaves, the evening they met. "So you went."

"I went. She tried to change my mind, right up to the day I left, but I was getting angry by then. I called her selfish and unreasonable. She told me she had a premonition, she was frightened. It was so out of character for her that I thought she had to be making it up. I told her it was hormones and to stop trying to manipulate me. I'd never talked to her like that before. I adored her." Cathryn could see his chest moving, as if it took all he had to let the air in and out of his lungs.

"I promised I'd be back in plenty of time. I was coming home twelve days before her due date, our due date, and I promised her I'd come sooner if there was any reason to think she'd be early, even though the doctor said that first babies were usually late."

He turned, at last, to meet Cathryn's eyes. "I promised her. But I was off in the jungle, and I let my phone die. I knew the battery was low, but I didn't care enough to stop and charge it because I was too consumed with the ideas that were swirling in my brain. I'd heard about this place where the sunlight came through the canopy in a particular way, illuminating the leaves with the transparency I was dead-set on capturing. I had to go there—that was the whole point of Costa Rica, to have an experience I could translate into glass. And I needed, wanted, to stay for twenty-four hours so I could see the cycle of the changing light. I wasn't thinking about my phone. There was probably no signal anyway, that far into the jungle."

Cathryn didn't dare to breathe. She knew, already, how the story would end.

Mack straightened his shoulders. "The baby stopped moving. She went to the doctor, and he said it happened sometimes—for no reason, it wasn't anything she did. The baby died inside her at thirty-seven weeks. It was fully formed, ready to be born. A boy. It just died. He died. They had to induce labor, and she wanted to be awake for it. She tried to call me, but I didn't answer. She kept calling. I saw that later, when I charged my phone. Fourteen missed calls. The labor went on for hours and hours, and she kept calling. She had to do all the work, without the baby to help. They wanted to anesthetize her, but she refused. She wanted to hear my voice when I called back, to have me with her."

He was trembling now. "I never called, not until two days later. She delivered a stillborn child and held him in her arms. She saw his face. His eyes were open, but he was dead. She buried him herself, without me."

His body spasmed with grief. "I tried to tell her how sorry I was, but she was done with me. As dead to me as my son. She never spoke to me again."

Cathryn's eyes flooded with tears. His pain, revealed to her at last. At first, it had pained her too, hearing about Deborah, but that no longer mattered. A well of compassion rose up in her, a spring that had been dry for so long.

She took his face in her hands and kissed him again and again. His mouth, his cheeks, his hair. Gently, she pushed him back down on the cot. He didn't resist. She kissed his chest, his stomach, every part she could reach. Even more gently, she drew his boxer shorts down along his legs and moved upward again to kiss the damp mound of his pubic hair. His smell, his taste. She took him in her mouth.

He shuddered, but responded, grief and sorrow and desire bound together in a single thrust, a single cry. She pulled off her jeans, straddled him, and took him inside her.

Shelter here.

Woman and mother, no thought or plan. Only herself, in this moment of need.

Shelter here. Inside me.

Twenty-Five

Cathryn had wanted to know about the darkness she'd glimpsed on Mack's face, and now she knew. He had kept his silence for two terrible years. If he had told someone at last, it might be because he trusted her, or because she had pushed him beyond the point where he could contain his grief. Either way, she couldn't go back and un-know what she had learned—about his sorrow, his guilt, and the woman he had loved. Still loved.

When she lifted herself, at last, from the too-small cot, Mack reached out to touch her waist. "You're a good woman, Cathryn."

That day at Mývatn, she had told him that a person could only be good in a specific moment. Whether this was one of those moments, she couldn't say. She had done the only thing that seemed possible—used the language of her body, because words were too small.

"You were hurting," she said, finally.

"It always hurts. I try not to feel it."

"I think everyone has something they try not to feel."

"Maybe," he conceded. "But some wounds are more innocent than others."

Cathryn thought of her own past. "I don't know. For years I was sure I'd played a role in my husband's death. I felt guilty and resentful.

Cheated. Not because he was dead, but because he'd marked me as a victim and a fool before I had a chance to turn it into something noble. There's not much innocence in that."

"Did you play a role?"

She hesitated. The brakes failed and the car rammed into a truck. "No." Then, with more conviction, she added, "No more than you played a role in your son's death."

"I understand that. But the other deaths were my doing." He looked away. "A part of Deborah died. A part of me died too."

Again, tears filled her eyes. Not just for Mack, but for Deborah, who had suffered so dreadfully. She understood Deborah, though she was angry at her. How could Deborah have closed her heart so utterly? Her loss was Mack's loss too; they could have shared it. Cathryn wanted to believe that, in Deborah's place, she would have forgiven Mack for his absence, but it was a stupid assumption. She hadn't forgiven Brian for betraying her; why did she think she would have forgiven Mack for what, to Deborah, was a greater betrayal?

Mack seemed far away now, yet she lingered on the edge of the cot. Common sense told her that she needed to leave. She had ruined his work—learning his story hadn't changed that—and there was no place for her anymore. *It's all right with me if you stay* only applied if the tacit part of the sentence held true. *As long as you don't destroy what I create.* She couldn't possibly assist him after what had happened, and any other role she might have imagined for herself was an illusion. Yet she could hardly bear to go.

Cathryn wiped away the tears, not wanting him to see. He wouldn't be sure why she was crying. She wasn't sure herself.

Somehow she found her voice. "What do you want me to do?"

He raised himself onto his elbows. "I need a day alone. To find another way to begin."

He didn't say, "Please don't go. Stay in Akureyri." Yet he hadn't said, "You were right, you need to leave. Go find the northern lights. Go back to America."

He had asked for a day to himself. A single day.

"Yes, of course." Cathryn slid off the cot and felt for her clothes. Then she turned and faced him again. "I'm so sorry about the sculpture. I can't tell you how sorry I am."

"It's happened to every glassblower."

"You're trying to be kind."

"It's a fact. It's bound to happen if you do this long enough."

She wanted to ask him to forgive her, but it seemed like a hideously insensitive request after the story he had told. Being factual instead of furious was already a gift, an absolution she didn't deserve.

"Glass breaks," Mack said. "It's the risk you take. This wasn't the first time, and it won't be the last."

There was so much she wanted to tell him. How beautiful the piece had been, and how it had felt like her piece too, because he had let her help him. How sorry she was that she wasn't Deborah and that the child she had saved in the fountain, Pétur, wasn't Deborah's child.

She wanted to reassure him: You can make the figure again, re-create the same design. But it wasn't true. He had explained it to her, the day they went to Hverir. *You let yourself be in the moment, feeling whatever you're feeling, and you let that truth pour itself into the piece.* That was why there was no re-creation. There was only the next thing, whatever it was.

There was no assurance, no solution she could offer. All she could do was to give him what he had asked for. This day, alone.

Cathryn decided to head up the Tröllaskagi Peninsula, the route she had taken when she left Akureyri that first time. There were places to explore that she had driven right past in her need to get to the next stop on her schedule, the island with the birds.

She didn't have a schedule anymore. She could walk along a cliff, collect wildflowers, do whatever she wanted. Take a photo. It didn't feel like she had the right to pursue her own art, not after destroying Mack's, but she put her camera and lenses into the daypack anyway, just in case.

Then she thought about Rachel, whose message seemed light-years ago. She would be at the house by now, asleep in her old room.

Cathryn paused, her hand still on the daypack. Maybe she really should go back to America—not to flee from Mack, but to be with her daughter.

Would Rachel want that? She couldn't ask, because Rachel's phone was turned off—Cathryn had tried, again, but the call went to voicemail and her texts to Rachel were still unread.

She grew more and more unsure. Should she be packing? Calling Icelandair? How was she supposed to know if her appearance would irritate a daughter who prided herself on being self-reliant, or if her failure to appear would hurt a daughter who expected her to come anyway?

She thought of the red scarf she had finally bought—and then, with a belated recognition of the obvious, understood. It wasn't the scarf Rachel wanted. She wanted to know that her mother was thinking of her.

Shit. Why was she so dense? She had spent two decades wanting Rachel to want her, and then she had missed the signal.

She needed to talk to Rachel or, if Rachel wouldn't answer, to Judah, who would have seen his sister by now. She looked at her watch. It was the wrong time to call, barely four in the morning in New York. She'd have to wait.

Well, if she wasn't going back to America—at least, not yet— then she had to go somewhere while Mack pondered a new design. It might as well be the Tröllaskagi Peninsula.

The drive along the Eyjafjörður fjord was more spectacular than Cathryn remembered. Green fields rimmed by snow-capped mountains, an occasional farmhouse. Sheep wandered freely. She didn't see many fences and wondered how people knew which sheep were theirs, or if they cared. Perhaps there were so many sheep that it didn't matter.

After a while she saw a small sign on the right that said Hrífandi. She didn't know what Hrífandi meant, but an arrow pointed to a dirt road in the direction of the fjord, so she thought it might be a viewing spot. On impulse, she steered the Kia onto the rutted lane. It led downhill, past wide grassy meadows and purple wildflowers. Across the fjord, Cathryn could see a ridge of towering mountains, streaked with white. Then she rounded a bend and saw a building with a red roof and a row of smaller cottages. She shut off the engine and got out.

The sky was enormous, as blue as the water. In the distance, a dog barked. She looked around, but there was no one in sight. Cautiously, she walked toward the shore. As she neared the water, she could see that the rocks littering the shoreline were actually chunks of lava. Their sharp edges caught the sunlight, flinging it back at her. She had never thought of lava as beautiful but it was, rough and pure. She picked her way to the beach. Slowly, she reached in the daypack for her camera.

Holding the camera aloft, she squatted near a cluster of black shapes. They were luminous in the morning light, the same luminosity she had seen in the apple the little girl held out to her on the church steps. A piece of fruit, a scrap of lava. What if the radiance was in everything, equally?

She remembered a story by Carson McCullers. An old man asks a boy, "Do you know how love should begin?"

Not with another human being, the most difficult and most sacred kind of love. No, he tells the boy. With a tree, a rock, a cloud.

Or a chunk of volcanic debris. She could love it, find the beauty that was already there, waiting to be loved. It was easy to be entranced by the jewels of Diamond Beach, but an artist could love anything, by really seeing it. Penetrating, and then revealing, the life within.

She adjusted her lens and took the photo. Then she looked around. Ripples of silver moved across the water in overlapping arcs. The shadow of a bird fell on the wet sand. The invitation to see was everywhere.

"Halló?"

Cathryn turned and met the aquamarine eyes of an old man in a tweed cap and woolen vest. She rose quickly. "Is this your property? I'm so sorry. I was passing through and wanted to take a picture." She had no idea if he understood English. Everyone seemed to, but she didn't want to assume.

"American?" he asked.

"Yes. American."

He nodded. "I always liked Ronald Reagan. Go ahead and take your picture."

"Is this your farm?"

"Farm and guesthouse. We rent the cottages. To the tourists."

She remembered the sign with the arrow; it was hard to believe that tourists could find the place on their own. "I saw your sign. What does the name mean?"

"Hrífandi? It means breathtaking." He pointed to the fjord, the mountains, the sky.

"A good name. It fits." Then, unable to resist, she asked, "Can you see the northern lights from here?"

"Of course." He straightened his cap. "We have the best view on the peninsula." He peered closely at her. "You find a better viewing spot, you let me know."

Just ask, Cathryn told herself. There was no harm in asking.

"Do you have a card, something with your phone number, in case I wanted to reserve one of the cottages?"

It hardly seemed possible, yet a wild hope flapped in her chest. *Our heart's desire.*

He searched in the pockets of his vest. "Here." He handed her a card. "Halldór. My wife makes the breakfast, though some like to do their own cooking."

"I'm Cathryn," she said. "Katrin." It was folly to think she would come here with Mack, but the man, Halldór, wouldn't know that. She could pretend, just for a minute. "It's a beautiful spot. I'd love to come back."

The old man eyed her sagely. "You'll come back if you want to."

"It's not really up to me." He gave another nod, and Cathryn realized that he was waiting for her to leave. "Anyway," she said, "thank you for your courtesy."

"No problem. An American taught me that. From California."

Cathryn dipped her head in a polite good-bye and made her way back to the Kia. She turned the car around, steered up the pitted track, and returned to the main road. After a few minutes she found a place to pull over. It was barely six in the morning in America—yet surely a mother could be permitted a six-in-the-morning text when her daughter was fleeing a dangerously possessive partner.

Assuming that Rachel had been able to flee. Suddenly she was frightened. She knew nothing about Ryder. Anything could have happened while she was running through the dark streets, straddling Mack, kissing his mouth and eyes.

She swiped to *R*, tapped on *Rachel*, but Rachel's phone was still off. Her fear mounting, Cathryn texted Judah. "Hey buddy. Just trying to find out if Rachel came to the house? That's where she said she was going."

To her amazement, Judah answered at once. "Yep. Elvis has entered the building."

"You're up?"

"Or sleep-texting."

"If you're up, I'm phoning. It's easier."

She was still frightened, but at least Rachel had made it safely. It meant the unimaginable hadn't happened.

She tapped on Judah's number. When she heard his voice, she said, "Why in the world are you up so early?"

"Hey Mom, and hello, and LOL I never went to sleep. Rachel and I hung out, and then I had a massive D-and-D game."

"What do you mean, hung out? She's okay?"

"She's okay. Mad as shit at that asshole boyfriend, but your basic Rachel."

Cathryn exhaled with relief. "You two really hung out?"

"We really did. Go figure. And yeah, she showed up, and she was pretty wired, which you probably knew, so I offered her a joint, and we ended up getting out all the old photo albums, you know, from when we were little? It was pretty hilarious, actually. We even got out those Disney videotapes—*Lion King, Little Mermaid*, who knew you'd saved all that crap?— and the next thing I knew, it was, like, two in the morning, and she was crashing on the family room couch."

Cathryn pictured her children laughing as they flipped through the pages of the albums she had arranged with such painstaking care, a lifetime ago. Halloween costumes. Tricycles and two-wheelers. Christmas mornings.

When we were little. That meant when they were a family of four.

Yet families changed. People died, terrible things happened. If you were unlucky, the damage pinned you to the moment. If you were lucky, you kept going.

"That's great," she told him. "I'm glad you two bonded."

"We kind of did. Who would've guessed?"

She wanted to ask if they had talked about Brian, and how it had felt to see the photos of their father. Then she thought: That was between the two of them. They didn't have to report to her so she could sanitize and explain away anything she didn't want them to feel. They got to have their own memories, their own resentments and regrets.

Her children had connected in her absence; that was the main thing. If she had been there, it wouldn't have happened, Cathryn was certain of that. The certainty let her off the hook, assuring her that she wasn't wrong to have stayed in Iceland. Yet that seemed too easy—or else, she thought, maybe there was more than one hook.

Then she tensed. "Wait. You never went to sleep? Don't you have to go to work today?"

Quickly, she caught herself. Judah was twenty-two years old. He knew he had to go to work.

"Yep, but it seemed better to just power through."

Power through meant do an all-nighter. Well, it was his life. She'd done all-nighters when she was his age.

She exhaled. "Right."

"I got this, Mom."

"Yes, I'm sure you do." She fought the urge to add a sentence of warning or advice. Instead, she told him, "Let Rachel know I called, okay? Tell her I love her."

"I will. And Ryder's a dick. In case you didn't know."

"I did know." Her voice softened. "I love you too, Jude."

"Well, duh."

Cathryn had to smile. Was there ever a more confident assurance of being loved? It meant she hadn't been a complete Snow Queen after all.

Twenty-Six

Cathryn didn't hear from Rachel until late afternoon, when she was back at the hotel. "Just letting you know I'm at the house and I'm okay," Rachel had written, "although BTW you might have mentioned that Jude the Dude was going to be there." Then, in a second message, she added, "It's fine, nice to have some company, even His Weirdness. Anyway, I'll figure out my next step and let you know."

The request was clear. *Give me space.*

Another person who wanted space. Rachel was her child, though, not a grown man. Did she get to decide how her mother was allowed to parent her?

She struggled not to text back: *I'll help you get through this.* That was the Cathryn McAllister way. Shoe repair on prom night, a ride home from a party that was turning sour—she did whatever needed to be done. No Dad? No problem. Mom will fix it.

I'm already on my way.

The irony was that for once she hadn't dropped everything when Rachel called that first time, wanting her to return to New York—to be the familiar reliable parent, on hand just in case. Instead, she'd chosen impulse and risk, the molten and unknown.

Yet she couldn't help wondering: Would things have gone differently if she'd flown back, as she was supposed to, and helped Rachel move into that new apartment?

Of course they would have. If you made a different choice, what came next would be different too. Rachel wouldn't have bought the black lace teddy that Ryder threw in her face; she herself wouldn't have given Mack the idea for the sculpture that she ended up shattering. It was impossible to unweave the tapestry of events and compare them to an alternate sequence that hadn't actually occurred. All you could say was that they would have been different. It didn't mean they would have been better.

Cathryn typed carefully, trying to match Rachel's casual tone. "Glad you're safe. Stay as long as you need to."

"Thanks, Mom," Rachel wrote back. "I'll figure it out. XOXO."

"Take care of yourself, honey. I love you."

"Luv U 2."

Cathryn sank into a chair as the notion that she ought to rush home to rescue her daughter fell away. If she left Iceland, it couldn't be on the pretense that her children needed her. If anything, they needed her to stay away.

Her children weren't begging her to leave. Mack wasn't begging her to stay.

It was up to her, what she herself wanted.

Cathryn thought of the lava she had photographed at Hrífandi, the twisted green treetops at the botanical garden. Her particular eye, opening again.

And Mack. A man with a huge laugh and a huge sorrow, whose art was somehow the portal to her own. She didn't know what he wanted from her, if anything. The only thing he had asked for was a day alone. She checked her phone but there was no text from him. A day was twenty-four hours, and it hadn't even been twelve.

For the second night in a row, Cathryn was alone in her bed.

By noon the next day, her impatience had spilled into anxiety. She kept reliving the events of the previous day, though she had no idea how they had settled in his mind. She had meant to offer solace when she covered her body with his, but it might have seemed like something else to him. With growing dread, she began to wonder if he had seen it as another iteration of her behavior when she returned from the waterfall. Selfish and greedy, a way to manipulate him.

Her anxiety spiked; thirty hours had passed by now. She needed to know what the day alone had brought him, and what it meant for her. She willed her fingers to type, "Wondering how you are and how your work has gone. Shall I come by?"

He replied at once. "Yes."

The same answer he had given her the first time. A single word.

Cathryn flew to the studio and popped the latch. Mack was arranging the tools on the bench, a towel slung on his arm. He looked up at the sound of the door, and smiled.

Her foreboding dropped away. A man who thought she had manipulated him wouldn't smile at her like that.

He began speaking at once, wiping his hands and walking toward her. Cathryn was struck by how much younger he looked.

"Even though I knew better," he told her, flinging the towel aside, "I still spent all day yesterday trying to re-create what was gone, I just didn't want to let it go. And then this morning I was ready." He opened his hands. "It seems so obvious, when I say it. All I can do is whatever will appear for me now."

"It's not obvious at all. It's natural to want to restore what's been lost."

"But futile."

Cathryn released her breath. "Yes."

"It will be something different. That's what I realized."

She couldn't help feeling the tentative offering in his words, the possibility, even if he was only talking about his art. "How can I help?"

"Let me show you the sketches."

He motioned her to the papers he had arranged on the table. Cathryn studied them, uneasy at first, then with a growing comprehension.

He had drawn an oval of slashed and jagged shapes, a mythic landscape ascending from a crater of blue ice. In the center were two shapes, one larger than the other. Their edges were mirrors, halves of a puzzle—as if the smaller shape completed the larger, or was hewn from it. Cathryn couldn't tell if they were stretching toward each other or pulling away.

Mack came to stand next to her. "You remember how I said I wanted to show the iceberg in transition? In movement, not static?"

She nodded.

"What's the most profound transition, other than death?"

"I don't know." Yet she did know, even before he told her. She could see it in the design.

"Calving," he said. "When a piece breaks free and leaves its parent."

"That's what they call it, calving?"

"That's the term. For glaciers and icebergs."

"A calf. It makes it seem so alive."

Emotion welled up in her. The words formed on her lips. She didn't know if saying them would hurt him, or if he needed her to say them for him. She waited, and then she whispered, "Like a mother giving birth."

Mack's voice was as soft as hers. "Just so."

"It's what you were trying to show about the leaves in Costa Rica. The moment of emergence." She swallowed, as a new word swelled to the surface. The enormous and complicated thing she was feeling had a name. No. She couldn't even think it.

"Calving is only the beginning," he told her. "I'm seeing a tableau, all the stages from birth to death, depicted in the ice—because ice is alive, living and growing and dying. I want to take a familiar idea and depict it in a whole new way, through something that people would never associate with birth and death."

Cathryn could feel him sizzling with electricity. If she had ever thought of holding back, it was too late.

"I'd like to start with the calving part," he said. "If you're up for it, that is. I could use an assistant."

"Yes. Of course."

Assistant, lover, friend. They didn't add up to *the woman I was meant to be with*. But here she was.

"Mack." She met his eyes. "Thank you for giving me another chance. This will be wonderful, but the other piece was too."

He lifted a shoulder. "I have to go forward. I don't see another way."

"Tell me what you need."

He pointed to the trays where the frits were laid out. "I want to add color in a different way—one color inside the other, to give a sense of mystery and depth."

Cathryn listened, tried to understand.

"It needs to be seen from the inside and the outside, together. It means the viewer is inside and outside too. Part of it. Because it's his story."

She held very still. She would pay attention, do better this time.

The afternoon light had faded. Cathryn looked at her watch, amazed to find that nearly six hours had passed. With her help, Mack had completed a series of sculptures, working with increasing speed as each piece appeared naturally, seamlessly, from the one that preceded it. Each was different, yet they belonged together.

She held the punti rod as he tapped, and the last piece broke free. He took it in his gloved hands. "I told you about the punti scar, right? The mark that shows where the object was attached to the punti while it was being formed?" Carefully, he angled the figure so she could see its irregular base. "Sometimes people like to smooth it down so it's barely visible, but I'm leaving mine just the way it is, with the mark of its creation."

Cathryn remembered how the punti scar had struck her, when he first showed her. "The bellybutton."

For a few terrible seconds, she was afraid she had gone too far, humanized it too much, but Mack didn't seem to mind. "Exactly," he said. "You wouldn't smooth out a bellybutton." He placed the piece in the annealer, removed his gloves, and strode to the spot near the glory hole where she was standing. "Thank you for everything."

"Pshaw. Just a lowly assistant."

"That's not what I'm talking about." She felt his gaze, piercing her. "You're a lovely woman, Cathryn McAllister."

She didn't know what that meant to him, feared it might not mean enough. And yet she couldn't help the swell of desire that arose in her. She raised her eyes and saw that he felt it too.

She wasn't Deborah, but she was someone, a person. He moved toward her, and she was lost already. She wanted him to lift her, carry her wherever he wanted. There was the chair, where she had used him. The cot, where she had tried her best to comfort him.

He brushed back her hair, kissed her mouth, and opened the top buttons of her shirt. Here? she thought. They were at the wrong end of the room, in the hot shop itself. Mack had never let passion for anything but his art enter the hot shop.

Until now. Heat radiated from the glory hole. Mack's skin was hot too; she could feel it through his shirt. Even his fingers on her nipple felt hot, exciting her even more. She started to say *oh God* and *please* when she felt his body slacken. His neck fell forward, unable to support the weight of a skull that was no longer supporting itself. Then he twitched, as if someone had jerked him awake. "Mack!" she shouted.

He hadn't done that in a long time. No, that was stupid. She hadn't seen him do it; that was all she could say.

He shuddered, releasing her. "Let's get away from the furnace. It's too damn hot."

She followed him to the far end of the room, and he sank into a chair. "It's my own fault, I let myself get dehydrated. I should know better."

Cathryn wanted to admonish him for being so careless and frightening her. Then she thought: Just be helpful. "Well, drink some water. Do you have any cold water?"

He motioned to the curtain behind the cot. "Back there."

She pushed the curtain aside and saw a mini-refrigerator next to a wire rack with a frying pan and a few mismatched dishes. She opened the refrigerator and took out a liter of water. "Here you go."

He twisted the cap and took a long drink. "That's heavenly. Which makes you an angel."

She gave him a wry look. "I'm pretty sure it takes more than opening a refrigerator to merit angelic status."

"Hey, it all depends on the context."

"Seriously. How are you feeling?"

"I'm fine. Trust me, there's nothing to worry about."

"I do trust you."

Mack reached for her hand and pulled her toward him. "Let's have dinner together."

"Really?" The dinner hour was their time apart. It was what he had seemed to want, and she had adapted.

"Yes, really. To celebrate the new series." He pulled her closer. "Indulge me."

Cathryn met his eyes— touched, wary, a jumble of emotions that made no sense. She wanted to say *It's not necessary,* scrambling for a counter-proposal so he wouldn't feel obliged to treat her to an expensive dinner that she doubted he could afford.

She felt the pressure of his fingers, the edge of his knee against her leg, as if his body was trying to tell her something.

He wanted to give her a gift. It wasn't her place to decide if he could afford it. She simply had to accept the gift, without telling him how to give it.

"We'll go to Rub 23," he said. "I've been wanting to go there. Mango chili, citrus rosemary. They even have sushi pizza."

She leaned into the space between his knees. "You're a bully, you know."

"I'll take that for a *yes.*"

Yes. It would always be *yes.*

Cathryn left the hot shop so she could shower and change before meeting Mack at the restaurant. The sun had already dropped below the horizon, and she could sense that the September days were growing short. Soon Einar would return to claim his studio. Mack would pack up his things and move on—to somewhere else in Iceland or, more likely, to his home, wherever that was. She would go home too. It was hard to picture any other outcome.

She wound her way back to the hotel and thought of her real home, back in America. So strange that her children were there together, without her. That had never happened before. Judah wasn't the sort of teenager she had felt comfortable leaving alone, with or without an older sister who made it clear that it wasn't her job to supervise him. By the time he was more-or-less trustworthy, Rachel was in college. Then Judah had left too, and Cathryn had been alone in a big house that remained unchanged for fifteen years. The same pantry with its louvered doors, the same copper kettle on the front burner and row of photographs on the family room wall—Rachel and Judah's school pictures, one for each grade, chronicling their transition from round-face kindergarteners to high school graduates. On the opposite wall, other photos. Soccer, ballet, family vacations. Brian was in some of them.

It had seemed wrong to change anything, as if the least she could do was to preserve her children's history in the walls and furniture. Bodies aged and were altered by experience; fathers died. But her children's home was intact.

Not that everything had been idyllic. Her children fought with each other, and she made mistakes, like every parent. At the time, the mistakes felt monumental, yet she'd been shocked, later, to find out that no one but her remembered—or, if they did, it was only as a goofy anecdote, not as evidence of her unforgivable failure.

She had needed so badly not to fail them, because it was her fault that they lost their father. Her fault, for sending him to the death she had wished for him, just for a moment.

She stopped walking. The hotel was just ahead. A couple was pushing through the revolving glass door; the woman's coat was bright green, like a Costa Rica leaf. The air was windy, brisk with impending autumn.

She had told Mack no, she hadn't played a role in her husband's death; if she hadn't been responsible, then Mack wasn't either. The truth was that she didn't know. Maybe you were responsible for everything, and maybe you were responsible for nothing. It wasn't Snow White's fault that she had fallen into a deathlike sleep; who would expect an old woman in a kerchief to hand you a poisoned apple? Nor could Snow White claim her own awakening. A servant had tripped. What mattered was that she was awake, and what she did next.

Cathryn pulled her jacket tight. Children lived or didn't live. Wives forgave or didn't forgive. You just had to go on.

She knew two things. One was that she would stay here, in Iceland, until it was clear that she had to leave, or until Mack told her to go.

The other was that if she wanted to love Mack—and yes, love was the word that had frightened her so much, earlier that afternoon—then she had to love Deborah too.

Twenty-Seven

Cathryn wrapped her wet hair in a towel and went to check her email before putting on a fresh outfit for dinner. There were two new messages, one from Renata Singer and the other from someone whose name she didn't recognize. She opened Renata's first.

"Hi there," Renata began. "Am I right that you're still in Europe? If you are, then today's your lucky day."

Cathryn leaned forward to read the rest of the message. "Stay tuned for an email from Nelson Whitley," Renata had written. "You might not know who he is, but take it from me, he's Mr. Modern Art in London and just about everywhere else. I gave him your name because of the fantastic job you did for us—and hey, now he owes me one. You can thank me later."

She had no idea what Renata was talking about but assumed that the second email—from Whitley himself—would provide some clarity. She clicked on the message.

"Good afternoon, Ms. McAllister. Renata Singer referred me to you, as I have a rather urgent need for someone with your particular skill set. I realize it's short notice, but I'm prepared to make it worth your while. Please refer to the links below to learn more about what I do. Might you call at your soonest convenience?"

Cathryn skimmed through the links, though it was clear immediately that Whitley was as well connected as Renata had indicated.
He managed several of London's most prestigious art galleries and
was on the boards of all the major cultural institutions. A person
like that had a world of resources at his fingertips. What could he
possibly need from her that was so urgent?

Her curiosity piqued, she dialed the number he had provided.
His voice was polished and crisp. "Nelson Whitley."

"Hello, Mr. Whitley," she said. "This is Cathryn McAllister. I've
just seen your message and I'm calling, as requested."

"Ah yes. Thank you so much." The crispness softened, became
more gracious. "I'll explain my rather terse email, if you have
a moment?"

"Of course."

"I'm reaching out to you because Renata spoke so highly of
your work, so I'll get right to the point." He cleared his throat. "By
coincidence, I have two significant shows opening at two of my
galleries here in London. One features a painter I've been promot-
ing for some time, quite high profile—and quite the prima donna,
between you and me. I'm the only one he trusts to show his work.
The other show will introduce two remarkable new artists, the first
major show for both of them. They're complements—it's striking,
actually, how the work of each enhances the other. In fact, they
bookend my major client beautifully. Three painters. Like the three
fates, only male."

Cathryn gave a vague murmur. She still didn't know what this
had to do with her.

"So," Whitley went on. "Here's the situation. My A-list client—I
won't tell you his name just yet, though you'll no doubt recognize
it when I do—has agreed to do a promotional feature with the two
emergent painters. It's a huge opportunity, as you can imagine.
Genius, across the artistic generations. An endorsement for them,
a sign of altruism for him—making them more bankable, and him
more likable. The problem is that I have a small window in which

to make it happen. Alain—that's the famous one, you can probably figure out his surname—wants to go to the south of France for a few days before the show opens, and what Alain wants, Alain must have. So we need to do the shoot right away."

"What does *right away* mean?"

"In the next day or two. It's a half-day's work, at most. I promised Alain he would have his three days in Antibes before he has to come back for the opening."

Cathryn squeezed the phone between her shoulder and jaw as she unwound the towel from her hair. "You mean you need a photographer in the next day or so? In London?"

"I understand it's an inconvenience," Whitley said. "But Renata thought it might be fortunate timing because you're so close. You're in Scotland, correct? Or is it Iceland? And, as I'm sure you can surmise, she raved about your work. You're an ideal fit, frankly, because you know how to photograph artists as well as art. We'll be placing the feature in all the fashion magazines—along with the Sunday cultural section, of course—so we need someone who can show the relationship between creator and creation."

"Iceland," Cathryn said.

"Iceland," he repeated. "Yes, well, it's two hours and change from Reykjavik to Heathrow. You'd be gone two nights at most. Hardly a blip in your vacation." He coughed delicately. "It goes without saying that you'll be well compensated. All expenses, first class, and triple whatever you normally charge. I quite understand the intrusion into your holiday and the last-minute nature of the request, and I have no issue making up for that. The truth is, Ms. McAllister, you can name your price."

Cathryn's head was spinning. This was much, much bigger than Nora Lang's dance company. Bigger than Shades of Blue, or any client she'd ever had. A shoot like Nelson Whitley was describing would more than make up for the fiasco with Elliott Fischer. Her reputation would not only be saved; it would soar.

She let out her breath. "This is all pretty sudden."

"I understand. It's sudden for me too. I didn't dare make any arrangements until Alain agreed."

She pictured driving to Keflavik, getting on a plane to England. "You're talking about a dash to London and back."

"It needn't be a dash. In fact, if you'd like to stay a few extra days once you're here, I'll be happy to introduce you to some of my colleagues. On my recommendation, I'm sure they would keep you well occupied with work—at the same level of compensation, obviously, and all expenses paid."

She remembered Renata's smug words. "You can thank me later."

Turning Nelson Whitley down would be crazy, but it was happening too fast. She needed to slow it down, think it through.

She held the phone with her left hand, opening the fingers of her right hand to separate the strands of wet hair. "I would have to make some arrangements. May I let you know in the morning?"

It clearly wasn't the answer Whitley expected, but his polite tone masked whatever he might be feeling. "First thing, please. If you can't do it, I need to know."

"Yes, I understand. First thing."

"I'm an early riser."

Cathryn had to laugh. "Point made."

"I'll be frank," he said. "The price of the paintings in both shows will skyrocket if we do this well. It's the kind of human interest feature that people love. So it will be good for all of us— financially, and for our careers. Yours included."

"You've made that point too."

"Sorry. I didn't mean to sound patronizing."

"You were being direct. It's fine."

"We'll speak in the morning, then. Thank you, Ms. McAllister."

She almost said, "Cathryn," but didn't. Switching to first names sounded like a pact, an acknowledgement that they would be working together. "Until the morning."

She disconnected the call. She was certain that Mack would tell her to go. It was the kind of opportunity that a free-spirited photographer with grown children and no obligations would kill for. Why hesitate? She could return to Iceland when it was over.

Yet she knew, with absolute clarity, that she wouldn't return to Akureyri if she went to London. It would make no sense to fly into Keflavik and drive all the way north again, and he wouldn't expect her to.

Her time in Akureyri would be over. It was going to end anyway. Did a few days really matter?

Her heart was pounding so hard that it hurt. She pressed her palm to her chest, as if that would stop the spikes of pain. Her wet hair fell to her shoulders like seaweed.

If she went to London, she would be rewarded. Nelson Whitley would be grateful. She had no doubt that the introductions and future work he alluded to would really happen. And if she didn't go? Renata Singer would be annoyed, although Cathryn was sure she could invent a plausible story. Other than Renata, no one would have to know.

She had told Whitley that she would call first thing in the morning. That meant she could have her night with Mack before she had to decide.

Relieved that she didn't have to settle everything right then, Cathryn dressed and set out for Rub 23, the seafood and sushi restaurant known for its spice mixes that combined flavors in unexpected ways. Mango chili, citrus rosemary.

It was a short walk through the center of the city. The sky was still light, but signs of evening began to appear as she made her way to the restaurant. Squares of lamplight shone in the houses with their sloping roofs and blue and green trim. The air grew cooler.

Then, all at once, Cathryn realized that she'd been mistaken. It was true that she didn't have to call Whitley until the morning, but she herself would have to know tonight. If she planned on leaving tomorrow, she would need to tell Mack—she couldn't just disappear, no more than she could have just disappeared when she ruined the sculpture. If it was their last night together, she wanted to know that, feel that.

The cold she felt had nothing to do with the wind from the fjord. It was coldness itself, pouring down her back.

You hardly ever knew when something was happening for the last time. All you knew was that something you took for granted hadn't happened in a while. She remembered how Rachel and Judah would run into the master bedroom on weekend mornings when they were small, jumping on the bed and pretending to be baby monkeys. Brian would make what were supposed to be gorilla noises, and they would climb on top of him, hysterical with glee. It was one of her happiest memories of their family life. And then one day she realized that Rachel and Judah hadn't done that in long while. She couldn't remember the last time it had happened, not specifically, and that had saddened her.

If this was her final evening in Akureyri, she wanted Mack to know it too. So that—what? He would beg her not to go? She already knew he wouldn't do that. All he had ever told her was, *It's all right if you stay*. Despite their passion, the moments of tenderness, the intimate hours working together in the hot shop—she wasn't the person he was meant to be with.

Cathryn was walking through the heart of Akureyri now. The Bláa Kannan, with its bright red towers. A shop window with the poster of Björk that she kept meaning to tell Rachel about.

The sidewalk was filling with people. A trio of teenage boys, two women with little white dogs, families. Cathryn saw a father carrying a girl on his shoulders. The girl had her arms wrapped around his neck, her cheek resting on the top of his head. The father held her feet; she was wearing red tights with bright pink hearts and tiny pink sneakers. Father and daughter were singing. *Dah-dee-da-deh. Dah-dee-da-deh.*

Brian had carried Rachel in exactly the same way. For a horrifying instant, the Icelandic father had Brian's face; the little girl was Rachel. They were singing *Daddy is dead, Daddy is dead.*

Cathryn couldn't breathe. Blindly, she reached for the side of a building to keep from stumbling. The father and daughter strolled past, disappearing into the crowd.

And then she felt it, after all this time. Brian was dead. Her children's father. The man she had pledged to love and cherish.

The grief she had never felt broke over her with the force of Goðafoss, and she began to sob. The cry, the howl, that had been stifled all those years ago.

It didn't matter whose fault it was—the keys, the brakes, their failure to love each other. What mattered was death itself.

Death was the end. It didn't care who you were, or how well you had carried on. It was forever, and nothing would undo it. She had understood that about little Pétur, who hadn't died. How could she have missed that simple truth about Brian, who had?

A Snow Queen. A girl, asleep in a glass coffin. Feeling no pain, and no joy.

She was awake now, and the enormity of her feeling for Mack meant that she had to feel this too. If you opened the door of your heart, everything came in.

What was said to the rose to make it open, was said to me.

Rumi hadn't revealed what those words were. Each person had to hear them for herself.

"Miss? May I help you?" A young woman in a tan beret put a hand on Cathryn's shoulder, her face full of concern.

Cathryn jerked. Then she met the woman's eyes. "It's all right. I'm fine. But thank you." She gave the woman an encouraging smile. "I'm fine, really."

The young woman looked unconvinced, but she nodded and moved away. Cathryn watched her stride across the street, onto the opposite curb, and pause under the yellow globe of a street lamp. The lamplight caught the curve of her neck and the dome of her cap.

Instinctively, Cathryn felt for her purse. Despite the grief that had overcome her, at last—no, not despite it, but alongside it— she yearned to pull out her camera and capture the image.

A woman in a hat, between gestures. A moment that would never come again.

The radiant perfection of a single moment, held in her hand like an apple or a rock.

Her heartbeat quickened. This was what she loved. Finding her own art, not photographing someone else's.

She didn't want to go to London. Not because of Mack. Because of herself. Because whatever was happening to her in Iceland would stop happening if she left too soon, before it showed her what her art could be.

The woman moved on, and Cathryn didn't take the picture. It didn't matter. There would be other pictures, if her eyes were open.

The restaurant was just ahead, a big red building like a farmhouse with a fan window over the front door. She hurried up to the entrance and went inside. She spotted Mack right away but he was turned to the window, in profile, and didn't see her. She was struck, again, by how different he seemed from everyone else. Larger, more roughly hewn.

There was no need to tell him about Whitley's offer. But since she knew that she wouldn't accept it, it would be wrong not to let Whitley himself know.

She slipped outside again, took out her phone, and hit redial. Whitley answered on the first ring. "It's Cathryn McAllister," she said. "I didn't want to make you wait till morning."

"Ms. McAllister." She could hear the relief in his voice. "I can't tell you how pleased I am."

"I'm afraid that *pleased* isn't going to be the most apt adjective. I didn't want to hold you up, because I'm not able to make it work after all. I won't be going to London."

"Oh no. Are you absolutely certain?"

"I am."

"Is there anything I can do to address whatever is in the way?"

She could almost see the gears turning in his mind. More money? A suite at The Savoy?

"No, it's a private matter."

"I see."

She was sure he didn't. "Thank you for thinking of me, however."

"I appreciate the quick response. Enjoy your holiday."

"I will, thank you." Then she added, "Nelson."

It took her a few seconds to realize that he had already hung up. It was rude, though it didn't really matter; they wouldn't be speaking again. People like Nelson Whitley weren't interested in being refused twice.

Cathryn dropped the phone into her purse and pulled open the door to the restaurant. She had given herself the only gift it was in her power to give. The gift of time.

Twenty-Eight

C athryn was glad she had dispensed with Whitley's proposal so there was no shadow over their dinner at Rub 23. She realized, now, that the question would have been with her the whole evening, tainting every moment with the possibility that it might be one of their last. Instead of making those moments more precious, it would have ruined them. Turning Whitley down had reclaimed the evening.

Mack was expansive, full of energy—discussing each item on their tasting platter with the waiter, making enthusiastic recommendations to people at adjacent tables. It was a Mack she had never seen, the Mack he might have been, or perhaps had been, before he wrapped himself in a cloak of grief and guilt.

They were alike that way, she thought. Oddly, she hadn't made the connection until now. And if Mack had brought her to life, maybe she had done that for him too. Their day in the hot shop, working on his new series, had filled him with an exuberance that was impossible to resist.

Cathryn felt irresistible too. For the first time, she felt inside her beauty, as if it had a meaning.

Around her, the world was sharp with its own beauty. The sheen of paper-thin cucumber next to a circle of glistening salmon. Black poppy seeds, seaweed on a white plate. The old man at the next table, the gray stubble on his cheeks that lifted and danced as he whispered to his grandchildren. Even the brass doorknob, as Mack held the door for her. The night air, the insects and fish and stars that were part of life, even if she couldn't see them. The sureness and power that coursed through her own body.

She saw everything, knew everything—just as she knew that Mack would pull her into an alleyway as they walked to the hotel and press her against the side of a building. He ran his hands down her arms and stomach and thighs, pressing his thumbs through the wrinkled fabric of her skirt, as if he needed to learn her anew, right then. Cathryn tasted the ginger and rosemary and lime on his tongue. The two nights they had been apart were like two lifetimes, or like nothing at all.

Cathryn was drifting off to sleep when the soft click of the closing door made her bolt awake. Mack had left quietly, the way he always did; she would register his departure in a vague drowsy way and go back to sleep. But this time she was wide awake.

The bedside clock said one forty in the morning. That meant it was evening in New York, a reasonable time to call, finally—because she needed to talk to her daughter. *Now*, no more waiting patiently. She needed to hear Rachel's voice and know she was all right.

Cathryn found her phone and propped herself against the pillows. After a dozen rings, she had almost given up when Rachel answered. "Mom?"

"Sweetheart. Oh, I've been longing to reach you. Judah said you were okay, but I've been wanting—"

"Mom," Rachel said again. "This is too weird. I was getting a glass of water, and then I was going to call you. Unless Jude already did?"

"Why would Jude be calling me?"

"I think you need to sit down."

"I am sitting down." Her pulse shot skyward. "What's going on? Did Ryder come after you?"

"No, no, nothing like that. I am *so* done with his shit. I sent him a text that we were finished, and he did that adolescent *good riddance* thing. Anyway, he has no idea where I am." She could hear Rachel take a deep breath. "No, this is something else. It's about the house."

"I'm glad you're all right, sweetheart. It sounds like you're well rid—"

"Mom, stop. You need to listen."

"I am listening."

"Okay." Cathryn waited. Finally Rachel said, "Do you want the whole story or just the bad-news ending?"

"*Is* there a bad-news ending?"

"I'd say so."

"The whole story, in that case." Cathryn braced herself for a tale about a wild party with Judah's friends, loud music, a neighbor calling the police. Then she thought: Damn it. If the police had come to her house, that was it. Judah's scrapes had always been the result of an infuriating passivity, not defiance of the law. If he had crossed that line, he was on his own.

"So Jude and I have been hanging out together," Rachel began. "I know, crazy, right? After all those years, when the last thing I wanted was to even share a last *name*. But he's okay, and it was kind of fun to regress. We even had a pillow fight."

"You did?" Despite the bad news that was yet to come, Cathryn couldn't help smiling.

"We really did. Not to mention singing the Barney song—I mean, that's how insanely regressive we were." Rachel snorted, then grew serious. "It all started because we were cooped up in the house. It's been raining nonstop, and we were literally stuck inside, hour after hour after hour. So finally neither of us could stand it and we got the crazy idea to make s'mores, like we used to do when we were kids, remember? But of course our lovely Whole Foods parent didn't have any graham crackers or Hersey bars, much less a single marshmallow, so we decided to go to the 7-Eleven, the hell with the rain, and get what we needed. It was, like, a ten-minute drive and we had to get out."

Overwhelmed with exhaustion, suddenly, Cathryn was having trouble following Rachel's monologue. She let herself slide down the pillow and stretched out her legs. "So what's the bad-news ending? The 7-Eleven was out of graham crackers?"

"Stop, Mom. Don't be snarky. Just listen."

"I am."

"We decided to take Jude's car," Rachel said, "so he could drive. You know how I hate driving in a downpour, but Jude was, like, I'm cool. He loves driving. Rain, snow."

Cathryn jolted to attention. Not another car accident. Dear God, it couldn't be.

No. Rachel would have said *It's about Jude* instead of *It's about the house*, or *I'm calling from the hospital*. Yet she couldn't halt the terror that was surging through her body. *The brakes failed. The car smashed into an eighteen-wheeler.*

"We were horsing around," Rachel went on. "We weren't even high, just stir-crazy and acting totally juvenile. So I said, 'Let's play car wash.' You remember how we liked to stay in the car when Dad took it through the car wash? Those giant swishy things on the windshield and roof, and all the water and suds pouring over everything? I told Jude, 'Just on the driveway.'" She paused, as if waiting for Cathryn to supply the rest of the story.

"And?"

"And I turned off the wipers. You know, so it was like a real car wash?" Rachel began to talk more rapidly. "I know it was stupid but he was going, like, two miles an hour, and I thought he would keep steering straight ahead."

Cathryn sat up, and the pillow fell to the floor. "Judah was driving in a downpour, and you turned off the wipers?" Fury vied with terror now. She wanted to scream at her daughter, "You're twenty-four, for god's sake, not ten. What the hell were you thinking?"

"We were on the *driveway*." Rachel's voice rose in defiance. "How was I supposed to know he couldn't figure out how to fucking *steer*?"

"What happened?" With the rational part of her mind, Cathryn understood that her children were all right, yet her heart was still racing. "You're both all right? You didn't get hurt?"

"We're both all right. But the car sort of skidded to the left, off the edge of the driveway onto that dirt area, you know, where the giant Sycamore is? Only it wasn't dirt anymore. It wasn't even mud. After all that rain, it was a fucking *lake*. So the tire sank right in, and Judah jerked the car into reverse, you know, so he could gun the engine and get unstuck? Only he couldn't see, and I guess neither of us was really thinking, so he slammed his foot on the gas and rammed into the tree. Then he shifted back into reverse and the car sort of jumped back onto the blacktop."

"Oh Lord. He bashed in the front end of his car?" Cathryn didn't care about the car—all she felt was gratitude that they'd been going too slowly for anyone to be injured—but she knew that Judah cared. "A bad-news ending for Jude, that's for sure. He loves that car."

"That's not the end of the story."

"Oh." Cathryn frowned. "What else happened?"

She could hear Rachel inhale before continuing. "You know how tall that sycamore is, right? I think it's, like, sixty or seventy feet tall. And how it has this super-wide, super-shallow root system? That's why the grass could never grow underneath it, just roots and dirt."

Cathryn didn't think she needed to answer. Of course she knew what the tree looked like. She steeled herself for the rest of the story.

"You wouldn't believe how soggy the ground was from all that rain—it was like a pond. And with the wind whipping it around, the tree must have been as loose as a kid's tooth. All it took was for the car to ram into it." Rachel paused, as if to give Cathryn time to prepare. Then she lowered her voice. "The first thing we heard was the noise. It was like a giant creak. We couldn't see shit, so we got out of the car. I've never seen anything like it. A seventy-foot tall tree slowly, slowly, tilting toward the ground."

"Toward you?" Cathryn's heart leapt into her throat.

"No, no. It was falling in the other direction. So, so slowly—until all of a sudden the whole root ball came right out of the ground, right in front of us, and the tree crashed forward. Like the Titanic, when it went all vertical. You know, in the movie?"

Cathryn pictured the driveway, the house, the tree. "I think you're about to deliver the bad news."

"It fell on the house, Mom. Right on the family room extension."

"No."

"Yes. Right through the roof."

Cathryn closed her eyes. "You said *through* the roof. Meaning, a big hole. In the pouring rain."

"A big hole. In the pouring rain." Rachel waited a beat. "We ran across the front yard, and it was weird because at first I thought, 'Oh, it's okay after all.' Everything looked so normal. But then Jude ran to the other side and he said, 'Holy shit,' and I could see where the tree had smashed into the roof. The sides of the house were fine—that was the weird part—so we opened the back door and went inside."

"You went inside?" Cathryn's eyes flew open. She wanted to yell, *don't go in there,* but of course they already had.

"Water was gushing in through these giant holes in the ceiling," Rachel was saying. "Plus leaves and twigs, huge chunks of dirt, and that sticky black roofing. You wouldn't believe all the shit."

Then she made a sound that seemed almost like laughter. "Judah was totally amazing. He yelled, 'Mom asked me to take care of the house!' Next thing I knew, he'd called 911, but they said wasn't a medical or police or fire emergency, so we had to call a tree service. A tree service, for god's sake. In a goddamn monsoon."

"So what did you do?"

Rachel's voice was full of wonder now. "You should have seen us, Mom. First we started dragging everything out of the family room, into the living room where it was dry. Most of the furniture was too heavy, so we hauled these tarps from the basement—from when you had the house painted?—and we covered the stuff that was too big to move. Then we tried to rescue whatever we could from the shelves, but most of it was too full of water. When we tried to pick up the books and art stuff, it all just fell apart, so we concentrated on the bigger things, like the lamps and that Kwan Yin statue. Then we nailed one of the tarps over the doorway, down to the floor, to keep the water from spilling into the rest of the house."

"You and Judah?"

"It was Jude, really. It was his idea. You wouldn't have recognized him, Mom. He was awesome. *We* were awesome."

Cathryn inhaled as the reality of the sycamore crashing through her family room penetrated her awareness. "You saved some of the lamps, and the pottery?"

"We did. Plus the end tables and the jade horses. And your Kwan Yin statue, like I said."

"The photos? The albums?"

"I'm sorry about that, Mom. I really am. We left everything spread out on the floor the night before, so they were totally wrecked. Along with the Disney videos. And Barney."

"The pictures on the walls?"

"I think they all just smashed to the floor when the tree hit. There was a ton of glass and shit on the carpet. Part of the general ooze." Rachel gave a sigh. "Anyway, the insurance people are coming first thing Tuesday morning. So that's why I'm calling. You need to be there."

Cathryn felt a chill spread through her body, as if she'd been dipped in the icy water of the lagoon. She should have seen that this was where the story led. From the moment Rachel said *it's about the house*, this was the inevitable destination. It wasn't like a job in London that she could decline. This was her home.

"What about the rest of the house?" she asked. "The living room, the bedrooms?"

"The rest of the house is fine. It's just the extension."

"You and Jude are really all right?"

"We're really all right." Rachel's voice caught. "I'm so sorry, Mom. This is a total clusterfuck for you."

Cathryn knew that Rachel was talking about the house. Her daughter had no way of knowing that the worst part of the story was *you need to be there.*

Her children were safe, that was the main thing. She couldn't let daughter feel that she was more concerned about leaving Iceland than she was about their safety.

"It was because ground was so soggy." Rachel sounded on the verge of tears. "Because of all the goddamn rain. We never would have been so stupid if we thought the fucking tree was going to fall."

You don't know what you've done.

Cathryn thought of the guilt that Brian had laid on Rachel's shoulders. She couldn't let that happen to her child, not a second time. "You couldn't have predicted what would happen," she said. "No one could have. And you saved as much as you could, so good on you for that. Good on both of you."

"You would have been so proud of Jude. He was all manly, like, 'Mom's counting on me.' I've never seen him step up like that. It was really something. I almost think the disaster helped him, if that makes sense."

"It does. Maybe it helped you, too."

"Me? How?"

"It helped you see your brother in a new way."

"Ha."

"And see? It made you laugh."

"Don't I laugh?"

Cathryn hesitated. Then she told her daughter the truth. "Hardly ever. You're too busy being hip and sarcastic and wry."

"That sounds so sad."

"It's not too late, honey. You can start now."

"Mom. Please."

"I'm serious. I changed. Why not you?"

"You did change. I can hear it." Rachel let out her breath; she sounded almost shy. "I love you, Mom. You're the best. I hope you know that."

"Dear girl, I love you too. I'll see you soon."

"When?"

Cathryn could hear a little girl's plea in the one-word question and knew she couldn't let an ounce of hesitation mar her reply. "I'll text both of you when I know my flight. I'll probably fly back on Monday morning, if that's okay. You're good over the weekend?"

It was Friday evening—Saturday morning, really. She knew Mack planned to work the whole day on Saturday, but she wanted the evening with him, and the night. It seemed little enough to ask for. On Sunday she would drive to Reykjavik, and from there to the airport.

"Of course," Rachel said. "I'll tell Jude."

And I'll tell Mack.

She had never spoken to him about her children, even after he told her about Deborah, especially after he told her about Deborah. It had seemed too cruel.

The irony struck her, then. Good thing she hadn't accepted the job in London. She would have had to cancel. A private matter, just as she'd told Nelson Whitley.

She ended the call and let her phone drop to the carpet. It hadn't been her choice, after all, about when to leave Iceland. Marshmallows and a rain storm had decided for her.

Oddly, she didn't care about the house. She had preserved it for her children, like an insect in amber, but her children didn't care if the art books were stacked on the coffee table with a precise symmetry or the ceramic figures were aligned on the shelf. The coffee table and shelves were gone. Even their childhood, documented with such meticulous precision in the albums and portraits—gone too. The image of it, anyway. Whatever they retained in their memories was up to them to preserve. Or not.

When she repaired the house, she would remodel. Or maybe she'd sell it. It was only a punti rod, the place where her children had been formed.

She rolled over and pushed her face into the mattress. Time, the thing she thought she could use as she wished, was zipping past, and she wasn't ready.

Five sleepless hours later, Cathryn got up and went to her laptop. There was a nine o'clock flight on Monday morning from Keflavik; with the four-hour time difference, it would get her into JFK at eleven the same morning. Enough time to get home, see her children—and the damage—and then, hopefully, sleep off some of the jet lag and be reasonably alert for the assessor.

She found a Marriott near Keflavik. The airport was a five-hour drive from Akureyri; staying near the airport the night before her flight was the only plan that would work. Eighteen hours from now, she would be hoisting her suitcase into the Kia and leaving Akureyri.

She made the reservations, then texted Rachel and Judah to ask if one of them could pick her up at Kennedy. Then she opened the file with the photos she had taken in Iceland, the ones that were supposed to catapult her into a whole new level of visibility. Mack, hatless, against the turquoise icebergs. In one of the photos, he was turned to the lagoon, framed by the jagged blue landscape; in another, he was looking right at the camera, at her.

The purple flower at the Lystigarðurinn, the photo that had nearly led to a child's death. The pictures of the waterfall at Goðafoss. The chunks of lava on the beach by the fjord.

She sat very still. Everything around her was still too, waiting for her to do the one thing she needed to do, and could do. With a single movement, she rose and found her purse where she had dropped it the night before. She emptied it onto the bed and found the card that Halldór, the owner of the cottages by the fjord, had given her. Hrífandi. It meant breathtaking.

With the card in her hand, she went to the computer again and typed *Aurora Borealis Current Conditions*. She selected *my location* and *tonight*.

Then she emailed Halldór. This one thing, before she had to leave.

Twenty-Nine

Cathryn pulled up in front of the hot shop at ten thirty, after checking out of the hotel and locking her suitcase in the trunk of the Kia. There was no need to return to the hotel. If Mack wouldn't come with her to Hrífandi—a possibility she could barely allow herself to consider—she would go anyway, on her own, and depart for Keflavik from there.

She popped the lock to let herself in. When Mack saw her, his face lit up. "How did you know I needed you this early?"

"I didn't. But here I am."

"Let me tell you my new idea." He waited for her to hang her coat and purse on a hook, then told her, "I need to start the tableau earlier in time. That's what I realized—not when the calf breaks free but sooner. Something dormant, embryonic, like a secret embedded in the parent. You can only see it if you get close, and even then you're not sure. The barest blue, deep in the iceberg. A part of time that hasn't happened yet."

Cathryn caught her breath. Or might not happen. Nothing was certain.

"These are just the models," he went on, "because you're right, I need to make this really large, something people can experience. I'll have to do that when I get home."

She met his eyes. "Where's home?"

"Vermont. A little town near Brattleboro, just over the New Hampshire border."

She had never asked; she hadn't wanted to think about his life outside of Iceland. It struck her, suddenly, that maybe he had felt the same way. Not indifference, but the wish to simply be here, in the present.

"What about you?" he asked.

"About forty-five minutes north of Manhattan." It seemed like a natural moment to tell him what had happened to the house, but she didn't. He wanted to make the new piece, and she wanted that for him. There was no need to dampen his eagerness. The family room would still be demolished when they finished the new sculpture. She would still be leaving Iceland.

She pulled her sweater over her head and twisted her hair into a knot. "What do you need me to do?"

"Just follow me. You'll know."

It was true, Cathryn realized. She was able, now, to anticipate his movements and sense what he needed. A real assistant, not a woman looking for an excuse to linger. A person who could watch and listen and see.

The new piece was small, but, to Cathryn, it was the loveliest thing he had ever made. A curled shape, like a sleeping bird, rimmed in flame-blue and fading to a luminous, nameless hue. She opened the annealer, and he placed the figure inside. "I'd like it to cool slowly," he said. "We'll see how it looks tomorrow."

She would be on her way to Reykjavik tomorrow. Like the paperweight, she wouldn't be there to see how it came out.

"Mack." Cathryn tried to steady her racing heartbeat. "I have to go back to New York."

He looked confused. "Why? Did something happen?"

"It did." She told him about the sycamore, about Rachel and Judah, the children whose names he had never heard and whose existence she had withheld. "I'm the homeowner, and I have to be there. I can't ask my children to handle this." She swallowed. "And I need to see them. Something happened, when they were together. Judah grew up. Rachel laughed." She knew Mack couldn't possibly understand what that meant, but she needed to share it with him anyway, the part of herself she had hidden.

"It sounds like they did a great job. And like you got lucky. If the tree had fallen on the center of the house, the damage would have been much worse."

Cathryn stared at him. "Lucky," she repeated. "I suppose."

He held her gaze. "When do you need to leave?"

"I have a flight from Keflavik first thing Monday morning. I'll drive down tomorrow, stay at a hotel by the airport."

"So we have today."

Her steadiness dissolved. "We have today."

"Cathryn—"

"And tonight." She had to say it quickly. "There's something I want to do tonight, with you. We talked about it the first day I was here." She fought to keep her voice from quavering. "Our heart's desire."

If he didn't know what she was walking about, she would feel like a fool, and it would be better to leave right now and go to Hrífandi alone. But he did know.

"The northern lights."

"There's a place we can go to see them," she said. "I found it by accident, and then I looked on one of the aurora websites and tonight is supposed to have really wonderful conditions."

"A place? You mean, a special viewing spot?"

"A cottage. Where we can stay the night, because you can't know exactly when the aurora will appear. It could be midnight or three in the morning." She knew what she was asking for. It seemed so little, and it seemed like too much.

Mack looked away. Seconds passed, and the thundering in her chest grew so loud she was sure he could hear. If this was so difficult, that itself was an answer, and she needed to turn and walk away before he saw the humiliation that was coursing through her.

Instead, he took her hand. "Come. Let's sit down." He kept her hand in his as they walked to the wooden table, the same table where the sculpture that looked like a dancer had rested for its brief existence. He motioned for her to sit beside him. "It's exactly right," he said. "We need to have that, and we will."

"I'm hearing a *but* at the end of that sentence."

"It's more of an *and*."

"Meaning?"

"Meaning that I need to explain why I haven't wanted to spend the night with you—no, that's not right. Why I *haven't* spent the night with you. Of course I've wanted to. In case it happens while we're together."

"It?" Her wariness shifted to alarm.

"I get these episodes at night," he said. "It's like I'm nowhere, not even in my body, and I wake up gasping for air, as if I've forgotten how to breathe. They're probably nightmares, but I don't have any memory of what they're about. I didn't want to frighten you—and, to be honest, I didn't want you to see me like that. I never know when it's going to happen. It started in the last couple of years, so I'm sure it's psychosomatic."

"Psychosomatic or not, it sounds scary."

"I've gotten used to it. That's why I sleep alone."

Her voice was soft. "But not tonight."

"No, not tonight."

Her eyes filled with tears at the three simple words. He was trusting her with this. How strange that they had each revealed something so important on their very last day.

Then she had a troubling thought. "Is it related to those daytime episodes? When you sort of blank out?"

"That's electrolytes. Dehydration. This is psychological."

"How do you know?"

"Like I said, they're nightmares. Not something I wanted you to see, but maybe you won't. It doesn't happen every night."

Cathryn wanted to insist that he needed a medical opinion, but how could she? She didn't have a claim on him. By tomorrow afternoon she would be gone.

"Tell me about the cottage," he said. "Do you think it might be free on such short notice?"

She gave him a smile that felt both clever and shy. "I already requested it, although I do need to check and make sure." She went to get her phone, but there was no email from Halldór, not even *sorry, we're all booked.* "That's odd. Maybe I should call." She retrieved the card from her purse and tapped out his number.

When she explained who she was, Halldór said, "Yes, I remember you, the one who knew Ronald Reagan. But I didn't see an email. Then again, I don't use the email much, we have such terrible service here. It's one of the few places in the country with poor internet, wouldn't you know?"

"I was wondering about a cottage," she said. "For tonight."

"Now that's a bit of luck," he told her.

Luck, Cathryn thought. The word seemed to mock her.

"Normally I wouldn't," Halldór said, "not on a weekend. But it's the shoulder season and most of the tourists are gone, so I do have one. It's the farthest from the farmhouse—that's where I live, with my wife. More of a hike for breakfast, which some don't like, but it has the best view. Right on the water."

"That's perfect," Cathryn said.

"You're not needing the Wi-Fi, are you?"

"No, no Wi-Fi."

"As I said, it's not very reliable. But most don't care. They come for the setting." He paused, and Cathryn could hear the pride in his voice. "The cottage has a full kitchen, you know, and a private hot tub on the porch. And, of course, the breathtaking view."

"Yes. You told me that Hrífandi means breathtaking."

"That it does. I named it myself."

"It sounds heavenly." She glanced at Mack and mouthed *private hot tub.* "So yes, please. For tonight."

"I'll take your credit card, then, to hold the cottage. When will you arrive?"

She knew Mack would want to keep working until there was no more light. The series was pouring out of him, and she would help for as long as she could. "Not till early evening, most likely. After seven."

"Well, that's no good," Halldór said. "I don't like to interrupt my dinner. But you can go ahead and give me the passport number now—along with the credit card, as I mentioned—and I'll leave the last cottage unlocked for you. That way, just come when you like, no need to stop by the farmhouse."

"Very good," Cathryn said. Passports were required wherever you stayed; she had never heard of someone taking the information over the phone, but if the old man wanted to do it that way, it was fine with her.

She found her purse and gave Halldór the numbers. Mack reached into his pocket for his wallet, pulling out a Visa card, but she put up a hand.

"Will there be another guest?" Halldór asked.

"Yes, there will."

"Another American?"

"Yes, American."

"I'll need that passport too."

"Of course."

She motioned to Mack. "They need your passport." He handed it to her, and she read the number aloud. His photo, birth date. Henry Malcolm Charbonneau. She'd almost forgotten that was his name.

When she got off the phone, he said, "You don't need to foot the bill for this."

"I do," she said. "I'm going to do something wonderful with my northern lights photos. I need the business deduction."

He grabbed her hand again and pulled her toward him. "You're a lovely liar."

"I'm not a liar. I'm really going to do that. My daughter's been nagging me about it ever since I told her I was going to Iceland."

"Aha. Is that why you came here?"

She was standing between his legs now, looking down at him. Her heart was beating madly.

She put her hands on either side of his head, spreading her fingers across his temples. She could feel the rhythm of his blood. "I came here for you."

Thirty

The cottage was exactly as Halldór had described. The last in a row of bungalows that led from the farmhouse to the edge of the fjord, it was angled away from the others, as if turning its back on them and claiming its privacy. The porch faced the water and the snow-topped mountains. Overhead, an enormous sky was strewn with stars. No haze, no clouds, only a sliver of moon. A perfect night for the aurora.

Mack lifted the lid of the hot tub, and Cathryn peered in. "My goodness," she declared. "When Halldór said *little* hot tub, he wasn't joking."

Mack put his hand on her waist. "I have an idea how we can both fit."

She remembered the first time they had made love, in the thermal pool at Mývatn; she knew Mack was remembering too. The cedar hot tub on the porch seemed like a fitting site for the last time.

It wasn't like the baby monkey game, when she hadn't been sure. She knew this was the last time.

"Really?" Cathryn tossed her head. "Have you worked it all out, à la Archimedes?"

To her surprise, the remark made him angry. "Why are you doing this?"

"Doing what?"

"Acting so brittle and false."

"What do you want me to do? Tell you how sad I am?"

"Cathryn." He turned her around and took her in his arms. "Let's just be here, together. Let's sit in this sweet little hot tub and watch the aurora."

"I know. I'm trying." Cathryn told herself not to spoil the short time they had left. She lifted her chin and blinked away the tears. "I need to set up my camera. And unpack a bit."

"All right. I'll scope out the place." He gestured at the hot tub. "And preheat the oven."

"Yes. Good." She went back to the car to get her daypack and the bag of groceries they had picked up in Akureyri. The farmhouse provided a hot breakfast, but she wanted to have breakfast with Mack in the cottage. To wake up next to him, make breakfast for him.

They had taken his Jeep. The Kia was parked in Akureyri, in its usual spot in front of the studio; her suitcase was in the trunk, ready for the flight home. It didn't make sense to drive to Hrífandi in two cars, since she had to backtrack nearly all the way to Akureyri to pick up the Ring Road that would take her to the airport.

Cathryn put the groceries away and got out her camera. She knew that capturing the aurora required the commitment of a hunter stalking its prey. The writhing emerald columns might illuminate the sky for twenty minutes or dissipate in seconds. They might never appear. There was no way to predict.

She set the aperture, ISO, and shutter speed. It was already dark so they could, theoretically, start their vigil. But she didn't want to, not yet. She wanted some time together first, in their temporary little home. She put the camera on the kitchen counter, next to her wallet and phone. Then she went to look for Mack.

He was on the porch, dipping his hand in the hot tub. "It fills up fast." He looked up at her. "Shall we?"

Cathryn's eyes met his. *Yes.* The word he had used to summon her, though she was already on her way.

She had said *yes* to him from the very beginning. Somehow he had opened her heart, and here she was. She hadn't expected to fall in love in Iceland. She had come here on a whim because it seemed regal and safe, not a place that would sear her with such passion and tenderness and pain.

"You're hard to resist."

"Then don't."

She opened her shirt, shook it off, and drew the tank top over her head. Then she undid her jeans, stepping out of them as she kicked off her shoes. When she was naked, she lifted a foot over the edge of the tub, then pulled it back. "Whoa, this really *is* hot. Let's wait till it cools down a bit."

"Don't back out now," he said. "I hear that making love in a hot tub is amazing."

Cathryn felt a surge of longing—for that day at Mývatn, when time didn't matter; for yesterday, an hour ago; for anything except tomorrow, when their time would be over. She ached with sorrow and desire and a feeling that had no name.

Mack took off his clothes and stepped into the tub. He lay back against the edge and reached for her hand. "Come to me."

She looked at him, the most beautiful man she had ever seen. Then she put her foot in again, wincing at the heat that really did seem excessive. She slid on top of him, opening her mouth to his. Opening to him forever.

She felt him jerk, and then his mouth went slack. Frightened, she pulled away. "Mack?" *Shit.* It was one of those dizzy things. She should have made him drink a glass of water before getting in the hot tub.

She waited for him to shiver and come out of it, the way he always did. Instead, he gave a low moan. "Mack!" She grabbed him under the arms, thinking she might shake him out of it. His head lolled back.

"Mack." Jesus. God.

He lifted his head and looked at her. She thought *yes, he's all right, thank goodness.* She wanted to weep with gratitude.

"Deborah," he whispered. "I'm so very sorry."

Cathryn stared at him. Time, the very thing she'd been dreading, no longer existed. It was now, and it was forever. She didn't know if he was seeing her or Deborah, if he even knew she was there.

She brought her face close to his. "I forgive you, my darling," she said. "With my whole heart." He looked into her eyes, took in her forgiveness. Nothing moved, not even the air.

Then his body went slack. She could feel him starting to slip under the water. *No.* Her hands were still under his arms. She grabbed his flesh, struggled to lift him. He was little Pétur, needing her to yank him out of the fountain. A boy in a red jacket who couldn't, mustn't, fall into the raging water at Goðafoss. Only he wasn't. He was a grown man, enormous, leaden, sliding out of her grasp. "No!" she screamed. With a desperate strength, she heaved his shoulders and chest over the side of the tub.

She scrambled out of the water and knelt beside him. Putting her hands on his face, she tried to breathe into his mouth. Nothing. Again. Nothing. *Don't give up.* She had to keep doing it, and eventually it would work. She pushed on his chest, commanding him to breathe. His head lolled to the side, eyes open and unseeing. His chest didn't move. She was shaking now, her teeth clattering. This couldn't be happening. She had pulled him out of the water, something that seemed impossible; she could do whatever else he needed her to do.

Terror coursed through her. She needed to get help, but she couldn't leave him. What if he slipped back in? She looked around the porch, her eyes wild, until she saw the valve to let the water out of the tub. She flipped it open and heard the rumble of the drain. With a sob of anguish, she pressed her body to Mack's. And she knew.

It was the stillness. Without breath, the body was empty. The same breath that he blew into the molten glass to give it form and beauty and life.

She covered him with every part of her that she could, knowing he wasn't there, doing it anyway. The horror, and the impossibility, poured over her.

Then she thought: What if I'm wrong? What if I can still save him?

She pushed herself off the floor and ran to the kitchen, grabbed her phone. There was no service. Halldór had warned her.

Fuck. She ran back to the porch, grabbed her jeans and shirt, pulled on her shoes. Ran into the night, to the farmhouse where Halldór had a land line.

She raced across the grass, along the edge of the fjord. Then something made her look up. There, overhead, emerald and magenta and blue, spreading across the sky like spilled paint. Jade-green dancers, lifting their arms. Luminous and surreal, burning its glory into her.

She began to sob, great wracking sounds that filled her body. She couldn't run anymore, could only stagger toward the farm-house as the aurora blazed around her. Hrífandi, a place that meant breathtaking. It had taken his breath, stolen it right out of his body.

She banged on the door, screaming, until Halldór let her in. A gray-haired woman stood behind him, wrapped in a plaid robe. "Call an ambulance!" she shrieked.

"What's going on, please?"

"Someone is in grave danger. We need an ambulance, right now."

"Your companion? In one of my cottages?"

"*Yes*, in one of your cottages." Oh, for god's sake. She wanted to grab him and make him understand how urgent it was. If it was urgent, it meant there was still a chance.

"I'll call the Red Cross," Halldór said. "They oversee the emergency service."

He motioned her inside. She needed to run back to Mack, so she shook her head.

The old man's look was sharp. "Was there an accident?"

Cathryn made herself calm down enough to speak. "He just—I don't know. A seizure, a heart attack." She started to shake again. "Please. He's not breathing."

Halldór dipped his head. Behind him, the woman said something in Icelandic, and Halldór retreated into the house. Cathryn could hear him talking in the phone. Icelandic again, so she couldn't understand. Her heart was crashing through her flesh.

He reappeared and told her, "Six or seven minutes."

"Six or seven minutes? That's insane."

He shrugged. "The nearest police station is in Dalvik."

"Why do we need a police station? All we need is an ambulance."

He gave her another keen look. "It's the law, here in Iceland. Especially since you're foreigners."

Cathryn had no idea what he was talking about. "I'm going back to the cottage." Before he could reply, she fled across the grass. The northern lights slapped the sky overhead, lighting her way.

When the ambulance came, it was accompanied by a police car. Cathryn rose from her vigil by Mack's body to greet them, though an ambulance seemed pointless. She had covered Mack with a bed-spread; she didn't want him to lie there, so naked and cold. The water in the tub had drained away while she ran to the farmhouse, and the night air was frigid.

"Thank you for coming." Her words sounded inane; their arrival hardly mattered anymore.

The medic knelt by Mack's side and checked for a pulse. Then he raised his eyes to Cathryn's. "You were with him when it happened?"

She nodded.

"Are you next-of-kin?"

Next-of-kin? "No," she answered.

"Do you know who next-of-kin might be, and where we can reach them?"

"I'm sorry, I don't."

"We'll have to contact the consulate, in that case."

The police officer stepped forward. "I should explain, ma'am. In Iceland, if someone dies when he's not under hospital care, we need to investigate."

Cathryn looked from one man to the other. "Investigate what?"

"The cause of death, when there was no physician present."

"I told Halldór." Her voice dropped to a whisper. "Something with his heart. He just—stopped."

"I'm sorry, ma'am," the officer said. He cleared his throat, then smoothed an eyebrow with his forefinger. "We need to follow the law."

Cathryn's eyes darted around the porch. What did that mean? Suddenly she was afraid. "I don't understand."

The medic answered. "We have to transport him to the hospital in Akureyri. A doctor needs to examine the body. And someone will want to talk to you."

"I'll need to file a report," the officer added, "and request a forensic autopsy."

She fixed on the word Akureyri, where they were taking him. Surely they wouldn't leave her here, alone?

The medic's face seemed kinder, so she directed her plea to him. "Can I come with you? Ride in the back with him? With Mack."

He gave a rueful shrug. "It's too small, just a van, really. And it's not permitted."

"If you have a car," the police officer said, "you can drive it, and I'll follow behind you."

They had brought Mack's car, the Jeep. The Kia was in front of the studio.

"Yes. All right." She was in a daze, yet understood that she had no choice. She looked around for Halldór, but he wasn't there.

"You can collect your belongings while we load the body," the medic told her.

The body. She wanted to punch him, then. It was Mack. *Mack.* And they were taking him away from her. She gripped the man's arm, digging her fingernails into the soft flesh above his elbow.

"I'm sorry, ma'am," the officer said. "It would be different if you were a family member."

No, she wasn't a family member.

She was no one.

Thirty-One

When they arrived at the hospital in Akureyri, the ambulance pulled up to an emergency entrance and two men in scrubs carried the gurney inside. Cathryn waited in the Jeep, wanting to follow but understanding that she couldn't. The police officer stopped his car behind hers, got out, and walked over to the Jeep. "You need to park over there," he said, indicating a half-empty lot. "I'll meet you in the lobby."

"All right." She was absurdly grateful that they were letting her inside, letting her have a place. She had started to panic when they took him away from the cottage—him, Mack, his body—but felt a bizarre reassurance to be sandwiched between the ambulance and the police car on the drive back to Akureyri.

The police officer led her to a small office. Cathryn wanted to ask if she could see Mack, but the grimness on his face told her to wait. "We'll need your help with some of the forms," he said. He pointed to a chair, and she sat down.

"I'm Inspector Magnusson," he told her, settling across from her and smoothing an eyebrow with his forefinger. A quirk, she thought. Mack's word.

"It's my job to write a report," he continued. "Order an autopsy, contact the US Consulate in Reykjavik. I have to wait for a doctor to issue a pronouncement of death before I can do any of that, so that's why we're here."

Cathryn was relieved that Magnusson spoke such fluent English. She wanted to help him. It seemed like something she could do for Mack—and for herself, to keep from shattering.

"Can you tell me what happened?" Magnusson asked. "You were the only witness? No one else was there?"

"No one else. Just the two of us."

"Can you tell me, then, in as much detail as you can recall?"

Cathryn looked at the man across from her. He had a broad flat face, expressionless eyes below the dark brows. Was she really supposed to share their last moments with this person? To tell him: "We were in the hot tub, naked. We were about to make love." To tell him that Mack had wanted Deborah, and she had given him Deborah.

No, those moments were hers. She told him, simply, how Mack had slumped forward and gone blank, the way he sometimes did.

"Did he have a medical condition?"

"I think he might have, but I don't know what it was."

"You were traveling in Iceland together?"

"No, not really."

Magnusson lifted his other eyebrow. "Not really? You didn't come here together, on a holiday?"

"No, nothing like that. We met here."

His expression was neutral now, revealing nothing. "How long, exactly, have you known Mr. Charbonneau?"

Cathryn met his gaze, determined not to apologize. "A few weeks." She knew what he was thinking. Single American woman, on the make. Well, fuck him.

Magnussen made a few notes. Then he sat back and folded his hands on the desk. "As I think I mentioned, in Icelandic law, any death that doesn't take place in a hospital or under a doctor's supervision has to be investigated by the police. So there's that. And then there are complications when it's a foreigner, especially if the person has no family member with him in the country."

Her head began to spin. "What are the next steps? You said something about the consulate?"

"It's tricky," he answered, "because they won't be open until Monday, not unless it's urgent, someone here on government business, that sort of thing, and it's only Saturday." He looked at his watch. "Actually, it's Sunday. In any case, everything has to wait until Monday morning. Luckily, Mr. Thorgrimson gave us your passport numbers, so we'll be able to trace Mr. Charbonneau's passport application to see if he indicated an emergency contact."

Cathryn realized that Mr. Thorgrimson meant Halldór. She tensed, wondering if Deborah was Mack's emergency contact.

"Then there's the forensic autopsy," Magnusson went on. "We need to establish the cause of death." His eyes fixed on hers. "Suffocation. Drowning. Poison. It could be anything."

Cathryn felt as if he had struck her with an ax. Was the man out of his mind? Making a sick joke?

The steel in his eyes told her that he was entirely serious. "What are you implying?"

He shrugged, though she didn't believe for an instant in the casualness of the gesture. Not now, after the coldness in his eyes. "That I have to do my job. As an officer would in America." She didn't answer, so he went on, "Unfortunately, that task will probably have to wait as well. Medical examiners don't like to do autopsies on Sundays. It's church, you know. So we won't have any answers about the cause of death until Monday afternoon, the earliest." He ran a forefinger along his eyebrow again. "At which point we'll know more about how to proceed."

This was insane. Was this man actually suggesting that she had a role in Mack's death? It took everything she had not to scream.

Then she remembered something else. "I have a flight to JFK on Monday morning."

Magnusson shook his head. "That won't be possible. I'm sure you can appreciate that you can't leave the country until this is settled." She stared at him in disbelief. "Not that we expect you would try," he added, "but we've put an alert on your passport. It's standard procedure. So you wouldn't be able to get checked in for any flight. Just to be clear."

Cathryn could scarcely breathe. All she wanted was to wake up from this nightmare. If she couldn't do that, then she wanted to be left alone to cry.

Finally, she whispered, "Can I see him?"

"I'm sorry. I'm about to file an order for a forensic autopsy."

And then she did cry. Great heaving sobs that felt as if they would never end.

After a minute, Magnusson coughed, signaling that they needed to move on. "We have your phone number from Mr. Thorgrimson, so we'll call you on Monday when we know more. I'll give you my number as well, in case you think of anything we might want to know." He stood and reached into his pocket for a card, offering it to her across the desk. "For now, you're free to go, as long as you remain in Akureyri."

In other words, she was dismissed. They weren't going to let her stay here, near him, but they weren't going to let her go home either.

"There's no need for you to remain at the hospital," Magnusson said. "I thought it was a convenient place to talk, since I had to come here anyway—to verify that the deceased arrived safely, that is."

Safely? Arriving dead wasn't arriving safely.

Magnusson coughed again, clearly waiting for her to leave. And where was she supposed to go? Not back to the cottage. There was no hotel to check into, not at two o'clock in the morning.

Then she knew. The only place she could bear to be.

"Very well," she said, taking the card and dropping it into her purse. She pushed out her chair, rose, and left the hospital.

She drove through the dark streets to the studio and parked the Jeep behind the Kia. She popped the lock as he'd taught her to do, and let herself into the building.

Mack was everywhere. The tools lined up on the bench. The blue-and-white sculptures arrayed on the shelves. She looked at the closed door of the furnace, and the unutterable thought bloomed in her mind that she had refused to let herself think.

That it was her fault. She had shut her eyes to the obvious fact that there was something wrong because she didn't want to act as if she had a place in his life, a role, that wasn't hers. But Mack's episodes, no matter how brief, weren't normal. She had known that, even if he refused to.

Then she told herself: No. Just because something horrible happened, it didn't mean it was someone's fault.

She gazed around the hot shop, taking each thing in with a piercing clarity. It hurt too much to be here, but this was where she needed to be. She walked to the end of the long room, to the cot, and stepped out of her shoes. Then she lay down on the place where Mack had lain, smelling him, feeling his presence. She wrapped the blanket around her body, the same blanket that had covered his, and spent the night with him, at last.

In the morning she texted Rachel and Judah, explaining that she wouldn't be flying back on Monday after all. A friend of hers had died unexpectedly and they wouldn't let her leave until all the paperwork was in order. They would have to postpone the assessor; she'd be back in touch when she knew more.

Then it struck her: Why didn't *they* talk to the assessor? They were direct witnesses and could tell him more than she could. She could follow up later, sign whatever had to be signed. Until then, there was no reason Rachel and Judah couldn't meet with him. She wrote a second message, telling them to get things started.

Meanwhile, she had to get through today. According to Magnusson, she would be here at least another day, perhaps longer, so she returned to the hotel where she had stayed before. The manager looked surprised to see her. "Do you want the same room?" he asked. "I believe it may be vacant."

The thought made her ill. "No. A different room, please."

She unpacked the Kia, took a shower, and booted up her laptop. There were pages of links for *forensic autopsy* and *what happens if a US citizen dies in Iceland?* Transfer of funds to cover the cost of shipment. Special caskets, since embalming wasn't permitted. Cremation only on Tuesdays. It was hideous, but she kept reading. Then she saw a paragraph that caught her attention.

"In cases where the deceased US citizen has no close family in Iceland at the time of death, a US consular officer will notify the next-of-kin, secure the deceased US citizen's personal effects, and assist in arrangements for the body. Pending instructions from the next-of-kin, the consular officer takes possession of all personal effects such as jewelry, personal documents, clothing, and other items belonging to the deceased."

Mack's art. They needed to treat it carefully; she had to tell someone how fragile glass could be. And the tools? No, they were Einar's. Did Magnusson even know where Mack had been staying? It wasn't a hotel where you had to register your passport. No one would know about the studio unless she told them.

Of course she would tell them. And someone would have to tell Einar. But before she phoned Magnusson, there was something she needed to do.

She walked the familiar route from the hotel to the hot shop. It was Sunday morning. She could hear the church bells, the pipe organ from the Akureyrarkirkja on the hill. Quietly, she let herself into the building and went to the annealer. The little piece was still there, the last thing they had made together, the infant iceberg, just before the glacier released it into the world. She had gotten to see how it looked, after all. Mack was the one who hadn't.

It was just as beautiful as she knew it would be. Carefully, she turned it over and yes, there was the punti scar. *I was here.* A glass artist left his mark on everything he touched.

She took a sheaf of dry newspaper and wrapped it around the glass figure before placing it in her daypack. She left everything else.

It was Mack's art. It belonged to the world, not to her.

Thirty-Two

Cathryn called Magnusson and told him about the studio. He thanked her and asked if she knew how to reach Einar. She didn't; she didn't even know Einar's last name. Then it occurred to her to mention Renata Singer and Shades of Blue. As Mack's representatives in America, they might have additional information.

"A useful idea," Magnusson said. He seemed friendlier than he had the night before, or maybe he thought a friendlier tone would make her more forthcoming. She didn't know and didn't care.

The hours passed with excruciating slowness. What was she supposed to do on a Sunday afternoon in a town whose every street she had already explored—without Mack to greet her at one o'clock, without Mack himself, the reason she was here? She thought of going to the hot shop again but didn't dare, now that she had told Magnusson about it. There was nowhere to go.

She hadn't expected Magnusson to call until Monday afternoon, but he phoned late Sunday evening. "I wanted to let you know," he said, "that we were able to run a search and find a scan of Mr. Charbonneau's passport application. He did indeed list an emergency contact—which serves, for our purpose, as next-of-kin. So we'll be reaching out and, hopefully, that will get matters underway. Aside from the investigative aspect, there are steps, documents, things that need to happen."

Cathryn was desperate to know who the emergency contact was, but she managed to murmur, "That's good. Thank you for telling me."

Magnusson wasn't finished, though. "Here's what I'm wondering," he said. "Sometimes the family member appreciates having a local contact to move things along, especially since there's always a time factor. We don't embalm here in Iceland, so decisions have to be made rather quickly. A face-to-face conversation with the mortuary can be quite helpful."

Cathryn was too stunned to be diplomatic. "I don't understand. On the one hand, you view me as a murder suspect. On the other hand, you want me to be a go-between for the family."

"I'm just covering all the possibilities. It won't be both, I assure you."

"Well, let me know when you decide."

"I will, Ms. McAllister." Before she could think how to answer, he had ended the call.

Instead of reassuring her, the conversation had unnerved her even more. She yearned to call someone and pour out everything she was feeling, the horror and emptiness and disbelief, but there was no one to call. Business contacts, but no real friends. Siblings she never spoke to. Her own daughter had called her a Snow Queen.

She thought of Rachel, and the fragile new connection they had forged. If only she could call her. *Hold me up.* You couldn't do that to a child—not unless she had already spent years coming to you for solace. But that hadn't been their way.

We'll do better, she vowed. I'll do better.

The hours were heavy as lead. Finally, at noon on Monday, Magnusson phoned again. "We've spoken with Mr. Charbonneau's younger brother," he said. "Paul Charbonneau, of Rhode Island. He was quite shocked, as you can imagine—to learn of his brother's death, obviously, and to learn that he was listed as next-of-kin. Apparently, the two had lost touch in recent months."

A brother? It was a reprieve—and, oddly, a disappointment. "He listed a brother on his passport?"

"It was a new application," Magnusson offered. "Submitted about a year ago. His old passport had expired."

That made sense. Deborah had divorced him by then.

"The medical examiner wants to speak with him," Magnusson continued. "There are some questions, light he may be able to shed. For now, however, I wanted to know if you might be willing to speak with Mr. Charbonneau—Paul Charbonneau, that is—if it seems indicated."

What Magnusson meant was, if we decide that you weren't a party to Mack's death.

It was all too oblique. "Whatever I can do to help."

Her heart hurt. She needed Mack to be alive. If she couldn't have that, she needed to go home.

The next call, late Monday afternoon, was from Benedikt Jakobson, the pathologist. "Ms. McAllister?"

"Yes," she said. "Do you have any news?"

"I do. Do you think you might be able to come in?"

"To the hospital? Of course."

As if she had anything else to do. As if they weren't keeping her in Akureyri, waiting for this very call.

She met Jakobson in his office. He was young, with a blonde beard and a wiry frame. Next to him, Magnusson, who was there too, looked bovine and coarse.

"Ms. McAllister," he said, shaking her hand. "Please sit down."

She took a seat on a black vinyl chair, forming a triangle with the two men. Jakobson sighed. "It's tragic to learn things when it's too late. But at least it allows us to make a diagnosis and determine the cause of death."

Cathryn waited. Magnusson's presence alerted her to say nothing.

"Paul Charbonneau was exceedingly helpful," Jakobson said. "I admit that we might have spun our wheels—that's the expression, yes?—without his input." He turned to the policeman. "So much was ambiguous. I think we can agree on that. A robust man, in excellent shape. As far as anyone knew, disease-free."

He returned his attention to Cathryn. "We ascertained that it was cardiac arrest, but that can have many causes. In Mr. Charbonneau's case—we're speaking of Henry Charbonneau, the deceased, not his brother—the cardiac incident was in the lower chambers, the ventricles. What can begin as a ventricular arrhythmia, an irregular heartbeat, can escalate in someone with Brugada syndrome into an abnormally rapid and dangerous ventricular fibrillation."

Jakobson gave a half-smile. "In plain language, each heartbeat is triggered by an electrical impulse generated by special cells in the right auricle, the upper right chamber. Tiny channels in each of these cells direct this electrical activity, which makes your heart beat. People with Brugada syndrome have a defect in those channels. When the electrical impulses are disrupted, the heart starts to beat abnormally fast, trying to pump more blood into the body—think of someone pumping gas into a car who can't tell whether any of it's getting into the tank. In a quick episode, the person might feel dizzy or faint, and then the heart rights itself. Sometimes an episode is so brief that the person doesn't even realize it's happened."

Cathryn could only stare at him.

"If it continues, however, and the abnormal heartbeat doesn't correct itself, sudden cardiac death can occur. That's what happened to Henry Charbonneau. It's why Brugada is called sudden death syndrome."

It felt unreal to hear him call Mack *Henry Charbonneau*. A crazy hope shot through her that maybe Jakobson was talking about someone else and Mack was still alive.

Magnusson leaned forward. "What did you call the condition?"

"Brugada syndrome," Jakobson said. "It's quite rare. Many people don't even know they have it."

Cathryn managed to speak. "So that's what Mack had?"

Jakobson eyed her keenly. "Did he ever faint or gasp for breath, particularly at night?"

Her own heart was beating wildly now, as the pieces came together. "He would slump and kind of space out, but it was over in seconds."

Jakobson nodded. "Yes, that would be consistent with the syndrome." He made a note on a chart. "And at night? People report waking up in the middle of the night to a labored breathing and a chaotic heartbeat."

She closed her eyes. "He told me about that. But he thought they were nightmares, psychosomatic."

"No," Jakobson said. "They were real."

She exhaled, then looked at the pathologist again. "How could he not know that something was wrong?"

"The symptoms can be quite minor, and people can mistake them for something else."

Magnusson spoke up; Cathryn had almost forgotten about him. "So why the big incident now? What set it off?"

Jakobson shrugged. "Most of the time, a serious incident like this—the kind that leads to sudden death—happens at night while the person is sleeping, so we don't know the precipitating factor. Heat can be a trigger as well."

"Like a hot tub?" Magnusson said. "Wouldn't they know not to do that?" He looked at Cathryn. She could feel him accusing her. *You did this to him.*

She raised her eyes to Jakobson's. "We were in a hot tub once before—well, a thermal pool. But it was fine."

He gave another shrug. "It's hard to know. Was there something different about the conditions, something that would have mitigated the heat?"

She remembered the way they had come together in a single inevitable movement, as the rain slanted down and the mist covered them like a shawl. Mack tearing her bathing suit and pressing her against the side of the lagoon, her legs wrapped around him.

"It was raining," she said. "And he wasn't all the way under. Just to his waist."

"It's hard to know," Jakobson repeated. "We can only try to understand the medical events that actually happen, not those that didn't. And even then, our understanding is incomplete." He looked from Cathryn to Magnusson. "Mr. Charbonneau worked in front of a furnace, yes? So he was exposed to intense heat on a regular basis. Perhaps he'd learned to accommodate. Perhaps, over time, it had weakened his ability to recover. Perhaps it was a matter of chance that the fatal incident happened when it did. It's impossible to say."

Magnusson put his palms on his knees. "All right. Cardiac arrest from Brugada syndrome. Just to close the circle, there was nothing that could have been done?"

Jakobson looked at Cathryn when he answered. "When an incident occurs, like the one that happened to Mr. Charbonneau— unless it takes place in a hospital where immediate intervention is possible—it's nearly always fatal."

A thought fluttered across Cathryn's awareness. "It usually happens at night?" she said. "While the person is sleeping?"

"That's right."

She was quiet, taking in the small mercy that Mack hadn't died alone. That she was with him, to give him the one thing he had asked for.

Jakobson was addressing the policeman now. "I'll submit the pathology report, and then we can release the body to the next-of-kin or the consular representative."

"Right," Magnusson said. "That's where we were hoping that Ms. McAllister might be willing to be of assistance. To Paul Charbonneau. The brother."

"You spoke with him?" she asked.

"We both did," he replied, indicating Jakobson.

"The brother was the one who led me to the diagnosis," the pathologist told her. "Apparently their uncle has the condition, though he never told anyone about it until a few months ago. Some notion of privacy—misguided, when a disease is hereditary, but people can have odd ideas."

"Mack didn't know about his uncle?"

"It seems not," Jakobson said. "Mr. Charbonneau—Henry, that is—had been out of touch with the family. However, when Paul

Charbonneau heard me describe what had happened, he understood right away."

Cathryn tried to follow everything he was telling her. "Does he have it too? Paul?"

Jakobson gave another faint smile. "He's on the alert now, you can be sure. Onset is typically in the early forties, generally in males."

She gave a start. "So it was Mack's age, nothing to do with trauma?"

"I wouldn't think so, not with a hereditary condition." He shrugged. "On the other hand, you can't really separate the mind and the body, can you?"

Magnusson didn't wait for Cathryn to answer. "I'll give Paul Charbonneau your phone number, as soon as Dr. Jakobson files his report. He'd like to get matters started. It's complicated for a foreign citizen to die in Iceland, especially outside of a hospital. Sometimes the families want cremation, it's less expensive, but the brother didn't want that. And with the artwork to be packed and shipped, well, that's another headache."

She hadn't even said yes, but of course she would help. She would get Mack safely home to Vermont, and she would make sure that his art found its way to Shades of Blue and from there to a gallery where others could see what he had created and who he was. The pieces weren't the size he had wanted them to be, but it didn't matter. They were huge in spirit, in majesty, in beauty and meaning.

She had to stifle a laugh that Magnusson and Jakobson wouldn't have understood. Mack had made something that conveyed a great idea about human existence—which meant, in his own definition, that he was an artist and not merely an artisan.

It would be a glorious show. Renata would want to highlight the fact—tastefully, of course—that he died while creating the very art featured on their new brochure.

Let her do it, Cathryn thought. What mattered was that the series would be seen.

Except for the one little piece, the piece she had kept.

Part Five: The Color of Ice

Thirty-Three

The flight from Keflavik to Kennedy was only three-quarters full, so the middle seat in Cathryn's row was empty. The aisle seat was occupied by a woman who opened her book as soon as she sat down and seemed engrossed in its contents. That was fine with Cathryn; the last thing she wanted was a talkative seatmate. She kept her eyes on the view from the window as they prepared for takeoff—an airplane pulling out of a nearby gate, men in Icelandair jumpsuits waving flags and pushing carts of luggage, the bright blue sky.

It was hard to believe that she was really going home. The last few days had been a frenzy of activity. She'd been the epitome of efficiency, taking care of everything that Paul Charbonneau asked her to do, and more, yet it had felt robotic and unreal. Under the watchful eye of a consular representative, she had supervised the packing and shipping of Mack's artwork and the few possessions he had brought with him. There would have been no chance to help herself to another item, even if she had wanted to. To her relief, Paul had handled everything with the mortuary in Reykjavik. There were documents to fill out and funds to be transferred, but no need for a local facilitator after all. The mortuary was used to dealing with situations like Mack's and knew how to obtain the required metal casket, secure approval from both countries, arrange for pickup and transport.

Paul had been grateful for her help. "You've been wonderful," he said. "Dealing with the legalities and funeral arrangements was about all I could manage."

"I was glad to do it. Besides, I really want the sculptures to make it back safely." She almost told him that she had been Mack's assistant, but was afraid that would seem as if she was laying claim to part of his vision. Then she almost explained that she had come to Iceland on behalf of Shades of Blue, Mack's agent, but decided not to say that either. It wasn't the reason she had been with him when he died.

"I hope you can come to the funeral," Paul told her. "It'll be in northern New Hampshire, where we grew up."

Cathryn chose her words with care. "I appreciate the invitation, I really do. But I don't belong there. It's for your family."

It was the same stark truth she had felt when Magnusson pointed out that she wasn't a relative: In everyone's eyes but her own, she was an outsider, no one at all. The people who came to Mack's funeral wouldn't think she had a right to mourn.

And yet, she had done everything she could, even waiting an extra day to make sure there were no remaining tasks before she left. She deferred her children's questions until she was back in New York, assuring them that she would explain when they were together.

Paul Charbonneau had tried to change her mind about the funeral. When she continued to refuse, he offered to compensate her for her time.

"I'm just trying to be the person Mack helped me become," Cathryn said. "Please let me be that."

"He helped you to be so generous? My brother?" Paul sounded incredulous. "That doesn't sound like him. I mean, I admired him tremendously, but he was a difficult man."

Cathryn didn't know what to say. After a minute Paul added, "I'm not a woman, but I imagine he could be rather charismatic. I hope he didn't break your heart."

She didn't know if he was being nosy or kind, but she gave the only true answer.

"No. He opened it."

They left it at that. The casket was delivered to the airport. Cathryn boarded her own plane a few hours later.

The flight attendant made her way up the aisle, reminding everyone to secure their tray tables for takeoff. The woman in Cathryn's row glanced up briefly, then closed her book and turned to Cathryn with a bright smile. "You're American? On your way home?"

Cathryn didn't want to talk, but she didn't want to be rude either. "I am," she said. Then, because it was expected, she added, "And you?"

The woman's smile widened. "Off to meet my newest grandchild. My son and his wife moved to the States a few years ago. I wish they would move back to Reykjavik so I could see them more often, but they have good jobs and I'm retired, so I'm the one to travel."

Cathryn could see that the woman was eager to talk; the book had been temporary. She braced herself to get through the pleasantries until she could excuse herself with the need for a nap.

"Were you here on a holiday?" the woman asked. "Iceland's a wonderful country, isn't it? What did you like best?"

I liked Mack best.

The pilot's voice came over the loudspeaker, telling them that they were next in line for takeoff. Cathryn gave a polite nod and told the woman, "The icebergs and the thermal pools. Mývatn." Then she turned back to the window.

Soon, Iceland would recede. There would be hours of ocean and sky, and then America.

As the plane moved into position, she had a moment of panic. Leaving Iceland would mean leaving Mack, as if he had only existed there.

The plane began to move forward. The engine grew louder, preparing for the ascent. It was too late to get off and go back to Akureyri. Mack was already dead.

It felt strange to be on American soil again. Not fire and ice, but earth, rooting her to the land where she had been born, raised her children, and was returning.

Cathryn waved her arm when she saw Rachel's car approaching the Passenger Pickup island. Rachel slowed to a stop and popped the trunk. Cathryn threw in her suitcase, closed the hatch, and pulled open the passenger door. "Hey, you," Rachel said, leaning across the seat for a quick kiss. "How was your flight?"

Cathryn looked at her daughter, stunned by her loveliness. Had Rachel always looked like that? "It's so good to see you, sweetheart."

"Well, Jude would have picked you up in your very own car, but he got called in for some kind of emergency job, so I said I would. He should be back by the time we get home, and then we can all have lunch, brunch, whatever you want to call it—or do they have high tea in Iceland?"

"No high tea."

"That's good, because we're ordering pizza."

"He's okay? Jude?"

"He's better than okay. I really think being Action Dude that night was a big boost to his confidence. He even looks taller."

"And you, honey?"

"Me?" Rachel's glance was, somehow, both bashful and coy. "I've been working on my laugh."

Cathryn smiled. "A worthy project." Then she lowered her voice. "How's the house?"

"The house." Rachel sighed. "The insurance people put up this plastic stuff to seal off the wrecked part until they decide how much they're going to pay. We're not allowed to go in there or change anything—you know, like preserving the scene of a crime? They have to figure out how much was from what they call an Act of God—because of the storm, which they're *not* responsible for, apparently—and how much is covered by your homeowner's insurance, and where the tree people come in." She paused. "And the car insurance people."

"Because Judah's car was damaged?"

"Not just that." Rachel gave Cathryn a sideways look. "At first we weren't going to tell them about the car wash business. We were scared they would say it was our fault and not give you any money."

"But you did tell them."

"Mostly. I said we couldn't see in the rain and went off the driveway and rammed into the tree."

"I hadn't thought about that part."

"It was okay," Rachel said quickly. "The insurance guy told us that trees were falling over right and left in the storm, and there was no way, on a regular dry night, that Jude's little car could have knocked over a giant tree. It was the wind and the rain, and the way the water had collected in that low spot by the driveway. The shallow roots."

"Is that really true?"

"As true as anything can ever be. I mean, it's always like that, right? A particular combination of factors, at a particular moment—and boom, a tree falls on a house."

Cathryn grew still. A combination of factors, at a particular moment. Yes, her daughter was right. "So they're working it out?"

"In their own bizarro way. It's the fine print on the policy, minus *shit happens,* multiplied by replacement value. Or something. Anyway, they need to talk to you. I explained that you were detained in Iceland because of a death."

Cathryn nodded. She might have to fight with the insurance company—or not. She could forgo the argument. Take whatever they gave her, unload the house, and move on.

"You *are* going to tell us about the guy who died, right?" Rachel said. "I have the feeling it was important."

Cathryn had managed to keep her grief at bay as she went through customs and searched the chaos of baggage claim for her suitcase, greeted Rachel, asked about the assessor—all of that had kept her occupied. Until now.

"Yes. It was important."

"Something happened in Iceland."

"Yes. Something happened in Iceland."

"I can feel it."

Cathryn looked at her daughter. "You've changed. The old Rachel would have turned that feeling into a clever remark."

"I guess I have." They were silent, and then Rachel said, "Will you tell me about it?"

"I think so. If I can."

"And Jude?"

Yes, of course. She wanted her children to know her, and she wanted to know them.

"Both of you," Cathryn said. "I love you two. You can't fathom how much." Then she gave a happy, embarrassed laugh. "Won't it be strange to be under the same roof, all of us at the same time? It's been years."

"Actually," Rachel said, "it's only for one night. Jude wants to get back to his apartment, I guess he settled the money thing. And I found a new place—just for me, in case you were going to ask, but we wanted to wait till you got back. We didn't want to leave the house empty. It seemed better for someone to be there, with the plastic and all."

"Yes, of course." Cathryn felt a pang of disappointment, but she knew they had their own lives, and she wanted them to have that. If she was about to be alone again—well, that was the life she had made. If she wanted that to change, it was up to her.

Judah was waiting for them when Rachel pulled into the driveway. "Aloha," he said. "Welcome home from the land of ice. Did you know that the name for Iceland in Iceland is actually Island? Weird, right? Though it really *is* an island, and it's not made of ice. That's Greenland. Which isn't green."

"Judah, you're the weird one," Rachel said, but her voice was affectionate. "Did you order the pizza for us?"

"Duh." He reached for Cathryn's bag. "Allow me, please."

Cathryn tried, over supper, to tell them about Mack and glass-blowing, but it was impossible to explain. In the end, she simply said that she had gotten to know someone special and it was terrible when he died.

Once the insurance company approved a settlement and gave the green light to begin repairs, Cathryn moved into an apartment to be out of the workmen's way. She wasn't going to live in the house again, anyway. As soon as it was fixed, it would go on the market.

She took a few freelance jobs, but spent most of her time on a series of photographs that she was calling *Fire, Air, Water, Earth*. Her idea was that she would offer them to Renata Singer, in the hope that Renata could find a gallery to show them. She would be the artist this time, not the one photographing the art.

In mid-December, she called Paul Charbonneau to ask for Deborah's email. He hedged her question about whether he knew how to reach Deborah, but she could tell that he did. "Why?" he asked.

Cathryn took a deep breath. She had wanted to wait until she was ready, but maybe she would never be ready. Anyway, she couldn't wait much longer.

"I have something to give her," she said.

Thirty-Four

When Deborah opened the door, Cathryn could see that she was wary. It was understandable; she had known about Deborah for months, but Deborah had only known about her for a few days. She'd asked Paul Charbonneau to explain that she'd been assisting Mack in the hot shop and was with him when he died. That was all Paul had told Deborah when he asked permission to share her email address; it was all he knew, really. Cathryn hadn't been sure if Deborah would agree to see her but hoped that curiosity would win in the end.

"Cathryn McAllister? Please, come in."

She followed Deborah into the brownstone. Like Deborah, the apartment was both exotic and understated. A black lacquer table with a porcelain vase at each end. Crown moldings against apricot-colored walls, and good rugs on the floor. There was no way to imagine Mack in a place like this.

Deborah was different than Cathryn had expected, though she didn't really know what she had expected. Petite, as Mack had described. Dark hair pushed away from her face with a tortoise-shell headband. Nervous hands and big haunted eyes. Cathryn had thought she would feel threatened by Deborah and she was, partly.

Deborah gestured at a dark blue couch, and then settled herself into a matching wing chair. "Can I offer you some coffee, tea?"

Cathryn shook her head. "No. But thank you."

There was an awkward silence. Then Deborah seemed to steel herself as she met Cathryn's eyes. "Paul told me that you were helping Mack. Are you a glassblower too?"

"No, I'm a photographer."

"How did you know him, then?"

Cathryn gave the answer she had prepared. "I had freelance job for the organization that represents him. So that's how I met him. In Iceland, where he was doing some work."

Deborah's wariness seemed to sharpen. "How did you know about me?"

"He told me."

Deborah stiffened. Cathryn could see her trying to mask the reactions that flashed across her features. Fear, that Mack had exposed her to a stranger. Anger, and jealousy too. "It wasn't like he went around telling people," Cathryn said. "I was the first person he'd ever told."

Deborah was motionless as marble. Nothing fluttered, not even an eyelash. Her hands rested in her lap, the hands that drew such celestial sounds from the cello. Bach. The unaccompanied cello suites. "He must have trusted you," she said, finally.

"I think he did. But he needed to speak, too, after all that time."

Deborah's penetrating gaze cut right through the composure that Cathryn was fighting to maintain. "You loved him," she said.

"I did."

"Did he love you?"

Cathryn hesitated. "A bit, I think. But mostly, he loved you."

A tremor passed through Deborah's body, and Cathryn could see that she was struggling not to give way to the emotions that were roiling inside her. The two of them, she thought, both trying so hard to sustain the illusion of control.

"I loved him too," Deborah whispered. "But I couldn't stand to love him anymore. It was too hard."

Cathryn felt herself tremble too, because Deborah had put into words what she already knew. Then Deborah said, "Tell me how he died."

Cathryn looked into the huge dark eyes of the woman she had feared and yearned to meet, the woman she had embodied in that final instant of Mack's life. There was no need to say anything about the cottage or the hot tub. Mack died because he stopped breathing, just as Brian died because his car slammed into the back of a truck.

"He had a rare heart condition called Brugada syndrome," she said. "He didn't know he had it, but it made him vulnerable to an arrhythmia that can, and did, lead to sudden death."

"Yes, I knew that part. Paul explained it to all of us."

All of us. The family. The people who had a right to mourn.

Deborah gave a loose shudder. "So frightening to think of a condition waiting in your genes like that, and the person having no idea."

"He had these tiny episodes," Cathryn said. "I saw it a few times, when I was with him, but he kept saying it was nothing. Then he had a major episode."

She gathered her courage. This was why she was here, in Deborah's apartment; it would be absurd to leave without saying what she had come to say. "Right before he died, Mack had a moment of what some might call delirium, but I can tell you that it was absolute lucidity."

Deborah's eyes were fixed on hers. Cathryn willed herself not to look away as she told Deborah what Mack had said, and what she had answered.

"He thought it was me?"

"It *was* you, in every way that mattered. You forgave him."

Cathryn wasn't sure if Deborah was going to slap her for her audacity. But Deborah stared at her, motionless—until she gave a single, terrible cry. She crumpled into the wing chair, her face in her hands.

When she lifted her face, at last, it was streaked with tears. "I wanted that baby so badly. I had to blame someone."

Cathryn began to speak, but Deborah stopped her. The tears

were still falling. "If I hadn't blamed him, I would have had to blame myself. I had to hold onto my anger. It was the only thing I had."

"The stillbirth wasn't your fault. I'm sure they told you that."

"It *was* my fault." Her words pierced Cathryn's heart. "I failed our son. I didn't keep him safe."

With a movement as swift and sure as a twist of the shears, Cathryn rose and knelt by the chair, gathering Deborah into her arms, letting her cry. Then she smoothed her hair and said, "I would have saved Mack if I could, just as you would have saved your child. But it isn't always up to us."

Deborah's voice was full of despair. "How can a person bear that?"

Cathryn thought of her younger self, tossing a set of car keys to a man she was angry with, but never meaning to send him to his death.

She hadn't pushed Mack into the hot tub. He had stretched out his hand. *Come to me.*

Deborah's baby died. Little Pétur didn't. There was no way to know who would live and who would die.

"We have to," she said. "There's no other way." Then she pulled away gently and reached for the purse she had placed on the floor. She opened it and felt inside for an object wrapped in newspaper. Still kneeling by Deborah's chair, she unwrapped the glass figure.

"He made this for you."

Slowly, Deborah extended her hand and took the sculpture. Cathryn looked at it, as if seeing it for the first time. The dark blue center, surrounded by luminosity, summoning the viewer inside, participant as well as observer. Mack had said that glass was special that way, the only material that let you look at it and through it. Deborah cradled the piece in her palm, her head bowed. Mack hadn't said it was for Deborah, but it was. Cathryn had wanted it for herself—had taken it for herself—but she wasn't the woman it belonged to.

"You're a kind person," Deborah said.

Cathryn gave a faint smile. "I wasn't especially kind before I knew Mack."

"That's because you loved him. Love makes a person kind. Or ought to." Deborah's voice caught. "I couldn't do it. I didn't have it in me."

"Not then. You were too distraught. You'll do it another time."

Deborah traced the edge of the sculpture with her finger. "This wasn't part of the show they're putting on? The one they've called *The Color of Ice*?"

"No," Cathryn said. "It was the last thing he did, so it was still in the cooling oven. Everything else was on the shelves." Her smile grew sheepish. "I kind of didn't let anyone know about it. I didn't mean to steal from Paul, who had the official right to everything. It was just because—well, just because."

Deborah nodded, still tracing the contours of the glass. Cathryn watched her. It wasn't hard to imagine those fingers on the strings of a cello, calling forth the music that had drawn Mack to her with such profound certainty.

Then Deborah squared her shoulders. She placed the sculpture in Cathryn's hand, closing her fingers around it. "You need to have it. Not me."

Cathryn's heart hammered against her ribs. "It's yours. He made it for you."

But Deborah shook her head. "Perhaps. But you gave him what I couldn't, and you gave it for me. So I give this to you, in return."

Fyrir þig. For you.

This time it was Cathryn who started to cry, and Deborah put an arm around her—tentatively, at first, then with a soft sisterly tenderness. Finally, when there were no more tears and no more words, Cathryn stood. She put the sculpture back in her purse and looked around the elegant apartment one last time before she left.

Deborah watched her go. What Deborah couldn't see, and didn't know, was that Cathryn was three months pregnant.

Cathryn's own show opened nine months later. *Fire, Air, Water, Earth*. Twenty-four photographs, the same number of images she had planned for the show she had abandoned all those years ago, when Brian died. The gallery owner had wanted to put each element on its own wall, but Cathryn had a different idea. She arranged the images in a zigzag procession that moved from one wall to the next, to show how each element changed the others. Water softened the earth. Air, filling the fiery glass, made it open and expand.

All four elements were part of glassblowing. She had seen that the day she made the paperweight under Mack's watchful eye. She remembered how he had laced his arms through hers to give the rod a twist when she lost her attention. "Nothing," he had told her, "not even the most interesting thought, can be more important than keeping the glass in movement." She could still feel him, surrounding her.

She had tried her best to digest what Iceland had given her and transform it into something usable and new. Whether or not she had succeeded—well, time would tell.

The gallery was filled with people she knew and people she didn't. Wine and cheese on silver trays, the flash of cameras. A list of the artworks, with different-colored stickers to indicate status and price.

Rachel came up beside her. "Mom," she said. "How are you doing? And *you*, you little pumpkin. Are you enjoying all the excitement?" She bent her head to nuzzle the infant who was tucked into a soft blue Snugli. Cathryn had one hand on the baby's back, holding him close, but he lifted his head to give Rachel a wide gummy grin. "See? I told you I was his favorite."

Cathryn laughed. "Everyone is his favorite. He loves the world."

Then Rachel motioned to the slender young man who was standing beside her. "Mom," she said, "there's someone I want you to meet."

Cathryn turned to the young man. He had intelligent eyes behind wire-rimmed glasses and a sweet smile.

"This is David," Rachel said. "And David, this is my amazing mother."

"I'm so glad to meet you," David told her. "Your work is extraordinary." His gaze moved to the baby. He held out a finger, and the baby grabbed it. "And what's your name, little man?"

Cathryn looked at the child. "Henry," she said. "It's a rather adult name, but maybe he'll pick a nickname later. It's up to him."

"That seems fair," David said. "It's his name, after all."

Rachel gave Cathryn a private smile. It was smug and shy and lovely. It meant: Isn't he wonderful? Didn't I do well, at last?

Cathryn touched her daughter's hand. Then she pressed her lips to the top of the baby's head.

For you, she thought.

Fyrir þig.

The End

Reader's Guide Questions

1. The nature of art is a central theme of the book. Early in the story, Mack insists that he's an artisan, not an artist. Do you think there's a difference? Was Mack an artist, after all? Was Cathryn?

2. Shortly before they meet, Cathryn reads what Mack has written on his website, "Glass is present and not-present. Both window and object, glass allows us to look through it and at it." The contradiction intrigues her. As she learns more about glass, she discovers an additional contradiction in its molten nature, which is both liquid and solid, withholding its "real colors" until the object has cooled. Is this sense of contradiction present in the characters, as well? What does it mean to Cathryn to be *molten*, as a human being?

3. Setting is clearly a key element in the book. Pivotal scenes take place at the iceberg lagoon, the thermal mud pots, the botanic garden, the Goðafoss waterfall. In fact, these places are so integral

to the narrative that it's hard to imagine the scenes taking place anywhere else. Which setting was especially powerful for you? In what way?

4.   The themes of age, aging, and agelessness also recur throughout the story. Beer baths, thermal pools, and special drinks boast of their power to keep a person from aging. At several points in the story, Cathryn is uncomfortably aware that she's older than Mack. In the end, do you think she embraces age or transcends it?

5.   Cathryn's daughter accuses her of being a "Snow Queen," frozen and remote. While Cathryn admits the truth of the image, she also sees herself as "Snow White," more asleep than aloof. Which metaphor captures her transformation, for you—is she someone who "melts" and grows warmer, or someone who wakes up?

6.   Cathryn's children have their own arcs of transformation. Do you think that Cathryn's personal journey helped each of her children to grow? If so, how? In what ways did Rachel and Judah take charge of their own growth?

7.   Children play an important role in the book, literally and symbolically—their birth, fragility, survival. At various points, Cathryn yearns to save or rescue a child. Do you think she succeeded in doing that? In what ways?

8.   There are two instances in the story when Cathryn is faced with a choice about her career as a commercial artist—once with Nora Lang, and later with Nelson Whitley. Was there something similar in both situations? How were they different? What did you think of how she handled each of the situations?

9. There are many references to *time* in the novel—time "folding into itself," blurring the border between past, present, and future; the desire for time to slow and "stretch itself;" the icebergs "shedding time;" photography "capturing time;" and so on. In fact, the story takes place in a very condensed period of time, a matter of weeks. What allowed Cathryn to undergo an intense inner journey in such a brief period of time?

10. The northern lights are mentioned in the book's opening paragraph, and several other times in the course of the story. Cathryn learns about the mythology surrounding them, the challenges of seeing as well as photographing them. Both Cathryn and Mack call the lights their "heart's desire." Do you think she achieved her heart's desire?

Acknowledgments

Gratitude beyond measure to all who helped bring this book to life:

To Sandra Scofield, writing mentor extraordinaire. Without Sandra's keen eye, tough love, and unflagging support, this story never would have made its way into print.

To Peter Bremers, glass artist, for sharing his experience translating the blue icebergs of Antarctica's "divine sculpture garden" into the medium of glass. When I discovered Peter's stunning *Icebergs and Paraphernalia* (https://peterbremers.com/portfolio/icebergs-and-paraphernalia/), it was as if the very essence of Mack's art had come to life.

To Ira Meyer, photographer, whose photos of Antarctica's blue icebergs (https://www.irameyer.com/category/icebergs) showed me a new way of seeing. Like Peter, Ira generously shared his insight and experience as an artist. Without the two of them, I wouldn't have understood how to write this book.

To Paul Swartwood of Glen Echo Glass Works, Jim Schantz of the Schantz Galleries in Stockbridge MA, and the glass artists of Hudson Beach Glass—Michael Benzer, John Gilvey, and Kathleen Anderson—for giving so graciously of their time and knowledge;

and to Andrew Lerman, photographer, for explaining so well what it's like to photograph the northern lights.

To Mikki Smith, Reference and Visitor Services Librarian, Rakow Research Library, Corning Museum of Glass, for her kindness in locating a wealth of material for me to explore during my visit to Corning.

To Vivek Y. Reddy, MD, Director, Cardiac Arrhythmia Service, and Professor of Medicine, Mount Sinai Hospital, for "finding" Brugada syndrome for me and helping me to understand its presentation.

To travel blogger Lauren Yakiwchuk, who shared an insider view of their time at a cottage near Akureyri overlooking the fjord, the inspiration for the Hrífandi Cottages. To Rachel Bovey and the staff at Borealis Basecamp, who provided the perfect context for understanding the Northern Lights and the northern light. To Jane Rosen for her help in conveying the calamity that befalls Cathryn's house. And to Tom Steenburg for his unconditional support—and our Iceland adventure, without which I never could have imagined this book.

To visionary publisher Brooke Warner and my savvy, ever-patient project manager Lauren Wise Wait, who had my back every step of the way. Together with cover designer Julie Metz, who knocked it out of the park yet again; the rest of the staff at She Writes Press; and my amazing publicist Ann-Marie Nieves—you have truly been a "dream team."

To Maggie Smith, Kay Scott, Gretchen Gold, Lilianne Milgrom, Sue Roberts, and Janis Daly who read early drafts and offered invaluable feedback.

I also gained much from Sarah Moss's memoir *Names for the Sea: Strangers in Iceland;* the Netflix series *Blown Away;* and Ken Burns' film about painter William Segal entitled *Seeing, Searching, Being.*

About the Author

Barbara Linn Probst is a writer of both fiction and nonfiction living on a historic dirt road in New York's Hudson Valley. Her acclaimed debut novel, *Queen of the Owls* (April 2020), is the story of a woman's search for wholeness, framed around the art and life of iconic American painter Georgia O'Keeffe. *Queen of the Owls* has garnered multiple awards, including medals from the Independent Publishers Association and the Sarton Award for women's fiction. Barbara's second book, *The Sound Between the Notes* (April 2021), explores timeless questions of identity and belonging through the unique perspective of a musician, and was named one of the Best Indie Books of 2021 by Kirkus Reviews. It was also the Gold Medalist for the Sarton Award and the Silver Medalist in fiction from the Nautilus Book Awards.

Barbara has a PhD in clinical social work and is a former therapist, researcher, teacher, and advocate. She is also a "serious amateur" pianist and has traveled extensively—including, of course, to Iceland. *The Color of Ice* is her third novel.

Author photo © David Heald 2018

SELECTED TITLES FROM SHE WRITES PRESS

She Writes Press is an independent publishing company founded to serve women writers everywhere. Visit us at www.shewritespress.com.

Fire & Water by Betsy Graziani Fasbinder. $16.95, 978-1-93831-414-8. Kate Murphy has always played by the rules—but when she meets charismatic artist Jake Bloom, she's forced to navigate the treacherous territory of passionate love, friendship, and family devotion.

Play for Me by Céline Keating. $16.95, 978-1-63152-972-6. Middle-aged Lily impulsively joins a touring folk-rock band, leaving her job and marriage behind in an attempt to find a second chance at life, passion, and art.

A Drop in the Ocean: A Novel by Jenni Ogden. $16.95, 978-1-63152-026-6. When middle-aged Anna Fergusson's research lab is abruptly closed, she flees Boston to an island on Australia's Great Barrier Reef—where, amongst the seabirds, nesting turtles, and eccentric islanders, she finds a family and learns some bittersweet lessons about love.

A Tight Grip: A Novel about Golf, Love Affairs, and Women of a Certain Age by Kay Rae Chomic. $16.95, 978-1-938314-76-6. As forty-six-year-old golfer Jane "Par" Parker prepares for her next tournament, she experiences a chain of events that force her to reevaluate her life.

Beautiful Illusion by Christie Nelson. $16.95, 978-1-63152-334-2. When brash and beautiful American newspaper reporter Lily Nordby falls into a forbidden love affair with Tokido Okamura, a sophisticated Japanese diplomat whom she suspects is a spy, at the Golden Gate International Exposition, a brilliant Mayan art scholar, Woodrow Packard, tries to save her.